I LOVE YOU IN FRENCH

I LOVE YOU *in* French

BY SARA NORTH

Story Boréale
Stratham, NH

Identifiers:
Library of Congress Control Number: 2023918890
ISBN: 979-8-9892125-0-7 (paperback)
ISBN: 979-8-9892125-1-4 (ebook)

First edition October 2023

Cover Illustration: Alyssa Miles
Cover Design: Taylor Waldron
Editing: Brittany Howard
Proofreading: Jenn Lockwood

Published in the United States by Story Boréale
20 Portsmouth Ave Ste 1 PMB 117
Stratham, NH 03885
www.authorsaranorth.com
@authorsaranorth

Note from the Author:

My heart is that you would feel comfortable reading my book. Because of this, please note that trigger warnings include: Death of a parent, discussions of grief, troubled parental relationship, and loneliness.

This book contains swoony kisses that aren't graphically described and implies intimacy between a married couple. This book does not contain swearing.

To everyone waiting for the full kind of love:
Take heart.

Dear One, I can now fall 'cause you'll catch me
Dear One, I can now dream 'cause I've seen your face
Dear One, I can now hope 'cause I've held you
Dear One, I can now sing 'cause you've let me near you

"Dear One" by Sara North

Chapter One

Sparrow

My fingers always smell like croissants. The real ones. The buttery ones. It's not ideal, but it helps to block out the other smells when I'm on the train home from Boston. I don't intend to smell like croissants. But when you work in a bakery—or *une boulangerie*—and a French American one at that, you don't stand a chance. And because we're in America, we also sell coffee and sneak in other pastries as we please.

I look to the overhead Lite-Brite style train marquee sign. Three minutes.

I slump further into my right hip—my former-ballerina posture taking a break—and observe the yellow, fluorescent lighting and cavernous tiles. Any remaining warmth from the outside world has stuffed itself beneath the earth and through the train platform as my fellow commuters and I wait.

A movement catches my eye as I see the silhouette of a fashionable man a few feet to my right looking my way. Today's the day. I feel it. He's finally going to talk to me. The last few months have been a dance. I see him but try not to let him know I see him. He tries to get my attention, and immediately, I put up all my defenses. He even left a business card near my seat once with his social handles so I could look him up. He's always been respectful, and you can tell he's a decent human. The man doesn't give off any creep factor. He just seems to know what he wants. Truthfully, he's swoon-worthy and handsome, but no. Just no. I have valid reasons for my standoffishness with men, even if my best friend always tries to convince me otherwise.

I adjust the earphones in my ears and try to pretend that we didn't make eye contact. The movement beside me tells me I'm too late. I grimace and politely point to my earphones. Not interested.

"Hi," he says.

I don't look his way.

"Okay, well, I'm sure you can hear me . . ."

I avoid his eyes and try to pretend I'm oh-so focused on my phone. It's no use. His cologne is strong enough to wake the swooned, as if he is prepared to both cause women to faint and then wake them up again. I sigh. This is happening.

"I've seen you here before. On the train. I'm not a creeper." He rushes the last part. Glad to know my inkling was correct.

"My name is Graham. Graham Winnings," he continues.

It sounds like he's prepared a pitch. I shift my stance and look up at the marquee light. Two minutes.

"I work in corporate law. I'm single. Never been married. No kids."

He tries to stay within view as a rush of commuters has us bumping shoulders. I turn and catch his eyes. It's confirmed—he is, indeed, very handsome. Not a Chris Evans type of handsome, but more like a my-town-would-be-thrilled-I'm-no-longer-single-and-he-probably-modeled-once type of handsome. Lily is going to have words for me for not accepting this one. I know it.

I nod my apologies and look back toward the tracks. "As I was saying . . ."

His voice isn't even annoying. But he's not the one. How do I know? Oh, I know. Took me two-point-five seconds to know. The smell of oil and exhaust surrounding us isn't distracting me from my mission of avoidance.

" . . . I'm thirty-two years old. I call my mom every morning because she lives alone, and I never want her to miss someone telling her 'Good morning.' And I don't have a dog, but I want one someday. A big one."

Oh, this comment makes women moan in frustration everywhere. The monster.

I slightly roll my eyes and hear a cough nearby. I look up to find a woman glaring at me with a look that says if I don't accept him, she will, and this could be my last chance before becoming a spinster. Yep, her eyes say all of that. I grin my apologies and try to focus. Mystery man—or now Graham—has continued listing off his qualities. I've missed most of them.

" . . . I own my house. I have never been arrested." He sighs.

I give him nothing. I can't.

"And it's not just because of how you look." My eyes widen. "Not that you aren't very attractive, but I just had a sense that we would hit it off somehow."

The truth is, he does seem nice. And I could see him somewhere in my world. Just not beside me. I've never been more certain.

"Um . . . I'm guessing by your lack of response that you don't care. I'm hoping it's not because you're married or have a boyfriend who is going to beat me up for talking to you."

I steal a glance at his face and see him staring at the phone in my hand. My earphones are not connected to my phone. The adapter is dangling in the wind. He stifles a laugh, which is polite.

"And I'm also guessing that you're not going to stop pretending that you actually have music playing in your earphones . . ."

I wrinkle my nose. I'd fail as an undercover agent.

"'May I ask why, with so little endeavor at civility, I am thus repulsed?'"

I grin at this. *Pride and Prejudice*. The movie. The man has taste. He's cultured. The once-glaring lady across from me nearly falls into the nearby cement pillar. A middle-aged man takes one look at Graham and starts to take notes on his newspaper. He catches my amused look and rolls his eyes. No one will let me travel here after this moment if I don't accept his hand immediately.

I turn slowly toward Graham. I shake the iciness out of my posture and try to be more human and less wounded—I need to ride this train. Lily is waiting on me at the store, and I can't mess this up just because it makes me uncomfortable to turn him down. It's not this guy's fault I can't date him. He's exceptional. He's well-dressed. But, nope, not the one. And something in me deeply wishes I wasn't so keenly aware of it.

"You seem like a nice guy," I say.

He startles, clearly not expecting to hear my voice. "I am."

I nod politely. "My friend Lily would be obsessed with you."

"I don't see how that detail matters at this moment . . . and, wait, did you say *Lily*?" His brow furrows, and I see a flash of something in his eyes before he shakes it off.

"But this is where you and I stop." I maintain eye contact and nod as if the conversation is over.

The alert sounds for the incoming train.

He clears his throat. "We're getting on the same train."

"Ahhh, but that's where you're wrong, buddy." Yep. I said it. It's metaphorical. Let's see if Mr. Millions of Bucks picks up on that cue.

He shuffles in his Italian leather dress shoes and crosses his arms over his broad chest tucked behind a camel-colored trench coat. An expensive designer scarf is even sticking out from the top of the coat, framing his strong jaw. I don't relent.

"It's not personal."

"It can't be personal. You don't know me." His eyes are amused while calling my bluff.

I grin again. "Well, it's not. I just can't date you."

The train car screeches on the rails. It's loud. The kind of loud that says they haven't greased these rails since the Boston Tea Party. Extreme? Not if you've heard this noise.

We wince. Once the train car stops, I turn toward him. I have ten seconds to get this right before the doors open.

I look into his questioning eyes. No doubt this will haunt him for a while. He checks every box, and he knows it. But he can't check the most important one of mine.

I square my shoulders as the door opens, and I step into the car. I turn quickly, the commuters already creating space between us.

"May I ask why not?" He amplifies his voice in a weirdly professional and acceptable way. Again, so very polite.

"Well, Graham, it's simple . . ."

He leans forward but doesn't attempt to get on the train car. I time the rest of my response. *Three, two, one . . .*

"You're not French."

His jaw goes slack as the doors close. We're taking off, and the force throws me onto the closest faux-leather seat. I can see his silhouette, unmoving, no doubt in shock from the one rule of my dating world: Date a Frenchman or date no man. And in case it's unclear, it hasn't worked for me so far.

I'm still staring at the closed doors in front of my face, my spine rocking and swaying lightly from the momentum of the moving car. Something is stirring my gut, but I try to push it down. I can feel the weight of the stares of the commuters around me, and I want to block it all out. I don't like the feeling of needing to explain myself. It would sound ridiculous if I did anyway.

So I scrunch my nose and turn to prepare for another battle when my eyes catch sight of the most beautiful frame of a man I've ever seen in my life. His back is to me, his head slightly angled to the side. He's within range and without earphones, so there's no way he didn't hear me a few moments ago. And this has me cringing with regret. Still, the curve of his shoulders under a bomber jacket and the way the pieces of his hair flip under a baseball cap has my mouth stuck together. This is ridiculous.

"Are you going to find a seat or not?" says an older woman with her eyebrows furrowed as if I got the last item she was looking for at a Black Friday sale.

My exhale is loud as I quickly attempt to move away from the embarrassment and her scorn and toward the only open seat I see, which is five rows behind Handsome Stranger. I don't need to see him to know his face would be devastating—his voice too, probably. Sometimes, you can just sense attractiveness even before you encounter it, and it's in this moment I recognize that the battle I'm facing today wasn't outside this train car. It's now.

I may have won my freedom by ensuring Graham won't ever ask me out again, but I most definitely have lost if it means this Handsome Stranger is not for me. I look out the window, warmth creeping up my neck and adding a new and unwelcome blush to my cheeks.

After waiting a few seconds to catch my breath, I glance again toward the back of his head (in case I blacked out and hadn't seen him clearly), but he's moved on ... because he's no longer in his seat. I risked a glance, and now I'm kind of wishing I hadn't. It figures the man I would want a better glimpse of is nowhere to be found, while the man I was trying to avoid has no problem approaching me. I should've known after the way this day started, even before my commute. The croissants didn't rise properly, and the sugar spilled all over my usually clean counters. It was a sign.

My thoughts drift back to Graham and the fact that my hands are still shaking. To say I panicked a few minutes ago is an understatement. Have I set my sights and hopes on one day marrying someone French? I mean, sure. It would be nice. My mother was French. My father was American. Somewhere in my deep well of memories, I can still hear my father saying, "Wait for the French kind of love." Of course, he was talking about my mother and not about a specific nation of people in general. I've never actually thought or told a man that I wouldn't date him because he wasn't French. In my distress, I just made that rule up.

Perhaps it has something to do with Jacques, a man who is most definitely French and has been visiting my bakery and coffee shop, Sparrow's Beret, for the past four or so months. He's basically a European version of

Graham, but instead of what went down outside of this train, he has never shown much interest in me other than to ask for his usual: a double shot of espresso and a *pain au chocolat*. For the past week, he has seemed to linger in the café a little longer than usual, but I could've been imagining it. Still, that hasn't stopped me from hoping he will see the light and ask me out one day soon. Though, these days, I would describe myself as more of a flashlight whose batteries are threatening to burn out.

I adjust myself in my seat, my heart still beating furiously after my outburst toward Graham. There's a draft somewhere on this train. I didn't dress warmly enough for the hint of fall in the air. So now I'm cold. I'm irritated at myself, and I feel the creeping blanket of my steady companion: loneliness. Not a great combination. Sure, I might have seemed calm and collected on the platform, minus my blunder of not having my earphones connected to my phone, but it's false bravery. Every time I have a close encounter with a man who's interested in me—not that it happens often—I tense. I panic. I'm always awkward. And I care about what people think of me way too much.

So, this has been quite the event. Who even am I? I know I'm too old to be pushing away perfectly acceptable men who quote Jane Austen and telling them ridiculous things like, "You're not French." I. Know. This.

Reaching into my oversized travel bag, I pull out an oversized cream sweater (yes, there's a theme here), and I snuggle within it. If only Handsome Stranger could see me now. Swallowed up by a sweater? Simply ravishing.

I intentionally connect my earphones to my phone this time—I don't yet trust earbuds—and listen to my favorite band, Histoire. I've been obsessed with their music for the last several years. I don't speak French fluently, but I understand it fairly well. And the lyrics get me every single time, like a frequency connected to my heart.

As the train grows quieter with each opening and closing of the doors, and since I still have about thirty minutes until I'm home, I let my thoughts drift to the metros within Paris that I've seen in pictures. Because with all my claims to be waiting for a Frenchman, have I even been to France? Sadly, no. Without my parents, I just haven't been able to bring myself to do it. I've booked a ticket no less than five times, and each time, I find a reason to wait. To delay.

The skyline of Boston catches my view, and I can't help but give a small smile for the city that is one of the reasons I exist. The leaves in the few trees I see whirling by are gathering orange and other warm tints at their edges, and it settles into my soul that there truly is nothing like New England in the fall. Even though I only go to the city every other Thursday morning and return on the eleven o'clock morning train, it's still a piece of home.

Home. What a concept. What a word. I like to think that words are like water or weapons. They give you what you're thirsty for or cut you at the heart. My mother, or *ma maman*, always said that words create your life.

I don't remember many words from my mother. From the photographs and my own vague memories, I know she was a force of elegance and strength. My father, who left this world nearly two years ago, was a hard-working man with a deep well of kindness and joy. I never got the full story of their love, only pieces that appear throughout my memories, like leaves falling to the earth. But they loved each other deeply and loved each other until the end. This I have always felt right down to my bones.

I do know that my parents met in Boston when they were sixteen. He was delivering bread in the city, and she was visiting America for the first time with my grandparents. It was an earth-shattering love from the start. They wrote to each other for a few years before my mother attended a university in America, and my father waited for her. They married soon after, and then I came along. I don't know how most love works, but you can sense when your parents love each other. And their love lives on in my system. I have to believe that.

My eyes stinging from the memory of them, I clear my throat. Without warning, our train car jerks violently and has some sort of shrieking fit. I jump as a guitar case flies from an overhead bin and lands to the right of my seat.

"You could've been *crushed,*" says the older woman from before. It's not helpful, and I think I detect a hint of mischief in her tone but hope for the best. The commuters surrounding us who are not on their phones look at the case, but no one moves toward it.

My gaze travels up the case and lands on a sticker that reads *Seb's.* Immediately, I think of *La La Land.* It looks just like the sign from the movie. I smile to myself and refrain from humming "City of Stars." I feel my eyes widen when I see another sticker—this one from CDG, Charles de Gaulle Airport, in Paris. I sit up and look around the train, but I'm now the only person in the car besides the unhelpful older woman and the snoring man wearing a New England Patriots sweatshirt across the aisle. He doesn't look like a Seb, but I've been wrong before.

I reach for the case to pull it out of the aisle when I suddenly feel I'm being watched. I turn to find a crew member with an intense brow who is new to this route heading my way.

"Excuse me?" I ask.

"Yes?" She turns toward me, clearly already annoyed.

I point to the guitar case and do my best to smile in a way that disarms her ability to hate life. "Um. . . Do you know whose this is? I don't know if it's been abandoned or not. It kind of flew at me, and I—"

"You're not stealing it?"

"What? No! No, I'm not stealing it—I think the case tried to kill me, actually . . ."

I swear I hear the older woman across the way whisper, "Crush," as the crew member grabs for the guitar and looks at the ticket above the seats, eyes narrowing.

"They're still here."

I laugh forcefully to try to dissolve the already awkward situation. My stomach dips at the thought that it could belong to the man I saw earlier. Because, of course, I'm being attacked by random luggage owned by someone (I'm hoping Handsome Stranger), who's possibly getting a coffee and not in need of a baggage manager.

"Great!"

She maintains eye contact as she walks away. As if I would steal someone's guitar. Really. The world these days.

"Seb," I whisper. A grin hits my face, and I realize it's the first time I've smiled all day. After my usual ritual in Boston this morning, combined with the emotions stirred up about my parents every time I'm in said city and a fleeting encounter with someone who thinks I'm unhinged for Frenchmen, my heart has been an overcast sky lately.

I pull out a book from my bag and attempt to hide

the cover. It's a Regency romance, so there's lots of pining and men in great coats. The cover doesn't do it justice really. But if *Seb* does come back, I don't want him to think I'm a hopeless romantic (I totally am).

I wait for five more minutes before I feel the rhythm of the train lull me toward sleep with the memories of the plans my mother and father once made for us to visit Paris.

Being jostled awake by a moving train car is not as glorious as it should be. I'm rethinking my love for travel because a train ride has never been a romantic experience for me yet. It's definitely not like the movies. Thankfully, I'm at my stop. I jolt upright in my seat, the scratch of my sweater still stinging my cheek, and as I search around my seat for my things, it hits me: The guitar case is gone. Looking up, I recognize the back of Handsome Stranger getting off the train. His brown hair lightly dances in the breeze beneath that blessed baseball cap. He adjusts his now-returned guitar case, which he must've retrieved while I was asleep. Fantastic. I hold my breath, praying luck is on my side to see a glimpse of his face.

"Please, please, please . . ." I whisper. "C'mon, Seb."

He hears me—I'm sure of it—and he starts to turn back toward the train just as a very large family barrels through from the train car next to us, completely blocking my view.

"No, no, no!" I grab my bag and slip out of the car, practically sliding off the steps and onto the train platform. I'm on my toes, trying to see over people— and now a baggage cart on the platform—when I realize there's no way I'm catching up to this man. He's gone.

And I didn't even get enough of a glimpse to give a report to Lily—or to commit his perfection to memory.

I let out a sigh that ruffles the fringe falling across my forehead and close my eyes.

"That was him, you know."

"Ah!" I jump and see the crew member with the intense brow beside me again. Why do I always attract people I don't want to spend the rest of my life with? I close my eyes and take a deep breath.

"You know? The one with the guitar case."

"Yes, I remember," I manage.

She inhales loudly, nails brushing across her pristine train vest. Are train vests a thing? They must be. "Quite a looker, that one."

I groan. I swear there's some amusement in her voice. She must get a kick out of these missed meet-cute moments all the time. If this were a fairy tale, she'd definitely be the villain—or at least the villain's sidekick.

And because I don't want her to feel the satisfaction of misjudging my frustration, I manage to quietly add, "How lovely."

I'm halfway to my car when I realize that if Mystery Man has gotten off at this stop, he's at least in the area. Maybe for an afternoon or maybe longer. He could have family in town, but that's doubtful, as I've met everyone who's a regular here at least four times. No one comes to Birch Borough without a reason. It's too small. Too off-the-map. Maybe there's still hope for a meet-cute after all.

Chapter Two

Sparrow

I just want to go to Paris and fall in love with a Frenchman. Is that really too much to ask?" I announce to the bakery. My bakery, to be exact.

A few customers look slightly aghast, but the regulars barely glance up. They're used to this sort of thing—my "announcements" into the universe.

The overhead bell rings, and I get hit by an overambitious child running out the door. No more croissants for him. His mother (at least I think it's his mother) looks apologetic before pushing me out of the way to catch her little escape artist. I nod my understanding and motor toward the counter where Lily, my best friend, waits. Her light-pink apron that reads *pain of chocolate*—a take on *pain au chocolat*—has seen better days. It looks like she was in a war with some chocolate this morning. By the smear over her eyebrow, my suspicions are confirmed.

"Why does chocolate hate you so much?" I ask incredulously. I wash my hands thoroughly and try to let the lingering mental image of Graham wash down the drain with the bubbles.

She sighs as she arranges the pastries in the front case. "It's not my fault chocolate is out to get me. But enough about me—who was he this time?"

"Huh?" I startle. Should've known I couldn't hide this one.

"Your face. You always have that distant look when someone, aka a man, gets too close to your castle."

"I don't have a castle," I reply. I do, though. I totally do.

She arches an eyebrow. "Look, I get it. You have very specific dreams and ideas about how your life is going to go."

"No, I don't."

"Yes, you do. Don't argue with me. Now my point is, you have ideas . . . but you can't plan your life like this."

"I haven't planned anything! Anything I've planned has been shot down like millennials and their side parts."

Lily huffs but turns back toward a vat of melted chocolate, her light-blonde hair swept up in a high ponytail. It sways as she walks and always will.

We met in the first grade and have been best friends ever since. I had lost my mother a year before and had withdrawn from the world. While in the reading corner of our classroom with a book about an American girl who goes to Paris, Lily was lying flat on a beanbag chair, looking up to the ceiling while having an existential crisis of her own. I asked her if she wanted me to read to her, and after a slight nod, she listened. It was meant to be.

When we discovered I was named after a bird and Lily after a flower, she made me a bracelet. We even have tattoos. I have a small lily on my left wrist, and she has a small sparrow on her right wrist. Neither of us has siblings, so that is what we are for each other. She's wild, and chocolate seems to hate her, but she's family, and I don't know where I'd be without her.

I always wanted to take over the bakery my father and mother had started—which my father ran on his own after my mother was no longer with us—and Lily loves chocolate. Case closed. There wasn't ever much of a discussion about it except to decide if we were going to change the signs (we didn't) or if we were going to update the aprons (we did).

Lily is the person I can talk to, or not talk to, about anything. Sometimes I think we've switched roles, and I'm the one now having an existential nearly-one-third-of-a-century crisis on the proverbial beanbag of life, while Lily is reading to me reminders of the dreams I've had and how to not lose sight of myself, even when all I feel are the burning coals of disappointment. Heaps of them.

"I think you need to tell me more about the man you met today."

"Ugh. You would've loved him, actually." Lily's eyes light up for a fraction of a second before they dim and resume their "not interested" type of look. Talk about a fortress. She accuses me of such a thing but never goes out with anyone. And I would know—she tells me everything.

She raises her brows and waits. Chocolate drips from the whisk she is holding as she makes eye contact. This is one of her stare-offs, and it will not go in my favor. As much as I wish there wasn't a little pool of melted dark chocolate forming on the industrial counter, Lily is focused, chocolate forgotten.

"He was perfectly . . . fine. Just not the person I'm

going to spend my life with."

Lily chucks the whisk into the sink and glares. "And. Why. Not?"

Honestly, she's terrifying when she gets into interrogation mode. I never had to worry about bullies or any other type of threat when we were in school with Lily as my best friend. Thank goodness I know which side of the line I'm on when it comes to her wrath, even if I do see glimpses of it every now and then.

I scrunch my nose and dip a spoon in chocolate. I'm going to need it. "He's not French?" I say while I shove the chocolate in my mouth.

"Of all the ridiculous . . ." Lily trails off. She rolls her eyes, and it's not the first time. "You must know you're not in an enchanted castle with magical objects wanting you to be their guest, right?"

We've had similar conversations before. And truthfully, I get why she's upset. Only my parents could've known the truth behind why I'm so hopefully set on giving my heart to someone who understands me when I say I feel like the Seine must be a character and not just a river.

"Gah!" She's got a spatula and is now stirring up the chocolate so fast I think it's just to break her own record for attempts at chocolate destruction. "The most frustrating thing is that you've probably opened a portal with your words because your little French crush, Jacques, asked about you today . . ."

I inhale sharply. "Really?"

"Yes, but don't get any ideas. You did not orchestrate his apparent and, dare I say, *new* interest in you with your 'man on the train platform refusal,'" she says as her arms flail about, melted chocolate bits raining to the floor. How it's gotten all over her arms too, I'll never know. "Got it?"

I wince slightly. She's not wrong.

Lily's eyes are slits, but I see her soften. She comes closer to where I'm standing with my chin held a little higher than necessary. With her hand on my shoulder, she looks into my eyes, and I see the same friend I found in the reading corner all those years ago once again.

"Rory, you know I love you." I'm Sparrow, of course, but Lily has called me "Rory" since we were kids. Somehow, because she's Lily, most of the town has caught on and call me the same.

I wait for the next part of Lily's commentary. There's always a next part. I raise my brows and tilt my head to signal for the rest.

"But . . . maybe what you're looking for is someone to really see those broken parts of you and love you anyway. To be perfectly free, not perfectly French."

I pull out a tray of cookies from the case and place them on the counter as Lily wraps her chocolate-covered arms around me.

"I love you too much to let you hide for the rest of your life."

I feel tears brewing, so I keep pulling out pastry trays just to do something with my hands.

When I look back, Lily is staring at the tray as if it personally hurt her. Sometimes I wonder if her mannerisms have a bite simply because she's hiding parts of herself too. I walk to her side, and she grins softly. There are bits of cookies on the tray from where I moved it a little too forcefully from the case. We each pick up a broken piece and take a bite.

Chapter Three

Sparrow

The music of the river rushing over the rocks below carries through the air. Walking around town as the sun sets and the night creeps in, I've already seen four bunnies and a chipmunk chirping from a rock. I love the way their whole bodies seem to move with their calls into the parting summer air. The light is starting to fade earlier each evening, and soon we'll be celebrating our Maple Fest.

I've never seen a town celebrate holidays like Birch Borough. New England is known, in general, for celebrating autumn like the whole season is a miracle. I love it so much. The maple everything, the pumpkin everything, the celebration of boots and sweaters . . .

I nod to my friend Ivy, the owner of the dance studio and dance shop in town called En Pointe, as I pass by its windows. I stop to take in the little ones running around in bunchy tights and slippers with their strings untied. The piano music makes me smile and brings back the memories of sweet days of my own at the barre.

I see Grey across the street in her family's independent bookstore, Marlee's Books. The shop's lights illuminate her as she stacks and organizes books. I don't miss how she peeks at the inside of each cover as she does. Grey and I went to school together, and I've always admired the way she tunes out the rest of the world and gets lost in a book. We have a lot in common, and she has always been very sweet. I make a mental note to reach out to her soon.

While Lily and I were always the best of friends, Grey and Ivy were our crew. In high school, we went down separate paths and no longer had many classes together. And then, when Grey's mother died and Ivy's family moved away, life seemed to get between all the details we should know about each other. But I miss the days of sitting outside Bette's Ice Cream, enjoying our cones and talking about crushes, books, baking, and nemeses (the nemeses were brought up by Lily, of course).

I keep strolling, waving to people as I go, taking in the way dusk has transformed the sky into an orange-and-gold glow and the feelings this town always brings out in me. As much as I've wanted to visit France, I can't imagine ever leaving this place for good. It's home.

And it's not just because my parents were here, and it's not even that I'm afraid to leave (okay, I would be a little afraid to leave). It's mostly because this place is a part of me. I love the rhythm of it all. The changes in the weather that transform the tone of our town. The way that Chester tries to sell bushels of apples in the fall and then lavender in the summer. The way that Angie from Angie's Pies tries to add extra cream to my coffee and extra whipped cream on my apple pie because she says I need the love. The way Ted from Ted's Pet Shoppe takes pictures of the local rescues every year and makes a calendar to raise money for even more pets to be able to be adopted. The way Mrs. Krutchens tries to sample wine at our weekly farmers' market, even though they only sell it by the glass.

People in high school were always talking about leaving this place. And except for the four of us girls, our class mostly did. But as much as I want to adventure to Paris, I've never wanted to escape Birch Borough. It's the most magical place because I've never had to leave it to know its worth.

This town is a place of belonging. It's a community that actually cares that you like pizza every Friday night and donuts every Sunday morning. A place that gives you the freedom to feel everything you're feeling. And while they'll send you soup when you're sick and put your bagel "on the house" when you're running late, they won't judge you for it when you're just . . . human.

Stopping in front of my store, I let out a little sigh. I'm so proud of it. I love what we've accomplished here and that it's still doing so well, even after the loss of my father. Sure, the first few months were tough, but the town rallied around me to make sure we made more money than ever, even after the weeks we barely stayed open.

But as I study the logo and the trim, I look for answers to the nagging feeling in my bones. The one that says I could do more. Not in terms of location but with the store. My father, in his final years, mentioned one day launching something online. Our town is not very tech-savvy, but I could see it. A way to get my mother's recipes and legacy to more people. A way to ensure this place lives beyond me as well.

I walk around the corner of Main Street toward the

back of my store, the uneven cobblestones pushing through the soles of my shoes, and see my apartment with the tin-roof door. It's not really a tin roof, but my father painted it the color of the roofs in Paris and did the same for our bakery and café so my mother would feel more at home. It's worn now, and the paint is chipped in several places, but it still feels right.

Gathering my mail and opening the front door, the tendrils of the crisp night send a chill down my spine. The only sounds I hear are the soft sounds of the stairs beneath my feet as I climb. My dancer training may have caused me to step lightly, but I'm convinced nothing can escape a creaky old floor.

I hesitate at the top, knowing that when I enter the apartment, I'm on my own. The store is closed for the evening, Lily is off doing Lily-like things, and there's no one waiting for me on the other side of the door. I take a deep breath and slide in, waiting for another night to pass.

I want love—the hit-me-in-the-guts-and-make-me-feel-something kind of love. A love that makes me forget these moments. This moment. The one where I'm thinking about which organic frozen meal I'm going to microwave for the fourth time this week and asking myself where I took a wrong turn to end up here.

I'm thirty years old. And in all the time I've lived, I've never once felt real love. Sure, I've had crushes and wished for someone's love, but all of that? That's really just pretend love. It's the kind of love that excites you because you want love so badly that you'll take the scraps. And somewhere in your soul, you know they're only scraps. But you take them anyway. And somehow, you end up thanking the person who gave you crumbs because you're starving, and they're the closest thing to love that you've known yet.

I've read enough romance novels to know that—somewhere—the love that makes you want to be brave is out there. It has to be. So many things have changed, but people still write about love, sing about it. Sure, I've spent more time with the heartbroken than the heart-whole, but I like to think it's taught me what love is not. And love is not this.

Don't get me wrong. I love a good night in, and the fact that I haven't settled, and that I'm sitting in my pjs with full possession of the remote control. But when I look in the mirror, I know I've never felt real love. Not romantically, anyway. And it bleeds me out, little by little.

There are very few moments in which I can fully remember my mother. But for some reason, a moment always seems to waltz into my mind from when I must've been three or four years old. We were sitting on a bench in Boston Common, and I remember it being sunny. And there were ducks . . . lots of them. I remember the sounds of people and families milling about and me looking up at *ma maman*. She was wearing a perfectly fitting white dress with brown strappy sandals, and her milk-chocolate hair flowed behind her as she drank from a paper coffee cup. I remember smelling cinnamon from whatever she was drinking and the taste from the madeleine cookie I nibbled—one of the buttery, golden ones. Whenever I recall this moment, I'm looking at the Swan Boats in the river, and then I look up at my mother, who stops drinking her coffee. A slow, blinding smile paints itself across her face, and when I follow her gaze, I see my father standing there.

The smile I can't seem to forget was for him. And I hope someday someone brings a smile like that out of me too.

I curl up on the loveseat in my apartment and play Histoire on my record player in the corner that is a CD, cassette, radio, and digital music player all in one. A candle glows on my coffee table, and a glass of rosé sits on a coaster that reads, *We'll be those dirty, filthy, almost-French, Stars Hollow girls.* Lily has one that says, *Oy, with the poodles already.*

A picture of my parents and me from when I was around three years old takes up space on a shelf on my built-in bookcases. I have all kinds of little figurines and memories that cover the gaps before the bindings on my books. My gaze falls to a picture of my father and me right before he passed. He's smiling, his little glasses perched on his nose, and I'm laughing at something he just said. Lily took the picture. I don't remember what was so funny, but really, does it matter?

I miss him so much it hurts. Sometimes I feel like I take up so much space, and other times, I feel like I'm alone in a great big world caught between two worlds, two stories, two cultures—my mother's and my father's—and neither one of them are here to tell me how to move forward or create my own future.

The microwave sounds with its annoying alarm, and I let it ding, not quite yet willing to move. My back has arched perfectly into the couch cushions, and honestly, the sound of Histoire's voices is doing exactly what I hoped it would—calming my nerves by hitting the right notes. The image of the guitar that was wedged between the train seats this morning puts a grin on my face. I wonder if the owner of said guitar appreciates how delightful Emma Stone and Ryan Gosling's dance numbers and duets were.

Suddenly, the meal heated through radioactive waves sounds even less appealing than before I sat down. So I take a sip of my nearby sparkling rosé and let the microwave down by ignoring its call and pulling the blanket from the back of my well-worn couch. I blow out the apple-crisp candle in one final slouch under the blanket and let the music wash over me, the memories of my father humming as he baked croissants calling me to dream.

Everything that could go wrong today has, indeed, gone wrong. There was a thunderstorm last night with torrential rain that reinforced my fear of freezing to death. I woke up to a thin layer of water all over my kitchen after accidentally leaving the window open a crack before falling asleep on my couch. Thanks, rosé, for giving me a sleep that meant I awakened to my music still playing with my alarm not even set.

I tried to make Nutella toast. It burned. I attempted coffee but realized I was fresh out. My hair, because of the aforementioned rain, is giving me such aggressive flyaways that another bobby pin is rejected as I watch it launch from my head and onto the floor. Even my shower was lackluster as I had forgotten to buy body wash, so instead of suds, I had one bubble's worth of soap. Really. One. Bubble.

Somewhere on the sidewalk from my apartment to the front door of the bakery, I stepped in something sticky, so the bottom of my shoe sounds like it is now trying to suction the earth. I didn't wash my favorite sweater, so I'm wearing my non-favorite sweater, which happens to have a mysterious stain on the cuff of my left sleeve.

Still, as I walk to my bakery, I can't help but find a fresh appreciation for all that waits for me inside. Thankfully, a year or so ago, we hired a pastry chef and an assistant pastry chef to manage the baking and opening in the early morning hours, so my schedule is on my own terms these days—a freedom I don't take for granted.

As I linger outside my store, I notice the things that make it as charming as it is in the morning light: the cream trim, the sign over the front door that was hand-painted by my mother, the café tables Lily and I chose that look like they belong in a French bistro and not in a tiny town like ours. We are situated by a river, though . . . so there's that.

I say a silent prayer that someday, someone else, a partner in this life, will love this place as much as I do—enough not to think I'm settling by being here. Enough to want to stay with me through the days and nights that I will keep these doors open. Enough to want to stay for more than the croissants (which are incredible, by the way).

I place my hand on the knob of the creaky old door and turn. If my parents had what it took to run this place, surely I can do the same today.

Chapter Four

Sparrow

Okay, name one thing that isn't perfect about Jacques?" Granted, I know he's not perfect. I'm sure Lily knows that I know that, too, but she's too kind to point out my tightly held nightly frozen-dinner habit. I'm pushing my luck with her by bringing him up again.

My friend makes a face and goes back to grinding coffee beans—rather aggressively, actually. I try to interject, but she grins and waits until the coffee beans are turned to dust. We couldn't use them if we tried.

"Feel better?" I ask.

"Lots." She grimaces as she looks at the coffee dust. She sprinkles it on a batch of cookies, confirming that she is a genius.

I shake my head and motion for her to get back to the conversation.

"Oh, I don't know," she begins. "Let's start with the fact that you don't really know him. And he's kind of . . . cold, no?"

I square my shoulders and lift my chin. "He's cute. Some people, who are drawn to model types, might even say he's beautiful."

Lily rolls her eyes. "Since when have you been into models?"

"Never," I mutter.

"But what if I subconsciously was saying what I want on the train platform yesterday? Because if I did end up with someone French, then it's like . . ."

"What your parents had," Lily finishes.

I nod as she closes the gap between us with one of her koala hugs. We can't call them bear hugs because she's too afraid of bears to allow it. She pulls away, and I start to organize the pastry case.

"What's so wrong with choosing a different path?"

I look up to see Lily leaning against the case, watching me work.

She grins. "I'm just saying . . . is this revelation about knowing what you want, or are you avoiding a real relationship?"

I bristle and work on grinding more coffee beans to replace Lily's coffee dust but end up watching as the coffee maker tries to sputter to life. I hit it with my palm as some nearby beans fall to the floor. The poor things are having a day like mine. Coffee grounds have claimed me and mark my apron, my hands, and—I'm pretty sure—parts of my face. I could've made a cup of coffee this morning with how many are glued to me at this moment.

"I don't pay you for therapy, you know. You're really on a roll lately."

"You've been grieving for two years. You're trying to hold on at this point."

I clench my jaw. "Let it go, Lily." The warning is the closest we'll get to fighting.

"So, you're really saying now that you're *only* going to go out with a man who's from France? Or someone who speaks French? I mean, *you* don't even really speak French! It's gotta be about more than that ... and, truthfully, it better be ... because your parents would want more for you."

"I am not being shallow. Lily, I go home to an apartment each night alone. I have no family, except for a great-aunt who's never written me back. I love this town, but everyone has their life—even you! So, what's so wrong with wanting to have something like my parents had? Why does it have to make sense? Life doesn't always make sense!"

I rearrange some bags of *chouquettes*—a choux pastry topped with pearl sugar—and recall a moment when I was little when my father handed me a chouquette and said he had sprinkled it with love, just like my mother would. I focus on the bags to keep up my nerve for the declaration I'm about to make. The bell over the door rings, and I will myself not to cry.

"You know what?" I announce. "I stand by what I said. And I now officially declare that I *refuse* to date anyone who isn't French. If they're not French, I'm not interested."

Lily drops a tray of macarons she is holding, and I watch them tumble to the floor.

"You sure about that?" she whispers.

I reach out to grab some of the ruined pastries and feel my forehead tap the edge of the counter. Great, a mark to encapsulate this moment. Lily still hasn't moved. I sigh and take in her frozen glance. She's a goner. I hold my head and grab a rag to try to brush myself off before turning to meet the new customer. If she's going to abandon me by becoming a statue, so be it.

Pasting a smile on my face, I turn toward where she's staring and freeze at the sight. It's a man. No, not a man. A man would be too pedestrian for the type of human before me. This is a Beyond Man—one you only see when you swear off all other men. And I'm pretty sure it's the same man from the train. Scratch that; it *is* the man from the train. I'd recognize the way the bottom of his hair flips anywhere.

"You." I let out a breath.

I'm taller than average, and even I have to look up to take him all in. Cinnamon-brown hair with natural highlights casually frames a set of forest-green eyes. Yes, forest green. The type of green only seen on the tall trees of a northern forest. The kind I've only seen in pictures.

His cheekbones and jawline perfectly highlight his full lips and stubble. His hair glistens in the sunlight. He's wearing a navy-blue t-shirt that hugs his shoulders and chest before meeting a pair of light-colored jeans.

He clears his throat, and I realize I've been staring for God knows how long. *Wait. How long have I been standing here?*

I stumble forward from the impact of Lily pushing me toward the register, where this human (at least, I think he's human) is looking at me. For a second, I think I catch a look of sadness crossing his face. But that can't be possible. He blinks slowly and then seems to mentally resolve something.

I catch a new glimmer of amusement in his eyes and feel my cheeks flush.

He's achingly handsome, but there's something about him that's also playful and unassuming. Realizing what I just announced to the universe, I immediately try to undo my declaration—or make it come true, at the very least.

Please be French. Please be French. The wish is on repeat. My whole body wills it to manifest. Now.

He narrows his eyes and looks at Lily and then back at me. I clear my throat and will myself to speak. I've got nothing.

"What can we get you?" Lily squeaks. Way to play it cool, my friend.

He seems to debate something as his eyes bounce back and forth between us before landing on me for good. "So, again with the 'only someone French,' yes?" No accent. But his voice sounds freaking angelic. Deep. Slightly raspy. Melodic.

"Wait. *Again?*"

He narrows his eyes playfully, and understanding creeps into my bones.

"You *did* hear me . . . on the train."

My cheeks are on fire, and my shoulders deflate, but I can't look away. I catch a twitch near his mouth, almost as if he's trying to will himself to remain unaffected. He doesn't break eye contact.

"Uh-uh," I stutter. I've never stuttered in my life. I feel a thump at my back and realize Lily has thrown a baked good at me to snap me out of it. What a friend. "You weren't supposed to hear that," I manage. "Either time."

He grins. "Well, I did . . . I have . . . and I don't think I'll forget it."

Lily chokes on something behind me. I love her, but she deserves it.

"What can I get you?" *Please say me.* I shake my head to loosen the thought. As if that would work.

"What do you recommend?" he croons. I stand by this description. His voice is, indeed, music.

A child screams in the corner, and I witness

chocolate milk explode somewhere in my peripheral vision. I ignore it. Let the whole place burn down. I'm locked in with an actual hallucination. This feels like a test that the universe is asking me to pass.

As if she hears my thoughts, Lily walks by and pinches me from behind. "Ow!" I screech.

Okay, so, not dreaming.

He clears his throat and lightly bites the edge of his lip. I mimic him, a flash of something warm and dangerous flooding my stomach.

"Wh-what?" I whisper. Excellent. Love how conversational I am now that my wish to be near him has come true.

If he's frustrated by my unraveling, he doesn't let on.

"How is your coffee ground?" And why do these words sound so seductive? Is he asking me out? Is this an innuendo?

"My coffee?" This time, my voice gives a squeak I don't recognize.

One of his sculpted hands signals to the front of my apron, and I follow the motion, suddenly remembering that this is real life, and I am, in fact, still covered in coffee grounds. This isn't TV, and I didn't magically get a chance to get wardrobe and makeup done before the leading man entered the coffee shop. Drat.

"Right, um . . ." I catch his gaze as my face flushes. "Well, the truth is . . ." I trail.

He lifts a brow. A perfectly sculpted brow. *I wonder if he gets his eyebrows done . . .*

"I do not, but thank you," he says softly, and I wince.

"Well, okay," I say quickly and steamroll ahead. "The truth is, I don't know because I didn't make the coffee this morning. I'm just wearing it, apparently. Because everything in my life seems to be imploding. Except the pastries! They're fantastic. So, a good choice is a croissant. I didn't make the coffee ... but I can make coffee! It's just that sometimes this coffee machine feels like it came from a level of hell because it really doesn't like me. If this were a movie, you just met my archnemesis."

I'm unhinged. I stop enough to see his eyes widen and motion to the behemoth of a coffee maker on the counter behind me.

He blinks.

"The coffee maker. Not me. To be clear," I add and inhale deeply.

He looks toward the pastry case and furrows his brow. "Is that ... a *maple* croissant?"

I smile wide before thinking. "You are in New England."

He rests an elbow on the counter and leans beautifully toward me, like he has ever since he walked into my bakery, as if what I have to say is the most fascinating thing he's ever heard.

"Okay, well, it's a croissant, of course," I begin. He nods encouragingly. "And I made a filling for it that's like the inside of a cinnamon roll, except maple. And then I dust it with maple sugar."

He stands to his full height, his eyes lit with interest (I tell myself it must be the pastry, not me).

"A maple croissant, please," he quickly replies. And then, a tentative look crosses his face. "Or sill vew plate?"

I cringe. *S'il vous plaît.* His attempt to say "if you please" in French was terrible. He cringes too, but I catch the way his eyes dance at his effort.

"Yes, the maple croissants are good. *Bon.*" I sort of wink, but I've never winked in my life because I actually can't wink. Lord only knows how my face just contorted. I just know it would look like one of those memes that show you Pinterest versus reality.

He reaches into his pocket and pulls out a debit card. Right. I need to ring him up now.

Lily is already bagging the biggest croissant we have and is placing it gingerly on the counter between us as if any sudden movement will redirect the other dimension we've clearly entered.

"So . . ." he continues as if I haven't lost all my dignity. Self-respect? Time of death: 10:01 a.m. "I feel like it's my job—my duty, really—to tell you that I'm a self-proclaimed coffee expert. I'm pretty sure that my body needs it more than water. I may even defy science."

He signals to his body in a non-suggestive way, and still, my jaw goes slack.

"Look, Mommy! The lady looks like a fish!" This beautiful observation comes from the chocolate-milk tornado from earlier.

I close my mouth and shake my head. "You like coffee?"

"Yes," he laughs lightly. "And I just moved into town, so I'm sure we'll see each other."

"You moved here?" I whisper. I know everyone in this town, and I could've sworn he would only be visiting. This news of his permanence has just officially shifted my world.

"Well, then! Welcome, *neighbor*!" Lily says a little too happily.

Somehow, he keeps his eyes focused on me.

"You can call me Rafe, *neighbor*." A dimple plays in the corner of his perfect, full mouth.

"You're not Seb?" I manage.

"Excuse me?" He smirks. He has the audacity to

smirk, and even that is a revelation.

"The—the guitar case. From yesterday."

He nods slowly. Gah, handsome men and their perfectly perfect names. Rafe. It's broody and suits him. Of course it does.

"Mm-hmm." Looking out the window, I again catch the way the morning light slowly shimmers across his stubble.

"What do you think?" he begins, and I freeze as he slowly leans forward, a smile starting to spread across his face. "Is it another day of sun?"

I feel my shoulders sink, and my mouth falls open once more. *Fish or no fish, this man just quoted* La La Land, *and I can never be the same.*

"Yeah," he whispers. "You spoke that out loud too. Don't worry. I won't ask you to sing with me." He looks to the ceiling as if he's remembering something that stings. "Also, I understand the choice, but I still always hope they'll end up together, don't you?"

And then he winks—a proper wink—and just like that, I don't care if I never see another Frenchman again.

Chapter Five

Rafe

I can't tell if the adorable woman in front of me is stumped, irritated, or frustrated. It's amusing the heck out of me. And yes, I'm describing her as adorable. She's the one who was on my train yesterday.

I got back to my seat, and in my peripheral vision, there she was, stretched out with a book featuring a picture of a woman in some sort of period clothing—I'm guessing something in the age of Mr. Darcy—and a man wearing a surprisingly great coat. She was spread out on the train seat, a slight grin on her slumbering face. If she had been awake, I would've asked for her number. Somehow, I think if I had seen her fully, I wouldn't have been able to.

There's a child with a volcano of chocolate milk erupting in the corner and a frantic mother trying to clean the sticky mess off the floor, but I don't even glance in their direction. Normally, that type of thing would draw my attention.

But I can't stop looking at the woman in front of me

who is annihilating my thoughts of anyone else I've considered attractive. I heard her declaration on the train yesterday, turned around, got my first look at the side of her face, and decided I couldn't look at her ever again if I wanted to keep a hold on my heart. And then I caught a glimpse of her sleeping. The way her bottom lip had parted just a bit as if she was ready to talk in her sleep. My chest warms, and I suddenly wish for the colder air outside. It's too hot in here.

Her hair is the color of dark honey, and her eyes are a river of melted chocolate. I was irritated when I heard her talking about wanting to date someone French—for the *second* time—but now, looking at her, I can't remember why it frustrated me. Oh, probably because it complicates any hope of a relationship with her *if* I wanted one. My heart and body are fighting it out with my mind right now. And my mind isn't winning.

"What else can I get you . . . Rafe?" she squeaks out.

Her eyes flutter toward the window with a grin, as if my name is satisfying to say. But then she shakes her head lightly and gives me a shy smile. When I gave her my name, I tried to be charming, but the hopeful look on her face when we first made eye contact shattered the second she heard me speak. Instinctively, I understand that she was hoping for a voice other than my own.

I think a part of me died, and I brought on some wrath from my ancestors when I butchered "please" in French. My whole mouth is bitter with the aftertaste of such a crime.

Maybe I should've handled this all differently, but when she was talking about wanting to date a French guy, I couldn't get the words out. And the reason sinks soul deep.

"Uh . . . " my voice cracks. This isn't doing me any favors.

The friend—*Lily*, I think her name tag reads—looks both riveted and confused. She glances at her friend and then looks back at me. Making a decision, she grabs a rag and heads toward the chocolate-milk kid. He may have left by now, for all I know, but who even cares at this point? The bell has chimed a few times, and there are definitely two or three people behind me, but again, I'm not moving. If this woman is looking at me, there's no chance I'm doing anything to interrupt her.

"I'll take an Americano, please?" Why do I keep turning statements into questions? I'm usually confident, able to accomplish anything I set my mind to—except for talking to this woman.

"For here?" she asks, and I manage to nod.

"That I can do ... I think," she whispers as she slowly turns away toward the machine. She mumbles something about shaking. Without her gaze on me, my shoulders relax a bit, and I breathe a little easier. I can finally take in my surroundings.

The sounds of the café bring a smile to my face. Suddenly, I miss the mornings of sitting in the corner of a *pâtisserie* with the smell of brewed coffee, the café tables on the sidewalks, the sounds of the city, the view of mopeds rushing by . . .

"Anything in it?"

ZAM. I follow the voice, and we make eye contact. I've been hit by lightning once again. I try to focus on anything but her eyes, probably looking like I don't usually drink espresso and am thrown by the question or that this is a cry for help.

I shake my head too excitedly and sigh audibly when she turns back to the machine.

"You should just ask Sparrow out," a voice behind me whispers.

I look over my shoulder to see a woman with whitening hair, a glimmer in her eyes, and a smirk as wide as the Atlantic Ocean looking at me. She nods toward the woman I now know is named Sparrow, and I feel my cheeks warm. I clear my throat. This must be what embarrassment feels like.

"I—uh—well, I . . . can't."

"And why not?" She's clearly not impressed with my response.

The reasons it wouldn't be a good idea to be involved with anyone right now filter through my head like a viewfinder: disappointed parents, writer's block, She-Who-Must-Not-Be-Named, nights in Paris, mornings in Los Angeles, an ominous deadline for a demo, that moment a few nights ago where I swear I did a very masculine version of crying myself to sleep.

"That will be three-fifty," says the angel voice from behind the counter.

My answer to the nosy customer behind me is cut off, and I'm glad for it. I pull out my wallet and pay for the drink. Usually, I would take it and rush out the door, but today, I just want to be near her a little longer. I walk around the counter, not without noticing a wink from Mystery Advice Woman. I move to the stools overlooking the espresso machine and pull one out to sit.

Well, I try to sit. I basically pull out the stool, attempt to sit, falter, and then finally make it onto the stool. Hopefully, she didn't see. Sparrow is placing the Americano—poured into a European-looking ceramic cup—onto the counter. I move to take it a little too slowly and realize I'm saddened our fingers didn't touch in the process. *What is with me today?*

She gives me a little grin, and I breathe deeply,

watching the steam from the cup dance in the air. My heart is beating out of my chest. Maybe it's all the movement in my life lately, or it could be this woman. I can't believe her name is Sparrow. I rub a hand over my heart to try to knead out the emotion that seems to have caught there.

I look up to see Sparrow making the next set of drinks, coffee cups already neatly stacked beside each other. I know she said the coffee maker hates her, but to me, she looks perfectly in her element. Like an actual angel dropped into the middle of a café. I'm wondering if she smells like croissants and coffee when she peeks over her shoulder at me with a look I don't know how to read.

And suddenly, I very much want to know the meaning behind every expression that crosses her face.

When I walked into this charming French café in search of coffee and croissants this morning, my plan was not to sit at a barstool, trying my best to not appear like I'm loitering. Now I'm writing in the notebook I carry around in my pocket, trying to pretend like I'm working, but really, I'm listening for the cheerful song of her voice, which I've already memorized. I'm usually one who avoids people. And it's not because I think more of myself than I need to, but in my line of work—and because of my family—being chased by women (and all people, really) comes with the territory. I knew this the minute I stepped in front of a microphone. Actually, I knew this the minute my father began caring about his image too much.

My family doesn't approve of me or what I do, and

it's been a point of contention for most of my life. They think I'll never be a good enough lyricist and musician to justify leaving the family business and legacy. They think my passion is a waste of time. But I want to make a name for myself on my own. After countless conversations where my parents sat me down for an intervention, and after years of being sent away through boarding school, university, and my own need for distance, I recognized that their dreams for me feel suffocating.

Lyrics and music have taken up space in my mind, rent free, since I was a boy. They are how I've processed everything in my life. They are how I know I'm alive. Fighting to find the right words to match the right notes so that I could convey what I was feeling became my obsession. As soon as I could write, I found scraps of paper and wrote out thoughts that could become songs. And as soon as I could read music, I added notes above the words like my own secret code. But it was only when I discovered that I found just as much joy in writing songs for other singers as I did in performing them on my own that I knew I was onto something.

I've been working to break into the industry for years, and a few years ago, I released my music with my—then—girlfriend. Not wanting to be in the spotlight at the time, I wrote the music and lyrics, and she sang the tracks. I trusted her with everything. I wish I had realized back then that she was more interested in the music than I was. And when fame started knocking on her door, she decided to take a different path, along with all the songs I had written. While I had thought we were sharing royalties and that the songs belonged to me, it turned out she made a deal to keep the rights— and the royalties.

Could I have sued her? Probably, yes. Did I have it in me to take her to court to fight for songs that were all about her anyway? No, I didn't. I had already given her full access to my life. Plus, my parents' warning that there would be consequences if our name got dragged through court for music and not fashion hadn't been lost on me.

It took months before creating didn't feel like shards of glass poking through my heart. Writing lyrics has been sporadic since. The words just aren't there. So, to keep myself distracted from the struggle of creating new music, I've worn myself out trying to find any other avenues open to a working musician.

There's too much at stake for me to do otherwise. Proving myself isn't even about pride; it's about making something of my life that matters. Something that makes people feel seen and not small. After the breakup, when it didn't hurt as much, I went back to see the comments on some of the music I'd written. Discovering that I could write words that others likened to a life preserver made me want to do that for others, even if I couldn't do it for myself.

I feel the need to be great—maybe because my parents don't think I can be. I'm not accepted by them, and somehow, that's bled into me not accepting myself. Not really. Oh, I know how to appear confident, and since music makes me happy, I can give a performance based on the memories of my past creativity. But a part of me always keeps a distance now. I wait for people to change me. To take the credit from me. To tell me what's wrong with me and what I'm missing. What I could do to be better. *And why do these thoughts sound like what the people closest to me have always said?*

I shift on the stool, distracted from my thoughts by

the woman who's now piping filling into macarons. She's brought out a tray so customers can see them being freshly assembled. She sells them even as she stacks them neatly into a macaron tray. The contented smile that plays on her face as she concentrates on the tiny shells has me reeling. I haven't felt this way since the last song I wrote.

I've been feeling like if another personal piece of my life leaks out—which is the essence of art after all—I won't be able to recover. My dreams are calling me to move forward, but I'm shutting down. I'm choking on all the things I haven't been able to say. And I don't know how to fix it.

That's why I'm in Birch Borough—for a change of scenery and something to make me feel like I haven't lost sight of myself after the last few years.

The New England way of life will take some adjustment after living in the City of Angels. To say it's been a culture shock is an understatement. Two days ago, I was looking at the ocean in Hermosa Beach on the pier (yes, the same one featured in *La La Land*, come to think of it). It was a clear day, and one of my favorite views in the world was before me: the ocean with the mountains in view. But I was burnt out creatively. I wasn't writing. And even the ocean couldn't ease the nagging feeling in my chest. When my friend called and said I should stay with him in his new place for a while, I jumped at the chance. It's even better that he got me a gig already—one that should cover the plane ticket.

I'm not a starving artist. I do quite well for myself, considering my family has basically disowned me, but I like to keep in the green each month. And unexpected trips across the country aren't normally in the budget these days.

Following my train in from Boston, I dropped off my luggage at my friend's house and crashed—hard. This morning, I went in search of decent coffee. I was jet lagged (still am), hungry, smelled butter, coffee, and the comfort that those things are for me, and here I am. It may be a small town, but I never thought I'd see this woman again. Does she live here? What's her story? And why do I even care?

Given the blush on her cheeks when we met, I can't be the only one feeling something between us. I swear I even heard her friend, Lily, say something about me to the effect of, "If he were French, you'd leave everything, and I'd never see you again." And there's the problem. If I had a dating rule, it would be: Don't let love leave you empty. All the external stuff? It means nothing when you're alone at night and find yourself wondering if the people who say they love you actually believe it themselves.

I may have lingered out of fascination for this woman, but Sparrow moved to the back a few minutes ago and hasn't returned. I hope she's not hiding, especially from me. I recognize that she's probably trying to search for the answer to questions like: *What to do if a guy has a sticker that's not his name on his guitar case.*

Do I even want her to know who I really am? Because if I can't share all of myself with her, then what am I even doing here? My parents' nagging voices telling me their name is the only thing I possess worth anything freezes me inside. Could my stay in Birch Borough be a fresh chance for people to see just . . . me?

The sound of my phone buzzing on the counter startles me back into the present. I see who's calling and ignore it. When it starts ringing again, I take the chance of leaving my stuff at the counter and head outside.

Better to get this over with as soon as possible. I shiver slightly at the temperature difference between here and what I've been used to in LA.

Still, the warmth of the sun hitting my eyes is a sharp contrast to the voice I hear on the other end of the line.

"Son."

I wince. Nothing like the sound of someone who should support you tearing you down instead simply by the tone of his voice. I already regret answering. I move toward the side of the building, just in case I slip and my native "Frenchness" breaks out. If I'm honest with myself—and I must be—I'm recently worn from pushing it down after all these years.

"Dad."

There's a pause on the line before I hear him clear his throat. The habit must run in the family. "Your mother wants you to come to dinner next Friday."

I'm stunned. I'm never invited to dinner anymore. There must be a catch. I look across the way to a store called Ollie & Sons Toy Shop, where an older man with a sunny smile is helping a little boy learn how to use a yo-yo. It's a nice distraction from what's happening in my mind.

"No, thank you," I manage.

"This isn't a game."

"Isn't it?"

"I've already had your social footprint erased with us. I can easily remove your footprint from your retirement fund too."

I know what he's saying. He's already disowned me (mostly), and he's ready to make it more official. I wish it didn't bother me that my father constantly finds the need to give me warnings and threats, but it does. Of course it does. So, I do what I always do. I disassociate, and somehow, I grow taller.

"One of these days, I'm just going to stop answering. If you're mad at anyone, it needs to be yourself."

My breathing is shallow as my father again ignores whatever he didn't want to hear.

"*Pffff,*" he slips in a familiar sound of frustration. "And speak *French*. This is not who we raised you to be."

I clench my jaw. My parents didn't really raise me at all. Still, my father likes to tell me what to do. He's not speaking French, and I know why. He's somewhere in America and doesn't want to exclude whoever is in the room. Amazing how he's more considerate with strangers than he's ever been with me. Unfortunately for him, I've made it my mission to scrub some memories—and much of my heritage—from my life. It's killed me little by little, but I've done it.

"No."

"Your mother has found someone suitable for you. Again. Well, I haven't met her, but she agreed to tolerate your little hobby—"

"Listen to me clearly," I interrupt. "The person I'll be with next will love me for *me*. Not because of my family, or my connections, or my talent—even though you don't agree that I have any."

There's silence on the other end of the line. I check the phone to make sure we're still connected and twitch as the time keeps ticking.

"I expect that you'll be on a plane sometime tomorrow. I'll even be generous enough to get you a ticket."

"Again, no."

He sighs audibly. "Give me a reason. If you're going to disappoint your mother once more, I need to have a reason. A valid one."

I look around the streets and find nothing that would be an acceptable reason to convince my father to let this go. I don't even know why I'm trying. Rubbing a hand down my face, I turn back to look at the bakery and see Sparrow has emerged in the front of the store again and is laughing with Lily over something behind the counter.

"I think I have one."

I hang up and hope that I'm right.

After coping with the call from my father with three more Americanos and a few macarons, I'm jittery enough to know that I may have made a mistake in leaving LA for this place—for no other reason than I've gotten way over my head by meeting Sparrow, and I know it. I've never had this much caffeine and sugar in one sitting, but my head was spinning, and my heart still felt heavy. Like some miracle, after my second Americano, I opened my notebook a few hours ago and started writing.

And now, the lyrics just keep flowing. I can't stop. The main themes seem to be honey and meeting someone on a train. If I didn't know any better, I would think it is because of a certain bakery/café owner (at least, I think she owns it). Lord knows my father usually drains inspiration, so it isn't coming from my earlier call with him.

The counter vibrates, and it takes me a second to register that it's my phone and not the coffee talking. I grin at the caller ID. The name on the screen started as a joke when we met while waiting in line at a restaurant in LA, and an actress told him he was handsome enough to be the lead in a Hallmark movie. I laughed, he was horrified, and we became instant friends. Turned out he was a lawyer. A good one. And I'm grateful to have him whenever I question just how much my parents could legally take from me.

Hallmark Hot G: Pizza tonight?

While that sounds perfect, I send the shrugging emoji just for kicks and tap my foot against the counter. He'll be annoyed, but I think it's time I shift my friend's comfort levels. He's gotten too rigid over the past few years.

Lily has started stocking the coffee bar behind me, and I wait until she's filled all the canisters and cream containers before I subtly try to get her attention. In the limited time I've been observing the dynamics here, it's clear that she may be the key to getting to know Sparrow.

"I like this place," I manage. "It reminds me of Paris a bit." She doesn't turn toward me, but I see her stiffen and then get back to cleaning and tidying up like she never heard me speak. A moment later, I feel her channel a different energy, and as Sparrow grabs a tray and moves to the back, Lily is next to me in a heartbeat.

"Keep writing," she whispers.

I glance around, trying to figure out why I'm suddenly in a spy movie, when her rag hits my knuckles.

"Ow!" I yell.

"I said . . . Keep. Writing."

"Okay, okay," I say and do as she instructed, although it's really only scribbles at this point.

"You've been to Paris?"

I nod quickly. "Quite a bit. I lived there for a while, actually."

"Did you like it?"

I hesitate. We're getting too close to the truth. "Not yet."

"You can't ruin it for her." She nods toward the back

kitchen. "Promise?"

I nod again.

"I need words."

"Yes," I swallow. "I promise."

Her swipes on the counter become less intentional and more lazy. "Are you going to break Rory's heart?"

My spine stiffens. "No."

"How can you promise?"

She gives me a moment to think as she walks behind me, peeks her head into the kitchen, yells something to Sparrow, and then rushes back my way. "Well?"

If I'm honest, being under her full gaze has me a little frightened. Lily's lavender-grey eyes are so intense and intriguing that they're like shining gems in a treasure mine. Though I feel no attraction to her at all, Lily is stunning. But there's an edge to her—a guardedness— and I don't ever want to be the one crossing anything or anyone she loves.

There's movement in the back, and I know I only have a moment to get this right. I've let other people dictate how I view myself for long enough. I also know I can't tell Sparrow I'm French and have it affect her opinion of me, for better or worse. My parents drop names, make plays, manipulate people's feelings . . . I'm doing my best not to be them. I feel like my secret could falsely change things between us, especially after her announcements on both the train and in this café.

I've had to defend myself from my father, but there are lines I won't cross. I've been heartbroken enough myself to understand that hurting someone intentionally isn't one of those lines. I won't use my heritage as a bargaining chip when it comes to love. So, I answer Lily as honestly as I can.

"Because I never do more damage than good." Lily

searches my face and gives a slight nod before turning away from me. I don't know if it was the answer she wanted or not, but I let out a breath.

Sparrow walks out to the main floor with a tray of cinnamon rolls, and Lily is already at her side, pulling it from her as if we didn't just share words that will stick with me for the rest of my life. I write it all down in my notebook while Sparrow laughs with a customer who just walked in. And I suddenly feel a stirring to be more creative than I have in a long time.

Chapter Six

Sparrow

The handsome man, aka Rafe, is back today. I was so embarrassed yesterday morning when he remembered me from the train, that when I saw him, I literally thought I was going to melt to the floor. Because, of course, seeing me asleep on a train wasn't enough. Hearing me announce to the world that I wouldn't date someone who wasn't French wasn't enough. TWICE.

No, he also had to see me covered in coffee and muttering my thoughts out loud. Because he's the most stunning man I've ever seen, and all the embarrassment thus far isn't nearly enough to right the impossibility of both of us being in the same space and there being any chance of keeping my heart in check. Have I been focused on Jacques? Yes. Does the feeling of meeting Rafe even compare? No.

I'm so frustrated that I've been furiously scrubbing a pot in the back of the bakery for the past ten minutes, occasionally leaving the sudsy sink and letting water drip on the floor as I peep through the window on the swinging door just to make sure he's still here. As of fifteen seconds ago, he is. I wish I could take everything back from yesterday. I never should've gone to the city. Except, I always do, so I did. Every other Thursday, I stop by the graveyard to honor my parents with flowers. I also bring the journal that holds my memories of them.

And then I sit in Boston Common, drinking a cinnamon-honey latte that I remember my mother liked (or really, that my father told me she liked), and I watch the ducks and the Swan Boats and try to remember at least one memory I have of each of them and write it down. It helps me to feel connected to them. It gives me a way to honor them. And I get to see life outside of my small town, even if it's only to keep myself from forgetting the world beyond Birch Borough.

What happened with Rafe is unsettling for several reasons. It's the multiplication of mortification for messing up something that could've been wonderful. It's the humming of change in the air before there's stillness, and you don't know if you muddled it up or made it better. It's the discomfort of Lily's words and the image of a castle with walls that are climbing higher with each tick of the clock because my heart is screaming that if I lose one more person I love from my life, something in me will permanently break. I've given up trying. I had to give up trying. I scrub the pot a little harder and try to ignore the burning behind my eyes. *Because aren't I breaking, regardless?*

I know what this is, the melancholy that floods my soul every so often, each time a little harder than before. It's the anger that layers itself on my heart every time I know my emotional walls ensure I'll still be alone when I get back to my apartment tonight. And it's the words that circulate in my head, saying that I'll never be enough for someone I'm attracted to. And life seems to keep reiterating this truth. Except for the bakery's account, which Lily runs, I left social media entirely because I couldn't stomach seeing people I know getting engaged, being in love, and having babies. Not because I'm not happy for them—I am happy—but because every time I see it, I'm confronted with the idea that maybe it won't happen for me. *Not everyone gets their happily ever after, right?*

I feel like I'm in a game where everyone got a manual on relationships, and I didn't. Like whenever God was handing out the instruction guides, I didn't hear my number called, or I was so focused on my grief that I missed the memo. I was absent when they covered this class in the school of life—the one where people seem to know how to talk to a potential partner and don't say sabotaging things like, "You're not French," to perfectly eligible men they might want to date. The one where people learn how to flirt (Ha! As if anyone has ever accused me of THAT).

Itching with the need to confirm if Rafe has felt the energy of my thoughts and finally decided to bounce, I chuck the pot to the counter (that's now clean enough to shine like a million suns) and sway toward the door. Rafe is furiously writing in a little notebook, occasionally stopping every ten seconds or so to tap the edge of the pencil against his full mouth. It's distracting. I'm out of my element, and I'm desperately trying to make sense of the effect that his hair curling under the rim of his now-vanished baseball cap has been on loop within my mind.

I realize there's no point in hiding back here anymore since we're about to have an afternoon rush, and I've left Lily by herself for the masses (aka our town regulars) to devour all the quiches, crêpes, and croissants we prepare each day, which will be chased by copious amounts of espresso. I take a deep breath, try to fix my haphazard low ponytail, and shove the swinging door open. Apparently, my newfound resolve is too powerful, as the door smacks the wall and almost takes me out before I dodge out of the way. My eyes are wide as I focus on Lily—and decidedly *not* Rafe—and cross to where she stands.

"Oy, finallyyyy," Lily huffs. "What have you been doing back there?"

I wrap my arms around myself and inwardly sink a bit with the truth. "I was cleaning a pot."

Lily's brow furrows. "One. Singular?" I nod. "There are, like, a million dishes stacking up in the bins, and the Music and Arts Committee is in the corner. We've got about fifteen more minutes of them debating on the right food truck choices and placement of the booths for Maple Fest before they're all going to bombard the counter."

I snap into work mode and start stacking some of our plates. They're cream with a little sparrow in the center of each one. "Oh, gosh—the festival! I forgot they're planning it today . . . even when I passed the pumpkins in front of all the shops this morning! How is that possible?"

My gaze slides over to Rafe right as he looks up at me, like we're already so in tune with each other that he knows my next move. He shrugs lightly, a grin ticking up one side of his mouth, and I find myself doing the same. Lily catches the exchange, and I can see she's about to squeal. If it wasn't so busy today, I'd banish her to the back of the store. Permanently.

I try to ignore him by taking stock of the store. Fall flowers on every table? Check. Tables cleaned and wiped? Check. Our adorable little boxes and napkins restocked? Check. Ability to ignore the beautiful man to my right? Absolutely none.

Rafe is still holding a pencil, and now he's tapping it on the notebook. The motion makes me think of teacups, the tiny ones that rest in my apartment. Suddenly, I remember the familiar smell of chamomile and the steam that would rise from the porcelain vessel while my mother wrote with a worn-down pencil in her journal or jotted letters back home to those she loved still in Paris. I haven't thought about that memory in years.

"Excuse me? Sparrow?" Dang, if that voice isn't as rich as a dark-chocolate ganache. And I think I was staring. Again.

"Mm-hmm?" I manage to get out—and wait, he knows my name?

Rafe nods with a grin, and my feet involuntarily move toward him. If he has a magnet specifically crafted for me on the other side of this counter, I won't be surprised. Dangerously, I place my elbows on the edge of the furniture between us and lean toward him. His thumb casually touches the rim of his coffee cup.

The fingers on his other hand brush the counter, seeming to move to a beat that only he can hear. I love these counters. They've been here since I was a little girl and are just the right amount of antique white worn down with a layer of charm. Rafe could be a model for these counters if they were available to the general public. But my father made them, so they're one of a kind.

"Don't ask me for another coffee." I grin. "I can't give it to you. I have my limits."

Rafe contemplates what I've just said by continuing

the tapping noise. I glance toward the rogue, familiar pencil, but it only picks up speed.

"I wanted to ask you . . ." he says, leaning closer to me. Our faces are only inches apart at this point, and I notice a dark-green ring encircling those forest eyes that seem to pull me in deeper the longer I stare at them.

"Mm-hmm?" Still nothing verbally creative happening here, folks. Keep it moving.

His eyes flicker to my lips for a fraction of a moment, and then they're back to my eyes, intensely trying to figure me out. So, of course, I lean a little closer. The bell on the door signals that a customer has entered the store. I ignore it due to the important work of trying to discover another color in Rafe's eyes. Lily can take care of the customer.

"Sparrow!" I hear my name spoken in a musical, French accent. *Or maybe not.*

I'm shocked out of the trance Rafe has me in and feel my cheeks blush. Rafe looks amused and clears his throat but not without sending a glare toward the man at the register.

"Jacques!" I hate how my voice cracks, but this man has had this effect on me since I first laid eyes on him. He's been in town to work with a French restaurant from Boston that is opening a location in Portsmouth, which is only a town away. I'm not sure why he decided to stay in Birch Borough and not closer to the restaurant, but I haven't been complaining. Portsmouth is typically full to the brim with renters, and we're the next best option.

I push disheveled hair behind my ears and try not to grimace when I realize it's already pulled back. Nervous habit. Rafe's brow furrows even more as he looks between me and Jacques. I pull away from Rafe and ease toward the register. Meeting Jacques' light-brown eyes, I take in his outfit: well-tailored pants (I'm guessing, since they're blocked by the counter, but he always wears them); a grey, button-down shirt rolled up at the elbows and showing off his impeccable, caramel-toned forearms; hair always neatly arranged. He's the version of a Frenchman that you'd see in the magazines. The one that most definitely has modeled at some point in his life (and I know this because Lily once looked him up for me). I mean, the man has literally been in a Chanel photoshoot . . . in *Paris*. And I . . . have never left New England.

I feel Rafe's interest but can't bring myself to look his way, not when there's so much at stake. I don't like how this is unfolding, but the man I've been hoping would ask me out for months is now here, and what if he's ready to give me something other than his coffee and pastry order? Lily told me not to focus on Jacques, but she also said he asked about me. So, guess what, Lily? This could be my moment. Maybe all the embarrassing events that have happened in my life up to this point could turn around. This could be redemption.

"Sparrow, I'm happy to see you back," Jacques says smoothly, his accent blurring the words in a pleasant way. "My heart stopped when you weren't here yesterday." A smile I haven't seen from him yet appears as he breaks the imaginary barrier over the counter. "Don't worry. I think it's working now," he says softly.

"Oh, gosh," I mumble. I immediately see his amusement and try to make it right. "I mean, I'm happy to see you too. So happy."

At this, I cringe. I chance a glimpse over toward Rafe, who looks confused, irritated, and like he's trying to figure out what's happening between me and Jacques.

Me too, Rafe. Me too.

Usually, I look forward to seeing Jacques. However misdirected and absurd, in my panic, *he* is the one I must've been thinking of yesterday morning during that critical moment on the train platform. He's the one I've been thinking of every morning since he showed up in town. And all this time, I've been hoping he would look at me in the way he's looking at me now.

I've been swearing to everyone (aka Lily) that Jacques is exactly what I need. What I want. I even declared it (sort of) to the world on an (almost) moving train. He's the very embodiment of what I've been waiting and praying for all these years. *I mean, isn't he?*

I think about all our interactions up until this point and quickly assess the situation. Handsome? Check. Fashionable? Check. French? CHECK. Single? As far as I know. Witty? To be determined. Personality? Possibly. Interest in me? To be determined. There was the time he mentioned that my croissants reminded him of the ones he used to get when he traveled to Cannes (yes, that place). Right now, he's making eye contact with me and isn't breaking it, so that's something. And yes, I realize the bar has been set really low for me to even have eye contact as a qualifying factor. But I'm also so embarrassed over all the events that have unfolded recently that my fingers are crossed that I can finally celebrate a win in getting Jacques' attention.

"Your usual?" I manage.

"*Oui, s'il te plaît,*" he says. *Yes, please.* Familiar. He's using the familiar tense, not the formal. He never uses the familiar tense. Are we familiar? Jacques knows I understand some French, so when he is here, he throws in words and phrases here and there. But it's always been formal. Is this a sign? It feels like a sign.

I get in motion to gather his usual order, my mind racing with possibilities. Surely this is how it begins. It must be. It starts with speaking French formally, and then informally, and then we're in love. Sounds about right.

I stare up at the clock. It's been exactly two minutes since Jacques walked into the bakery, and I'm shaking. My nerves are absolutely not because Rafe is watching my every movement as I grind espresso and take a *pain au chocolat* from the case. It's not because of the way Rafe's navy sweater stretches over his shoulders. Or the way I want to run my hands through his hair like I'm folding pastry dough. *Wait, what?*

"Sparrow, what have you been up to?" Jacques asks, looking at me over the pastry counter as I pull shots of espresso. He's moved out of the way so Lily can take care of other customers—much to her not-delight—and I crinkle my nose. I have to get Rafe out of my mind so that I can focus on this situation.

"Oh, you know . . . this and that." I shrug.

"D'accord." *Okay.*

A sound comes from Rafe that sounds suspiciously like laughter.

I shoot a pleading look at Rafe and pray that this awkward interaction will be over as quickly as possible. Or that Jacques will ask me to marry him and solve both the question and the problem in the form of the man on the barstool behind me.

Placing the *pain au chocolat* in a bag and with the to-go coffee cup in hand, I pass them to Jacques. His gaze shuffles toward Rafe, and I watch his jaw tense. I wonder what he thinks of the handsome newcomer.

Suddenly, he turns back toward me, and his smile is a bit—dare I say—unsure. I don't know whether to enjoy his newly found attention or run from it.

"Sparrow, I've been meaning to ask you . . ." he begins. Jacques has never been one to stay at the bakery longer than necessary. While always polite, he's usually glued to his phone. I didn't know he'd ever noticed me. I feel Rafe leaning in for this conversation as much as I am, and it's distracting. *Sabotage.*

"Yes?" I manage to get out.

Jacques does the most incredible thing. He gives me a full smile. Yet another smile I've never seen before, and it's alarming how much I'm *not* melting right now.

"Are you seeing someone?" His voice echoes throughout the café. Croissants are held mid-air. Coffee cups clatter.

And this is the moment where I believe that there are other dimensions. As much as I've been wishing this would happen, there's no way this can be real life. I feel vindicated. I feel affirmed. I feel . . . confused?

"Oh—I, uh . . ." I begin.

Lily is frozen too, completely in awe of what's unfolding. Thank goodness the person beside her is Emma from the art studio, or this would be a bad review waiting to happen. The whole bakery has hushed. And it's like I can see outside of myself, the way my body looks tense, the way I'm chewing on my lip . . .

And, people of the world, *this* moment, much like the one on the train platform, is one that I will never understand. The moment that, when asked my relationship status by the man I've been waiting to notice me for months, instead of saying "no" or "*non,*" I look over to the man I met less than twenty-four hours ago instead and find that he's looking at me too.

Chapter Seven

Rafe

Sparrow is looking at me. Her eyes are wild and a bit cautious. Jacques just asked if she is single, and I thought I would have to endure the frustration of seeing her jump around and squeal with Lily at how the world must be perfect because she is finally about to be asked out by this *other man* from France. I've never wanted to play the *I'm-French* card more in my life. If you ask me, I think the man is enjoying being someone with an accent women swoon over—but no one's asking me.

Instead, I'm caught in a moment where the clock doesn't move, and it's just me and the terrible decision I'm about to make for my heart as I focus on Sparrow. I see something I can't name flash across her face. Without breaking eye contact, I hear myself say, "Sorry, Jacques. She's with me."

Whatever she thought I was going to say, I can promise that was definitely not it. Sparrow's mouth is hanging open, and the same child from yesterday pipes up from the corner. "Look, Mama! That lady looks like a fish again!"

I cringe, my eyes darting between Lily, who looks like she wants to (happily) punch me in the arm; Jacques, who looks like he'd try to punch me in the face; and Sparrow, who I suddenly can't read at all. Did I miss some sort of cue here? When she said she wanted someone French, did she mean *this* French guy? I thought I had channeled Schmidt at Cece's arranged wedding. I swear Sparrow was talking to me with her eyes and asking me for a way out, but maybe I really have been watching too much TV lately.

"*Je suis désolé,*" Jacques says. Yeah, I bet you're sorry, pal. "I didn't know."

Now I want to laugh because . . . I also didn't know. But here we are. And there's no way I can think to rectify this situation, unless singing could solve something . . . and that seems inappropriate.

Lily quickly turns to the customer who left money on the counter and bolted when I made my announcement. Suddenly, the bakery feels empty. It's like an old Western where everyone clears out when they sense a brawl. Even the child with an affinity for fish has left with his mother.

Jacques is looking between Sparrow and me, and when he takes a break from me, I motion to her that her mouth is still open.

She snaps it shut and turns toward Jacques. I am curious to see how this plays out. My fingers are itching to write down lyrics because a song will be written from this, no doubt.

"Jacques, will you wait one moment?" Sparrow holds up a finger to Jacques to signal for him to wait.

She's next to me before I can even blink. How she traveled that quickly without making noise is a mystery.

Before I can fully grasp what's happening, she's pulling me toward the back kitchen. I'm thrown through the door by her suddenly superhuman strength and turn to face her. It smells like butter and sugar in here, and I'm distracted by all the equipment before I can focus on a very unnerved Sparrow in front of me. Parts of my body feel like they've been electrocuted where they've made contact with her, and I really hope I can still play guitar if I ever get to touch her again—not that I expect to.

"What are you doing?" she wildly whispers (which is apparently a thing).

Through the door's small window, I can see Jacques standing by the counter with his brow furrowed.

I smile. "He's looking," I say through my teeth.

She pulls me away from the window as I give him a small wave.

"Of course he's looking. Why did you do that? What did you think—?" She shakes her head.

I wish I could go back to a few minutes ago, when I was happily trusting and channeling Schmidt from *New Girl*. But I can't. And so, it's time to attempt to fix this fiasco.

"Look, you're into him, right?" I ask. I hope she says no, but I don't think that's what I'm going to get here. She shakes her head both up and to the side, which is confusing.

"I mean, yes, of course—did you see him?" she says softly.

I make a face and shrug. "Well, of course I did, but honestly, I don't get the appeal."

A frustrated noise escapes from her throat. I gently reach for her hand in an attempt to comfort her, but when she looks at my hand like it could burn her, I drop it immediately.

"But you like him," I say the next part quickly, "and I thought you needed me to help you."

She tilts her chin up and takes a step closer. I try not to notice the way the air is crackling between us. "Why would you think I needed you to help me?"

"Because you gave me these eyes that were, like, 'Help me!' or something." I slide my hand through my hair and feel my eyes narrow as I brace for impact. Instead, she blinks. "I mean, I don't know you well enough yet. So maybe that's not what you meant?"

"Of course *not*," she huffs. And I hate how adorable she is to me right now. "I'm a lone croissant—and I was going to tell him!"

She rises on her toes so we're closer to eye level. She's still shorter than me, even though she's tall, and I think that if we don't turn this around soon, I'm going to kiss her.

"Sparrow," I begin. I hold up my hands in surrender, and she lowers onto her heels again. "You're upset with me for saying something that prevented him from asking you out?"

She nods quickly. We're inches apart, and I've never wanted to scoop someone up in my arms more than this woman in front of me. "You were really going to say yes to him?"

She hesitates, then nods once. It's slight, but I caught it.

"Then I just have one question." She exhales and puts her hands on her hips. "Why did you look at *me*?"

Her neck tilts as her eyes scan the front of my chest frantically. It's like she's searching for the answers or a superhero symbol right in front of her and can't seem to find either. She drops her shoulders and sighs. "I don't know," she says quietly. When her eyes finally lift back to mine, I see the corners glistening with tears. "I don't know," she says again.

Something scratches at the back of my throat. I can't tell whether I'm irritated or grateful that I now know she smells like caramelized sugar and dreams.

"Okay, well, we can work with this," I say softly. Partly because I can't handle seeing her cry right now, and partly because I'm apparently eager to get my heart run over.

Sparrow quirks her head to the side. "How?"

"Do you want me to tell him it was all a misunderstanding?"

"That's even more embarrassing."

"Well, Jacques is still standing out there. Kind of a bad look on his part, but there he stands." I cringe and motion to the front of the store. "Which tells me that he's jealous."

She scoffs like the idea is unbelievable. "Jealous? Of whom? An orphan who owns a bakery and can't seem to keep coffee grounds off her clothing?"

It's clear she didn't mean for me to hear the honesty she just threw down between us. I reach out and touch the side of her arms, pushing through the delicious sear of pain the touch brings. I look at Jacques through the window. It's infuriating. He doesn't deserve her. Sparrow catches my look of scorn and narrows her eyes. Now I'm glaring at him like I have superhero powers I could activate and eliminate him all at once (for the record, I wouldn't hurt him ... just move him to a different planet).

"So, let's date. You and me."

She blinks again. And again. I expect her to refute it, and so I use the opportunity to dig myself in even deeper.

"Fake date, of course," I add, only to break the silence. My new roommate and friend, aka Hallmark Hot G, is going to have so many words for me. If anyone knows about contracts and messy agreements, it's him. But here I am, second day in town, making a mess and betting on being able to convince him that I have a good feeling about this and that it's worth the risk.

Sparrow searches my face with an intensity I've never seen before. Her eyes catch on a piece of my hair that's hanging near my eyes. Her hand lifts toward it while tension in the air hums. She shifts her gaze toward her hand as if she doesn't know how it got there, and then it falls in a smooth move around her back while her other hand rests across her middle. She's all wrapped up in her own embrace. Whether for comfort or protection, I've yet to discover.

"Oh, um—and why would we do that?"

Interest seems like a good sign, so I start to pick up steam with this idea. "Well, you saw how he reacted just from *thinking* that we're together."

I must be making sense because she nods.

"Imagine how much more it will get to him if he *sees* us together. Holding hands. Out around town. We fake date," I mumble nonchalantly. "In a few weeks, we'll pretend to break up, and then your Frenchman out there can swoop in." But I'm dying a bit inside. Because from the moment I met her, I knew she was worth my time. I pride myself on not needing anyone anymore, but I think we may need each other. I already don't like Jacques, but I also know I'll do my best to put a smile on her face—even better if I can do it more than once.

"Won't he just meet someone else if I'm taken?"

"Possibly. But has he been around here for a while?"

She nods.

"Well, then . . . if he didn't ask you out the second he met you, I question his life choices."

Her eyes laser in on mine. "You didn't ask me out."

My lungs deflate. "No, I didn't." I want to tell her why. I want to tell her it was a mistake. I can't seem to do either. "Sparrow, I . . . I know we just met. And you have no reason to believe in me yet. I am sorry I messed up your plans, but I'll do my best to help you fix it."

I cringe at the words that just came out of my mouth. I'm wrestling with them because it all would've been so much easier if, yesterday morning, when I saw her on the train, I had thought of leaving a note in her book with my number that read something like: *You're adorable. Call me.*

Instead, I'm in the back of her bakery with what I hope is butter on the back of my pants after being pushed into the counter while proposing that I fake date the woman I genuinely want to date so that I can help her get a man that I want to fly back to France immediately. I'd even drive him to the airport. All while not telling her what I should have said the moment that she announced her dating resolution—both times. But I can't even think about that part right now.

She peeks out the little window to the front, and I see when she spots Jacques. She gives him a slight wave, although the smile doesn't reach her eyes. But when she turns toward me, I see a spark. I swallow as she lifts her chin.

"Okay," she says.

"Okay?" My stomach both sinks and lifts at the possibility.

"Yes. We fake date. And then we'll both get what we want." She pauses and looks up at me again, a brow raised. "Wait—what do you want? You know I want to go out with Jacques, but what do you get out of this?"

I suck in a breath and stare into the chocolate eyes that will stick with me in my dreams tonight. Discovering that there are gold specks in her irises nearly has me on my knees. "Uh . . . just to help you after I misread the situation. I'll make good on my word."

Her brow furrows. "That doesn't seem fair. You don't even know me. I can't—"

"You can." I smile, the one I know will show my dimple. Hopefully, it shows her I mean it. This wasn't the plan, and I don't know how I'll ever recover from this, but I really do want to help her. "Plus, I'm scared of Lily."

At this, she laughs. "Aren't we all." She smiles but then it drops. "Wait. No. I . . ." she begins.

My heart actually twists.

"If we do this, we have to do our best not to get our hearts involved."

I feel my jaw go slightly slack. I don't know how I could possibly not get my heart involved when I stare at her sweetheart of a face. "I can't promise that."

Her eyes widen as she steps back. "Then we can't do this."

Sparrow turns toward the front of the store, and I lightly grab her elbow. A zing shoots through my arm. I might be already addicted to what it feels like to be near her. How am I supposed to pretend we're dating if I can't touch her without giving myself away? It feels like she's a charger for the low battery of my heart, and I don't know if I'm losing percentage or gaining at this point.

She studies my face, and I'm too stuck on the current still pulsing through my arm to say anything. Her shoulders bend forward a bit. "What is it?"

"My heart will be involved, Sparrow. Because I do everything with my heart. And honestly, I don't have much to give you. But we'd be in this together."

"And it ends when you leave?"

I nod. "It ends when I leave." Those words spark something visceral.

"I don't tend to trust people," she admits. "Except Lily. I'm stuck with her until the end." A small, sad smile plays on the edge of her mouth.

Her eyes turn back to me, and I see the path her gaze follows . . . from my neck, they snag on my mouth before flitting up to my eyes. I swallow. I'm willing myself to say more but can't seem to do it.

When I don't respond, I hear her mutter, "It's okay. I knew this was too good to be true . . ."

Her hand is already on the door when I come to my senses. "No!"

She turns. "No?" The swinging door stays in place with the tip of her foot.

"I mean, yes, I want to do this. I just . . . I . . ."

"Yes?"

"I don't tend to trust people either." Sharing this part of myself has me grasping for anything in a room full of kitchen equipment and baking ingredients. The truth is, something is stirring in me again that I thought was long gone. I think of what it would mean to really feel again. The discomfort. The want. The happiness. If I'm ever going to become the lyricist I want to be or remember what it was like to find joy in creating music, I need to be able to feel. And I've been a shell of myself for too long.

I think of what I would do, of what I would say, if my heart was light and the boy who dreamed he could be fully loved was still a part of me. He would believe that someone out of his league might want him too.

I settle into the moment and try to remember what it's like to follow my instincts and . . . *play*. Just for the fun of it. "If we're dating, you probably need a nickname," I say.

If her nose scrunching wasn't so adorable, I'd be laughing at how light I feel right now. I've been anchored in pain for far too long. She crosses her arms, lightly clasping her elbows.

"What do you mean a *nickname*?"

My heart is beating strongly, and I'm beginning to remember what it means to want someone again. "When you're dating, don't people tend to have nicknames for each other? It happens in France too, I would imagine," I encourage. We totally have nicknames for each other there.

Sparrow narrows her eyes and makes a noncommittal sound. She starts smearing the semi-dried coffee grounds on her apron in an attempt to get them off. I have to remind myself, again, not to smile. And not to notice her curves.

I clear my throat. "I can't call you *Sparrow*, and I can't call you *Rory*."

"Why? That is literally my nickname," she mutters. Her hands go out in front of her like she's stuck pulling two baking trays from the oven.

I grin. "Because everyone calls you that."

She holds her breath and slightly shifts the bottom of her lip. It's distracting. I feel the heat creeping up my neck and avert my gaze. Through the kitchen window, I spot the trays of macarons in the front of the store that she was attempting to pick up from the floor when we first met. Next to them are bags of *chouquettes*, their bright-white pearls of sugar a contrast to the caramel-colored choux pastry underneath.

An idea hits. It's bold, but I have a feeling I have to go all in for this woman. I remember the American movies I tried to watch as a kid. Some of them Westerns. Some of them rom-coms. I remember how I used to pretend to be smooth. I need a bit of that version of me now.

"Okay, it's Sugar. I'm gonna be the one to call you Sugar."

Her eyes widen, but I see a hint of light flash through them, and the dimple on her right cheek makes an appearance. "You will not." She doesn't hate it.

"Actually, I will."

We're in a stare-off, and it's the most exciting thing I've been a part of in ages. A bobby pin shoots to the floor. She lets out a frustrated sound. She leans down to pick it up, and a crescent moon of skin peeks through the line between her shirt and pants. My mouth goes dry. She stands to her full height, her face a bit flushed, and pulls up the rogue piece of hair with the pin she's reclaimed. I let my emotions leak onto my face and stare at her like she's my next lyrics to the song I haven't figured out how to write yet.

"Sugar."

"Yes?" I grin.

"What are you, Southern?" she counters.

I shake my head slowly. Southern France doesn't count here. Besides, most of my childhood was spent in Paris. "No, just a man who has a sweet tooth." This time, I laugh at the way her mouth parts and her eyes simmer. I can admit how ridiculous I sound, but I stand by it.

Sparrow surprises me by grabbing my hand and pulling me behind her into the front of the store before letting go. Jacques is still waiting (a patient man, I'll give him that). She nods at him, and I don't miss the moment she rubs the hand I was holding with her other one.

"Listen, Jacques," I start. I don't dare touch Sparrow again, so I lean in a bit closer toward her and hope it's convincing enough. "Why don't you come to my show tomorrow night?"

"I'm already going to a show tomorrow night. And I was going to ask . . . " He looks at me and then toward the poster now hanging on the bulletin board. I don't know who posted it, but from the grin on Lily's face, I'm guessing I know the answer. Where she got it from is a mystery.

Jacques looks between me and the poster. "Wait— is that you? *You're* Rafe?"

I put on my meet-and-greet face and smile. It's not fake, but it's not the full me. I shrug my shoulders. "Guilty."

"You're the one on the poster? *That* poster?" He's pointing at it like it's vermin.

I want to laugh, but I refrain. It should also be noted that I've only wanted to laugh this much since I've met Sparrow. It's like she's released something in me that feels like joy. I didn't know that would be possible for me again.

"I am—although, not my best look, if I'm honest. But there will be some singing. Guitar. That kind of thing."

He looks between Sparrow and me, the expression on her face still choosing how to emote itself.

"You write your own songs," she says, looking toward me. It's part question, part statement.

"Ah—I do, yes. And some covers. But only if it's a song that means something to me, of course."

Jacques shuffles his feet. "Well, I have tickets. I

probably can't return them, so . . . sounds good."

Does it, Jacques? He starts to move toward the door.

I feel Sparrow's hand wrap lightly around my arm, and I'm not sure if it's to keep herself steady or to further sell the fake-dating thing, but I'm here for it.

"*A bientôt!* See you tomorrow!" Jacques calls. The door shuts, and I look down to see Sparrow's hand still wrapped around my arm. She peeks up at me, her eyes once again catching on a piece of my hair that must be out of place (it's always out of place), and I notice the blush creeping up her neck as she pulls her hand from me. To break some of the tension, I hurry behind the counter (even though I'm certain I'm not allowed back here) and reach for a muffin from a nearby tray as I do. Because I'm now a thief and a musician.

I walk back around the counter in a sort of spin move, allowing myself to fully smile when I'm turned from her view. I take a bite of the muffin in my hand. It's delicious. It shouldn't even be legal for her to sell these things. When I turn to face her, I feel the crumbs on my face and hear myself let out an appreciative moan. It's cinnamon and sugar, but it's light and buttery. I peek over my shoulder to see her eyes light up.

"You like it?"

I nod and really sell how much I'm enjoying it. "So much so that I'll leave a ticket for you at will call. Do you want one for Lily too?"

"I have a thing!" Lily yells from the back. Yes, I definitely should be scared of that one.

We laugh, and I lean a little closer to avoid Lily's listening ears. "So, see you tomorrow night, Sugar?" I whisper conspiratorially.

And just like that, I'm using a nickname for the woman I first met on a train and never expected to see again. I freeze as a soft smile plays on her lips.

"See you tomorrow tonight," she whispers back. She turns from where we are standing, grabs an empty canister of what was probably cookies from near the register, and moves toward the kitchen, but not without throwing me another smile as she moves through the swinging door.

Chapter Eight

Sparrow

My stomach has been fluttering all day. I would say it's butterfly wings, but it also could be the three cups of coffee I had with a croissant. I couldn't eat much today from the nervous energy in my system. I was hoping Rafe would stop by, but he didn't. I don't know why he would've, except to see me. Or to eat one of our amazing pieces of *mille-feuille, a thousand leaves or layers*, which consists of really thin and crispy layers of puff pastry that we fill with a rich vanilla pastry cream and powdered sugar. They're more common in patisseries than a boulangerie, but it's my mother's recipe. It's flaky and buttery and scrumptious, and maybe I've just convinced myself my stomach has more *mille-feuille* flakes than butterfly wings.

I don't know what's happened to my life in such a short time. When Jacques asked about my relationship status, I panicked. I've been doing a lot of that lately. And all I could see at that moment was Rafe. And then I was too embarrassed by the whole debacle to go back out and tell Jacques I'm single. But I need to tell Rafe that we can't do this—we can't fake date. As much as it would be a dream in many ways—because let's be honest, I can't deny he's dreamy—I need to rein this whole charade in before it gets out of hand.

"He's not staying," I speak out loud, thinking maybe if I hear it back, it will stick. My heart has been set on Jacques for months. I need to get out of this mess so that I'm free again to date him—even though I was never taken in the first place. And while pretending to date Rafe doesn't change that, I don't like entertaining what's not real. I've learned it can be dangerous to pretend. To try to convince yourself that you're not as alone as you are. And while I'd never want to hurt anyone in the world, maybe this is my opportunity for Jacques to finally recognize my worth and for me to be a step closer to finding a love I haven't dared to hope for lately.

That's why I'm pulling down a skirt that's shorter than anything I think I've worn in my life, besides when I danced ballet. Granted, it's only inches above my knee, but it might as well be a swimsuit for how much of my legs are showing compared to how I normally dress. Lily insisted that if I get to go see a man as beautiful as Rafe, as his pretend date or otherwise, then I might as well give other women a reason to cry (her words, not mine).

I don't think it's working, but I appreciate her confidence. I've managed my hair as best I can; two small braids now flow into a messy knot at the back of my neck. Between my new red lipstick, a shimmery nude eyeshadow, and a plumping mascara that—once again— Lily insisted on, I'm standing a little taller. I insisted the dress be flowy and that I could wear my ballet flats with ribbons, and she let me. Besides the length of my dress,

I still feel like myself, which I appreciate.

The little venue—Nostalgia—where Rafe is playing tonight, is one my father and I would venture to each summer. It converts from a music venue to a makeshift movie theater of sorts. They often feature Old Hollywood films or classic movies, and our favorite happened to be *Sabrina*. My father was a Humphrey Bogart fan, and I, of course, adore Audrey Hepburn.

The memories bring a smile to my face as I see my lovely town shine in the glow of the lanterns and fairy lights hanging from the venue as I approach. There's a group of women talking to each other, their faces animated as they chat. It's then I notice what they're looking at—an image of Rafe behind one of the theater's glass-enclosed poster spaces.

I move around them to get a full glimpse and feel like I can hardly breathe. How does one go from living a life in which you don't know someone exists to not understanding how that was ever possible? The man photographs WELL. The poster features him sitting with his guitar on the edge of a stage, his hair slightly disheveled, a five o'clock shadow on his face. I take a moment to really drink in the sight of him. It's my opportunity to study him without the variability of his movements or words. Now that I'm researching his face, I realize his expressions are almost sculptural. You could pause his face at any moment, and it's a study of human emotion. This photo must've been chosen for its ease and playfulness. He's looking to the left and laughing, his forest eyes dancing with whatever he's seeing off camera. I feel the warmth in my stomach as I think of *that* man—the one that I'm seeing on a poster—when his arm was around me. And suddenly, I'm wishing to be fully held by him.

The lights flicker overhead with my cue to go inside, and I head to the ticket booth. The outside is a bit antiquated but clean, much like our town. The gold accents have dulled a bit over the years, but it feels worn in a way that honors the past while time keeps moving forward. The person on the other side, Gladys, is the same woman who has been there since I was a child. She likes to start shenanigans in town and has a thing for our macarons at my shop. We're also close because of her consistent communication with me via text message. Bless her, she loves to send me pictures of good-looking men once or so a week with messages such as, *Thought you'd like these attractive men reading books* or *Here's a fireman holding a cat*. I'd like to think it's sweet, but really, I think the photos are more for Gladys than me.

"Hi, Gladys!" I say lightly.

She takes one look at me, and I see amusement in her eyes. "You too, huh?"

I furrow my brow. "I'm sorry?" My heartbeat pulses through my ears at the thought that I must've been caught during my art lesson back at Rafe's concert poster.

"Let me tell you, honey, I don't blame you in the least. In fact, I encourage it. You've had too much heartache in your life, and this could be our dear Lord just giving a little love back to you."

The theology is misguided, but her heart is in the right place. I open my mouth to ask her about my tickets when I realize she isn't done with her little pep talk.

"I saw a glimpse of that man earlier today as he was getting some of that musician stuff out of the back of a truck, and I could've stared at him for the rest of my life. And that was just from behind! The way those jeans just fit his—"

"Gladys!" I yell before she can finish the sentence. *Oh, Lord, please don't let her finish that sentence.*

She grins, fully knowing she's got me flustered, and hands me an envelope. "Well, you look pretty if that's what you're worried about." Oh, the blessings of being in a small town.

I let out a deep breath, enough for my bangs to catch some air before they land back on my forehead. I grin and shake my head, the smell of popcorn whirling through the air. "Thank you, Gladys."

I cup my hand toward her as if we're conspiring and watch as she excitedly leans closer to the glass between us. "I hope you get a look at him again, even if it is from behind," I whisper before biting my lip to keep from laughing as she falls back in her chair with a dramatic flourish.

"From your mouth to God's ears, honey. From your mouth to God's ears."

I head toward the doors and move to pull out my ticket when I see a note, barely visible, scribbled on the side.

I'm singing for you tonight, Sugar -R

My cheeks hurt from smiling so much when someone knocks into my back. I guess standing in a doorway will do that to someone.

"I'm so sorry," I mutter, my heart racing and lifting simultaneously. I don't know Rafe enough to know if he's left notes and given nicknames to other girls when he's toured. The thought sparks an ember of envy, but I extinguish it as fast as it appeared. And though, by the looks of him, the likelihood of such a scenario is high, his eyes are sincere. And my father always said one's character is all in the eyes if you know how to look.

It may just be pretend, but tonight, someone's

waiting for me.

Once inside, I grab a drink and head to the corner of the room. I forgot how much I love this place and the feeling it exudes of a theater that's seen and heard creativity in its proper time. While the floor creaks a bit, the acoustics are wonderful here. And the anticipation of seeing Rafe on the stage in front of me is a bit heady. My seat is right by the stage, and I will be near Rafe while he sings. I'm so close that I can see the scratch marks from shoes and equipment etched on the stage.

The lights go down, and suddenly, there he is. He walks onto the small stage, his head high and confidence humming through his frame. I don't know how to describe him except to say he's a vision. His hair is unruly with a few pieces cascading over his forehead. He's wearing a white t-shirt under a brown bomber jacket that I recognize from the train and jeans that are tight in all the right places. Even his Converse high-top shoes scream *my kind of guy*. Vintage high tops. I honestly don't know how I'll last the night.

He settles on a stool and signals to the rest of the band, whom I'm just now noticing. As the opening chords start to play, I catch him sliding his gaze to the floor, across the stage, and lifting his eyes right to me. He knew I was here the whole time. He grins, and I feel my cheeks heat.

Without breaking eye contact, he speaks into the mic, "This one's for a girl I saw on a train, and lucky for me, I got to see her again."

He winks at me, and I'm shaken. His fingers start strumming his guitar, and I go to another dimension. In a moment, I picture my mother sitting with a guitar, me dancing around her feet as she strums. Tears brim in my eyes. I had missed that memory somehow. How could I have forgotten it? The beauty of it is that when his voice hits the air, something deep within me shifts a little more. His voice is heavy cream swirling in a cold-brew coffee. It's the crackly top of a perfect crème brûlée. My soul wakes, and I know I can never un-hear the way his heart is melded into every word and note. Or the way his voice is twirling around my lungs and asking them to hope again.

For a brief moment, I let myself think it's only the two of us here. Rafe is a natural onstage. Even during the songs that make me want to hug him through them, it's unnerving how raw he can be but also so funny and animated. His lyrics are poetic and symbolic, and I want to dance to them. I haven't touched a barre in years, but my feet seem to keep tapping to everything he's playing. I brush a tear from my face as Rafe sings about a love that moves along without him. Somewhere moving, always moving, and when it feels like love may be seen in the distance, love still moves ahead of him every time. The beat is light, a contrast to the weight of this heartache, and I realize that he is a merging of two worlds. Old Hollywood meets current trends. Indie artist meets an A-list smile. Soft strumming with loud significance. A voice mixed with grit and grace.

Rafe catches my eyes at the end of every song and sometimes in between. He doesn't look at me when the songs speak of sadness, but I see him glance my way whenever there's a lyric about hope or moving forward. If I had any thoughts about calling this off, they're getting weaker with every chorus. Before I know it, the set is over, and I'm standing on my feet with everyone else, clapping frantically and smiling so much my face may freeze like this. Rafe gives a wave and a humble nod to the crowd. I don't miss the grin he throws my way over his shoulder as he steps into the wings.

"*C'est beau ça!*" It's beautiful. I hear the phrase coming from somewhere to my left.

I scan the room to find the French-speaking attendee and notice, three tables over, Jacques. I can't believe I didn't notice him before now. I've been distracted by Rafe but can't forget that it's my mission to find what my parents had and to live, as my father would say, with the "French kind of love." Jacques is sitting with a stunning woman. I would expect nothing less, but seeing them together still causes my stomach to stutter with a spark of jealousy. I don't think I'm insignificant in the looks department, but I also don't think I can compete with her perfect beauty. But as the lights go up, I find myself asking, *Do I even want to?*

The show ended about two minutes ago, and as I gather my clutch and stand, I notice a guitar pick hovering near the edge of the stage. It must've fallen during the set. I know it's Rafe's because of where it fell. I think of bringing it back to him, even though it's probably ridiculous. Don't musicians have a thousand of these? I hesitate another moment before finding some courage and heading toward the stage. Maybe he needs it or maybe he doesn't. I reach for the guitar pick and feel an imprint near my thumb. Upon a closer look, I see an "R" etched into the custom pick. I smile lightly, glad to have grabbed it, and slide it into a hidden pocket within my clutch. I'm moving toward the entrance to leave when I see my phone light up with a message.

Unknown Number: Wait for me, please?

I don't have to guess who it is, but even if I did, the

next message clarifies.

Unknown Number: Gladys gave me your number. Hope it's OK.

I laugh and feel the *mille-feuille* version of butterflies in my stomach start to flip. It was one thing to see him onstage. It's another to know he wants to stand beside me again. We didn't make plans tonight except for me coming to the show. And while I should tell him that we need to back out of this whole fake-dating thing, after seeing him tonight, I'm conflicted.

So, I pull out my phone to text Gladys, seeing the most recent image she sent of a man in a very tight shirt, reading a book while holding a cup of coffee, from some account called @hotdudesreading. It has remained unanswered because responding can be a bit like a jack-in-the-box situation—you know what's coming, but her responses still surprise me every time.

Sparrow: I'm going to assume giving out my number was a moment of temporary insanity.

My phone immediately lights up with a response.

Gladys: Proof.

It's a picture of Rafe leaning into a truck bed and pulling something out. I squeal and drop my phone.

"Everything okay?" His caramel-like voice cuts through the air.

Oh, gosh, no. I'm going to give that woman a piece of my mind when I see her next. I watch as Rafe bends to the ground to pick up my phone, and I look away before he stands up. He's looking at me with a smirk as he hands my phone back to me.

"Looked like something either shocked you or burned you."

Oh, you have no idea.

"Clumsy, I guess," I manage to get out. Thankfully,

he didn't see the screen, but his expression tells me he's enjoying the reaction he's getting from me in this moment.

He's about to say something else when I hear a thick French accent getting louder behind us.

"Sparrow!" Jacques yells, and Rafe flinches. Interesting. Jacques approaches and does a weird handshake thing that Rafe clearly has no idea what to do with.

Rafe makes a face, and thankfully, Jacques misses it as he pulls the woman I saw earlier closer to his side.

"Sparrow, this is Vivienne." He smiles tightly.

She briefly dismisses me before she looks Rafe up and down, and I feel my hands clench into fists. Yes, he's beautiful, but he's more than a face and a body, for crying out loud. That's why I'm still planning to talk Gladys into more appropriate usage of her smartphone camera.

Rafe must take my look to think I'm jealous of her since she's with Jacques, when, honestly, I'm more upset at how she's looking at him. He moves closer to me, and my world tilts as he moves his arm around me and pulls me closer. Jacques' eyes slide down, taking in Rafe's arm around me. Right, our fake date. I attempt to pull my brain back to the purpose of this charade: to make Jacques jealous. But I'm distracted. Even as tall as I am, I fit perfectly under his shoulder, his arm casually wrapped about my waist. Except, there's nothing casual about it. I'm undone by his touch. I whip my head toward him, but he's focused on whatever Jacques and Vivienne are saying, though the slight quirk of his mouth tells me he's aware of the reaction he's getting from me.

Well, two can play this game, buddy.

I feel like I'm on fire, but I will myself to wrap my

arm around his waist, and oh good Lord, is this man made of muscle? I slip my thumb through the side of his belt loop to avoid actually touching him and applaud myself for holding it together. I may think Jacques is attractive, but even I can admit he's got nothing on Rafe. It's like comparing the sun with a lightbulb. Both give light, but only one is worth writing songs about.

This close to him, I smell cedar and a hint of something else I can't name. Slowly, I close my eyes and let myself enjoy the moment, not caring if I become a statue. Just let me live here, people. Turn me into a monument if you have to.

"Sparrow?"

"Hmm . . .?" I open my eyes and notice that Jacques is gone, along with Vivienne, and I was in such a trance that about half of the room left with them too.

Rafe gently turns me to face him, and I don't miss the moment his fingers casually brush the fallen pieces from my updo as I move. "Are you okay?" he asks, his brow slightly wrinkled as if he's worried.

"Uh—yes. I'm okay?"

He visibly relaxes even though I answered with a question of my own. Because I realize I may not be fine at all. My lungs constrict. *What am I doing?* My eyes rove over his chiseled face and notice the scar in his eyebrow, the tick in his jaw. The man before me is an invitation to cross a line into an unknown world. Perhaps in Rafe's world, I might not be as terrified to leave the comfort of the cage I've built around my heart.

"Good. I wasn't sure when I saw Jacques here with someone if that would be hard for you. I mean, it must be, right?"

I look into his eyes and melt a bit at his concern.

"Oh—of course, yeah," I muster. "Super hard."

He nods in understanding and sighs. "Okay, well, are you hungry? My friend told me there's only one diner open at this time of night just outside of town. I couldn't believe him when he told me how early everything closes here. I'm used to places being open late, but at least there's an option close to here."

I look up at him questioningly. "I—uh—I'm not sure . . ." I trail off. I should call it. Let the chips fall and let this handsome no-longer-a-stranger tiptoe from my life. And suddenly, that feels wrong. So wrong.

"I just thought we could go over the terms, you know?" he says quickly. "If we're going to be fake dating, I'm sure there are some rules we need to discuss."

Rules? Right. I guess there should be something *if* we're fake dating. But now, looking into his eyes as he waits for an answer, I see something I haven't seen before: the sparkle of an adventure. And it's right then and there I decide that I'm not going to pass on this opportunity to be close to him—even if I know I won't be able to give my heart to him fully. I'll try to remind myself again that Jacques is what I need. Wasn't it only days ago that I would melt for *him*? I shake off the truth that I've never reacted to a man like I have the one near me now and that Rafe is willing to help me have a chance at the life I imagine, even though I'm already blatantly aware of the cracks in its foundation.

Rafe's deep green eyes are a little hopeful, a little cautious. And something in me pulls at how maybe—impossible as it may seem—he might need me as a friend while he's in town. Maybe, just this once, I can give myself permission to pretend that I'm less alone in the world than I am with a man like Rafe beside me.

"Oh, sure—yes. Let's do it." I make a weird gesture—like a thumbs-up but with my index fingers—

and quickly hide them behind my back.

He laughs in reply, and it's stunning. His laugh is hot chocolate on a cold night. It's the sound of crunchy leaves on a crisp fall day. My eyes widen as Rafe leans closer to me, the tone of his voice a secret I now want to keep.

"Careful, Sugar. Anyone watching might think I'm still trying to win you over. I may need to work harder to convince you this isn't a mistake." His inflection is light, but his gaze is steady.

As we leave the venue, the weight of his hand on my lower back and the glow of the twinkle lights adding to the dreamlike quality of how this evening is unfolding, I find myself looking at Rafe to make sure he's still beside me. The sound of his laughter is echoing in my mind, and it's almost as if I can hear Rafe's voice whispering for me to believe this isn't a mistake at all.

Chapter Nine

Rafe

Well, this was stupid. Agreeing to fake date—actually, scratch that—being the one to come up with the *idea* to fake date someone I want to kiss into oblivion is pure torture. And we haven't even really begun our charade. But there's something about Sparrow that makes me want to be near her. I'm already terrified.

Being a singer and starting to tour—even in small venues—there was never a shortage of bright-eyed young women who were asking me out or telling me they were perfect for me. I respected their confidence, but I've always found myself drawn to someone who doesn't have to announce who she is to light up a room. Someone I want to write about simply because she exists.

Sparrow is sitting in the passenger seat of my temporary roommate's car (that I am borrowing for the evening), a look of both contentment and nervousness on her face. Of course she's nervous. In one night, I brought her to my show, wrapped my arm around her, and then told her I know of a diner. Who says that? I'm not Luke from *Gilmore Girls* and never will be. The man is a legend.

I may not have grown up in New England or even LA, but I thank boarding school for my vast knowledge of American culture and niche shows that find a way of moving hearts and spreading love. Sparrow reminds me of an Old Hollywood star who should've made it to the big screen. But if she had, she'd be the one looking for ways to avoid the camera and keep her life private. This realization makes me wince. I'm not well-known like my parents, but my dream is to have my music touching lives around the world. Sparrow may not want that kind of attention, even indirectly.

We pull up to Train Car Diner (which looks exactly like it sounds—a train car converted into a diner) when I let out a sound somewhere between a grunt and a sigh. Sparrow seems to have been lost in thought too, because it takes her a full breath to notice neither of us is moving.

"You okay?" I ask her, suddenly questioning every life decision I've made up until this point.

"Yes, of course," she says as her hand finds the door latch, and she softly pushes it open. She casually drops one of her legs toward the outside ground, her skirt riding up in my peripheral vision, testing my ability to keep my eyes lifted. The light breeze from outside has me swirling in her scent—caramelized sugar mixed with amber tonight. I close my eyes briefly, and when I open them, I see Sparrow semi-turned toward me, her eyes carefully peeking over her left shoulder. The best part is that she's not trying to have this effect on me. Every move she makes is the most genuine, easy-going action. She's a casual surgeon, and I feel another stitch move through my heart.

Before I can overthink it, I pull out the Polaroid camera I keep on the backseat and see her eyes widen. Thankfully, instead of being concerned that I just pulled out an actual camera that doesn't exist on my phone, she leans her head back against the headrest and gives a smile that would stop the world. It stops mine for a second. And I hope the film knows how to reflect what feels like gold.

A look of amusement crosses her face. "Do you normally take pictures of your fake girlfriends?"

I swallow. "No."

She hums and then looks toward the diner, a glint of *something* in her eyes.

"I'm not weird if that's what you're thinking. I mean, you can have it if you want. I just like to capture moments." I look at the film and see the outlines of her form making it through. The light was perfect, the bright neon lights from the diner shooting through my car window and lighting up her face in just the right way. Like she knew how to angle her smile so it wouldn't be forgotten.

Instead of waiting for it to fully develop, I place it on the dashboard. Hustling out of the car, I walk toward her and see she's already closed her door. *Must get faster at this.* I rush to hold open the diner's door for her, and she smiles shyly, her shoulders lifting slightly in a tiny shrug as if to say she understands *this* may take a minute for us to figure out. I walk into the diner behind her, a bell announcing our arrival, the smell of pancakes and grease happily hovering in the air, along with a side of coffee.

"Sit anywhere!" a woman with peppered hair and a pencil behind her ear yells as she walks to a booth in the far corner, her hands full of plates holding the biggest burgers and stacks of fries I've ever seen.

I look at Sparrow and see her eyes are sparkling. She looks around the room and then hesitantly looks at me. I stick my hands in my pockets and try to figure out what I should do next. There are not a ton of people here, but one section seems to be fuller than the other. I've been on plenty of dates before . . . and this isn't even a real date. But all my knowledge of how these things are supposed to go suddenly leaves my memory. Shouldn't I be looking for a draft in the air in case she's cold? Would she be more comfortable with the quieter spot or the one with more people? What if she doesn't like a window seat? Would she want the stools? Do we sit on one side of the table if we're only pretending to date?

A light touch on my forearm stills my overthinking brain. Sparrow nods her head toward the quieter section of the diner. "That booth looks nice," she says as she tugs my sleeve for me to follow with a look asking if it's okay. I nod and am grateful when she picks a side, and I can slide into the booth across from her.

"Hey, darlins," says the woman who greeted us when we entered. Her name tag says *Lucy*. I see the moment when Sparrow spots her name, and she releases a smile once again. I wish I knew what brought that reaction.

We nod our thanks for the water and both order coffees. I'm grateful for something to do with my hands when they arrive and move about fiddling with sugar packets and small creamer containers.

As if reading my thoughts, she shuffles in the booth, amusement tugging her face. "One day, ask Lily why the name Lucy makes me smile, okay? It's from one of our favorite movies."

I manage to nod, noticing the way she mentions

there will be a "one day." It's also ironic that she's holding a sugar packet, given the new nickname I gave her, but I don't point it out.

"Speaking of Lily, how long have you been friends?"

Sparrow taps the table with her fingers as if she's calculating. She gives up. "Oh, ages," she says. "We met when we were tiny. She announced we were friends, and that's been it. I've never been more grateful."

"Or more terrified?" I manage.

"What could you possibly be worried about?" Sparrow says while a smirk plays at the corner of her mouth. "She likes you."

I scoff. "I don't believe it."

"Well, has she thrown chocolate at you?"

I'm both confused and intrigued. "No."

"Then you're fine." As Sparrow looks about the space, a wistful look crosses her face that I want to chase. "In high school, my friends and I would come here. There are really four of us—Lily and me and then two others I suspect you haven't been in town long enough to meet yet."

I shake my head.

"We would come here and sit in a booth and chat about, you know, our crushes at the time, and our parents—well, in my case at the time, *parent*—and we'd plan our movie nights and sleepovers. It was the best."

I've seen pictures in her café of her parents but just realized there is only one of both parents with Sparrow. The rest were of her and her father alone. "Have you always lived here?"

She nods. "Mm-hmm . . . my parents started the café and bakery right after I was born . . . my namesake, of course. Berets can be cliché, but my father bought me one for my third birthday. There's a picture of me in it somewhere . . . Anyway, that's how it got its name, and I couldn't ever leave it. And I'm okay with that. Some people need to go off and be in the world, and I respect them for it. I mean, look at you; you've just come from LA!"

If only she knew all the places I've been, calling them home but never feeling at home.

"I love where I live. And except for wanting to visit Paris—which is where my mother was from—I have no desire to live anywhere but here."

We're interrupted again by Lucy, and I order an omelet and fries (I insist it's far better this way than with hash browns), and Sparrow orders the same. I'm not used to eating with someone in a way that makes me feel nervous and also like I've put on a comfortable sweater. I know what it's like to travel with a band, but I'm usually the lone man out. I've never realized how much that bothers me until I notice how nice it is to sit across from someone who wants to be here with me and isn't trying to only talk to me about key changes or chord charts. Someone who's content with the moment. As Sparrow gazes around the diner, her eyes crinkled in the corners like maybe she's enjoying herself too, I realize how much I could get used to this.

"Absolutely not," I mutter.

"Oh, I agree," she says matter-of-factly as her eyes meet mine over her steaming cup of coffee. Lucy refilled our coffees a minute ago after clearing our plates, and now I'm trying to find reasons for this night not to end. "I may be partly French, but I cannot bring myself to eat a snail."

I smile at her rambling ways and try to think of something else to get her talking. It turns out she's not as shy as I thought she was. I think she just needs to know someone wants to listen.

"Here, lovebirds," Lucy sings as the biggest sundae ever, with bits of warm apple pie melting the vanilla ice cream through the chilled glass and a swirl of whipped cream and cinnamon, is placed between us on the table. Sparrow's mouth has formed a slight O, a blush nestled on her cheeks. "On the house," Lucy says and winks while walking away, all before I can remind her that we never ordered dessert. With the smell of cinnamon and apples swirling around us, I don't seem to mind. It immediately reminds me of *Chaussons aux Pommes*, the apple turnovers I grew up eating.

Sparrow shrugs as she reaches for a spoon. She digs in for a bite, a spoon full of melting ice cream and pie hanging mid-air as the bell jingles. The look of shock on her face is enough to tell me who it is, even before I hear the French accent.

"*Bonsoir!*" Well, it *was* a good evening. All I want to tell him is, *"Au revoir."*

I try not to let my emotions show as I attempt to catch Sparrow's eye. Her mouth is still slightly parted, the sundae forgotten, but she seems calm. Kind of.

"Uh—Jacques," she says. Without overthinking it, I stand and do a hovering move over the table to swerve next to Sparrow. Except, she still hasn't moved, so part of my backside is not on the bench. I look at Sparrow, but she's focused ahead, her eyes still tracking Jacques.

He walks our way with a scarf around his neck that makes him look so very … French. His face looks delighted as he takes in my right leg awkwardly extended from the booth. He's studying me closely, and I'm praying fervently that he doesn't out me. I hope he doesn't ask my last name. Or see a bit of my father in me. It's only then that Sparrow seems to notice my new location and the situation we've found ourselves in.

"Oh!" she whispers. A pink blush creeps up her neck, and I grin as she slides closer to the window, her hand still holding the spoon of (dripping) ice cream.

"Hi, Jacques," I say, my fake media smile plastered to my face.

He nods briefly but then looks to Sparrow. They begin chatting about something to do with the bakery and croissants, and I notice the woman he was with at my show—Vivienne, was it?—creep up behind him. She's looking at me like we're not in a public place, and since I don't want to give her any wrong ideas, I take the opportunity to study Jacques myself. To try to figure out why Sparrow wants him so badly. It takes me five seconds to realize that I will never understand her attraction to him. He infuriates me. And so does his date with her unsettling attention on me.

A slight burning feeling is happening on my left side, and before I can register what's happening, Sparrow's hand is on my shoulder. She's close enough that I can smell her scent wrapping around me and the warmth of her fingers through my shirt. I clear my throat and decide that if she's going to be close to me, I'm going to enjoy every moment. I do my best to let my body relax and slide my hand up her back, stopping at the nape of her neck. I begin playing with her hair, which I've wanted to do for the past hour, and smirk when I feel her hand grip my shoulder a little tighter. I don't miss the way her voice cracks a bit as I wrap a tendril of her hair around my finger, wrap it, release it, and then do it again. This is my new favorite game.

"You should meet us at the art gallery," Jacques says while glancing at his date, who's still smirking at me, before focusing more attention on Sparrow. I suddenly want to pull a Thor and send my coffee mug to the floor. Except, I wouldn't be yelling, "Another!" as other less-savory words circle my mind. I don't know what to do with this new feeling of wanting someone to myself.

"Darling, do you want to go to an art show?" Her voice breaks me from my thoughts, and I turn to look between her and Jacques (and decidedly not Vivienne). Sparrow's mannerisms are full of amusement, but her eyes tell me she really wants to know. And all I'm stuck on is that she just called me *darling*.

"Right now, anywhere you are is where I want to be," I manage. And I mean it. Dropping my arm from her neck to the curve of her waist, I pull Sparrow a little closer to me and feel her ribcage expand with her breath.

"Gallery. It's a gallery," Jacques corrects.

She grins, and I return the gesture until we're just two grinning people crammed on one side of a booth, making Jacques and his own date uncomfortable while they stand at an awkward distance. He mutters his goodbyes and some directions to a place I won't remember, leading Vivienne slowly away from us, and my body refuses to move. We're still leaning toward each other, her eyes searching mine for a clue as to what's happening. But instead of letting her in on anything, since I can't define what I'm doing either, I reach for the spoon with the abandoned sundae.

I get a new bite's worth on the spoon and hold it in front of her face. Her eyes never leave mine. I remove my arm from her waist and feel myself smile when she lets out a little sigh. I cup my hand under the waiting spoon and hover it near her red-painted mouth.

"What are you doing?" she whispers, her eyes still trying to figure me out.

"Feeding you." A drip of melted ice cream hits my palm.

"Why?"

I move my gaze from her perfect lips to the spoon and back again. "I don't know."

She furrows her brow. "Oh, I thought maybe Jacques was still watching."

"Hmm," I hum. "That would've made more sense."

I will my hands to put the spoon down and walk away with as much dignity as possible when Sparrow grasps my wrist. Her touch pulses through my arm and toward my heart again, like she just can't help but check on its condition. Instead of turning away, she takes the bite from the spoon, whipped cream and a hint of apple filling now lightly resting near her top lip, and closes her eyes in delight.

"Good?" I choke out, my pulse pounding.

"Wicked good." She grins, and I find my thumb brushing the cream off her face ever so lightly. She stills and then settles into my touch.

"Kiss her already!" Lucy cheers from behind the counter.

Sparrow's eyes widen, and the spell is broken as I realize how close I was to doing just that. What was almost a movie moment now feels like Lucy pouring a pitcher of ice water on my hopes and dreams. I must pay attention so I don't forget who I am and what I want. And while it looks, sounds, and smells like the Sparrow sitting next to me, and I wish I had met her before Jacques, we both know I'm not really what she wants.

Still, I look to Sparrow, who is looking at me with what can only be described as whispers of hope breezing through her eyes, and I want it to stay. I lift my hand, and she holds her breath as I grab a piece of hair falling near her eyes. She stays still as I lightly twist it between my fingers and set it right again, never pushing it back. A smile plays at the corner of her mouth, and I think this must be a glimpse of what it feels like to be cherished and seen by someone. And even if it's pretend, something about this doesn't feel pretend at all. In fact, it's so real it aches a little.

I clear my throat.

"Um . . . so, did you want anything else? Another coffee?" Lucy says while fanning herself with a pot holder in my peripheral vision.

I open my mouth to say something but close it again just as quickly. Sparrow raises an eyebrow. Without looking away from her, I find myself softly saying, "I'll settle for that, for now."

Chapter Ten

Sparrow

We never did talk about the rules for our fake-dating charade. And I don't want to worry about them. Because even though fear is beating around my heart, the thought of putting a rule in place like, *Hand holding only when in public unless a kiss is necessary* or *Must appear to like each other*, etcetera, seems too constricting. I'm learning that Rafe is more creative than I imagined— not just in music but in how he moves through life.

Last night felt like a dream. After our ice-cream-and-pie-eating moment at the diner, Rafe brought me home. He opened my car door and even walked me to my apartment. I left the Polaroid he took of me on the dashboard, not hating the way he looked at it before getting out of the car.

After hearing his music last night, I downloaded his playlist on my music app. There were a few singles and some covers. I may or may not have fallen asleep with his music playing (I did). Since I don't have social media (I know, I know) I managed to text Lily to check him out for me. She sent me beautifully candid photos of him recording in the studio, playing his guitar, and even a few where he's making ridiculous faces. His playfulness might be the most surprising attribute for someone as attractive as him.

I reach my hand inside my front apron pocket and feel the guitar pick I placed there from the show last night. I plan on giving it back to Rafe today. When I feel the imprint of his initial on the pick once more, I sigh.

I'm walking toward the flower market to meet Lily when I spot Jacques. He is so French it hurts. He's chatting with someone who looks very important on the corner, his dress shoes and jacket giving the impression he just stepped off the runway. He spots me and leaves the conversation, moving toward me with purpose.

"Rory, *salut!*" Huh. He's using my nickname. Where did he hear that? I flash to the memory of Rafe's nickname for me and feel my cheeks heat.

"Hi, Jacques. Good to see you." His eyes look warm and inviting today, in contrast to the cool, aloof demeanor he wore when we first met. "How's Vivienne?"

He winces slightly and shakes his head. "Oh, we're not together. I just didn't want to go to the show alone." He gives an adorable shrug, and I feel his reason. Because I don't like to do anything alone either.

"And . . . she's okay with that?"

He nods affirmatively. "Yes, of course. We both agreed it wasn't a date."

My mind flashes to my own agreement with Rafe. "Oh."

He leans toward me, the scent of his French cologne revealing his sudden closeness, and my breath catches. "I'm only interested in one woman right now." I startle at his directness and focus on my brand-new fascination with the pastry case between us.

"How is Rafe?" he says, but I notice the way his hands clench the sides of his jacket.

"He's . . ." I start. How do you describe someone like Rafe, who appeared and seems to read you like a favorite poem? "Good. He's good." That's all I manage to say.

"Don't forget, Rory. I know I was . . . distracted before. I asked you out too late. But if things change— not that I wish them to—but *if* they do, give me a chance, okay?"

He wants a chance with me. I find myself nodding slowly because what else can I do? Rafe was right. The plan to fake date seems to have already gotten Jacques' attention. The question is, when it comes to Rafe, why does it feel so uncomfortable to think of calling the whole thing off?

I make it to the flower market and catch Lily looking reverently at the flowers around her. She's lost in her own world because—no surprise to anyone who knows her—Lily loves flowers. And since it's officially the start of fall, Lily has recruited me to the market to create a fall-themed bouquet "while the flowers last," she'd said dramatically. Every Thursday, our town holds a farmers' market—outdoors when it's warm, indoors when it's cold. Today, there's a chill in the air, so I'm surrounded by flowers in a tent-like structure with a view of Town Hall when you exit.

"So, about Rafe . . ." Lily begins. Wow, she really isn't wasting any time.

"What about Rafe?" I try to avoid eye contact while also pretending to be unaffected by the mention of his name. By the way Lily grins as she selectively picks Gerbera daisies, I don't think it's working.

"I saw you."

I glance up enough to see her eyes meet mine, a knowing look hovering within them. "I mean, you've met, so . . ."

Lily walks around to where I'm looking at bunches of sunflowers and lightly stops my hand from picking up an additional bucket of them. I was too busy comparing Jacques with Rafe to notice my arms frantically grabbing flowers like I'm hoarding them for spring.

"What are you even doing? Who needs this many sunflowers?" Lily scoffs. "I mean, I love them, but this is too much—even for you."

I'm too proud to stop my motions, so I just keep avoiding her gaze and own the fact that, at this rate, I will be handing out sunflowers to the entire town.

"Sparrow, stop."

I sigh and watch as Lily takes hold of most of the stems and softly places them back in their container. They're back to enjoying their buckets with all the water they could need, and I'm back to holding a reasonable number of flowers again.

My hand shakes a bit, and I grip it in the other to avoid Lily seeing, but suddenly, I don't have the strength. I blame the cloudy weather for relaxing me too much. "Jacques asked me if I was single. And instead of answering him, I looked at someone else."

Lily grips my hand to pull me closer to her. "You did. And you must at least promise me this . . ." Lily declares as she brings my handful of sunflowers to the register and pays before I can protest. I watch the brown paper wrapper contrasting with the golden-yellow petals and feel like the brown packing string as it gets knotted before becoming a bow. "Try to keep your heart open. You suddenly have two men in your life by some gift from heaven. So, try to have some fun. You do remember what that is, don't you?"

I search my mind and try to remember the last time I remember having fun for the sake of it. My subconscious takes over and flashes a series of images. Apple pie ice cream sundae on a spoon. Disheveled cinnamon-brown hair. A baseball cap. Slightly crooked bottom teeth. Stickers on a guitar case. I take a breath.

Lily hands me the flowers and flashes a knowing little grin.

Two days later, I'm standing in the bakery's kitchen. Waiting. I know he'll be here at any moment. Yesterday, I saw a few guitar picks sticking out of his messenger bag, and I was struck with what could only be described as brilliance. I grin to myself. I'm normally not the type to play. When your heart has been broken enough, I think you forget how to chase joy. But with Rafe? I'm trying to remember. Besides, it's his own fault. His perfectly tossed hair and sequoia-forest eyes are just begging to be messed with, and I've decided that I'm more than up for the challenge. This is new. But it's *fun*.

The swinging door catapults open, and I put on my best poker face. I don't actually have a poker face, but I'm going to act like my dignity depends on pulling this off. Rafe's been frequenting the café (aka living here while it's open), probably going broke from drinking cups of coffee and eating pastries. He even brought his guitar this morning and played some light music. Lily gave him permission as long as he gives her a portion of the tips she saw people placing in his empty coffee cup as they left the bakery.

"Okay, where are they?" he mutters. His eyes flash, but he's dangerously close to grinning. He's wearing a sweater beneath a blazer and looking way too good to be in the back of my café. Still, I take in the scruff that lines his face before meeting his narrowing eyes.

"I don't know what you could possibly mean," I say, possibly a little too adamantly.

He slowly saunters toward the counter and runs a hand through his hair. It sticks up like leaves in a pile, and my hand just wants to jump in it. This experiment is already a success.

"You seem so upset. Are you coming down with something?" I unhelpfully add. I hide a grin and continue making a tray of macarons.

"Woman, how do you expect me to be able to play guitar if you keep stealing my picks, hmm?"

"Hmm . . . so, I'm 'woman' now and not 'Sugar'?" I ask innocently.

"This act of yours is not so sweet." His hands are on his hips, and his foot is tapping as I continue piping circles of the light-green pistachio batter, or *pistache*, onto a Silpat mat.

"Hmm, sounds like you have a real problem."

He sighs. "I do *not* have a problem. I have never misplaced so many guitar picks in my life since arriving here. And it's only been days."

I continue to pipe, swiftly circling the pastry bag across my baking trays. "Oh my, that does, in fact, sound like a problem."

His foot taps more rapidly. He's almost infuriating

he's so attractive.

Hovering a finger over a circle of batter on the tray, he waits, an eyebrow raised.

"Don't," I say simply and continue to pipe. Something came over me when I decided that, as long as he's here, I'm going to soak up the warmth that he brings. Winter will be here before we know it after all.

He huffs and starts pacing. He's all bark and no bite, pretending to be a pirate while he's really a prince.

"Did you try The Music Store?" I manage to say while focusing on the tray, so I don't see his reaction. It really is called The Music Store. Sometimes, in a small town, it's function over flair.

"I would, except given the size of this town, there is only *one*. And they're closed."

I grin. "Ah, yes, Liam does like to sleep in on Wednesdays. Something about shooting reels of his cat. He's famous, you know."

He's beside me in two seconds, the heat radiating off him and causing my hands, and thus the piping bag, to tremble. I toss it to the side and turn to face him.

"You took them," he says matter-of-factly.

I scoff. "Sure, because between running a bakery and my own life, I have so much time on my hands that I just get a kick out of somehow stealing your guitar picks and hiding them. Yeah, sure . . ."

"Sparrow, are you *playing* with me?" His eyes flash before they catch on something above my head, and I realize my mistake.

I should've turned the raccoon so he was facing the other way. I watch as Rafe's jaw shifts back and forth. He's so cute when he's irritated, but I feel the energy of him trying to prevent himself from laughing. Rafe ever so slowly shifts his gaze to mine, and I feel my eyes widen.

"What is that?" He points over my head.

"What is what?" I ask innocently.

"That—that over your head."

"What's over my head?"

"On the wall, near the order sheets. What is that?"

I hide my hands behind my back to distract myself. *Don't laugh, don't laugh* ... "Really, Rafe, I don't know what's gotten into you today."

He crosses the space between us and the wall at record speed. I keep my back turned. He'll be back. And I'm right. After some shuffling and sighing, he's in front of me again, the smell of him invading my space.

"*This.*" He's pointing to one of his guitar picks—because I hid one back here.

"Huh," I say.

"Huh? That's all you have to say for yourself?"

"So strange that it would be here ..." I swirl my hand in the air as if to pull down answers from the sky. Suddenly I'm a dame in one of those Old Hollywood movies. I think about putting him out of his misery, but honestly, I'm still having too much fun. "Rafe, have you been sleepwalking or something?"

A mischievous look crosses his face, and I swallow. Seems like he's ready to play too.

"Sleepwalking to the point that I manage to walk across town, break into this store, walk into the kitchen, and somehow decide to hide ONE guitar pick on the stuffed-animal thing that's ..." He looks up again to study it. "... wearing a beret and holding a croissant?"

I throw back my shoulders and lift my chin. "It's a raccoon. His name is Philippe, as it is pronounced *in French*. If you press his paw, he says, *'C'est incroyable!'*" His mouth drops. I dare him with my eyebrows.

"I will not touch his paw."

I wave my hand again. "Your loss."

His eyes dart from the back wall to me again before his shoulders slump slightly. "Fine, that little critter can have it. This time." He looks at Philippe as if he would like to crush him if he could. "Isn't that unsanitary?" he asks.

"It's stuffed."

He winces.

"Lily got him for me."

"Of course she did," he sighs.

He moves away from me, and I already miss his warmth. The dimple comes out to play as he starts to inch toward my sheet pan rack of finished pastries. "You win this time, Sparrow."

I watch as he lifts the bottom of his sweatshirt into a makeshift pocket and grabs a handful of macarons from two of the trays but not before stuffing a coffee-colored one in his mouth. "Hey!"

He walks backward toward the door to the front of the bakery, a look of triumph on his face. "Mmm, espresso," he says to himself before looking back at me, a little amusement matched with indignation flashing in his eyes. "Oh, and Sugar?"

I turn to face him with the most innocent expression I can muster.

"Quit stealing my guitar picks." The twitch on the side of his mouth betrays him. He's enjoying this as much as I am.

When the door swings shut, I finally let out a laugh. It's relief mixed with elation. It's floating after worrying you may sink. I don't want to keep the man from his music, but I regret nothing. It turns out that he has multiple colors of his engraved pics. Good thing I looked online to find out how I could order them to replace them if he doesn't find them all.

But if I can see that face of his getting so worked up a few more times, it will be more than worth it. I'm still smiling as I finish the tray and pop the macarons into the oven. My phone vibrates on the counter, and I know just who it's from.

Rafe: This isn't over.

Grabbing a pumpkin macaron from the tray he sampled, I smile and take a satisfying bite. Just wait until he realizes where I hid the rest.

Chapter Eleven

Rafe

I hum quietly to the pieces of a song playing through my earphones. I'm hooked up to a sound booth sort of situation in the back of The Music Store. Liam, its owner, is younger than I expected. I looked him up, and while he is renowned in this region for jazz music, he works with musical artists across multiple genres and is a multi-instrumentalist. Apparently, his father was a drummer in a famous band in the eighties, and while Liam never wanted to tour, music is his life. I can relate.

Being attached to an instrument in the studio is where I feel the most at home. It quiets the noise and makes me feel things I otherwise wouldn't let myself feel. I've been in therapy over the years, my parents insisting upon it when they thought I wasn't pursuing my best life by refusing to go into fashion with my father. Little did they know I used the time to process how to distance myself further from their disappointment. It's the music notes that have always been my haven.

"Man, this is sounding good," Liam says into the microphone behind the plexiglass. Birch Borough is not Nashville or LA, but I like the vibe of this place. Here, it feels like music is all that matters, and I can get behind that. I've been scribbling for days and had to get the sounds out, so I stopped at the store. Liam and I connected over a love of recording music, and here I am, trying to hide away while counting down the moments until I see Sparrow again.

Usually, I can lose track of time in the studio. But while the song is coming along, it's not quite there yet. I think I need to live a bit more to find out what it needs. Or perhaps I need to be around a certain someone who seems to both inspire me and take up all my creativity.

"We should lay down some vocals soon. What do you say?"

I nod and grin, the tension starting to ease from my frame. When I was fifteen, I realized that the only way to get my music into the world was to do it myself. I couldn't just go up to a famous singer and ask them to sing a song I wrote. But getting music into the world is my passion. I've always felt like everyone has something to give to the world, and the something I have to give involves music. I've learned to use alchemy to turn disappointment into my fuel for creativity. But lately, that creativity has been running out—until Sparrow.

Speaking of Sparrow, she has no reason to think I will stick around, and that's bothering me way too much. Tell people you're a singer, and they automatically assume you want to be famous. I don't. I just want famous people to sing my songs. And I believe, one day, they will. The journey has cost me too much. And just like the others, this song has to count. It will count. I can't afford for anything I create to only be "good" and not reach its full potential. My heart demands more.

"It needs a bit more work, but I think I know where to find more inspiration."

Liam gives a knowing grin as he steps into the studio space. "You seem to be spending lots of time at Sparrow's Beret."

I will myself to keep my face in check. "Good coffee. Great pastries. What's not to like?"

He doesn't say anything, letting me settle into what we're not saying: I've got a thing for the person who owns the bakery.

"I've lived here a long time. Went to school with the crew—the four women who are becoming the backbone of this town," he says with a smile, confirming that we are around the same age and when it comes to this group of friends, he's got wisdom to share. "Are you patient?" he says unexpectedly.

I nod.

"Good. Because your girl likes to hide. She's brilliant and beautiful, but you'll have to work to get under her layers."

I must give him a look, because he shakes his head with a laugh. "I've never felt like that for her, just telling you how it is. It's probably nothing you haven't figured out."

I nod again because my throat is feeling tight.

"But she hides."

"Do you know why?" I ask because I've made some guesses, but it's startling to me that I've been all over the world, and the woman I wouldn't have believed existed has been tucked away in this small town, content to call it her home and yet aching to go to Paris.

"The same reason most of us hide, I think . . . wanting to be seen and being terrified of it at the same time."

I jump when I feel Sparrow's hand against my face, lifting the side of my headphones so she can talk to me.

"You're humming again," she announces.

She's gotten a bit more friendly with me the last couple of days, and while I know I can't read too much into it, she's only adding to my level of attraction. We barely talk about the premise of fake dating but have somehow fallen into an understanding and a rhythm of being together. She's the drum beat to my life right now, and I am here for it. I've been here for less than a week, and I'm already tired of seeing how she's put into a box in this town. They love her, but they label her. She's the steady creator of their coffees and croissants. They don't see her as someone who could completely change someone's world like she's already changed mine. And I think it's time she was given a new reputation.

I slip off the headphones and turn to see her in what I think to be a fourth position in ballet but with her hip relaxed and arms crossed in front of her. I grin and shake off how sweet I find her faux ballet positions. She's like a ballerina who just won't let herself forget that her resting posture is undeniably elegant. She says she's clumsy, but it's mixed with grace.

"I don't get why I'm still tired. It doesn't make any sense. I've had about four of these today." I tilt the coffee cup on the counter to show her its emptiness. I've been here for hours, and I've had so many coffees. Too many coffees. I stretch on the stool and rub my eyes. When I open them, I watch Sparrow's eyes widen as she clears and cleans the counter around me but avoids my gaze. "Sparrow?"

She doesn't stop moving, and I notice her nose scrunching in an adorable way.

"Please, look at me."

She keeps cleaning.

"What have you done?" I whisper.

Dramatically, she walks over to the coffee maker and starts examining the containers of beans she has. "Hmm . . . that's interesting."

I cross my arms in a surly pose, but I'm trying not to smile. Her playfulness is delightful. For some reason, it keeps surprising me every time. "What? What's interesting?"

She grins at me in what can only be described as a wicked manner and pretends to examine the coffee containers. I know she's pretending because she doesn't need to check them—they've been there for decades. "Sorry. Guess you've been getting decaf all day."

I moan. "Sugar, why do you keep doing this? Why?"

She did this yesterday too. After my third cup of coffee, when I felt the lack of caffeine weakening my resolve to create, she confessed to switching out one of the cups with the drink of despair: decaf. My shoulders are slumped, and I'm holding my face in my hands. I haven't been sleeping as a result of the woman standing in front of me. I need her to just give me the coffee goods, and for some odd reason, she's been holding out on me.

She leans closer to me, her addicting scent of caramelized sugar, vanilla, and something spicy today lingering in the air. I inhale deeply and hope she doesn't hear. Yep, I definitely need to write a song about the way she smells—in a totally non-creepy way, of course.

"Some of us like to keep our customers alive and not

set them loose from here as a destruction to both themselves and the world."

I do my best to squint menacingly, but given the way she's biting her cheek, I imagine it's not as ominous as I would wish. "Half-caf. You couldn't give me half-caf?"

Sparrow surveys the little coffee cups with a valiant effort.

"*Non*," she says with a French accent that makes me grateful I'm sitting and not standing. Sparrow speaking French is going to cause me to implode. It's not painful when it comes from her.

"Let me ask you this," she says, holding a finger in the air. "How many cups did you have before you got here today?"

I shift on the stool. "Well, I don't see how that's relevant . . ."

"How. Many."

I lift my gaze to hers and lose myself in the swirling chocolate of her eyes. They're stormy right now, like when she makes truffles or melts the chocolate over the double burner and swirls it around before dipping the madeleines. Not that I've been paying attention. I inch my way closer to her and hold my breath as she leans in toward me too. Her eyes fall to my lips, and I hold myself so still before the spell is broken. The sound of the bell over the door has us turning our faces toward the noise. And there, in all his French glory, is the man and the menace, Jacques.

"Him," I mutter.

Sparrow turns to me, her eyes riveted. A look of amusement passes over them as I realize my error: Jealousy has come out to play.

"*Salut, Rory!*" he calls.

She turns to face him and walks away from me but

not before I see her grin my way.

"*Salut, Jacques! Que veux-tu manger?*" What would you like to eat? She doesn't speak French often, but why she hasn't tried to speak French with me—other than saying *non*—knowing full well I've lived in Paris, is beyond me. I thought for sure Lily would've told her. Maybe it's simply because of the awful way I first said *please*. I know I still haven't recovered.

Little does she know, the more she directs this part of herself away from me only makes me crave it more.

"*Pain au chocolat et un café, s'il te plâit!*" A chocolate croissant and a coffee, please. She can do that.

"*D'accord!*"

I sink lower on the stool as Lily walks out from the back and heads my way. She leans an elbow on the counter between us and gives me a knowing glance like she can read my thoughts about wanting to throw the chocolate croissant he ordered across the room.

"Well . . . " she starts. "What's your move, D'Artagnan? Sitting here like an idiot isn't going to work well for you, no matter how attractive you are."

"D'Artagnan?" I inhale at the thought of my secret being revealed sooner than I realized if Lily has already figured out I'm French. "Why would you call me that?" I'm not proud of the way my voice cracks.

"Traveling the world, swashbuckling tendencies . . . trying to be a part of this town and win over a woman. I wouldn't put it past you to want to win a duel with a sword, probably against Jacques." She pins me with an intense look. "Also, I'm referring to the vibes from the 2014 British TV drama series, of course."

I take a deep breath. "Lily, did anyone ever tell you that you are . . . " She gives me a stare that stops my train of thought. "The most incredibly perceptive, can't-live-without, sunshine-like person on the planet?" I shift my shoulders as she grins.

"I couldn't have said it better myself."

I tap my fingers on the counter.

"Oh, for The Three Musketeers' sake, just put a guitar in your hands and start playing music. She can't resist a brooding artist. I blame Eric for playing the recorder in first grade."

I raise my eyebrows. "What did you say?"

Lily motions toward Sparrow. "The woman you can't take your eyes off of . . . " She stops herself before finishing her sentence to redirect. "She has a thing for music. She also loves to dance. Can you dance?"

I nod, narrowing my eyes. This could be a trap.

"Ask her to hang out with you after the Maple Fest. She may even want to go to the pumpkin patch."

I start at this. "What's a pumpkin patch?"

She laughs. "Look it up. It's about ten minutes from here. But I don't care what you do . . . just ask her." Lily aggressively wipes the counter space around me.

"Lily, why are you helping me right now?"

Lily rolls her eyes and then grimaces when her eyes land on Jacques. "Because *that* man is not who Sparrow needs."

"He's French," I add unhelpfully as if the fact wasn't obvious.

"Oh, so what?"

"But Sparrow said she wanted someone French."

"She doesn't always know what she wants."

"And you do?"

"Mm-hmm. You don't know someone for most of your life and consider yourself an amateur."

"We're only fake dating." My words sound half-hearted at best.

"Ha! Good one." She shakes her head as if I've cracked. "Sparrow is incapable of faking. Once, in the fourth grade, we had a Thanksgiving performance—one of those truly terrible ones that scar you for life and make you wonder if you have any purpose when you remember your teacher thought you'd be best playing an ear of corn or a pumpkin."

"I never had that experience."

"Of course you didn't. And be glad for it." She scrubs a nonexistent stain on the counter and mutters, "Stupid turkey."

"Okay . . . well, Lily—wait—what was Sparrow?"

"Oh, right." She veers back on track. "She was supposed to be Plymouth Rock." She scoffs, and I smile. "But she told the teacher there wasn't any way she could possibly be a rock because rocks aren't human, and she couldn't pretend she wasn't."

I let this little revelation sink in.

"So, you see? Sparrow is who she is. What you see is what you get."

My heart lifts. If that's true, I really like what I'm seeing. But I'm not sure if she will like my own story. "So, if she can't pretend, what is this all about? What does she need?"

My hope is that Lily will spill something, anything, that will give me a clue to the reason Sparrow has built such thick walls around her heart. I think they are cracking, but I'm worried it's not enough. The pictures on the wall indicate that she's at least partially French, so maybe it has something to do with her heritage. But that can't be the only reason she declared to the universe that she would only consider dating a Frenchman. It just can't be. I think I notice one of my guitar picks peeking out of a canister of coffee when Lily turns toward me.

"Nice try, D'Artagnan. But no. I don't spill heart secrets."

"Lily . . ." I almost plead.

"No. If you don't figure it out, then you don't deserve her." She grabs my plate, a half-eaten cookie still on it.

"I was still eating that!"

"You weren't," she says while wrapping it up in a tiny box and putting it in front of me. And I wasn't. The thing's been untouched for the past thirty minutes. She points to the empty espresso cups in front of me. "And those?"

"Don't. Even. Say it," I mutter.

Lily slowly backs away. "Decafffff," she whispers.

And I sigh. These women . . . the one I can't get out of my head and the one who acts like her bouncer . . . they'll be the end of me. I just know it. An idea swirls through my mind. It'll be me laying down one of my cards. And trusting Sparrow won't take the whole hand.

Chapter Twelve

Sparrow

I watch a lot of shows on YouTube in French. I can't really understand what most of them are saying, but I'm super proud of myself for understanding a lot of mannerisms and picking up more words lately. It's hard to explain why it's comforting, even when I'm not entirely sure what they're saying, but it is.

Some part of me must remember my mother speaking to me in French when I was little. My father only knew how to listen—he never tried speaking French, except for a few words to my mother. He said that he knew he didn't have the sound, so it wasn't his role to try to pretend he did. He wanted to leave that to her, but without her, I'm afraid that sound I could have had left me before it even had the chance to flourish.

I pull the dough I've been stirring off the stove and prepare my piping bags. I love the feel of piping choux pastry, or *pâte à choux*, onto baking sheets. My father loved it too. At two or three in the morning, I would smell melted butter and a mixture of flour and eggs. It was the smell that often woke me up from my dreams. And when I would tiptoe down the stairs, my feet in socks so I didn't alert my father that I was also out of bed, I would see him in the kitchen with a dozen or so pastry sheets surrounding him.

He wore an apron that still had embroidery from my mother on the pocket, and he would be standing there, piping rows and rows of *choux*, the dough that makes up everything from eclairs to profiteroles, or cream puffs.

His large hands gripped the distressed pastry bag with such precision and grace it was like a farmer tending a garden or a surgeon utilizing their skills but through pastry.

I would sit on the little step leading down to the bakery from the back door and watch him work. He always hummed. Usually, they were songs from my mother, and usually, they were French. Sometimes, I would also catch him humming classics from Simon & Garfunkel or The Beatles. I think baking was his therapy.

My father never wanted to own the bakery on his own. When he started it, the goal was to make my mother's dreams come true. It was never his dream to own such a place, even though he was a master baker. He never went to culinary school. Everything he knew how to do, aside from bread, he learned from my mother.

But he treated the café and bakery with the same care and intention with which he loved my mother—and taught me a lesson in what it means to do something and keep doing something with all your heart.

I once asked my father what he would've done if he hadn't met my mother. And he said that he would probably still be baking bread somewhere in Boston and eating toast with two pats of butter and nothing more.

He said knowing that *pains au chocolat* existed because of my mother made all the difference in his life.

When we ate breakfast together, he would often say, "Sometimes some of us settle for what we know, and we think that butter is so great on toast because we've never eaten a croissant. Be someone who knows the difference."

I walk to the front of the store, a folder in hand. As I look about my bakery, I guess what I'm wondering is, even though I've never been to France, at what point do I get to feel more French? Maybe this was something my mother was supposed to assure me of, and now, I have to settle for what I am: a French American woman who has learned to hide the fact that hearing French makes her want to cry. That choux pastry was one of my first foods, and being surrounded by chocolate creme and butter is as familiar as breathing. Or that I sometimes dream in French. Because when I wake up, I'm Sparrow, a woman who lives in a tiny New England town, has wild hair, and still dreams of seeing Paris.

This is what I'm thinking of as I hover over an application to submit my bakery to be featured in *The Seacoast Gazette* magazine. They often feature bakeries, and I've been waiting, sitting on applying or getting the word out about my store because I don't know what would happen if a piece of my life made it into a world bigger than my own. Rafe makes me want to believe the wait is over.

Something about him as he works on his song makes me reflect on my passions—what I dream about. And it's always the same: to keep my parents' legacy alive while I can, when I can. I think I've done a fair job of it so far with the store, but what if their story could be told to even more people?

The bell jingles, and I look up to see Rafe walking toward me with a hesitant smile. He walks up to the counter, and I push myself to my full height. We don't say anything, simply staring at each other, the sounds of a French café playlist swirling around us. I notice his forest-green eyes are a little darker today, something that shouldn't cause my stomach to clench, but it does. He raises an eyebrow, the one with the scar, and I want to trace it and ask him how he got it.

A throat clearing makes me jump a bit. Gladys is in the corner of the café, her eyebrow raised. Rafe turns slowly toward her, which I'm certain he regrets when she signals for him to get on with whatever he's here to do. I bite my lip and notice his eyes catch on it before moving up to my own.

"I heard there's a pumpkin patch thing happening?" he says in a question. He's fidgeting, his hair bouncing with every move. If I didn't know better, I would say he's nervous.

"Yes, there's a pumpkin patch, over at Wicked Good Farms."

"Huh," he says, a grin starting to play near one side of his mouth. He puts a hand on the back of his neck and rubs it slowly, shifting the top of the light-grey hoodie he's wearing. It's unfair how good he looks right now. "And there are pumpkins . . . at this patch?"

I try to hold back a laugh at how certain I am this is the first time he's ever said that word in his life. I nod instead. "Did you want a coffee?" I ask him, and he shakes his head, convincing me immediately that something is up. "A pastry?" Again, his head shakes.

He shifts from side to side, his hands now doing a tapping thing on the front of the counter.

"Ask her out already!" Gladys yells from the corner.

Clearly, she's had enough. "This isn't Dunkin'. You don't just order a regular coffee with cream and sugar and call it a day."

I sink a little. "Rafe, are you asking me out?" I ask breathlessly. It seems odd he would be nervous to ask me something I would clearly say yes to, especially because we are supposed to be fake dating.

He clears his throat. "I, uh . . . Well, I was going to see . . . if you wanted to—you know, go because we're dating. We can go after the Maple Fest. Maybe there will be pumpkins." He winces at the last bit. He's usually the sort that is so composed, so easygoing. But I like this side of him a little too much.

"Yes, I'd love to go."

He lets himself smile in a way that warms me up from within. I move to the pastry case and pull out a maple croissant with a piece of brown bakery tissue, hovering it between us. He takes it, the edges of his fingers meeting the edges of mine, and I hope he doesn't notice the little shiver that hits me when we touch.

"Thanks, Sugar," he says so softly, as if we're sharing a secret. And I suppose we are. "I'll meet you after I sing."

It's officially Maple Fest, and my heart is so full. This is one of my favorite days of our entire year here in our small town, and it's one where everyone (and I do mean everyone) celebrates the start of fall. Maple is our mascot. Even people from the surrounding cities and areas drive to experience what it's like to be in our town and celebrate the scenery and festivities along our river.

There's a park adjacent to one side of the river—the stiller segment. It looks like a giant lake there, but you can hear the rush of the river on the other side of the shops where it's rocky and not as smooth. People even paddle board into our town via the river. They'll get some lunch and then paddle back to wherever they started from.

It's a beautiful, sunny day, and I'm wearing a long sweater dress and boots to kick off the celebration. With the addition of my trench coat, it's clear I put in a little extra effort in my appearance today. I'm going to say it was to represent the bakery well for a special day, not to impress anyone in particular. We have a booth in the long lineup, and I'm hoping I've baked enough croissants and *chouquettes* to make all the families happy with a little piece of French-baked goodness.

"Hmm. Someone's looking foxy for a certain musician."

I whip around to find Lily walking up to the booth with a satisfied smile on her face. She's wearing all black, and her hair is in a haphazard bun.

"Lily, please. It's really not like that." A few people overhear and turn toward us, but thankfully, they're tourists and no one I know, so we're safe.

She puts on her apron, which somehow already has chocolate on it even though I know it's just been washed, and gives me a knowing grin. "Where is your main man, anyway?" she mutters, looking around.

"I haven't seen Jacques," I reply politely. My whole body cringes because we both know that's not who she was referring to, and it's certainly not who came to my mind when she mentioned "my man." She rolls her eyes, and we start to set out our signs and pastries. I found several adorable sparrow statues at a consignment shop recently, and Lily somehow found tiny berets to put on them. I think she made them herself, but she'll never admit it. She does seem to have a look of pride when she looks at them, though, so I'm pretty sure my theory is correct.

It's only when she elbows me that I look up and follow her gaze to see Rafe walking through the building crowd with his guitar case and a smoldering smile. His focus is on me. I start to stand a bit taller when we're both derailed by Alfred Hughes, one of the board members of our Music and Arts Committee, intercepting Rafe. He talks hurriedly to Rafe, who nods politely, and they start to move toward the bandstand on the other end of the park. I grin at him, and he shrugs like he's truly sorry. I laugh a little when he makes an absurd face with his eyes crossed over his shoulder, setting down his guitar case. He points to himself and mimics strumming a guitar, points at me, then to the bandstand, and then holds his hands as if in prayer. He's asking me to visit him while he's singing.

I tap my mouth with my finger and look up like I'm thinking about it. Lily interrupts our adorable and silent communication when she hits me with a bag of marshmallows and yells, "She'll be there!"

Rafe laughs and picks up his guitar case, looking at me over his shoulder with a heartbreakingly beautiful smile.

I smile back at him and then look down, trying to remember what I was doing before that moment. Lily is helping a customer with an order of macarons while I'm trying to will the blush out of my face and out of my heart.

Hours later, we're nearly out of pastries, and we have a dozen new pickup orders for the next few weeks. We've even received an order to supply maple croissants for a new inn opening in Portsmouth. The event was a huge success, and more than once, I was asked about plans to expand and my thoughts on people being able to have our products shipped to them. Even though I'm now exhausted, the day has given me a lot to think about when it comes to the next steps for my bakery.

I roll my neck around to try to get some of the tension out. Lily and I have started to pack up, and I'm just pulling down an edge of the back banner when she stops me.

"Hey, I've got this. Go see your man. Isn't he playing soon?"

I look at my phone. It's 3:54 p.m. Lily's right. Earlier, I may have bent down under our table and looked up the band schedule for today's event. Sure enough, they added Rafe, and he's playing at 4:00 p.m.

"He isn't my man," is all I manage to say as I abandon the banner to pull boxes from under the table to organize some of the packaging.

"He wants to be."

I look at her, but she hasn't given me a face. She's calmly starting her part of the tear-down process, which means she isn't teasing me. "Rory, go. I've got this, really. And Liam already offered to take some of our stuff back to the shop. So, I'll be fine."

"You don't want to go listen to music too?"

Lily shakes her head. "I'm peopled out. As much as I love good music, I'm ready for a glass of wine and the latest episode of *The Man is a Rake*. Who needs a show by the river when I can be home and watching a man rile up the womenfolk with a good trench coat and his fortune of ten thousand pounds a year?"

I laugh. She isn't wrong. I think one of the funniest things about Lily is that she's obsessed with Regency romances. I like them, too, but she's the one who got me interested in them. It's such a contrast to her sometimes-spiky personality that I forget she's really a homebody and someone who would prefer to be away from the crowd.

It's now four minutes till. The truth is, I don't want to miss Rafe's performance. I take off my apron, set it neatly in the bin near our table, and wrap Lily up in a hug while she says, "Don't get sappy on me."

I laugh and walk toward the bandstand. It's a darling, raised platform with a roof and a lattice designed across the lower third of the structure. It's just big enough for a band. A grassy section surrounds it where people have already stretched out blankets and lawn chairs to settle in for the show. I hear strumming and the sounds of musicians warming up. As I get closer, I make out three people on the stage. There's Rafe, who has my heart hammering in my chest, and two men I haven't seen before—a percussionist and a violinist. I'm so intrigued by this little group that I wander toward the back and near a line of trees.

I wave and say hello to people I either met at my booth or have known since I was a little girl and try to compose myself. Thermos of coffee in hand, I close my eyes and inhale sharply when Rafe's voice breaks through the air.

"Good afternoon, everyone. Thank you so much for being here and for being willing to listen to some of my music."

I open my eyes and see the effortless way he's settled in behind the mic. It's clear that he's at home, and this is just an extension of who he is more than a show. He's the same both on and off the stage. And this brings more comfort than I expected.

"I did write all of the songs you'll hear tonight—and you may recognize one covered by a small French band known as Histoire." Rafe is laser-focused on me.

I drop my Thermos and scramble to pick it up. He

writes for my favorite band. How is that possible? It makes no sense. I've looked them up. There is a Durand. There is a Noémie. There is a François. Besides the image of their lead singer, Noémie, no one knows who they are (unfortunately)—at least no one I've met, and especially no one in my small town. But this means Rafe knows them. And I can't even begin to think of what a small world it must be for this to be true.

Rafe starts strumming his guitar, and I'm spellbound. If I thought that the first time I heard him sing was magical, this is proving that it only gets better as I know the man better. I'm learning new things every moment now too.

Things like the way he scrunches his nose when he needs to hit a note in the higher range, or the way his hair looks in the setting sun, and the outline of his frame with the backdrop of the river behind him. He's free, and he's wonderful. I can't help but think of how at home he looks not only with an instrument in his hands but also here in this place. I try to picture him not in Birch Borough any longer, and a chill hits my system. It just doesn't seem possible that he'll ever leave. How quickly meeting someone can change our lives, even when we least expect it.

From LA to the City of Light
Stay with me through the night.
Rafe's lyrics are so . . . him.
I've hoped all my life
For you to see me, need me
Take away the pain and hold me as I am
Love me as I am
And find a way home.

The crowd claps song after song, and I realize that everyone is falling in love with him as much as I expected they would. He's stunning. His voice is a mix of rugged creativity and softly spoken love letters. He's everything good in this world, I'm convinced. Perfect? No. No one is. But beautiful? Without a doubt.

"Honey, you keep looking at him like that, and we're going to need to get you to a doctor."

I turn to my right and see Gladys in a lawn chair with an empty one beside her. I was so focused on Rafe I didn't notice her arrival. Or did she pass by me? I'm honestly not sure. She motions for me to sit and hands me a blanket. I'm grateful for the warmth and the company. My movement must've shifted something for Rafe because he noticed. And as we make eye contact from across the lawn, he smiles—wider than I've seen him smile yet—and closes his eyes with a grin, like he's committing however he saw me to memory.

"Sheesh. Now I understand." Gladys is fanning herself, and I'm trying to keep the blush from my face (unsuccessfully). "So, how does he kiss? He's a good kisser, isn't he?" I'm too tongue-tied to answer. "Ah, of course he is. With a mouth like that and the voice of an angel, there's no way that man can do anything badly. I mean, just look at how he plays that guitar."

I try not to think of her tone, and the way she's implying much more than kissing, and attempt to focus back on the music. It swirls around us, and a sense of peace falls around me.

"You like him."

It's a statement, not a question. I hesitate.

"And don't have the audacity to try to make it less than it is." She huffs and takes a sip from her Thermos, which from the smell of it, may be a little more than hot chocolate. Brow furrowed, I manage to break my watch on Rafe and turn to look at the woman I've known my whole life. Her eyes are dancing as the lights come on around us. "Why are you fighting it so much?"

I swallow and play with the edge of the blanket. "Why do you think I'm fighting it?"

"Because, child, you're back here instead of being right in the front, showing those groupie wannabes that there's no competition."

I peek toward the stage and cringe. There are several single women, some just out of college, I'd guess, and some quite a bit older than me, swaying to the music and trying to get Rafe to look their way. I take some satisfaction (okay, a lot) that he's not.

"Take it from me, Rory. Life is too short to be waiting in the wings, hoping one day you'll be ready for love. Because love isn't something you're ready for. It's something that finds you. So don't miss it when it does, yeah?"

I swallow and think of all the ways I've missed having someone older than me really speaking into my life. Sure, I have people who look out for me, but wisdom and greetings are not the same thing. I nod lightly to her because I can't lie and tell her I don't have feelings, and I also can't promise that I can carry through on the feelings Rafe might have for me.

"Good," is all she says before looking back to Rafe's band in the stand.

"Thank you, everyone. For this final song . . ." Rafe's speaking voice cuts through the brisk air as the crowd starts to lovingly shoot the idea down. Apparently, they don't want him to leave either. "I want to dedicate this to someone who has changed how I see the world in a very short time."

My heart beats faster in my chest. There's no way he could be talking about me, yet my body knows he is.

"This person has become someone very special to me." He clears his throat, and I feel tears sting my eyes. "And they don't even know how sweet they really are." Leaning closer to the mic, eyes focused on the ground, he whispers, "This one's for you, Sugar."

And then I am carried away by a melody wrapped in lyrics with talk of birds taking flight, and hearts becoming homes, and cities of lights not comparing to the love they're finding through the night. It's only when the crowd cheers and starts to pack up their things or disperse that I realize I have tears streaming down my face.

Gladys has the decency not to comment on my emotional state and waits patiently while I stand and help pack up her chair.

"Thank you," I tell her before giving her a hug that's been long overdue. She pats my back gently and winks at me when she catches someone's eye behind me. But I already know who it is. My body told me a few seconds ago by the increase in energy through my veins and the sudden charge in the air.

"Thanks for taking care of my girl," he says quietly. *My girl.*

"You're welcome," Gladys replies as I turn to face him.

Rafe's hands are in his pockets, and if not for his confident posture, his expression would tell me he's nervous. He wants to know what I think of his performance. And this thought has me feeling far cozier than I expected.

A teenage girl interrupts us, asking for photos and a selfie. Before we know it, the last clusters of people want signatures and photos and are just dying to know who the song is about. Rafe doesn't tell them, but he does give me a wink. It's only when we're (almost) alone, nearly a half hour later, and the only people left in the vicinity are our town's cleaning committee, that I get the chance to tell him what I've wanted to tell him all night.

"Rafe, you were . . ." And that's all I manage to say. Nothing else comes out.

Instead of teasing me, he pulls me to his side and wraps his arm around my shoulder. He leans down to kiss my temple and takes a deep breath. It's comforting more than sensual, but my body is buzzing just the same.

"Wait!" I yell. "You wrote with Histoire?"

Tension crosses his face. "I did." A pause. "Do you . . . know of them?"

I take a step back, as hard as it is move away from his embrace, to look him fully in the face. "Do I know them? Do I *know* them? Rafe, they have my favorite songs of all time. The music. The lyrics. The way they speak to the soul . . ." I pause to see that my words have thoroughly unsettled him. His looks are changing like a viewfinder from delighted to processing to unsure.

"How do you possibly know them?" he whispers.

I rock back on my heels. "Oh! My father. When we found out he was sick, we'd sometimes listen to French radio. He said it reminded him of my mother . . . and there was this one song he couldn't get out of his head. Lily helped us track it down, and it was Histoire! Their music made the hard days less hard." I hesitate. "Do you think you could let them know? Not about me . . . but just that their music helps people heal?"

With a smile and a slight look of relief, Rafe nods. "I'll tell them."

"Sparrow, I lived in Paris for a while," he says, the words rushing out between us. A look of what can only be described as pain flashes through his forest eyes. As shocked as I am to hear his confession, within a few breaths, the information settles and starts to make sense.

"The CDG sticker," I whisper. "On your guitar case."

He nods as we slowly make our way away along the river and toward the shops, his fingers holding mine a little more tightly than before.

"It wasn't a good place for me," he confesses, and my stomach drops. Rafe turns to face me, both of his hands now holding mine between us. "Sparrow, I—a lot of people have left my life. People I trusted. People I should've been able to trust." The cost of it is written on his forehead and etched around his mouth.

I want to ask him more on the subject, but I'm mesmerized by his touch and the intensity in his gaze. Instead of more questions, maybe all he needs is to be heard.

"I know I mentioned the pumpkin patch, but tonight, how do you feel about pizza?" he asks, slivers of sunlight hitting his stubble and lighting one side of his face like rays of light through tree branches.

I nod and take his hand, his fingers warm as they weave through mine and offset the chill in the air. Perhaps the warmth is also because when we touch this time, I know it's not for show.

When we end up back at the studio later, Rafe is laughing, a pizza box on his lap, eyes dancing with happiness. He's been playing songs and making me guess them—it seems I can only remember nineties boy bands tonight. Little does he know I've already hidden a guitar pick on the side of the snare drum in the corner when he wasn't looking.

"Rafe, why are you really here?"

"For my birthday?"

"Your birthday is soon?"

He gives a slight nod. "But I'm supposed to be gone by then." The air becomes heavy.

"When is it?" Ignoring his comment about leaving, I grab a scrap of abandoned lyrics off the floor and a pencil from near the piano.

"I—uh . . ." He clears his throat. "The fourteenth of November."

I write down the date and immediately tuck the paper into the pocket of my coat. He's playing with the edges of the pizza box, like he just can't help but make music somehow.

"Sparrow, what's with Jacques?" he asks suddenly. "Do you really like him?"

I hesitate, surprised by his question.

"Because, since you know he's French, and he seems interested in you, I'm struggling to see why you wouldn't have just asked him out yourself?"

My shoulders tense at his inquiry. "You make it sound so easy."

"Then help me understand why it isn't." I hear the pleading in his voice, a statement to help me not fly away without him knowing the truth.

"He's what I've been waiting for, I think. I—I know I said I want to be with someone French, but it isn't for shallow reasons." I whisper the words. He opens his mouth to speak when my phone buzzes, and I scramble to catch it. "Oh, gosh—look at the time! I'm going to go because I should just go . . ." I whisper.

My heart deflates. I gather my things without making eye contact.

"Sparrow, I . . ."

He stands to move toward me, but I give him a grin to ease his worry. "No need to walk me home. I'll be there in less than a minute." I make it to the door and peek over my shoulder, the light catching his face as my eyes adjust to the night around me. "Rafe, for what it's worth, I feel sorry for the ones who've left you."

He looks up to catch my gaze.

"They have no idea what they're missing."

Chapter Thirteen

Rafe

I'm walking through crisp air, my mind replaying moments with Sparrow. It smells like maple, cinnamon, and the musky-sweet scent of the red and orange leaves circling my feet. After she left the studio last night, all I could think about was my birthday—and the fact that she wrote it down.

I freeze. For a moment, I feel myself sitting on the wood-grooved cutting room floor in my father's design studio, watching scraps of discarded fabric hit the floor. If I stand, a view of the Arc de Triomphe can be seen from the balcony. We're in Paris before going to London. My father is meeting with a famous celebrity on one of the floors above, but I'm under one of the tables, waiting for someone to acknowledge my eighth birthday. It isn't until the end of the night that my father hands me a sweater from their new line. It is far too big. At bedtime, my mother kisses me on the forehead, tucks me under some blankets, and turns out the light without remembering.

I pass by the Ollie & Sons Toy Shop, and focusing on seeing Sparrow, I almost miss the man sitting in front of the store, rocking away in a chair positioned on the sidewalk. It's the man I saw before. He's melded to his chair in a way that tells me this is routine. Though he's older, I catch the sparkle in his eyes as he motions for me to sit. The truth is, I could use a moment to gather my thoughts. I lower myself into a nearby chair and get to rocking beside him. When I feel the cool air and see the people milling about the street, I think he has the right idea.

"Morning, son."

It's weird the effect the sentiment has on me. I freeze slightly and give a small nod.

"I've been waiting to meet you. The new guy." His brows dance, and I grin. "Your jaw okay?" he asks, and I immediately feel more at ease. He sees me.

"You own this store, sir?" I nod toward the toy store that hasn't opened for the day. He nods with pride, his movements steady even though he is advanced in years.

"I do. And my father did before me. And my grandfather before him." He pauses and crosses his arms.

"Wow, that's quite a legacy." I can't imagine staying in one place so long. Images of my father trying to pass down his legacy to me leaves me with a sinking feeling.

"It is." He studies me, and I let him. A piece of me is desperate to know what he's thinking. "Son, I think you've got something a lot of kids lose these days."

"And what's that, sir?" I flinch a little bit at his use of *son*, but the word doesn't make me bristle like I did a moment ago.

He grins knowingly. "Imagination."

I blame the sudden moisture in my eyes from

allergies or something in the air. It's definitely not because of this gem of a human sitting next to me.

"Your girl has seen a lot. Felt a lot. Her dad was my best friend, you know."

I look at him. His eyes take in the street. I know exactly who he means, and I'm loving that he just called Sparrow mine.

"Any advice for me, sir?" I ask humbly. This man is quickly becoming a legend I'll tell my kids about, I'm sure.

He lets out a laugh. "Well, other than not calling me sir . . ." He gives me a pointed look full of amusement before his face becomes solemn. "Let her know you see her. Just because everyone knows her doesn't mean she feels seen."

Don't I know the feeling. Maybe what Sparrow needs is what I need too. Maybe we need each other. I clear my throat and lean back a little more, the rhythm of our rocking chairs becoming more in sync.

"Do you mind if I call you son?" he says into the morning before us.

And I find myself saying, "No, not at all."

How I ended up in this kitchen as Sparrow bakes and I . . . stand awkwardly, I'll never know. Oh, wait. I do know. It starts with Lily and ends with . . . well, Lily.

When I first walked into the bakery after meeting Ollie, all I got was, "She's in the back," and a motion to head there. I moved toward the kitchen, and as surprised as I thought Sparrow would be, it turns out she has a great poker face. She looked up from her work with only a slight blush on her cheek. Then she handed me an apron and motioned to the sink. I nodded to the stuffed raccoon (who still holds one of my guitar picks), and that was that.

Now I'm standing between the oven and a counter, the oven warming my backside and making me regret wearing one of my nice sweaters. Sparrow seems to like when I wear a sweater, so I thought I'd make an effort. I'm glad I did, even though I can feel my neck growing hot. I brush the hair from my forehead and, for the third time, try to put my hands in apron pockets that are nonexistent. If she's noticed my awkwardness, she hasn't said anything, which is a small blessing.

Sparrow mixes various elements together and effortlessly floats from each ingredient's location to the stainless-steel equipment surrounding us.

"You move very . . . gracefully," I say tentatively, already kicking myself for using a poetic word and giving away another glimpse of how romantic my heart can be. There's a reason I write song lyrics for a living—I often forget how much I like picturing the world as an opportunity to love someone.

Her chocolatey eyes, which look like Swiss chocolate today, captivate me. Sparrow has tiny freckles dancing across her nose and the edges of her lightly flushed cheeks.

"I'm glad my years of pliés and relevés have given me a distinct way to move through the world."

Ah, I was right. She was a ballerina. I take in her hair, which is pulled into a bun like it was always meant to be held in such a way, and observe the curve of her neck, the set of her shoulders, the way I never hear her shoes clicking across the floor, and I'm so happy to have discovered this about her.

"Okay," I say much too cheerily, nearly knocking

over the container of flour in front of us. I find myself mirroring her small smile.

"Okay," she says in a lower octave than normal, which causes my heart to beat again in a way I'm not familiar with . . . but could get used to. "Since you're with me today, and Lily won't have it otherwise, you can help me make these muffins."

I watch as long as I'm allowed before she looks at me, those pretty eyes slamming into mine. I lean closer without realizing it, and she makes an amused sound. Somehow, I've shifted so close that she can no longer move her right arm unless she leaves her station. Instead of embarrassing me, she smiles softly.

"If you want to grab the sugar, that would be helpful."

I clear my throat and look for a bin of sugar, or *le sucre*, but all the containers look the same. Without looking over her shoulder, she says, "The one on the top right, with the 'S' written on the lid."

I find it and set it near her, careful to keep my distance this time. Standing in the back of the bakery like this, watching her work, I feel more of a sense of what she's lost. She has never mentioned her parents to me, but I know they're no longer here. And I know firsthand that a person can only carry so much before they lose themselves in the process. But even though she's experienced what must have been deep pain, she's strength meeting a soft heart, and I'm in awe of her.

Sparrow uses the sugar to magically create a concoction of flour, sugar, salt, baking powder, and some brown stuff that looks like cinnamon. "This is nutmeg," she explains, catching me eyeing her progress. "It makes vanilla batter taste better, in my opinion." She grins, and I find myself grinning too. Her hands carefully weave together milk, eggs, and melted butter. "Could you please hand me those muffin tins?"

I nod and grab the muffin tins and a stack of what appears to be paper cups of some sort.

"And the muffin liners," she adds. And I stand a little taller, knowing that I somehow knew she would need them too. She raises a brow when she sees I already have them in my hand and effortlessly lines the tin and scoops most of the batter like it's easier than an inhale. I watch her mix what I think is another cinnamon mixture. "This is cinnamon and sugar. And we'll melt some butter to dip them in when they've baked. But first, let's get these in the oven."

"Allow me," I say in a way that makes me wince. She laughs lightly, though, and I'd say it a thousand more times if it meant she would make that sound again.

While the muffins are in the oven, I lean against the counter and try to appear calm. I can make small talk. I have the thought that if I can make her see I'm not awkward in her kitchen, she'll see I won't be awkward for her heart.

We chat about her favorite things in Birch Borough and how my songs are coming along, the timer keeping a steady rhythm to our conversation like a game show without the pressure. She asks me about my time in Europe and when I started playing music, and I'm careful to give her the parts of me that I'm ready to have her see. We're dancing a fine line between me revealing everything or holding back. Because the truth is, she's already been breaking down my defenses. They're crumbling. But I'm trying to believe I still have a choice whether or not I allow her in all the way.

We've switched back to the topic of baked goods when she casually mentions, "These are called French breakfast puffs."

I furrow my brow. "Huh. I never heard of them . . . when I was in Paris."

She grins and leans closer to me as if we're conspiring. "That's because they're not really French." Sparrow scrunches her nose, and we laugh. I absolutely know they're not French. "Carrying them in the bakery was my father's doing," she explains. "It's a bit of a French fry situation, this . . . and this is who I am." She shrugs. "Very American, but sometimes French . . . and these muffins are not one of those times."

I nod, only half-listening as I watch her hands orchestrate these everyday ingredients into the start of a batter.

"My father knew they weren't authentic but wanted something new to add to the menu. These made the cut." She hums. "They are delicious . . . my best seller after maple croissants, but I don't love the name. Puffs should be reserved for cream puffs."

"What happened to your family?" She looks at me slowly, her smile sinking. And I immediately wish I could take back my question. "I'm sorry, you don't have to answer that, of course . . ."

"No, it's okay. I actually can't believe it hasn't come up . . . you know, since we're dating and all." She grins, and I know that we're okay. "It was his heart. And for my mother . . . we lost her in an accident."

She looks up at me, and I can see the silent request to refrain from asking anything more right now. I nod but can't let the moment pass without saying, "Sparrow. Tell me when you're ready, okay?"

Her eyes are glassy as she gives me the saddest, softest smile I've ever seen. It's time for me to return to my nonsense over the muffins. "So, why don't you just call them French muffins?"

"What?" She's amused but tries to keep it in check.

"Well, we have English muffins . . . why can't we have French muffins?"

She laughs, but I can see the wheels of her beautiful mind turning. "I'm not sure my father would've approved of it." I know my father would hate it. She looks up into the corner of the room as if she'll find the answer there. "Actually," she laughs, "he probably would've loved it."

"So, why are you rejecting my idea to call them French muffins?" I dip my finger in the bowl and watch as she intently follows the journey of the batter to my mouth.

She catches my gaze and quickly shakes her head. "Because this is a bakery—my family's bakery. And I'm trying to elevate things a little, so calling another baked item something so pedestrian feels a little bit like . . . I don't know . . ."

"Not French?" I finish the sentence for her.

She nods shyly, and I grin.

"So, you're the type of girl who binges *Emily in Paris* but is also kind of mad about some of the inaccuracies?"

Her mouth drops open.

"You *have* seen every episode . . ." I put a dish into the sink and turn to face her. "Haven't you?"

She tilts her chin up, and I see her resolve to call her own bluff.

"I mean, wasn't Alfie just the dreamiest?"

Sparrow turns around so fast a puff of flour gets thrown onto the counter. "No, Gabriel!"

"Ha! I knew it."

Suddenly, magic happens as she bends away from me, her shoulders shaking silently. When she rises again, she's wiping tears from her eyes and laughing. Her smile lights up the whole room, and I never want this radiance to fade. I thought she couldn't be any more lovely, and here she is, lifting the limit on what I thought possible.

"And just what is so funny?" I ask, my arms crossing over my chest.

"It's just ... you," she laughs. "*Emily in Paris* references."

Little does she know I've binged the show too. (And love to hate it.) I'm grinning as she smirks and begins to wipe up the flour on the counter. I move over to help her, and soon, my hands are covered in flour while she has a neat little pile in front of her.

"I mean, who knows? You could even call your new French boyfriend a French muffin."

At this, her nose crinkles, and she tilts her head to the side. Her hands go a mile a minute as she remembers something that she finds exciting. "Oh my goodness! In college, there was this couple on my floor, and she was American, and he was English, and she always called him her *little English muffin!*" Her mouth opens in shock while her eyes light with amusement. "I couldn't possibly," she says, more like Audrey Hepburn than Sparrow.

I lean closer to her and wiggle my eyebrows dramatically. Her eyes widen. "I'll be your French muffin." The funny thing is, I'm not joking. I would totally let her call me her French muffin if it meant I could be near her like this more often.

The smile falters on her face. Her eyes scan me as if looking for something she hasn't yet found the answer to. "But you're not French," she whispers.

I swallow. "What if I was?"

Now she swallows, and her teeth pull on her bottom lip, brow furrowed. "But you're not."

My heart sinks a little, and I feel the urge to get away from this pressure building in my chest as quickly as possible. The batter left in the mixing bowl in front of us calls to me, and when I see her pick up a few items and turn toward the sink, without overthinking it, I smear my thumb in the batter and paint her hand with the mixture. She freezes and turns to me, her eyes wide again and mouth slightly open.

I force myself not to look at her lips as I hold back a laugh.

"How. Dare. You." Her eyes send warning flares, but I see her holding back another laugh. I don't break eye contact and dip my thumb back into the bowl in slow motion. Her mouth opens wider as a big heap of batter rests on my thumb, and I wait.

"Don't!" she warns as the blob of batter lands directly on her nose and catches in her eyelashes. I watch it drop from her face to the top of her t-shirt. When it rolls to her apron like a Slinky toy, a laugh escapes me.

"That's it!" she yells as she reaches for the rest of the batter, but I block her before she can reach my face. Instead, her hand swipes across my chest and stains my blue sweater with a handprint of muffin batter.

"Ugh!" she's yelling, and I'm laughing more than I've let myself laugh in ages as she successfully gets another handful of batter and smears it in my hair while I double over. She's ruthless.

I stand to my full height and watch as she waits for me to retaliate. Instead, I change tactics and step closer to her. The smell of the batter and her distinct scent of caramelized sugar is a heady combination. Her eyes darken slightly as we stare at each other. A few drips of batter from our messy fingers flop to the floor. I reach for her hand, the sticky batter gluing us together. Our fingers intertwine, and I never want to let her go. Even though the moment is chaotic, it's wonderful.

My heart rate accelerates, the sensations in my hands heightening, and I feel my eyes taking in each detail of her face. She tips up her chin, and I watch, mesmerized, as her eyes land on my lips. She's trembling slightly, and I gain courage in knowing I'm not the only one about to explode from the heat in this kitchen. Finally, she lifts her eyes to mine, and I know it's my moment.

If I don't kiss Sparrow right here, right now, I may never recover from the regret. I stare at her lips and commit to memory the moment they part slightly. I lessen the space between us but pause as my mouth barely brushes hers. Inhaling shakily as the very edges of my lips burn deliciously, I know I'm about to be a changed man.

BEEP! BEEP! BEEP!

Sparrow jumps back and stares at our muffin-battered hands woven together. She gasps and shakes her head slightly. I let out a breath. The moment is gone.

"Oh, don't burn!" she pleads, searching everywhere for something to grab the muffins. Little does she know I'm already toast. I see a pot holder on the counter in front of me and clear my throat.

"Can't talk about it right now!" She rushes toward me. Seeing the pot holder, she grasps it frantically and flings open the oven doors. The kitchen smells amazing, and nothing seems to be burning except for me. She places the tins on cooling racks, and I see her slouch over like she just ran a marathon and didn't just do what she's done thousands of times before.

I walk up and stop right behind her, the intensity between us still humming. The moment may be over for me to kiss her, but it isn't too late to let her know I'm not done with whatever is brewing between us. Lightly touching her arm, I reach for a towel on the shelf above her. She stiffens but doesn't move. Her breath catches, and I close my eyes for a moment, relief washing through me. My reaction wasn't just one-sided, and I didn't dream whatever just happened only moments ago.

I wipe my hands and reach for another towel. Gently, I capture her shoulders and turn her toward me. I need her to know I won't push for anything. Instead of holding her close like I'd like, I reach for her hand and begin carefully wiping away the batter that's crusting onto her skin.

"Baked goods are a serious business," I say, my voice raspier than usual, while she focuses steadily on our hands.

"I think the pot holder is shot," she whispers. "It never did fit right." The opening of the item she's referring to is nearly sealed shut from the batter that transferred when she hurriedly put it on without washing her hands first.

I look around, and at least a dozen of the same pot holder lines the shelves near the oven. She has things in her kitchen that she doesn't even like. It's infuriating. In the short time I've known her, I'm convinced this woman deserves to be surrounded only by things that bring her joy, especially when she is so content with the smallest details.

I don't know what her dreams are quite yet, but if I can make them happen, I will. Like those pesky pot holders, I think she is holding onto ideas that need replacing. From everything I've seen so far, she's got the wrong narrative of who she is and what she deserves. I won't stand by and let her believe the lies anymore. We may not be ready to face the full truth between us, but what I feel is honest. I decide then and there that I'm going to be the one she finds shelter in, as much as possible, for as long as possible.

"If you didn't like how they fit, why did you keep buying them?" I ask softly.

Her eyes get a bit glassy. "Um . . . because they were supposed to be what I needed."

"And they weren't what you hoped for?"

She shakes her head and moves her feet into first position. She seems to find comfort in ballet poses. When I'm almost finished wiping away the wayward batter, I lightly wrap my hand around her wrist and move the towel back and forth across her fingers. There's nothing else there, and we both know it, but she's not moving, so I take a chance.

"Well, maybe there's one out there that fits better." And just like that, I'm not talking about the pot holders anymore, and she knows it. Sparrow searches my eyes, and I let her. I'm not sure whether five seconds or five minutes pass, but I won't move until she finds what she needs. I almost hope she discovers my secret. When she seems satisfied with her search for now, she nods slightly and releases our hands. I don't miss the extra press of her palm into my own before she moves to the sink and turns on the water.

I thought this had everything to do with her wanting someone French. It doesn't. She's waiting to move forward . . . She just doesn't want to do it alone. If she needs a dance partner, I'm ready to volunteer.

"Don't worry, Sugar. Even if there were ten Jacques here, fighting for your love, they would never be worthy of you," I find myself saying. "And I'm on a mission to make you believe it."

Chapter Fourteen

Sparrow

The shop has long closed. Rafe told me earlier over his croissant and coffee that the studio in town is booked tonight and asked if I minded him using the bakery. I told him as long as he remembers me when his songs make it around the world, it's a deal. His invitation to stop by probably has nothing to do with knowing what it feels like to have a lightness in your lungs and hope in your heart again. And just like when you're caught in the flash of a camera, I don't know how I'm going to see clearly when he's gone.

His comment about ten Jacques not being worthy of me had me speechless. It won't quit my consciousness. And I think his math must be wrong. Because I'm starting to believe that ten Jacques could never equal one Rafe. *Oh, what have I done?*

In this moment, I'm just doing my best to feel a little more like the woman I would want to be if he were mine and we were meeting or going out for an evening instead of the coffee-laden woman always offering baked goods.

I love her, but she's not the feeling I want tonight.

I find my blue dress, which I haven't worn since my father was alive, and pull it over my head. It feels casual but looks elegant. To be warm, I throw a cashmere sweater over the top. I tackle my hair, gathering it in a hair scarf and creating a messy low bun. Throwing on some boxed-toe flats with satin bows, a coat (even though I only have to go fifteen steps), and some of my favorite red lipstick—the very same one I wore when I first saw him sing—I rush down the stairs.

I hope I look classy and like I'm trying in the five minutes it took me to put this together. But this is me. I take five minutes to get ready. Maybe it's the former dancer in me, but give me anything that feels like satin and add lipstick, and I'm ready to take on the world.

Pausing just outside the back door to the bakery, I clutch my waist. My breathing has turned shallow, but I'm instantly at ease when I hear a sound from inside the café. Rafe is humming, and the strumming of his guitar casts a spell around the space. I open the door and see that, in the short time I've been away, someone else has been busy too.

The lights are off, and a few candles are lit throughout the front of the store. Rafe must've brought them. He's also changed into a light denim button-up shirt under a mahogany-colored jacket, dark-blue jeans, and his signature, vintage-style sneakers. When he sees me enter, he stops strumming and stands. He walks over to me with his hands outstretched to take my coat. I slip it off, still a bit chilled from the brief encounter with the cold, and smile. He drapes the coat over his arm and places it carefully on one of the stools before turning back toward me.

I don't miss the moment his eyes scan my body in a polite but lingering way. His dimples are on full display as he gives me a closed-mouth smile. His eyes crinkle slightly in the corners, and I nearly melt. If I thought he looked great on the stage, it's nothing compared to seeing him by the soft light of the lamp in the corner mixed with candlelight.

"You look beautiful," he says. And the way he says it so sincerely, so effortlessly, I actually believe him.

I motion to his guitar. "What were you playing?"

He rubs the back of his neck with his hand, and his eyes sparkle. "Oh, just a cover I'm working on for my next show." Rafe doesn't move, and I can't help but adore how we're both just kind of lost in this moment.

I move toward his guitar.

"May I?"

This earns me a full smile, and I almost fall into the instrument. Rafe catches me, his arms sturdy beneath my own. We each let out a breathy laugh.

"Do you play?" he asks, thankfully ignoring my clumsiness.

We haven't yet let each other go.

"No," I say seriously. "But you do."

He laughs, and as I reach for the guitar, he tugs me closer to him. "How about we play something else right now?"

I look into his eyes, which are a mixture of mischief and vulnerability. "What do you have in mind?"

He moves to the corner and turns off the lamp so that only candlelight illuminates the space. "I thought it was safest if you could see where you were going when you first arrived." He closes the space between us in a few steps. His hands glide softly along my arms until his hands are loosely around my waist. He grips a bit of fabric from my dress and, with his index fingers and thumbs, pulls me an inch closer. "Dance with me, Sugar?"

It's not what I was expecting him to say. I haven't danced since my father was alive.

"Only if you want to," he says, probably noticing that words have failed me. He's already playing music from a Bluetooth speaker resting on the coffee bar, the sounds of French jazz floating through the air.

"I mean, full warning, I'm not an expert—I've never had official training . . ." he continues. I want so badly to join him. This is pure romance. I wrap my arms up and over his shoulders, my fingers lacing at the back of his neck. The ends of his hair brush the tops of my fingers, and we hover in front of each other, inches from being pressed together.

"You've convinced me," I say quietly. He chuckles, gazing deeply into my eyes.

"I'm so glad."

We have just started to sway when he breaks the silence, his voice a whisper through the charged air encircling us. "I don't think I've told you yet, but this place is special, Sparrow. I mean it. Your boulangerie could rival any place in Paris."

I feel my jaw drop a bit. "You can't mean that." I know we've been blurring some of the lines between fiction and truth, but this is something I would hope would be clearly true.

His face shifts. There's not a hint of amusement now. "I'm serious. I wouldn't lie to you about that."

I want to believe him. The music has stopped for some reason. My guess is the occasionally spotty Wi-Fi, but I don't mention it. We seem to be moving with or without a track. "Why don't you ever call me Rory?"

He shifts back, and his shoulders shrug as he wraps my hand tighter in his. Cradling it near his heart, I feel the beat of it against his chest. "When I was little, we went to church every Easter Sunday. It was memorable because it was the one day out of the year where my parents let me be me—there was no pressure except to attend. I just got to focus on the music and the words from the priest." He pauses, and I think I've lost him in the story until he shifts back to me. "There was a verse spoken once . . . about not worrying about our lives. That if God watches over the sparrows—"

"He'll watch over us too."

He gives a sad smile.

"I've heard it," I say simply, emotion creeping up my spine. It's hard to picture a young Rafe who needed a reminder that he was seen. "That must've been comforting for you."

"Yes . . . always stuck with me." He holds my hand a little tighter. "Actually . . ." he continues, and I don't miss the hesitation in his voice.

"What is it?" I whisper, my body warming as I go deeper into the forest within his eyes.

"I—well, I should probably just show you." Hesitantly, he releases me and starts to unbutton the top of his denim shirt. My mouth goes dry, and my heart starts kicking my ribs. I remind myself to breathe when he stops a third of the way down.

His beautifully calloused hand, its tan a contrast against the lightness of his shirt, reveals a spot of skin over his heart. I lean closer without thinking and stop myself. His eyes not only give me permission; they ask me to see for myself. I let the tips of my fingers trace the tattoo, and I shiver at the sensation. Raised skin. Electric feelings. And the image of a small sparrow tattooed over Rafe's heart that will forever mark my dreams.

"I got it when I was angry for being sent away for another year of boarding school. I went for a walk and sat on a bench. A sparrow landed beside me. It just sat there. I don't even know for how long. I don't know, it . . . it felt like a sign." He gives a sheepish smile. "I was underage, so I made a fake ID." He smiles. "But I got the one thing I thought I wouldn't mind having on me for the rest of my life."

I trace the outline of the most perfect little image I've ever seen. I don't know quite what it is about this man—who can hold up the world and yet still notice all its details—that has me undone. Realizing I'm still touching him, I move my hand away. He starts to slowly close the buttons, and the image of the sparrow flies away within his shirt.

"That's why you're Sparrow to me, and I just can't bring myself to call you Rory. Not sure I ever will." He reaches out his arms, and without hesitation, we're back to swaying in the silence.

"Rafe?" His intensity surrounds me. "Never call me Rory."

He drops his head closer to mine with a smile, his unruly hair brushing mine. "What about Sugar?"

"Oh, well, that's just a given."

He laughs, and I join him. Until we still, and it's so quiet again, there's only the sound of our breathing and the sliding of our shoes across the bakery floor.

"What about the music?" I whisper.

We continue to sway as he replies, "Oh, I know a guy."

At this, Rafe begins to hum. And I'm mesmerized. I can feel his body vibrating with the sound, the way his breath moves in and out of his frame, and I feel the workings of his mind through the energy of his hands. He's a living instrument, and I feel it all around and within me.

The tune he's singing is a classic, a song my father used to play to remember my mother. He said they danced to it when they needed a break from the world. I still have the record from the great Édith Piaf, except Rafe's adding his own touch to it and has slowed down the tempo enough for us to move steady and slow.

Quand il me prend dans ses bras
Il me parle tout bas
Je vois la vie en rose

In the song, a woman speaks about a man taking her in his arms and speaking softly to her, making her see the world differently. He pulls me a little closer, and this moment feels like magic. If it was wonderful hearing him sing to a crowd, it's infinitely better when he's singing only to me.

And as he plays with the edges of my sweater near my waist, I know it's a moment I'll remember for the rest of my life.

Il me dit des mots d'amour
Des mots de tous les jours
Et ça me fait quelque chose

He slows even more, and I lean back to catch his gaze. The song speaks of words of love being spoken and that they are everyday words that do something. And his words have been doing something to me since we met.

Before I think better of it, I reach a hand toward the scar through his left eyebrow. He holds his breath as my hand hovers. I almost touch him and then pull back. His eyes search my face, and he nods. Ever so gently, I trace my thumb across the mark, and he breathes again. His eyes slowly close before they open again to burn through me.

"What happened?" I ask into the quiet space.

"Hmm, you're just getting all my stories out of me tonight, aren't you?"

I nod enthusiastically as he laughs.

"It was a fall when I was little. I tried to help my mother bake muffins in the kitchen, and I fell off the counter with a wooden spoon."

"You did not!" My mouth opens as I try to process that the scar I find so appealing happens to be from one of my most-used baking utensils.

"I did too." He pretends that he's suddenly realizing we're standing in a bakery. "It's amazing I can even stand in here without twitching." A grin covers his face. "It took a few stitches, but I kind of like the look. Gives me an edge, you know?"

"Definitely."

"But you're sworn to secrecy now."

"Am I? I don't think I agreed to that."

"I can't ruin my reputation."

"Ok, fine."

He grips my waist a bit tighter. I don't think I'll ever get over the feeling of being held by this man. It's like I'm anchored and no longer wandering.

"That easy? You're not going to make me work harder to convince you?"

I lean my head on his chest. "Not as long as you keep singing."

We sway without music for so long I lose track of time. At some point in the silence, without a note to be heard within the room, Rafe has taken most of my weight and is allowing me to lean on him as we move back and forth.

"What do you dream of, Sparrow? When you are by yourself, and no one needs anything from you . . . what do you dream of?"

I inhale deeply, uncomfortable with the attention but also realizing this is what I've been craving. Who typically has the courage to ask us what we dream about? And I can tell from the tension in his fingers around my waist and the way his breathing has quieted in anticipation of my answer that he really wants to know.

"My father and I had a plan to expand this place." I catch his gaze and notice the way his brows lift in response. "Oh, not a franchise. But expand into possibly creating a book of my mother's recipes. Move online so we could ship items beyond our little town."

He brushes my fringe bangs away from my forehead with a hum.

"Except . . ." I begin. And this is the part that's the hardest for me to admit. He keeps us moving, not a hint of impatience at my delay. "Well, I think I've lost my courage." I avoid his eyes. "I wanted to submit the bakery for a regional magazine feature, and I can't even look at the papers without shutting down. He's gone, and he was all I had left. I just . . . it was rough for me. For quite a while. Lily is the reason I've been able to keep moving. Lily and this town. Because they keep making sure I'm not drowning in grief, even when I have felt so alone, I could hardly breathe."

As if to make my point, I release a breath. His grip only tightens.

"Do you feel alone right now?"

I meet his gaze. "Not at all." I shrug lightly, a weight lifting with every sway and step of our feet. In a minute or ten, he breaks the silence.

"What is it about someone who's French exactly?" He stiffens slightly though keeping the rhythm of our movement.

"Well . . . my mother was French." I pause. "She

was . . . elegant. Magnetic. Beautiful."

"Sounds like you," he whispers.

My eyes burn from his words.

"My mother's accident. It was sudden. She just went out to pick something up . . ." I take a deep breath. "We spoke French together when I was little. And then, when she passed . . . well, the sound of French in our home sort of died with her."

"And your father?"

"Two years ago. Their love . . . it was *something*, you know. I felt it. I just remember my father always said to wait for a 'French kind of love' because he had my mother. And I know that wasn't literal, but with Jacques, and before that, with the guy near the train asking me out . . ."

"The guy near the train?" he says stiffly.

"Yes, another man asked me out the day before we met . . . on the platform in Boston. And I panicked and said I couldn't date him because he wasn't French." I rush the last part. "That's what you overheard in the café when we actually met. I didn't want to admit to Lily that I made a mistake by turning him down."

Rafe's hand draws a distracting pattern along my spine. Somehow, the silence feels like a safe space. He feels like a safe space.

"I've had tickets, you know. To Paris."

"Why didn't you go?" he asks without judgment. Just a question. I shake my head and meet his eyes.

"What if I don't fit in there?"

Gently, he cups his palm around my jaw, and I feel myself lean in.

"You would fit there," he says. "And you wouldn't just enjoy it; you would add to it. Paris would be brighter with you. I know it would." He leans down, his cheek brushing my own, and I feel his breath on my ear, the smell of spice and cedar calling me deeper.

"I'm not very brave," I whisper into the little space there is between us.

"You're brave. You are. And Sugar?" Rafe asks, his voice low and raspy from the late hour and something else I can't quite name.

"Mm-hmm," I manage.

He stops swaying, my face gently turned to his as he brushes his fingers behind my ear and rests his hand on one of my shoulders. "If you keep showing me your heart, I'm going to forget this is pretend." His thumb traces a slow line across my collarbone before he reaches for my hand to hold it against his heart. As we continue to sway, he turns his stubbled cheek to rest lightly on my head.

"Who says I'm pretending?" I confess.

I feel one of his calloused hands travel up my back and lightly rest against the nape of my neck. He cradles my head and holds me close to him before placing a soft kiss on my forehead. The tenderness of it all has me pushing the burn from the back of my throat and the sting of tears from my eyes.

I don't want to try to interpret what he means. I just want to enjoy this moment. A moment of feeling safe. A moment of not wondering what else is out there, because it feels like nothing is missing right where I am. So, instead of arguing or figuring out what we're doing or what the outcome will be, I hold on to one of the best nights of my life and one of the best men I've ever met.

"Sing to me again?" I request.

And he does. With the candlelight long extinguished and the rosy pink of a morning sky peeking through the night and announcing a new day, we dance, the sound of Rafe's voice swirling all around us.

Chapter Fifteen

Rafe

I knock on Sparrow's door, not sure she's even awake yet. Lily swore this would be a good move, but I've noticed Sparrow avoids the bakery on Thursday mornings, so I'm not sure what to expect. I wore my best cable-knit sweater and my lucky Converse and threw on my camel-colored trench coat for warmth. It felt like the right move. I've run my hand through my hair so many times I'm sure it's sticking up, but this is important.

I woke to a call from a recording studio telling me we may have a deal on a demo I sent and seven missed text messages from my father. What I haven't told Sparrow yet is that my father has made it his mission to ensure I'm not able to work anywhere around him. He's called all his connections and told them I'm not worth their time. Unfortunately, a call like that from someone of his caliber is to be believed. So, moving forward is a big deal. It has to be.

I'm startled from my thoughts by the door opening and the sight of Sparrow in her oversized sleep dress and knee-high socks. My mouth goes dry as I take in her disheveled hair and the way one side of her face has what can only be a pillow mark. My face heats as I clear my throat.

She lets out a squeak as she wraps her arms around herself. I hold up the coffees and pastries I brought as a distraction before she decides to shut the door. But then I realize that maybe she really is uncomfortable, so I turn around to give her some privacy. I hear a giggle from her, and I feel my shoulders relax.

"I'm sorry. Lily . . ." I trail off.

"Enough said." A pause. "You can turn around, Rafe."

I turn around, a grin playing on my face. She has a trench coat wrapped around her now, the socks and hem of her pajama dress still peeking out from beneath. "Morning, Sugar."

Her eyes are bright as she scans my outfit, a small smile on her lips as she takes in my sneakers. She motions for me to come in, and I step into her apartment, which instantly feels like home. I try to notice as many details as possible. The French elements throughout, the pictures of her and two people who must be her parents, the way it smells like her.

I put the coffees and pastries on her farmhouse-style countertop and look at the tiny clock in the kitchen. It's French blue with a little sparrow in the middle.

"My father gave that clock to me," she says simply, a trace of pain laced with comfort in her voice.

"I like it." I start to open the box of pastries and notice Sparrow hasn't moved yet. There's a furrow in her brow. Just when I'm tempted to reach over to smooth it, she looks at me with such certainty I almost take a step back.

"Rafe," she begins, "would you like to go to Boston with me today?"

The offer is not what I expected, to say the least. But I feel myself grin as I motion to the pastries. "Good thing I got them to go."

Her eyes are closed, and I take the moment to hungrily take her all in. The freckles dancing across her face and the way her bottom lip is slightly fuller than her top lip. The way her lashes seem to hover over her cheeks like butterfly wings. There's nothing pretentious about her. She's classically stunning, her beauty mesmerizing me like a sunset. Seven wonders of the world? Please. I've traveled the world and never seen anything this moving in my life.

We're sitting on a bench in Boston Common, looking at the pond. Sparrow is beside me, a cup of coffee in her hand. The scent of cinnamon and honey combined with her own sugary fragrance invades my senses. Rogue leaves still cling to the trees, the sun patchy as it reaches through the branches, creating a trail of shadows all around us.

The air is crisp and cool, filled with the scent of the nearby ocean and the sound of children playing across the way. Tourists paddle in Swan Boats on the distant pond, taking pictures and enjoying an iconic fall day in Boston.

But my only focus is the woman beside me. The top half of her face is now etched with a look of pain, her brow still furrowed, a slight crease between her eyebrows. Despite her emotional turmoil, a slight grin attempts to emerge on one side of her face. It's not enough to bring out her dimple but enough to let me know she's not about to cry. Whatever she's feeling, it's not my time to step in or rescue her—she doesn't need that. What I sense is that she just needs me to be near her so she's not alone.

After Sparrow invited me to accompany her today, she took a shower, and I went for a brisk walk around town. There was no way I could be in the same space with her, knowing that only a door would be between me and her with no clothing. I respect her too much to let it be otherwise. When I returned, I was ready to take on the world, and she looked like my newfound dream. She's wearing a dress that wraps at the waist with boots and a trench coat that nearly matches mine.

We ate our pastries and the reheated coffee on the train to Boston (side-by-side, this time) and laughed the whole way here. It turns out that traveling with someone you're falling for is actually . . . fun. While she travels, Sparrow loves to comment on the potential lives and secrets of the people that happen to be on the train. She kept me fully entertained. We didn't converse too deeply—I still don't know why we are here, except that this is a day she tends to repeat every few weeks, and Lily thought Sparrow could use the company.

I wasn't expecting to be invited when I knocked on her door this morning, but I did want to give her something to keep her energy and spirits up for whatever she seems to encounter every time she makes the trip to the city. The last time she returned to the shop after a notable absence on a Thursday, she seemed a little sadder than usual.

The sun shifts again, a sliver of its warmth crossing my face. I close my eyes and allow my head to tilt back, a feeling of peace settling over me. It's being beside her,

I think, that's making such a difference. I used to feel anxious all the time, as if my legs had to keep walking and my fingers had to keep moving, but she quiets that restlessness within me.

I'm surprised when she breaks the silence.

"My parents met in Boston," she says, without looking to see if I'm listening. She knows I am. "My mother used to bring me here. I remember her grabbing a latte and a treat for me at the café we just visited. She would bring me here, and we would sit on this bench. And my father would walk up and around and across the bridge over there . . ." She nods toward the Public Garden Foot Bridge, a pedestrian bridge that crosses the lagoon, where a Swan Boat floats underneath it with passengers. "And when he reached the middle of that bridge, he would wave at us. And we would wave back."

She clears her throat, as if she's not used to saying the words she's speaking between us. "And then she would wait for him. We would wait for him. And she'd point out the ducks. And the weeping willows that I still love so much. And we would watch them dance in the wind."

I look toward the weeping branches, their delicate leaves rustled by the invisible wind playing between them. And then I look at Sparrow, her hair almost mimicking the movement—strands of it flying up and swirling around, as if part of her has been weeping too. I know it has. I reach out and pull her close to me, her head easily nesting into the crook of my neck.

"I come here every other Thursday because that's the day of the week they met. My father did so after my mother passed, and I kept it going after . . ." She stops. "It helps me to remember them. And it reminds me that there's a world bigger than the one I'm used to. One that's full of more possibilities. Where a woman from a small town in France and a man from a small town in America can somehow meet, and make a life, and write a story that's worth repeating."

"Thank you for telling me." The simple words feel like enough.

She nestles in a little closer when a brush of wind rustles through the trees. I'm not sure how long we sit on the bench before I feel her nod against my skin. I take a deep breath. She shifts back but reaches for my hand to maintain our contact and lifts her brow as if it's my turn.

"It would be easier if I could sing it to you," I murmur. And I wish I could tell her what I want to say. What I know, one day, I'll need to say. But I've had too many experiences with heartache, and I don't feel brave enough yet. I'm not ready.

"Hmm. I'm sure I would love to hear it. But I think, in this moment, it would mean more if you'd speak it to me."

I love that she sees my way of moving through the world and is asking me to give her something I couldn't give anyone else. It's easy for me to sing out my feelings. Much harder to let them be known without music.

I laugh lightly and pull her back beside me. She doesn't fight it. I think she knows that having her closer to me will help me say the words I need to say—well, most of them. My heart is racing as anxiety starts to creep in. I feel a lot, but I often don't let myself feel it like this. So honest. So open. My jaw clenches, but somehow, I find the courage to begin. I know I need to give her more of myself. "My father is a fashion designer."

She lets out a sigh. "Ahh, yes, so that's why you're

always so well dressed." The amusement in her voice makes me grin, as if she finally figured out the answer to a question she's had since we met.

"I suppose so." My hands are cold, but I don't want to move the one wrapped around her, so I settle for one in my pocket and one exposed. As if she can read my thoughts, Sparrow glances to my hand around her and pulls it closer so that she can wrap her gloved hands around my palm. Better. "He's been on runways across the world. And, well, my whole life has been people trying to know me in order to get to him. Or people trying to know me in order to get seats or take selfies. Or get free clothes."

She scoffs at this but then catches my face, and I see when she realizes I'm not joking. "Would I know him?"

I shake my head. "You've probably heard of his designer name. But that's why I just go by Rafe. It's why I've traveled so much. Why I've lived in a few different cities. If I wanted a chance at my own art, my own life, and to make a name for myself on my terms, it had to be completely on my own. My father made that clear as well."

Sparrow grimaces slightly. "I'm sorry." She pauses for a moment, shuffling the fringe resting on her forehead. She faces me with a look that would level any man. "There was a woman too, wasn't there? Her influence is all over your music."

I don't want to ruin the image of the band she loves so much, so I simply whisper, "It was in Paris."

She nods almost imperceptibly, and then her brow furrows. "French?" she mumbles.

"I thought we loved each other. Really, she only wanted the fame, the lights . . . another guitarist I knew. And she wanted my songs. I thought I was *in love* with her."

"Thought? You didn't really love her?"

"Thought. Being in love and loving someone are very different things."

"Yes, I suppose that could be true."

I hold my breath, my mind racing with what she could be implying. "Could be? Have you not ever been in love?"

She closes her eyes for longer than a blink and then shakes her head. I can't believe it. This woman is taking my heart piece by piece. I want her to fall in love with me just so I know she can shake her head *yes*, and I could be the reason.

"I was heartbroken at the time, but now I realize I was mourning something that wasn't alive in the first place." She hums, so I continue. "I've traveled around the world. I've lived in Paris. When I was thirteen, I was sent to boarding school."

"In America?"

"Yes. In America. It was one that had a prestigious art program. My parents thought I was studying design. I was not."

"Music?"

I nod. "Music. It's the only thing that has ever made sense for me." *Until now*, I almost say, but I don't. She grips my hand a little tighter. I must figure out the science between this connection because I swear she knows what I'm thinking most of the time, which is dangerous and strangely comforting. "I do not have good memories of my parents, Sparrow. People think it's glamorous to be at all the parties. To have a name that people know. I just felt like I was drowning."

"Did they hurt you?" she whispers.

"Not physically." It's the most I can say without going into all the details of how much they've cut me internally over the years. "But I'm a disappointment to them."

"That can't be true."

"It is," I say roughly. Not from anger but from emotion. "As long as I pursue music, I'm cut off from them. I'm not allowed to pose with them in any pictures unless they arrange it for a photo op. My inheritance is being held hostage. And they have decided that unless I apologize, marry someone they think is worthy of our name, and join the business, then I'm not worth their time."

Sparrow sits up, and her movement somehow pulls us closer. We're inches apart, and I hold my breath as one of her gloved hands moves toward one side of my face. She's cupping my jaw so sweetly, so tenderly, I feel another piece of my heart shift. No one has ever touched me like this. I've been with women, but having Sparrow beside me, I can see how clearly they were all imposters—trying to be the real thing to me but never actually seeing me. She sees me.

"Listen to me and listen well." I nod, the intensity in her eyes new and blinding. "You are not a disappointment. You are creative. You are kind. You're the most beautiful man I've ever seen in my life—and not because of your looks—because of who you are. You actually see people. You're so funny. You care deeply. You give so much of yourself. You pour out your heart through your music, and you make it so that others can feel something too. We haven't known each other long . . ." she says.

I shake my head because I feel the emotion behind my eyes.

She removes her gloved hand from my face, and rather than letting go of me, she pulls off her glove with her teeth and lets it fall to the grass beneath our feet. "Gosh, I'm just so happy you exist." And then her warm hand is wiping at the corner of one of my eyes. I must be crying.

She's looking at me as if her look alone could convince me that a lifetime of not being enough for the people I wanted to love me the most could be erased. She looks at me like I haven't yet dreamed what's possible for me. The roots of what my parents have sown grow deep, but she's shining the truth over the shadows. I'm not sure how to hold on to her words, but she makes me want to believe. I didn't think someone could love me, yet she is making me think there's a possibility I was wrong.

We don't speak for a while after that, other than to point out amusing people and circumstances happening around us. For someone who has had so much pain, she sees the world in such an interesting and amusing way. She never makes fun of people, but she does see the humor when people are so very . . . human.

We spend the rest of the day in Boston, her hand never leaving mine. We stroll the walkways in Boston Common. We window shop and wander as far as the North End, where we eat lunch in Faneuil Hall and walk through Christopher Columbus Waterfront Park to catch a glimpse of Boston Harbor. We end up at a coffee shop before catching the T so we can make it to South Station for our train back home.

Something shifted for Sparrow and me today. And there were moments as we explored Boston when I knew I'd remember this as one of the best days I'd ever have. I wanted to take a Polaroid of it, to use my old-fashioned camera that actually prints pictures so that I could hold on to it and have a stack to hide in my guitar case for inspiration.

I know that what I'm holding is fragile. It's the crunching of leaves between my fingers; it's the colors on the trees already changing. As much as I want to hold on to the woman within my arms, the urge to put what she needs above what I want is haunting. I know what I need to do when we return to town. She deserves someone who can stay, and I don't yet know if I have it in me to be in one place without running again.

It's when we're riding back on our train car to Birch Borough, as the quiet seeps in and the lights contrast with the darkness outside the windows, that I let myself daydream a little more, even if I know that I'll wake up to reality soon. Sparrow is leaning against my chest, her peace easing through me. She fell asleep about five minutes ago, her breathing calm and even, and I've been trying desperately to will my whole body to remember this feeling. The one where I'm allowed to be a place of safety for her, and she's a place of safety for me.

I let my finger trace the soft skin of her forehead lightly, brushing a piece of her dark, honeyed hair to the side. "Sparrow, I'm in love with you," I whisper into the still air, only the steady sound of her breathing and the train on the tracks beneath us as we move through the New England night.

Chapter Sixteen

Sparrow

I still have the application for my shop to be featured in *The Seacoast Gazette* hovering in my mind but haven't yet applied. Online shop? Recipes of my mother's? It's swirling uncomfortably in my mind. Despite the irony, Rafe has been the only one who brings me a sense of peace these days, even if I'm melting because of the tension between us. I find myself hoping that he'll stop by the bakery today, which explains why I'm hovering at the front of the store, grabbing things from the back so I can keep my eyes trained on the entrance.

I've been doing my best not to completely lose sight of the fact that Rafe is going to move on. He has to. And he's not French. (Can't forget that . . . even though that argument of mine wasn't sound from the beginning.)

Lily is rolling her eyes so much I'm sure she's going to do some damage if I don't get this situation under control. And if she was here right now, she'd have me blaring a playlist about not needing men and being independent, but because I'm me, I have soft French café music surrounding us (me and the few regulars here). I'm rearranging a tray of salted caramel macarons for the fifth time in the past fifteen minutes when I hear the door open. My eyes bounce up to find Grey and Ivy walking in, and I feel my smile grow at the sight of them.

"Rory!" Grey yells.

I wave and lean over to give them hugs across the counter. Grey's light-brown hair is pulled up in a messy bun, her wide, cat-eye glasses peeking out from under her bangs. Ivy's dark-golden hair is nestled under one of those headbands with the knots on top like a vintage icon. They're both wearing long, cozy sweaters and boots, a sign that fall is certainly here. It makes my heart happy to see them because it's been way too long.

"So, any men from France hanging around here these days?" Grey asks, her eyes wide and hopeful. If anyone would recognize a storybook romance, it's her. She's constantly surrounded by books and is the fastest and most prolific reader I've ever met. She's been mostly single in the time that I've known her, although I suspect it might be because of a mutual friend of ours, but she's a romantic at heart in every way.

Right now, I know she's talking about Jacques, but her words don't get my heart fluttering like they used to. Ivy grins a bit, her husky voice breaking through the air—the type of voice you want to read to you or sing on a cold winter's night in front of a fire. She's always had the coolest voice of anyone I know.

"Or, you know, any other men hanging around here?" She shrugs. "Doesn't have to be French." Ivy and Grey share a look.

"Okay, so, you know about Rafe, clearly . . ." I start.

They are practically giddy as I turn to get their usual

orders: a pumpkin spice latte for Grey and a hot chocolate for Ivy. She really is like a Christmas card come to life, now that I think of it. I set to steaming the milk and allow the familiar sound of the steam frothing to settle my nerves.

"I understand why people would be so fond of him. I mean with his hair . . . and his eyes." I sigh and lean into the counter for a second.

"What about his eyes?" Grey asks, a hint of amusement in her voice.

I pour a splash of house-made syrup into the cup and grind more espresso while I give her question some thought. "Oh, gosh . . . his eyes hold secrets. An enchanted forest full of them, saying you'll get lost, but you'll have fun along the way." I pour the steamed milk—perfectly frothed, might I add—into the coffee mixture, content with the hint of pumpkin meeting crema at the rim of the cup, a heart in white foam clearly outlined. I put a lid on it and work on the hot chocolate. Ivy's voice breaks through the routine.

"Hmm . . . sounds dreamy. Anything else about him?"

I pour some of our homemade chocolate sauce into the cup, add a little steamed milk, and mix so that it's integrated before pouring in the rest of the milk. I put in a pump of house-made, salted caramel syrup for good luck.

"Well," I begin. "I mean, I know he's not Jacques, but he's his own version of a dream. The hair, the height, the way he dresses. You know, his style is kind of like a classic, Old-Hollywood-meets-boy-next-door type of vibe." I drizzle some chocolate over the top in another heart design. So many hearts to match the ones I'm sure are in my eyes. I grab two of our to-go bags, light-brown patisserie paper with our logo stamped on the front, and insert a sampling of macarons in each one. I also package up some croissants in an attempt to make up for our lack of time together lately.

"And I just have to say . . . " I start, adding the treats to a bag with a satin ribbon handle. I put the drinks in a to-go carrier, gathering everything together. "I don't know, sometimes I just want to tell him—"

"Tell me what?"

I jump at the sound of the voice behind me. I nearly knock over the drinks but recover in time. Even with my eyes tightly shut and my back to the man, I know who is behind me.

"Please wake up, please wake up. . ." I whisper.

"You're awake," Grey assures me.

"Yes, very awake," is the added (non-helpful) encouragement from Ivy.

I take a deep breath and roll back my shoulders. When I turn toward my friends, I also spot Rafe grinning at me. Something is clouding his expression, but I'm too focused on the fact that he's wearing glasses. As if he needed yet another reason to make him more heart melting, he now has solid frames accentuating his green eyes. I clear my throat and focus on my friends, who are standing wide-eyed and slightly slack-jawed at the sight of Rafe. I know, friends. Hard to believe he's real. And the glasses really take it up a level. He is not making this easy.

Feeling my eyes take on a bit of a "help me" glint, they finally turn to face me. They're a step behind Rafe, and with his eyes still on me, they use this opportunity to both give me a thumbs-up sign. Before I can manage another word, the little traitors grab their treats and are out the door, but not before I see them through the window peeking back at me. Ivy fans her face while the to-go bag swings wildly from her wrist, and Grey pulls her away from the window.

"How long were you standing there?" I ask while pretending to reorganize some pastries. Again.

"Not long. Except, tell me, what do you think of this shirt?"

I look over to see him in a sage-green V-neck sweater, his eyes illuminated with amusement. "Do they bring out my forest eyes?"

I roll my own eyes and try to act unaffected. "First of all, you don't know I was talking about you. I could've been talking about Jacques."

"His eyes are brown."

"So?"

"So, the forest is brown?" His eyebrows furrow, but it's a little too whimsical to be taken seriously.

I put down a tray of *chaussons aux pommes*, or French apple turnovers, a little too forcefully. I realize in that moment that I can either run away (which won't work because Lily's shift hasn't started yet, and I need my pastry chef to keep working on a wedding order in the back), pretend that I'm not talking nonsense (which won't work because I totally am), or own it. I choose none of the options by changing the subject.

The overhead bell rings, and in walks Jacques. I'm expecting a standoff, given the way I've seen Rafe giving him looks whenever we're about town. Instead, he nods at him and moves out of the way to sit at his usual spot at the counter. He doesn't order anything.

I look at Jacques, confusion on my face. Something is definitely different about today.

"Sparrow, I . . . " Jacques starts.

We're interrupted now by Gladys, who's coming in

hot. Of all the moments for her to stop by, of course it would be now. I swear I saw her bang a uey (a u-turn, in New England language) on her way to the flower shop. It's not even her usual time for coming into the store. And the way she's heading toward Rafe, like a kid with a chocolate bar within reach, I'm certain it's for him.

Rafe braces for impact, but like a barnacle, Gladys attaches to him. I'd warn him, but despite her meddling and complete lack of awareness at times, she really does mean well and has a heart of gold. I'm just hoping she doesn't break out the messages she sent me of Rafe at his show. I shudder.

"What can I get you, Gladys?" I give her a warning glance, but she ignores me, instead keeping her focus on Rafe.

"What are your intentions with our girl?" she demands.

Thankfully, Rafe has the good sense not to laugh. I set about making a decaf pour-over and add a handful of madeleines to a plate—some toffee, some coffee— and try my best to listen.

"I promise they're honorable," Rafe says, his jaw tight, gaze set. He's looking her right in the eye, and even I believe him. Not that I doubted.

Gladys rises up on her tiptoes as if she can threaten him with her intensity. I lean back a bit because it's working on me, at least. Except, Rafe doesn't move. He's committed. And instead of trying to run, or scoffing, or acknowledging how absurd this is, he has the audacity to grin.

"Ms. Gladys," he begins. "I know how much Sparrow must mean to you—and to this town—because it's clear that if she has people coming to check up on my intentions, she's dear to you. And I respect that. And

I respect her. And while I have a suspicion that she may have stolen another guitar pick of mine the other night . . ." He glances over at me on that part before returning his attention back to Gladys. "I can assure you that this short time with Sparrow has already been the best I've ever had with a woman. And not because of anything physical, but because she has as much heart as she does beauty. It's in how she moves. It's in when I make her nervous, and she overfills a coffee cup. It's when she's so passionate about her work that she doesn't realize she's covered in flour. It's in the way she smells of caramelized sugar and dreams. It's also in the way there's a piece of hair that falls over her eyes, no matter how much she pulls it back, and all I want to do is tell her to leave it right where it is because it's perfect. I know I can't be the one she chooses in the end because, the truth is, I'm not sure I deserve her. But anyone would be an idiot not to try."

"Well," Gladys says, wiping her eyes. She lowers her heels back to the ground and grips the counter, much like I'm doing while I stare at this man—this wonderful man who just gave the most beautiful speech I've ever heard. She reaches out and lightly takes Rafe's hand before picking up her coffee and madeleines and walking away.

I reach for him too, except now he's standing. He walks over to Jacques, not making eye contact with me, though I'm begging him to.

"Rafe," I whisper.

I see him swallow, his hand extending to shake Jacques'.

"Be good to her," Rafe says, his jaw clenched.

"Rafe!"

He doesn't stop until he's at the door. The grin

marking his face is forced. The waves of his hair fall in an arc over his forehead. He nods, and then he's gone, putting on his coat as he walks away, the sun marking his steps.

"Sparrow," Jacques continues while I'm reeling from the interaction that just unfolded. "Rafe told me it was a mistake."

I lean onto the counter, my heartbeat thumping in my ears. "A mistake?"

"Yes." He nods. "I thought you two were dating, but he told me you were just friends. He says he knows you need someone to be here for you."

"Friends. Someone here," I repeat, my fingers going numb.

"I do really want to know you more, Sparrow."

"I—I'm sorry, Jacques. I just . . ." I begin as he pulls a piece of folded paper from his jacket pocket and hands it to me.

Opening it slowly, I note the smudges of ink in the corners and the creases of notes that must've been written over the paper I'm holding now before it got to these words: *I still believe you're brave. And I'll keep singing for you, Sugar.*

I clear my throat and fold the paper, tucking it into the pocket of my apron before lifting my eyes to Jacques.

"Will you go out with me, Rory?"

And this time, with Rafe not in sight and the note clenched in my hands, I nod my head and feel a bit shattered as I do.

Chapter Seventeen

Sparrow

Lily! I have nothing to wear!" I yell via speaker phone. "You have loads to wear. Actual loads, Rory. I've seen you do your laundry."

My sigh bends me forward enough to place my head on my dresser, its half-open drawers pressing into my hips. My phone is resting next to my head so I can hear Lily in a muffled yet endearing sort of way.

A ribbon hairpiece I haven't seen in a few months is stuffed toward the back of the open drawer, and I shut my eyes before I notice anything else that's gone missing. There's too much weighing on my mind for this event.

I hear some music playing softly through the phone. Lily has a nineties boy band playlist going at the café— she does that sometimes when I'm not there—and I don't even have the heart to tease her or tell her to switch it. "Lil," I start.

"I know, Rory. I know."

And we both know that she's not talking about the music.

Somewhere in the conversation, I've turned and slid to the floor, my bed to my back. This is one of the moments I remember it's true that grief shows its face when you least expect it. Speaking of grief, I look at the flowers on my bedside table. Because I'm a masochist, I put the bouquet Rafe gave me earlier this week in a vase beside my bed so I can look at them and think of the look on his face when he told Gladys that he couldn't be the one I'd choose in the end. The look that will haunt me. I had him close to me, and I didn't go after him. I know I let fear win this time, and if I didn't have tonight to distract me, I would be banging on his door for forgiveness. But what would that change?

"Ro, why aren't you with *him* instead?"

I don't have the luxury of hiding from someone who's walked with me through the most difficult parts of my life. "Because this was always supposed to be the plan, wasn't it? Apparently, Rafe had an enlightening conversation with Jacques. And then Jacques asked me out. How could I say no?"

"And? I sense an *and*," is the response I get from the other end of the line.

"Anddddd Rafe's not going to stay in this small town forever." It hurts to say his name. Whereas normally, it's sweet and like honey on my tongue, it now feels scratchy.

"Well, have you asked him that? I mean, have you said, 'Rafe, what are your plans for the future'?"

"He told me. He said that he was here to get his music back on track. But he's been to Paris and London and just came from LA, Lily! LA."

"So?"

"So, I love it here, but I know there's no way I could ask him to stay. Not when he wants to reach people with his music. He's everything good in this world. He deserves to be on a bigger stage."

There's silence, and I know she's giving me her full attention. "And you can't leave."

I shake my head, even though I know she can't see me. My eyes catch on a framed picture of my parents and me at my fourth birthday. The cake is a few feet toward the center of the table, so I'm on my elbows, leaning over the table, my lips pursed to blow out the candles, my eyes closed to make a wish. The cake is white with pink roses and trim, and my parents are behind me, my mother smiling and my father grinning at my dedication to making wishes. I've always made wishes. I just didn't believe any more of them would come true. "And I can't leave," is all I say.

Lily hums in acknowledgment, and then it's quiet on her end of the line. I know she's giving me space to work through this moment. I wipe my eyes—because at some point in this conversation I started crying—and I stand up from the floor. It's time to move forward. Rafe has been a distraction—a beautiful distraction—but I can't commit to someone who won't be able to fully commit to me. Who shouldn't. And I would never ask. So, I ignore the dread in my stomach and decide a different distraction is exactly what I need. Besides, isn't this what I wished for?

"Let me ask you, Rory—because I love you too much. You want someone to fight for you, and I get it. But what if he needs someone to fight for him too?"

"He got to you too, didn't he?"

Lily sighs, but I can feel that she's not going to give away anything easily. She's a beautiful vault and fights fiercely for people she cares about. So, if she's not telling me something about Rafe, it means she's also come to care for him too. This thought makes me smile.

"He didn't *not* get to me. He's okay. I guess. But most importantly, he makes you smile like I've never seen. Ever. I don't know whether to hate him a little bit for it or name one of our coffee drinks after him—decaf, of course." She laughs at herself. "But if you really need to see this through with Jacques, I'll support you. I just think you need to be really careful about what you could be losing in the process."

"I can't lose him. I never had him." Something tastes sour about those words. "I have to know, Lily. Don't I have to know?"

She hums a bit, and I can feel she doesn't wholeheartedly approve, but she also won't stand in my way. Sometimes just knowing someone will support you in the trying is enough to add some courage.

"Okay, Lils, here's what we're going to do." I can hear the smile from Lily on the other side of the line.

"There she is," she whispers.

This new confidence has me pacing back and forth, really seeing, for the first time, my entire wardrobe sans the homecoming dress still hanging in my closet because I refuse to ever part with it. My father decided I needed a dress that went with my eyes, so he chose a mocha color, and I've never forgotten how happy he was that I wanted his opinion, never mind that I actually followed through with it. I was like an awkward teenage chocolate truffle, but my father's expression of pure love was worth it all.

My eyes catch on a pair of black tights with tiny black hearts printed on them. Like a constellation forming, I focus on my black ankle boots, my black skirt, and a cream-colored blouse with the style of sleeves that are loosely fitting but cling in a cuff at the wrists.

This is my outfit.

"Got it!" I whisper-yell into the phone and hear the warped sound of Lily's cheer. This is what it means to have best friends. We wait, comfortable in the closeness and process, until one of us can see clearly. And even if we don't agree, she'll show me she's rooting for me just the same.

"Tell me everything," is all she says before hanging up the phone. I run into my tiny bathroom, past the shelves with a Chip mug from *Beauty and the Beast*. I reach inside and pull out my gold necklace, from which dangles an image of the rose in a bell glass from the same film and featuring little petals that rise from the bottom of the necklace as if they just fell. My father gifted it to me when I was around thirteen years old, and it's what I wear for courage. Most people don't recognize the symbol. It's elegant and not a jewelry piece for kids. I put it on and get dressed, only glancing at myself in the mirror long enough to notice the dark circles under my eyes and the way my ribcage seems to want to cave in under the heaviness I feel inside.

Jacques picks me up at my place, and we take his fancy, European car toward the Downtown area of Portsmouth. He looks stylish, and his modeling skills are in full effect as I sit across from him at an upscale restaurant. It's an Italian-fusion place, and while it smells incredible in here, the moment we walked through the door, all I could think about was the pizza Rafe and I shared at his studio. I will myself to focus. But it's so hard when I feel so out of place. Unsettled. Unsure. These are the words that are floating through my mind as I dip some homemade bread into a plate of olive oil and salt.

Although Jacques has been perfectly polite, I feel like I need to be a different version of myself. Like somehow, if he saw the one who questions everything at midnight each night and has a stack of cards (already stamped) by her fridge and still forgets to send them, he wouldn't be able to comprehend it. He's only seen business-owner me—the slightly flustered me. Not the one who would hide a guitar pick in a stuffed raccoon just to see Rafe's reaction. Or the one who owns candles and sometimes never lights them but collects them simply because I like the look of them.

I'm studying his face now—the symmetrical perfection of it, and it's grating on me that his eyebrows are perfect. Whose eyebrows are perfect? I think it's a ridiculous thing to be distracted by until I remember the scar through Rafe's eyebrow. I grin to myself and clearly am distracted since Jacques has to call my name.

"*Ça va?*" I find him looking at me hesitantly. I'm not sure how many times he's called my name, but I missed it at least once if his expression is any indication.

"Mm-hmm . . ." I manage. "*Ça va, merci.*" The piece of bread I was dipping is completely soaked. It's a vessel lost at sea in the middle of the plate. I poke at it and then push the plate to the side. No point in trying to rescue it and getting oil all over the table.

"So, Jacques, tell me about what you do?" I take a sip of wine and will myself to breathe. His accented-English is stunning. Musical. I've never understood why American movies feature French characters with the worst accents I've ever heard. It's abominable, really, to butcher the language in such a way. Why not just hire people who are actually French? I find it all so alarming. There's a cassette tape of my mother reading me a bedtime story. It's about a girl who lives in a tree and wishes that she could be a bird so that she can fly away. My mother said that's why she named me Sparrow. So that I always know I never have to be grounded. But hearing her voice, the melody of it all as she switched between English and French, has forever changed how I hear the language.

I snap back into the present and listen as Jacques talks about how he got into business and about all the places his work takes him, but my mind drifts to Rafe when he was in LA, and I wonder how many times he's sung in Paris. I have to shake myself out of this because here—right in front of me—is a real-life Frenchman who is smart, interesting (to someone, I'm sure), and downright handsome. I can't sabotage this.

His phone chimes. *"Excusez moi."*

I nod and really take him in while he's focused on something on his phone. The way his face is all European—you know the type; you look at them and immediately know somehow that they're not American. If he's amused or annoyed with the cultural differences between us, I can't tell. It's then I decide to give it a chance. A real chance.

It's at this moment he puts his phone on silent and hides it away inside his suit jacket. Because, of course, he's wearing a perfectly tailored outfit.

"Sparrow, I'm so glad you came here with me tonight," he states while the fancy food is brought to our table. I thought I had ordered a simple pasta dish, but looking at it, I severely underestimated how elaborately pasta could be made.

"My mother was French," is all I manage to get out. And my focus is now on the chunks of tomato in the sauce. I hate chunks of tomato in a sauce. Blend it or make it a margarita pizza where one knows what one is getting, but for the love of all that is good, don't make tomato sauce chunky. In town, Lorenzo knows how I like it. I start to move the pieces around the plate to find a bite I'd be comfortable with and am not having much luck.

He notices me playing with my food but has the courtesy not to say anything. So, I ask him about Paris, and his eyes flicker with excitement.

"Oh, when we're in Paris, I just have to take you to this place my mother loves. It's a fashion house called Durand, and it's *magnifique*."

I nod and get back to picking at my plate. I mean, is it kind of strange he's already talking about us traveling together? Sure. But his confidence is one of the things I am attracted to.

"And I'll take you to the gardens, of course. And shopping on the *Champs-Élysées*. Do you like fast cars?"

I look up and try to process what he was saying. Because that's not the Paris that I had in mind at all. I think of sitting in Montmartre and having an artist sketch my portrait along with the others on the street. I think of crowded cafés and walking over bridges that hover above the Seine. I think of standing under the Eiffel Tower just so I can be right in the middle of it. I take a sip of wine and leave his question hovering in the air. This wine is . . . good. He's . . . good.

Jacques is still politely waiting for my answer, and I grin. Maybe what he and I can have is good, and I just won't know until I keep trying. Maybe he can open up a different world to me that I hadn't really considered yet. I fix a piece of my hair and put my hand down a little too forcefully. It nicks the abandoned bread and olive oil situation, and the piece of bread that I thought was gone forever manages to fly off the plate and catapult a few drops of olive oil toward Jacques. It's a direct hit.

And he smiles. He actually smiles. I look around the restaurant, but no one seems to care that I've just gotten food on a former model.

"Oh, gosh, I'm so sorry," I mutter as I stand to . . . what? Try to wipe it off him? I'm not sure what I'm doing anymore and move to sit back down but then think better of it since he can't see the mess near his shoulder. I hop and drag my chair over toward him, and he's laughing again.

"Wanted us to be closer, yes?" He chuckles, and I let a grin break through. Maybe he will be okay with the clumsy parts of me. Grabbing a clean napkin, I dip it in water and attempt to help the situation, but all I'm really doing is getting a better sense of the cologne he wears. He captures my hand and slowly brings it to his mouth instead of letting me continue. A soft kiss lands on the edge of my knuckles, and I swallow. It's a movie moment, to be sure. But I'd be lying if I said there were sparks. Where are the sparks?

I clear my throat and try to push back, but the chair gets stuck on the carpet, and my life flashes before my eyes. I let out a little squeak and stand quickly, taking my chair with me.

"Miss, do you need assistance?" The waiter is next to me, clearly concerned for my welfare.

As am I, young man. As am I.

"I'm fine. Thank you so much."

He doesn't believe me, but thankfully, he walks away anyway.

Jacques is amused and starts to eat his food, all politeness and refinement, and nods at the waiter as if it was perfectly reasonable to ask me such a question and perfectly reasonable for me to have almost wiped out a moment ago. Jacques is still smiling, but it's at this moment I realize Rafe would've laughed. Actually, he may have thrown a piece of his own food back at me just so we'd be even. And this thought makes me ache.

"So, Jacques," I say, attempting to distract myself . . . again. "What do you think about Birch Borough?" I know he's in the area for the next few years at least, as he mentioned as much when he first arrived.

"It's . . . quaint." Huh.

"Does this mean that you don't expect to stay?"

He shakes his head adamantly. "No, of course not. I'll be here another year more to gain business experience in America. It's a good choice for me to be here now. But France is home."

I smile politely, and inside, I'm sunk. Wasn't I just telling Lily that the reason I can't be with Rafe is because he is leaving? And didn't I partially choose Jacques tonight on the pretense that he . . . isn't? "I didn't realize that."

He nods, and I think of all the ways I may have seen this situation incorrectly. He's stunning, yes. On paper, he's what I wanted. But off paper . . .

"Sparrow, I have to tell you, you make me so nervous."

What did he say? I make *him* nervous? I stuff a forkful of pasta with hardly any sauce into my mouth to buy some time. I point to my mouth in the universally acknowledged sign for "hold please, I'm chewing" (actually, that may not be true, but it was worth a shot) and wait while my brain races. I take another sip of wine to buy a few more seconds, and then I look him in the eye.

"Why?" is the devastatingly clever answer I manage.

He grins and leans a little closer. "You're beautiful.

You own a business. You're very funny." I shrug at this. "You're like light. You make people feel good—they want to be around you. I want to be around you."

To his credit, these are very kind answers. And still, I'm disappointed. The words seem right. They should feel right too, shouldn't they? But they don't.

"Thank you, Jacques. You've definitely made me nervous too." Because he has. The past few months I was frozen when he walked in. "If you're not staying here . . ." I start, "then, um . . . what are we doing here? Tonight?"

He shifts in his seat, his brow furrowed. "You mean to date?"

I nod. He smiles. "I would like to know each other. See what happens. Next year, I'm going back to Paris. And if things are good, we could go together? No matter what happens, if you want to be in Paris too, I can help. You could even sell your business. It's what I do."

My shoulders slump slightly. I stare back at the face I have been hoping to see in front of me, just like this, for all these months. Now that we're here, I realize a very important thing: He doesn't see me. And I wouldn't even know this to be true if I didn't know what it's like to be fully seen by someone else.

Jacques is kind. He's a decent man. My mind gives me images and ideas of touring Paris with him, and as incredible as it would be to be there and feel like I was with someone who knew the culture and the language, I'd rather stumble through and discover it all with Rafe.

"That's very kind, thank you." I smile and resume eating. It's pleasant enough, but I keep my words few and my smiles sincere but generic. As fancy of a place as this is, as elegant as the company, as delicious as the dessert is when we get to that point of the meal, I want to hoard all my words and my full smiles for a man who is not here, and yet I feel him as if he were.

At the end of the night, I get a kiss on the cheek from Jacques in that *faire la bise* type of way, with a promise to see each other around town from me and a hope we go out again from him. But we won't.

Chapter Eighteen

Rafe

Another tree branch hits me in the face. "Ow!"

"Would you quiet down back there, D'Artagnan? You're going to cause a scene."

Lily and I have already been around town, trailing a romantic date that makes me feel like my insides are being ripped out as I watch. I was sitting at Graham's tonight, trying to work up the energy to order a pizza, when Lily texted me, saying that Sparrow needed my help. Turned out, it was all a ruse for us to follow Sparrow and Jacques around on *their* date.

We've been to a fancy Italian place (and driven all around Portsmouth before we found said Italian place). We went through a drive-through (Lily insisted she had a craving and needed fuel for the mission). And now it's dark, and we're parked back at Lily's apartment, walking behind some of the shops in town and through some (very sharp) tree branches extending from almost barren trees. Clusters of birch trees, the namesake of this town, stand out against the night sky, moonlight reflecting off their trunks from the river rushing to our left, its steady presence a comfort.

"Lily, why are we doing this? Do you just have a sick sense of humor or something, because this really isn't fun for me."

She turns to face me, a milkshake cup dangling from her hand. I didn't see her take it from the car. How did it even get here? And when?

"D'Artagnan, repeat after me: I will win my woman's heart."

"Lily," I begin.

"She has feelings for you. I know she does."

I lean in carefully, trying not to disrupt Lily's train of thought. Her openness toward me right now is like a rare creature you stumble across and don't want to run away. But the words she just spoke shake me. "What do you mean?" My pulse is pounding so hard I feel it in my throat.

"She's finally coming to terms with her fear."

I nod my head in, hopefully, what appears to be a thoughtful manner when, really, I'm spinning. "And— what would that happen to be?"

Lily laughs. She actually laughs. I'm a man in pain, and she's laughing. "She's afraid of *you*, D'Artagnan." This time, when she swings her arm around, chocolate milkshake flies through the air and lands on my coat.

I open my mouth in mock horror. "I've been wounded."

That earns me a grin. She pulls napkins from her coat and finishes her milkshake before throwing it away in a nearby dumpster.

"I don't want her to be afraid of me."

She waves her hand about, the chocolate staining one side of her hand. "And I'm guessing you've tagged along with me—the best friend—on this date to try to see if anything can be done about the fact that you're actually in love with her?"

"I never said . . ." I freeze at her expression. She dares me to deny it and . . . I won't.

"Yes."

"Lily, I trust you." Her eyes narrow as if she's assessing whether I mean it. I do.

She suddenly exhales, and a warm smile breaks over her face. It catches me so off guard that I look over my shoulder to make sure I'm still the only one receiving her attention. Lily laughs while shaking her head.

"There's something you should know," I mumble.

"Spill," she orders.

My heart starts to beat wildly, and I grimace. My pulse has moved upward to thunder in my ears, and the weight of the truth stuns me momentarily. I'm about to level with the best friend of the woman I love.

"First off, are you leaving?" Lily demands.

I shift as the hoot of an owl calls in the distance. "Might have to go to Nashville for a bit. I sent a demo in last week, and it's getting some traction. And I will have to get things settled from LA, but I would never take her from here."

She nods, satisfied. We take a sharp right through an alleyway to cut through toward the front of the shops, the light from one of the streetlamps revealing more of Lily's expressions.

"And about the other thing? You confirmed, but I need to hear you actually say it," she urges.

"Uh . . ." The scratch in my throat causes me to wince. I clear it loudly. "You're right . . . I'm in love with Sparrow," I breathe out.

"I KNEW IT!"

"Shh, shh," I grit out as I channel my inner librarian, like I'm the only one preventing a room full of teenagers from making out in the reference section, even though we're outside. My jaw clenches, which is the complete opposite of the expression on Lily's eager face. "But . . ."

For as fast as Lily's excitement appeared, it evaporates just as quickly. Her eyes narrow. "But. What." It's not a question. It's a demand.

"There's something about me she doesn't know. And I don't know how to get around this. I really don't." I look into Lily's eyes, and for the first time, I see that she's really rooting for me. It's time to go all-in. "Lily, the truth is, while my family did a number on me, and my ex did the same, I was scared. I hid. I didn't tell Sparrow who I really am."

She studies my face, and I hold my breath.

"She knows I'm a musician. And she knows I've lived in Paris, which is true. But she doesn't know the one thing I can't change about myself."

"Should I be really concerned right now?" she starts. "Because if you so much as cause her one tear that's not from happiness, I will come after you. Don't you think I won't. She's my girl. She's my bestie. And you don't spend over TWENTY years of your life with someone to have her go down because a beautiful man comes into town, with the voice of a freakin' angel and lyrics that would soften hearts of stone, all to have her—"

"Lily," I plead. I look about the sidewalk and motion for her to lean in. She cautiously does as I ask, and I move to whisper in her ear. I tell her the secret I've been holding since I arrived in this town and watch as Lily stills.

She looks at me with her jaw open before letting out a cross between a yell and a shriek. "WHAT?!"

Lily grasps my jacket and pulls me toward the sidewalk and out into the open. A couple in the distance turns to look at us, and I feel my face redden. A few lights turn on above some of the quiet shops. I won't be surprised if we are brought in for questioning. Lily doesn't care in the least, her eyes bright. She locates a snack-sized candy bar freakishly quick and starts smacking me with it.

"Ow! Lily!"

"Why." *Smack.* "Didn't." *Smack.* "You." *Smack.* *Smack.* "Say." *Smack.* "Something?" *Smack.*

"Ow!" I step away from the madwoman with the violent chocolate. She motions for me to come closer again. *SMACK.* I'm an idiot for falling for it. "Lily, please stop hitting me."

Despite the fact that the chocolate has melted considerably from her body heat, Lily takes a bite, the evidence sticking to her fingers. It seems to do the trick in dissolving the tension in her system. "That was for my best friend. At ease."

I rub my arm where she zapped me. "I'm sorry I didn't tell her right away."

She scrunches her nose.

"Or you . . . before now."

Lily gives me a nod of approval. "People have . . . you know, only gotten close to you because of this?"

I nod.

"Well, this really puts a wrench in things, doesn't it?" She pulls out another candy bar and leans against the brick wall, her eyes tracking a car that slowly moves past the nearly empty two-lane road that runs through the middle of town. "But . . . I *kind of* get it," she concedes. It's my turn to be surprised. "Kind of," she concludes.

"I can work with kind of," I admit.

Lily looks me over and nods as if I passed some unknown test. She looks out at another passing car and speaks into the night. "Sparrow keeps people out, especially men. She's had lots of disappointments with dating in the past. Her way of coping has been to build walls and create unrealistic scenarios . . . to ward off her suitors. Kind of puts you in a sticky situation right now . . ."

We look at each other, and I see the moment that tears fill her eyes. Hope fills my own. I didn't realize how gentle Lily's heart could be until now.

"I don't want to give her a reason to keep me out. Not anymore," I say.

Lily wipes the moisture from her eyes and nods. "I'm sorry I got the mean reds for a second," she mutters.

"*Breakfast at Tiffany's.*" I grin.

She pauses and arches her brow. I see the laugh trying to escape from her mouth. She's at war with whether to be really annoyed at me or really impressed. And I'm just waiting to find out which one it will be. She reaches into her jacket pocket and pulls out another candy bar, throwing it toward my chest. I catch it in one hand, aware that she's debating, and decide to throw down my last wish.

"Help me get her for real, Lily? Please? I want her more than I've ever wanted anything in my life."

Lily's eyes glisten again, and she gives me a full smile. "Oh, the drama." She sighs. "I'm too young for this." She uses a napkin to attempt to clean the long-gone chocolate milkshake that somehow also got on her phone. It does nothing but smear further, but I appreciate the effort. She winces.

"I really don't get why chocolate hates you so much . . ." I begin.

She sighs, but I see the amusement in her eyes.

"Listen. You're only going to hear this from me once. *Once*. Got it? I never thought I'd find someone worthy of her, but here we are."

I feel my eyes widen. That's more than I ever thought I would hear from her. Emotion starts to stick in my throat. Oh, stars, am I going to cry too? This can't be happening. Lily won't let it.

"Get it together, man. I hate to break it to you, but she's not afraid because you're some big scary man." I nod, a bit of relief coming to my spine. "She's afraid because she loves you—you ridiculous, always French, mostly American-acting, and sometimes funny man."

"She really loves me?"

A bit of a growl escapes her throat. She's taking us farther down the street and back to another set of shops, leading the charge into the night.

"Why are we still back here?"

"So she doesn't see us!" Right. Because this isn't suspicious at all. Two people near the dumpsters along the town river late at night.

"You're not the first person to tell me that, by the way."

"Uh—tell you what?" My voice is raspy and strained. I really do think I am going to cry, but I'll try to hold it in until I get to the studio or to Graham's.

Lily wipes something from her face and then freezes. She turns slowly, and it takes everything in me not to laugh. Who am I kidding? I start laughing. The emotional energy from sharing my secret with someone else has gotten to me, and Lily is standing there, chocolate milkshake smeared across her face like it has marked her to be an American football player.

"Chocolate really does hate me," she says, defeated. And there's nothing I can do but agree. "So, here's what you do. You really should pay me for my help, by the way." She grins and pulls me toward the corner of the street, where we hover between a Thai restaurant and a Southern kitchen with a clear view of the bakery. "You're going to take Winnings' advice."

"Winnings? You know Graham?"

She flinches a bit but waves it away. "Not important." I see the way her jaw tenses. Got it. Another time. "Here's the thing. This isn't *La La Land*. Rory loves that movie, but it's so depressing."

I scoff. "It's beautiful."

"This is why you're perfect for each other, but that's not my point. My point is that you're both acting like this is the end. Like you've missed your chance. You've kept something to yourself. She's doing the same with her heart. But you don't need to move to Paris, and she doesn't need to stay behind."

"What?"

"*La. La. Land.*"

"Yes, right."

"This isn't a movie. And if you don't want *La La Land* to be a self-fulfilling prophecy, you're going to do everything you can to get your girl. You're not going to let her slip through your hands, even though it's hard." I'm nodding furiously. "But your pursuit of her needs to be heartfelt. Your grand gesture needs to create a memory. Sparrow is all about the things she can hold on to. The ways that she can tangibly know she's seen. So, what've you got?" She motions for me to spill again. I've got nothing left to spill.

"Uh . . . flowers?"

She makes a frustrating buzzer noise.

"Ok . . . well, chocolate and baked goods are out. Although, croissants . . ." I grin at the idea of Sparrow holding a croissant as Lily interrupts with the buzzing sound again. "A note?"

She nods her head up and down. "Better, but . . ."

I hold up my hand to stop her, and still, she makes the buzzing noise.

"Please stop doing that."

"I'll stop when you come up with the idea."

I wince. "A trip to Paris?" Lily buzzes.

"I already wrote her a song . . . several of them." I run my fingers through my hair as, you guessed it, Lily buzzes.

"Keep going . . ." she continues. Lily snaps her fingers as if it will hurry the process.

I think of everything I know about Sparrow. She holds on to things that remind her of people she loves, which must be why she keeps taking guitar picks of mine. She sees everyone, and gives to everyone, and never expects to get anything in return. Halloween is just around the corner, just like our hiding spot, but that's beside the point. Because while she's with my unspoken rival, Jacques, I'm wondering if I can come up with something special enough to win Sparrow's heart.

Just then, a fancy car pulls in front of the bakery. Under the reflection of the streetlights, I can't see anything at first. When Jacques steps out, dressed in a sharp suit that looks familiar, I'm immediately miserable. He rounds the car and opens the door for the most stunning woman. Sparrow takes his hand and steps out, her red lipstick accentuated by the dim lighting.

I turn away, but Lily is gripping my arm. She's with me. They say goodbye, kissing on each cheek, and Sparrow walks around the back of the store toward her apartment. Jacques drives off, but I see Sparrow stare at the door as if she needs a little more courage to step through it alone. My heart hurts for her, but a spark from a flame of hope stirs in my soul. It doesn't look like it was the best night of her life after all.

"What is she doing?" I whisper.

Lily looks at me, a furrow in her brow. "Being Sparrow."

Once she walks through the door to her apartment and is out from the cold, I know what I need to do.

"You've got it?" Lily asks. I nod. I assume she's going to give me a hard time, but she must see the determination in my face. "Okay, then. Do what you need to do. I'm rooting for you."

She holds out her hand for a sort of high-five type of thing, but instead, I awkwardly lean down to pull her into a side hug. "Thank you, Lily," I say quietly. She's stiff, but she nods with a grin.

As I turn fully to head back toward Graham's apartment, crushed leaves under my shoes and dried milkshake on my coat, I hear Lily call to me. "Go get her, D'Artagnan. On behalf of all the heartbroken, change the ending."

Chapter Nineteen

Rafe

I haven't seen Sparrow for four days. I would say it's because I'm too busy writing and getting ready for another show, but that's not entirely true. I've written, sure, but I've also been as distracted as I ever remember being. I joined the gym in town just to try to wear myself out and lift really heavy things without people wondering what was wrong with me. It was horrible. So now I'm sore and can't bend my legs too much. But the worst pain is the one that's pulsing near my lungs. She went out with Jacques.

My phone rings. I think it could be her but deflate as soon as I see it's my dad. I know he'll keep calling if I don't answer, so I accept. He wants something.

"Son," he says. "Another article came out here about your band. Talks about trouble in our family. Your mother and I need you to meet us in London. The family needs to be seen together for a photo op."

I clench my jaw so tight something pops near my right ear. "Ow," I mutter.

"What was that?"

"Nothing." He wouldn't care anyway. "And my answer is no."

"You need to be there," is the response. There must be people around for him to speak so vaguely.

"Can't do that." I don't even apologize.

"Is this because of one of your shows?" he seethes. I hear the meanness breaking through his civility. It's only a matter of time before he'll completely crack.

"Listen, I'm going to let you go. Thanks for checking in. Hope all is well. Do tell Mother I said hello." And with that, I hang up.

I put my head in my hands and wait for the text I know is coming. My phone pings, and I turn over to check . . . because I still can't seem to fully separate myself from my parents—no matter how hard I've tried.

Dad: I'll send you your flight information.

My thumbs type furiously.

Rafe: Don't waste your airline miles. Can't be there. Wear your blue suit. Looks better in photos.

I shouldn't have added the last line to twist the knife, but I'm so sick of feeling like a pawn in my father's dreams. And I won't let them keep overtaking my own.

The image of Sparrow getting out of the car with Jacques still has me in knots, but I did this to myself. It's what she said she wanted. All I wanted was to see her happy and to show her that I'll get out of the way if it means she gets to live her own dreams. And it feels ridiculous to think I could try to make this situation go in any other direction.

Graham and I had a solid heart-to-heart last night, and he told me I have to remember that I'm leaving. *I am leaving, right?* I've never considered trying to pursue music outside of a major city. And while I haven't had it in me to return to Paris yet, and living in LA felt like a piece of my soul was sinking bit by bit, it has always been my plan to return when I found the courage. Except, it doesn't feel like home anymore. Home suddenly feels like weird, small-town activities and the river that changes color depending on the weather. It feels like the tiny studio in the music shop on Main Street, where Liam has a cup of coffee waiting for me when I arrive. It feels like Lily giving me slightly hostile advice and Graham answering every time I call. It feels like a box of croissants and eating pizza in a studio. It feels like a woman slow dancing in my arms.

I stare at myself in the mirror. I'm wearing a crisp white dress shirt with my solid black tie. A suit jacket hangs from one arm. This is what came to mind when Lily advised me to make a grand gesture, not because I think it could sway her but simply because I'll do anything for her to smile like she means it. I've gelled my hair in a classic Hollywood way and parted it to one side. I'm clean-shaven tonight. I've even got the shoes right— the Oxford ones—to look like I just stepped out of a 1950s film. I'm dressed as Seb from *La La Land* because I think Sparrow will like it. While Graham asked me if I was auditioning to be a Frank Sinatra impersonator, I know she'll get the reference immediately.

I am trying to be charming, and I don't think I've ever tried to be charming—not intentionally, anyway. So I'm not sure what to do with this new part of my personality, but it's too late to back out now. I promised Graham I would show up to this little town Halloween Happy Hour thing, and so I will.

Standing near the gazebo in the town square near Main Street (yes, this is real life and not a movie set), I take in the little kids walking around with their parents. It's all smiles and oversized costumes. It's attempts at being fictional characters and sticky hands from candy already being snuck from their orange plastic pumpkins. It's the way the masks don't quite fit where their tiny eyes should be looking out. The effect is . . . adorable.

I clear my throat. I'll try to say it's from the cold, but this town is getting to me, as is the sight of parents holding hands with their little ones. A thought of Sparrow as a little girl, holding her parents' hands and asking for candy, hits me so strongly. The people she held on to are gone now. And I wonder if she wants to have a family and take them trick-or-treating too.

This must be a great town to grow up in. While I was falling asleep under tables at fashion events that lasted until 2:00 a.m. and sneaking *hors d'oeuvres* as my dinner, she was waking up to the smell of croissants and sprinkling sugar on chouquettes. While I was begging my parents to come see me at a show or a game, she was a comfort to her father in their grief. And while I was running as far away from Paris as possible, she's been dreaming of booking a ticket since she knew that she could.

We're from different worlds, and yet I think we could balance each other out. Be the one the other needs. When my eyes catch on a bright-yellow dress, I know I'm right. It's got capped sleeves, cinches at the waist, and flares out. It's vintage. It's Sparrow, and also, it's Mia from *La La Land*. We look like we've each tried to recreate the movie poster with our costumes. She sees me and stills, a sweater thrown over her arm. I thought it would be okay to see her, but my heart is screaming at me for being this close to her. It's both a comfort after days without her and a new level of pain.

I scuff my shoes on the concrete beneath them, not willing to break eye contact. She takes a deep breath, and I don't miss the way her mouth slightly turns up, and she shrugs as if to say, *Of course we did*. While I was secretly getting ready for my role tonight to make Sparrow smile, she was doing the same for me.

I try to avoid getting in the way of tiny princesses and cowboys as we meet in the middle of the street. It's closed off for the event, and it's far too crowded on the sidewalk. As we get closer to each other, I take in her hair, which she has perfectly styled in a vintage way. I note her bold lipstick and the fact that she's also wearing Oxford shoes. I want to hug her and tell her how much I love how the lights are casting a glow around her that I'll never forget. Even if I had my camera, I don't think I'd try to get a picture since I know you can't always catch magic with a lens.

We stare at each other for a moment when a flash goes off to my right. Startled out of our focus, I turn to see Lily with a smug look on her face. Looks like we got a picture of tonight after all. And now all I'm thinking about is how to convince Lily to let me see it. Although, it may not be the same as I remember it, I want something to confirm that Sparrow might have been looking at me the way I thought she was. I remember Jacques and wonder if he's around here somewhere. I give a quick glance around but don't see him in the crowd.

A little girl in a princess costume has distracted Sparrow enough that she's eye level with the little one and helping to arrange a barrette. She knows everyone in this town. Every time I've been with her, it's like we're walking on the streets of a theme park, and I'm just waiting for someone to stop us to get their picture with her. I hope this is always how it is. I pull my eyes away from her long enough to get another look at our surroundings and any Frenchmen in sight when I feel Lily tug on my suit jacket.

"He's not here," Lily whispers to me.

"Hmm?" I manage.

"Your nemesis. He isn't here."

I'm cut off from asking more when Sparrow stands up, a bright smile on her face. The little girl has run off while a small snowman waddles, more than runs, behind her. He falls and can't get up immediately. A man, who I assume is his father, bends down and scoops him up over his shoulder, the orange foam carrot of a nose bouncing in the night air. I chuckle a bit.

"That kid's gonna need therapy," Lily says, a serious look on her face. I can't disagree, but it's cute at the moment.

"So, Lily, to what do we owe this pleasure?" I tease and motion away from the town. "I'm surprised you're not out there trying to get your fill of frightening things."

She swats at me. "Who needs to visit a haunted house? Just go on a dating app."

"Truer words may never have been spoken." I laugh as Lily gives a slight bow. And then I'm laughing again as Sparrow looks between us, a hesitant smile on her face. Appreciation seems to pass over her face as she looks between us, but it's gone before I can hold on to it.

"I'm here to watch the insanity that is this town's events," Lily counters.

"You love it," Sparrow suggests. "You've never missed one. Not even when you had pneumonia in fourth grade."

"This town needs me," is Lily's response. I also can't disagree with that. Whereas Sparrow is the heart of this town, Lily is the feistiness, its keeper of levity. I'm sure her personality is to disarm people, but it sure as heck is amusing.

"Well, Graham's going to be missing this one. He texted me a few minutes ago saying that he got caught up at work, and it's a code red." I slide my phone back into my pocket.

I swear I hear Lily mutter something like, "I'm sure it is," before she changes the subject entirely by saying, "Let's get a drink."

We nod in agreement, and the three of us walk toward Aesop's Tavern. When we arrive, I hold the door as the ladies walk through. I'm not doing very well at ignoring Sparrow's legs showing from underneath her dress or ignoring the way she smells more of caramelized sugar than usual . . . actually, there's a new smell. Could it be marshmallow?

Clark at the bar gives a wave, and we head to a high-top table in the corner. Although the place is completely full, there's a little reserved sign on it, and I grin. This is because Sparrow is here. Apparently, Clark was a good friend of her father's, and when she wants to go out, she just tells him, and he reserves a space.

"So, Lily, do you enjoy Halloween?" I'm trying to bring her into the conversation. One, because I like her as a person and want to stay on her good side. Two, because she's still the best friend of the woman who has completely overtaken my life. And three, because I don't have strength yet to talk to Sparrow without asking questions about Jacques. And I don't know if I want to know those answers. So avoidance is fine for now.

Sparrow's amusement is enough to distract me, though. She's biting on the edge of her lip. She ordered a margarita with salt, and I'm just realizing that there must be a piece of salt stuck to her skin from the way she's shifting her mouth as if she wants every last bit of salt but is also savoring it. And I wonder if a salty version of her lips would be better than sweet. My face starts to heat, and my heart pumps harder. I clear my throat because there's absolutely zero chill with me when it comes to this woman.

I move to take a sip of my hard cider and nearly knock it over. A few drops hit the table, and Lily's eyes give me a strong sense that she knows exactly what I was thinking, and I need to BE COOL. But I can't. Take me to Paris and put me in LA, and I'll have people thinking that I'm suave. Under control. Unattached (words from the press, not myself). And then stick me in front of Sparrow, and I can't seem to get it together. She unravels me, and I . . . love it.

Sparrow wipes the remaining droplets off the table with a napkin as she looks at me with a grin so casual it's as if my insides aren't falling apart from having her near. I shift in my seat, my knee lightly brushing hers, and it's pure fire. I catch Lily leaning back in her chair and making a sign with her finger and her throat like I need to kill whatever vibes I'm putting off right now. She's not wrong. I look about the space and see it: an old piano in the corner.

I leap from the table and give a weird nod before heading to the bar to find Clark. After asking him if I could please play out my feelings (really, I just ask if he minds me playing the piano), he heartily agrees. So now I'm sitting on the warped wooden bench that creaks beneath my weight, and I feel good. This is good. This is a piece of what will ground me in any situation.

Without looking at Sparrow, I allow my energy to go into the keys. I play until I feel sweat through my undershirt and at the sides of my hair. I'm playing out every single feeling that I've been feeling since I arrived, which is . . . a lot. It's Halloween, and I feel the whisper of the ghost that I let near my life. The one who crushed my creativity. I was hollow for so long, and now I'm starting to come back to life. But just as when a limb starts to awaken after falling asleep, the pain is hitting every nerve ending. And all I can do is play it out.

So, I don't notice the way the bar goes silent. Or the way that people lean in and hang on every note. I also don't notice when Sparrow gets out of her seat and makes her way to stand beside me, her head propped on her hand as her elbow leans against the top of the piano.

I'm vibrating with the energy and the mood of the music. Finally, I look to her to get a read on what she's thinking or feeling. I don't expect to see her eyes warm with what can only be described as pride. Her eyes are glassy too, as if I've struck a note that she needed to hear. She gives me a slow, beautiful smile, and I shift over on the piano bench. Without missing a beat, I motion with my head for her to sit beside me, and she does. A sweater is now draped loosely over her dress, the yellow peeking through the holes. It's a glimpse of how she lives—her femininity shining through her attempts to hide. I'm undone at the sight of her. I shift the song I am playing into one that came to me after we danced in her bakery. It's a song about whispers and things I wish we could be.

It's sweet, and it's slow, with pieces of us both mixed throughout. I've been trying not to touch her too much as I move my hands over the keys, but I don't mind the few times our shoulders brush. I feel her gaze move from my hands to my face, and I turn to take her in. Her lips are slightly parted, her eyes are slightly wide, and suddenly, her head is on my shoulder. I transition the song to one that's a little less intense and compose the melody as I play. It's the sound of the smell of her so close to me; it's the feeling of her hand now resting low on my knee; it's the unwavering truth that I'm completely in love with her. And I never want this dream to end.

Suddenly, I picture her in a cream dress with tiny polka dots, gold earrings hanging against her slender neck, her hair pulled up in a loose bun, and bracelets wrapped around her wrists. She leans against one of the stone walls on the *Pont Neuf* and watches the Seine rumbling beneath, a look of joy and wonder on her face. And all I want is to be there, with her, to see it.

It's nearly nine o'clock before the three of us walk back to Sparrow's apartment. Sparrow and I didn't drink much, but I offered to walk them back to her place since Lily declared, two glasses of wine in, that they were going to have a sleepover. She's asked me a few questions about my roommate, sometimes calling him *George* and not *Graham*, with a hint of amusement on her face. I'm not sure what that's all about. But as we're walking back the few blocks it takes to reach our destination, I take mental images of the hand-carved, lighted pumpkins on every porch. This town is completely invested in the holiday, from each decorated storefront to the Halloween tinsel that hangs from the lampposts. While the kids have all gone home, the sound of light music and people enjoying each other's company filters through the air. Since it's a small town, not many places are open at this time of night, but the homes look friendly and warm.

When we arrive at the door, Sparrow unlocks it for Lily and allows her to head upstairs first as she hands her the keys to the door at the top of the stairs. "This one," Sparrow says firmly. Lily nods, her face slightly scrunched, and reaches into her pockets. A handful of Halloween candy appears in her palm.

"Lily, where on earth did you get those? Have they been in your pocket all night?" Sparrow laughs as Lily shakes her head.

"One of the superheroes gave them to me." She throws the candy between us, giving me a wave before finding her way up the stairs. It's not exactly graceful, but she's managing better than I thought she would.

Sparrow turns her attention back to me, and I smile. We each choose a piece of the fun-sized candy, and I shove the rest into the pocket of Sparrow's sweater. Opening the wrapper, I take a bite and realize, once again, how sweet the candy is here in America. I make a face and put the rest of it in my pocket, trying to will myself to remember it's there before it melts further. Sparrow is finishing off her candy and licking a hint of chocolate off her mouth, weaving a web of desire over me.

She looks up at the stars above, her eyes taking on a peaceful look. I step beside her and look up too, amazed at how bright the earth's shining memories above us seem to look on a clear fall night.

"You dressed as Seb tonight," she says happily.

I smile at this and turn to face her. "I did."

As our eyes meet, she shifts her sweater closer around her, and a dimple appears on her face. I hold my breath and watch it release into the air with a puff of white from its warmth. If she notices I'm nervous, she's being kind by not pointing it out.

"Good choice."

I nod and dare to reach down and take her hand. I shift my fingers slowly, one by one, through hers. Now, it's her turn to inhale and hold her breath.

"Is someone watching?" She doesn't move her eyes from mine, and we both know she's asking this question strictly to see if I'm pretending.

"I'm sure they are," I say with a grin and without confirming. My shoulder still feels the weight of her head from the tavern. I can't hold in my curiosity anymore. I need to know what happened. Now that I'm holding her hand, I can't and won't do any more before I have the facts. "Sparrow, what happened with Jacques?"

She lifts her chin a bit and shifts her mouth to the side. "He ... I ... nothing," she says with a defeated sigh.

My free hand clenches into a fist while the one holding hers softens. "Did he hurt you?"

She shakes her head.

"Reject you?"

Another shake of head.

"Sugar, you're killing my heart here."

Her feet inch a bit closer to mine, our breath now close enough to mingle between us. "You don't need to find creative ways to get rid of him if that's what you're asking."

I let out a little sigh of relief but keep my voice clear. "It is."

"No, he just ... he wasn't ..." she starts. *You.* That's what I want her to say. And I suddenly wish I could read her as easily as I can read music. When she's hiding, I can't. I see her, but none of the notes make sense. And I have no idea what she's trying to tell me right now.

"You should get inside," I say as my voice cracks.

"You don't want to get cold."

"I'm already cold," she whispers.

Her sweater has shifted off her shoulder, and before I can think too much about what I'm doing, I release her hand to reach over and nestle it back around her, the texture of it branding my fingers.

Her chocolatey eyes peeking up at me are warming me through. I take a deep breath, my arms sliding down. I see her hand start to extend like we're puzzle pieces, needing the other to feel whole. But instead of lacing my fingers through hers again, I pull my hand back, leaving some space between us.

"You're . . . disappointed?" I ask while hoping she isn't. Again, she shakes her head. And before I realize what's happening, Sparrow's arms are wrapped around me. She tucks her ear close to my heart like it's the thing she's been wishing to do all night. Her hands grip my shirt. At first, I think it's because she's still cold. But then I realize she's just fine, her frame warm against mine. I rest my cheek on the top of her head and hold her close.

I know her enough to know that she wouldn't hold me like this if she really was interested in Jacques. I know she wouldn't hold me like this if she didn't want something more. And like a Magic Shell topping, sweetness cracks over my heart.

When it comes to her, all my words are still stuck— so easy in my mind and so difficult to get out. There are moments in life where, no matter how much I've worked through healing the hurt from the past, sometimes a haunting memory will bring me to my knees. And I'm frozen.

"Sparrow," I finally whisper when five or twenty minutes have passed.

"Hmm?" She hums.

"You really see me?"

She stiffens slightly. A chill from a gust of wind rattles through my spine, the scent of her vanilla meeting the smoke that laces the air from a nearby fire.

"*Oui.*" The word echoes through the still quiet night all around us. I grin as we grip each other a little tighter, the sweetest thing I could have ever hoped for wrapped around me.

It turns out, long after we left each other, I am up until three in the morning, trying to find the right notes and words because I have to be sure to somehow never forget that one of the most magical moments of my life was seeing Sparrow studying the stars and choosing to hug me under an autumn night sky.

Chapter Twenty

Sparrow

I'm on my way to grab something for dinner at our local farmers' market, still humming "La Vie en Rose" from our slow dance in the bakery and trying to concentrate on something other than Rafe dressed as Seb. It's not working well. Especially not after the way he played the piano at the tavern and realizing he seems to know how to hold me just right.

The problem is that I'm scared. Terrified. And even looking at life through rose-colored glasses isn't going to wipe away the years of hiding and the deep desire in me to somehow know, with certainty, that I can have the kind of love my parents shared.

"A good song," a rich voice says behind me. I freeze and turn to find Jacques with some farm-fresh eggs in a tote bag and some locally made jam.

"Jacques, hello—or *bonjour!*"

He grins sweetly. *"Bonjour,* Rory!" He looks at my tote bag of nothing and grins. "Looks like we had the same idea, although it doesn't look like you're having much success."

I smile at him and try to push down the anxiety creeping up my spine.

"My mother used to sing that song," he says. Unlike when I'm with Rafe, something in me constricts, and I can't find the words to mention my parents.

"How's work?" I ask, attempting light conversation.

"Good, good. I'm thinking of signing a contract— to stay after all." A look of questioning crosses his face, like he's very interested in my reaction, before I see it fade.

And I do my best to stay composed. Because if he stays, that means there could've been more of a chance for us to get to know each other after all. And Rafe is still leaving. Something I've had trouble holding on to lately.

"How was Halloween?" he asks.

I can't contain the smile that crosses my face. "It was . . . magic."

Jacques gives me a puzzled grin, his button-down shirt and classic cardigan advertising his good fashion sense. At the moment, all I can think of is how Rafe would wear it better. And my heart does a little skip. As much as the man before me used to occupy my thoughts, I think of Rafe telling me I'm brave. I think of how it felt to be in his arms. Even though we agreed not to get our hearts involved (well, I came up with the idea, and he went along with it), my heart is very much involved. And I know what I need to do.

"Excuse me, Jacques? I'm so sorry, but I need to go."

He looks rightfully confused. "But you didn't get anything."

I let out a laugh. "I'm not so sure about that yet."

My fingers fly over my phone, and I just hope that the man who held me last is close by enough to see it.

It's been a rush since I first laid eyes on Rafe. And something in me has snapped.

How anxious I am without him is the degree of peace I feel when I'm with him. My stomach twirls as I feel a pull to see him and be near him. And little does he know that I wait to see him every day. That when I'm not seeing him, I'm hoping to see him. I'm always waiting to find any valid reason to ask him to stay or come back.

I turn the corner of the store to climb the stairs to my apartment, and there, sitting on the steps outside my door, is Rafe. His hair is slightly disheveled, like he's run his fingers through it a few times. His denim-blue t-shirt is wrinkled in one spot, another indicator he's been pulling on it. Could it be that he's just as nervous to see me as I am to see him?

He's here. I give him a slow smile and walk to my door. The energy crackles between us, and I don't miss the addictive smell of him already filling the space outside my apartment.

He grins and stands, a look of relief in his eyes and a box of pastries beside him.

We walk up the stairs, him trailing behind me, and already I can feel tingles moving up my back and through my fingers. I stop at the door and pray he doesn't see how my key shakes in my hand. I get my answer when the key knocks against the lock before I can insert it. I wince but set it straight and get us through the door.

I motion for Rafe to put down the pink pastry box

from the French bakery in Boston that I love and watch as he carefully puts it on the counter. He handles them like they're valuable—yet another reason I'm undone. I don't even know when he would've gotten those, but I tuck away the fact that he even did.

We haven't said a word to each other yet, and I don't know what the rules are right now, but I fear that any sound will break whatever magic is happening between us. From the look on his face, Rafe understands and feels the same.

He points to my empty tote, and I just shrug. I'll worry about dinner later.

Rafe rocks back and forth on his heels and moves his hand to run it through his hair before he stops and puts it back at his side. A boyish look crosses his face as he clasps a hand behind his back while grabbing his other arm. He's adorable, and I don't know how I will ever get over the way his hair falls lightly over his forehead. The way his eyes can tell me the weather of his heart. The way I now crave him, like I've been hungry for love for years, and he's the first glimpse of it I've ever actually seen. He turns his perfect profile toward the window, and I take the opportunity to soak him in, the parting sunlight outlining his lashes and his full mouth.

Rafe is gorgeous, but he doesn't seem to know it. It's disarming. And he's not immune to aging, but it adds character. The slight lines around his eyes are more etched when he laughs. The scar near his eyebrow pulls and shifts his face when he raises a brow. When he smiles, the indents near his jaw only make his dimples shine more. I think of how much more handsome he'll be as he ages. The way the creases and lines will only make him more endearing.

He turns toward me, his eyes intense and a little

hesitant. Whatever line we've crossed, we both know we're not leaving the same way we entered this apartment. The least I can do is give him caffeine for the journey.

I point toward the stovetop coffeepot, and he nods slightly. I move close to the stove and stop when his arm lightly crosses me. He points to himself, and I nod. He wants to take care of it—take care of me. As he fills the pot with water, I allow myself to watch his movements.

I watch his hands move, carefully measuring and methodically in motion. He does everything with intention. From the notes he chooses to each word in the songs he sings. The way he moves through this world is like music because everything he does *is* music. Fast, slow, unsure, confident . . . it's all beautiful.

For a moment, I think of how normal this feels. Him being in my home. Him *being* my home. I've never felt this way for a man but have also rarely ever felt like this—as if I want to stay a while and not wonder about the world I'm missing because this, being near each other, is enough. And it's then that I realize that the gnawing feeling of loneliness I've felt here in my home isn't wrapped around me now. Feeling empty is like a memory with space between me and the constant companion loneliness used to be.

We're still playing the no-talking game as he gestures back toward the pastry box. I nod, and he opens it, revealing the croissants that are the best found in the States—the only ones better found in Paris. I wouldn't know that to be true myself, but I remember my father taking me there where my mother thought they were the best. He said he could tell when she really missed Paris and those croissants were the cure every time. It's hard to imagine that Boston, of all places, would be the place that puts croissants on the map for me, but I trust what my father told me.

My eyes burn at the gesture Rafe has made. He went to Boston just to get them, and now, as he holds out a croissant in his hands, I swear I suddenly catch a glimpse of who he must've been as a young man. Slightly shy. Timid. Uncertain of the world. A flash of anger moves through my heart at the idea that his parents have had years with him and never really seen him. They still don't see him. I suddenly feel robbed of all the days I've waited for him, not believing someone like him was walking the earth too.

His eyes shift to the floor, as if he's also thinking about something, before he meets my eyes again. As I reach for the croissant, our hands touch, and neither of us pulls away. The pulsing through my body starts at my fingers and charges up to my heart, which is suddenly beating so loudly through my chest that I'm certain Rafe can hear it.

My eyes travel quickly to his heart to catch it beating so strongly it's shifting the fabric of his shirt. *Ok, so I'm not the only one.* He grins, using his free hand to rub the back of his neck, as if to confess that he's caught.

I release some air I've been holding, the sound of my exhale the only noise besides the ticking of the clock on the wall and the coffee now brewing on the stove.

Rafe reaches into the box and pulls out another croissant. Bending to catch my eyes, he lifts back up to his full height and lightly taps our croissants together. Cheers.

We smile softly at each other and move in to take a bite of the beautiful, buttery wonders. It's only two seconds in that I recognize how big of a bite I just took. My cheeks are slightly puffed out, and I'm trying to cover my mouth with my hand, my cheeks reddening at my own clumsiness. I was so distracted by whatever is happening in this moment that I bit off more than I could chew. Literally.

Just when I think I have it under control, I feel his hand wrap around mine, tiny dots of the flaky pastry stuck to his rough fingers.

I swallow the bite and steel myself to look up. When I do, it does not disappoint. Forest-green eyes meet mine, and suddenly, I see everything. Like I'm waking up for the first time and realizing that how I was seeing the world is nothing compared to how I could see it. He's unlocked whatever he's withheld so carefully from me before. There's no guardedness. Rafe is letting me see him fully, and if I thought the gesture of bringing my favorite pastry was sweet, this gesture takes my breath away.

It would take me years to decipher what he's showing me in this moment, his layers vaster than the galaxies above this tiny apartment. I inhale sharply and watch as his eyes lock in on my lips. He stares so intensely that I feel myself being pulled closer to him.

Without breaking his focus from my mouth, his finger circles around his own mouth to gesture that there's something on my lips. I breathe in slowly and lift my hand, my fingers brushing over croissant flakes. Tons of them. Like they are my new form of lip gloss. I try to chuckle, but really, the embarrassment takes over. Before I walked home, I applied some lip balm to protect against the cold air. I now regret this decision as I realize that the croissant has stuck to it like sugar on a powdered donut.

I manage to wipe some of the crumbs from my mouth, my hands trembling and my lips pulsing from the friction. When I meet Rafe's gaze, expecting to find laughter or pity, I find reassurance. I don't think another human has ever looked at me the way he is at this moment—appreciating me despite my blunder and staying close. His feet move a fraction toward me. One would hardly notice, but it was movement just the same.

His eyes shift again to my mouth, and he swallows. I reach my fingers to brush away more of the offending flakes when Rafe's hand meets mine. This time, he doesn't let go. He laces his fingers through mine, and when our palms touch, I suck in a breath. If I wasn't alive before, I am now. So very alive. I should be embarrassed, but ... I'm not. I'm actually liberated. I don't have to be perfect with him, and I force my eyes closed to etch this feeling into my bones. I'm wishing and willing it to sink in and never leave me.

He takes the arm with our hands and fingers entwined and wraps it around my back, pulling me closer to him.

I open my eyes to look up at him, an element of desire radiating out of him that causes me to shiver. His face is hovering just out of reach, his warm breath sweet and buttery, his skin radiating with that cedar-and-coffee smell that is just so him. I've never been so still in my life, waiting for what will happen next.

He tilts his head toward me, asking my permission.

I hitch my own breath and nod slightly, the heat from him warming not just my body but my soul. Rafe steadily breaks through the barrier that's hovering between us, his nose lightly brushing my cheek as he tilts his head and slightly nuzzles the side of my face, his scruff marking my skin. I inhale when I feel his eyelashes flutter closed and grip his hand around my back even tighter. I'm desperate to know what his kiss feels like.

I'm aching for it. If I'm going to be crushed by the feeling of love when he leaves, I know that having this memory of him will be worth it.

With his free hand, his calloused thumb swipes stubborn croissant flakes from my mouth so gently I almost miss it. He slowly traces my bottom lip, and I lean into the movement.

"I've got you, Sugar," he raggedly whispers against my mouth before his lips meet mine. Warmth moves through my system, and the magnetic pull that we share intensifies. He slowly moves from one end of my mouth to the other, tiny kisses touching stray flakes of buttery pastry, and I'm dying. His lips are like warm rose petals brushing against my skin and melting the butter leftover from the croissant. My heart is thrumming. I sway lightly from the emotion of it all and feel pulses of light as his palms guide my hips to rest gently against the counter.

He kisses me slowly and gently, and I feel him trembling from the intensity. He's layering me with affection. Layers and layers, like the pastry that started this otherworldly experience. Rafe stops kissing me for a moment, and I lean into him. I don't want to beg, but a small sound escapes me. I feel his breath moving in a staccato rhythm over my mouth, smell his warm scent, and still feel my lips pulsing from the ghost of his kiss. Our hands come unclasped but not before he pulls me closer to him so that we never lose contact. I search his eyes, now dark as a night sky over a forest with only hints of light. The universe is in them, and he's holding all the stars I've ever wished upon.

It's then I make a choice. I'm not ready to let him go just yet. So I wrap my free hand into his hair and feel when he lets his head relax into my touch. I let my fingers flow lightly through the tousled strands, then slide them down his neck and around until my fingers trace his stubble and the curve of his jaw. He moans softly, and I'm convinced it's the most alluring sound I've ever heard.

Now it's my turn to ask him for more. I tilt my head, any hesitation I may have had politely on pause. He nods and then shows me how much he'll meet me when I ask him to by lifting me up so that my legs wrap around his waist. Feeling his strength as he carries me breaks a wall in my heart. I feel tears sting my eyes as I pull him closer. I press my lips to him and start to tell him all the things I haven't had the courage to say before. How much he's changed my life. How I never knew there could be anyone like him. How scared I am. With his hands under my thighs, he guides me back gently to sit on the counter, our mouths never losing contact. He meets everything I'm telling him and tells me, in his own way, how much he's in awe of me. He's wanted to do this since we met. And I've unraveled him in the best way.

His calloused thumb—suddenly my favorite thing— traces my spine where my high-waisted jeans end and my skin begins, and I'm branded. I've never been kissed like this in my life, and just when I feel like I should probably put on the brakes and hide, I do something I never thought I would—I let my heart move even closer. We started to see the shoreline, and I threw us back into deeper water.

My lips part to invite him in, and when I finally taste him, everything is light and comets and things I've never dared to dream. It's gold and stardust. I let out a content sound and feel the effect it has on him as his hands move to trace the flow of my hips, the bend in my waist, and the curve of my neck. He's on a mission to map me, and I let him explore. I run my hands up his chest, over his tight shoulders, and feel how he plays me in a way that's art. Like his hands would play his guitar, finding the notes and melodies, all his focus on making the perfect song—so he is with me. He's learning and finding what would make me sing.

When I finally open my eyes, his face is all that I see. Everything I want to see.

I look into his eyes and repeat the motion he did to me earlier, hovering in front of his face, allowing my eyelashes to brush his cheeks. Except, this time, I softly leave a trail of kisses for him to remember and trace back when I'm no longer with him tonight—on his stubbled jaw, the scar on his eyebrow, and finally, the dimple in his cheek. It's not nearly what he's given me, but I do my best to make him feel cared for too.

His hand gently covers one side of my face, and with the back of the other, he wipes the tears streaming down my cheek. Sometime during the past several minutes, which I can now say were the best moments of my life, I started crying. I started healing. And the man in front of me is the reason.

Rafe's face is a mixture of awe, intensity, and care. I grin softly, my body still pulsing with emotion. He studies my face and then surprises me in the most stunning way. Instead of pushing for more or speaking a word, he hugs me.

This isn't a hug for the faint of heart. He wraps a hand in my hair and cradles my head against him. Even though his breathing is shallow, his pulse is steady and sure beneath my ear. I wrap my own arms around him and hold on for dear life. Every argument I've put between us now feels exposed and weary. The protection of his hold and the reverence of this moment allow me to take a deep breath. He's letting me breathe.

I let my walls down when I kissed him senseless, and now he's protecting me—telling me I'm safe with him and letting me rest in the warmth of being held by someone who wants nothing more than for me to feel how much he wants me to glow.

Chapter Twenty-One

Rafe

I sit in my room at Graham's house, a coffee mug in one hand and my face cradled in the other. Whatever I thought my life was before Sparrow is completely undone. When I left her yesterday, I had never been more grateful for a series of moments in my life. I didn't intend to kiss her—I wanted to, of course, but I didn't intend to. I just wanted to share the same air. Now, we've shared much more. After talking to Lily, I was ready to tell Sparrow everything.

Yesterday, I met with another singer in Boston while he was in town for a stop on his tour. He wants me to write a song for him, and we had an amazing brainstorming session. I think it might be one of my best songs yet. He invited me to meet him in Nashville next week, and since it lines up with my other meetings there, I would've been a fool to say no. So, I didn't. I'll have to leave a few days earlier than planned, but I'm hoping Sparrow will understand.

I know that it's partially from being here that I have

this new confidence, but I couldn't get Sparrow out of my mind. So, when I remembered the bakery specializing in *viennoiseries*—a perfect blend of bread meets pastry—and the croissants she loves so much, I knew I had to stop. Had to.

I was disappointed when she wasn't home, but right as I was about to walk away, she sent me a text. I had given myself thirty minutes to wait, and twenty-nine minutes later, the door opened, and like the angel she is, she appeared. I also didn't mean to stay so quiet, but the silence felt necessary, given all that I was feeling.

When we started another sweet dance of silence, I leaned into the moment and saw on her face what I hadn't fully seen before—that she wants me too. She wants me for *me*.

When I finally saw what I hoped for, something in me broke. And I spent the next several minutes lost in a world we were building all on our own. I memorized the feeling of her hips under my hands, the gentle slope of her waist, and the way her soft lips can feel like both a feather and an avalanche. I keep replaying her hands in my hair and the sound she made when I traced her spine. I couldn't even bring myself to change my sweater last night—it smelled like her. And the way she traced kisses across my face . . . well, I'm pretty sure I forgot to breathe for a bit.

And after we were wrapped up in each other, pushing and pulling—it was so much that all I could think to do was hold her. To show her that she doesn't have to stay in a castle on her own. That I can be her safe place. The best part was, she hugged me back. No one has ever treasured me the way she did in that moment. I swipe at my eyes, thinking about it. I've always been a poet with my songs but not much of a crier—until moving here.

"Get it together, man," I mutter.

I don't think I can. Even if I leave Birch Borough next week, which was always the plan, Sparrow now holds a part of me. What started as a moment on the train and an impulse to step in and help her get the man she wanted—which, I can admit, was stupid—has given me what I never saw coming: a glimpse at a life of love.

I sing about love for everyone else, and I've never had my own. Noémie played a game with my heart. I wasn't enough, so I had to keep chasing it. Earning it. Making myself worthy of it. The same is true with my parents. With Sparrow, I can feel it kindling. But I don't know where her heart is at. I don't know if what we shared completely derailed her considering any other options but me. I'm not even sure she'd take me if she knew the truth. It's one thing to see me the way she did; it's another to discover the parts of myself that I've yet to share. And after feeling what it's like to kiss her and have her in my arms, I'm terrified to know the answer.

I pace across the floor for God knows how long until I hear a rap at the door.

"Rafe? You all right, man?"

Attacking the door like it might hold the answer to my questions, I swing it open to find Graham home early from his business trip. He winces.

"Sorry, I'm stressed."

He looks me over and shakes his head with a slight smile. "Man, you look terrible." He looks at me again, and I don't know whether to laugh or punch him for how he's sizing me up. "You're in love," he finally concludes.

I hang my head at how easy it was for him to guess. Taking a brief look into the rest of the house to ensure no one else is lurking, I pull him into the room and slam the door. Everything outside is scary and unknown. I'm breathing heavily like I just ran from something chasing me.

Putting down his travel bag, he sits on the edge of the small couch in the corner and clasps his hands together, a little concerned and a little amused. "So, what are you going to do about it?"

A weird laugh escapes me. "I don't know!" I'm unhinged, and I don't even care anymore.

Graham is smug. It's decided. I definitely want to punch him.

I start pacing. "Should I write another song?"

He shakes his head.

"Tell her?"

He shakes his head again.

"Take her on a date?"

Graham thinks about this but then quickly does the move I hate the most right now—he shakes his head.

"Graham, I swear if you don't stop with that . . ." I shake my hands toward him. "That . . . stupid shaking-your-head thing." He raises his eyebrows, and I stop pacing to sink into the couch. I shut my eyes tightly and take a deep breath. "I'm sorry. That was uncalled for. I'm just . . ."

"In love?"

I crack open my eyes slightly to see Graham looking at me without judgment. He really is a solid guy. It makes me feel even worse for wanting to punch him a minute ago. I rub my face, disheveling myself even more.

"I don't know what to do about it. She drives me nuts. Hides my guitar picks. Declares she'll only marry a Frenchman to the world—I mean, who does that?" My question is rhetorical, so I keep going. "Makes the best muffins I've ever had. Kisses like a freaking miracle. Has me so nuts that I'll end up with coffee stains on me for the rest of my life because I'll try to keep them off of her."

"And this was supposed to be fake, or at the very least, you weren't planning on staying . . ." he summarizes. And then he seems to hear what I said only a few seconds ago. "Wait. You *kissed* her?"

"Yes! I don't know what the heck I was thinking, but she's got me so upside down . . ." I trail off. My hair feels like it could hit the ceiling it's been pulled so much.

Graham leans back on the couch and rests his arm on the armrest. Thankfully, because he's a gentleman, he doesn't rag me about it or ask for details. "But you haven't told her the truth?" I fix him with a glare, and he holds up his hands in surrender. "The whole truth."

I shake my head slightly.

"Why?"

My jaw clenches so tight it will be a miracle if I don't have to visit a dentist after this conversation. "You know why."

"No, *you* know why. I don't, actually."

I sigh and pull out my guitar. Nothing seems to calm me like the guitar, apart from Sparrow. But she also drives me wild. So, guitar it is.

"Is she familiar with your father's brand?"

I shake my head. "It's not me."

"But it *is* a part of who you are. It's your last name."

I try to deny it, but he's right. My heart is beating faster, and I wish there was a way that I could skip all these uncomfortable bits. I wish I could calm the anger brewing within me. And I realize I'm so angry because I let my fear surrounding my parents interrupt my fear of telling Sparrow the full story. I haven't even given her a choice.

"I left everything behind and moved to LA to have a life so I wouldn't be defined or controlled by my family. How do I even talk about it? Because she lost both of her parents, and they loved her. My parents are still here, and they hate what I'm doing with my life."

"That can't be true."

I casually strum my guitar, and Graham nods for me to continue.

"It's true." That's all I can get out.

Graham lets out a slow whistle. "I'm sorry, man."

I put the guitar aside because it's making me remember the way I played my fingers on Sparrow's spine, like my favorite chord progression. That woman has invaded my life. I stand and start conducting the air with my hands.

"I still live in LA! I have an apartment. I have a car. I've lived around the world . . . this is a small town. I have my music to think about . . . I'm here to write! She makes me want to leave everything behind . . ." I'm now so worked up that I do the best thing I can think of—I take another sip of coffee.

"And you want to tell her," Graham observes.

"Of course I want to tell her!"

"And it seems like she's the reason you're able to write again." I growl in frustration at how insightful he is and resume pacing. "You still need to tell her." He's right, of course. Graham gestures toward my pacing and lifts a brow. "What's the truth here?"

I groan. "The truth is, I saw her, and everything stopped. It was like all those sentimental movies we've seen and called fake have laughed in my face. Our connection was so real it felt like lightning. Even when I'd only seen her on the train, I couldn't get the image of the woman with the big sweater and the darkest honey-colored hair out of my mind." I'm wearing out the floor with my movements, and Graham just keeps listening.

"I never thought I'd see her again. And then, BAM! There she was. And when her eyes met mine, my heart danced. I mean, I write love songs—and even I thought it must be a joke. Nothing could be that real. Nothing could be that scripted. But then she said she would only date someone French—for the second time—and I froze."

I am tired at this part of the story, so I sit back down and keep my gaze focused on the floor. "It was like I forgot everything bad in my life just at the sight of her. If I had told her my last name then, I would have felt like I was cheating. Like if she knew who I really was, I wouldn't have earned it. I wouldn't have known that she truly liked me for me and not because of my family or the fact that Paris was home for a long time." I try to add a lighthearted touch. "I could've used that to my advantage, you know."

Graham sees through my bull. "Oh, I know. Good thing you're too upstanding of a guy."

I scoff lightly. "It felt dishonest. But now, because she doesn't know everything about me, I still feel dishonest."

Graham stands to his feet and rolls up his sleeves while he looks out the window, still thinking. Always thinking. "I get that. I do."

I nod with relief, and he holds up his hand.

"However," he starts, and I pick up my guitar to attempt to do something again with my racing mind. I'm really going to have to go for a run or something to help with this chaos. "How can she like you for you if you don't actually tell her who you really are?"

My hand slips on my guitar with a scratching sound that makes us wince. He sure knows how to punch someone with his words.

"You made your decision with the knowledge you had at the time. But if she doesn't know all of you, then I don't think it's love at all."

I know he's right. But I also don't miss how his jaw tightens, as if he knows from experience. "G, what happened to you?"

I see a flash of fear cross over his features. I've never seen a crack in his armor. He's always the polished one, the clever one. He says everything straightforward and matter-of-factly. He's funny if you can get enough time with him to wear down his stoicism. I didn't think it was possible for him to have a secret he hasn't told me, and I realize how much I've missed him. He's been my best friend even though we haven't lived in the same place since we both lived in LA. He's been the one I could turn to—clearly, since I'm now living in his apartment, staying here until I figure my life out. He told me to come here, no questions asked, and he's always been that way with me.

"Another time," is all he says before focusing back on me. "Seems to me that you know something needs to change if you think Sparrow is worth it." I nod aggressively, and he nods back. We're on the same page. "Ok, so what are you going to do about it?"

"I don't know. Telling her of my true heritage right *now*, after all that's happened between us, just doesn't seem like enough."

Graham crosses his arms in the stance I've seen him use when he means business. "You need to make a move."

"Well, I kind of did . . ."

He raises his brows. "A kiss isn't enough."

"You weren't there. Not that I would've wanted you there, but this was not a normal kiss. I can't . . . words aren't enough." I don't even hide the grin on my face. It was the best moment of my life, and I'm not ashamed of it.

"Wow. You two kiss one time, and the musician and lyricist is stumped."

I nod enthusiastically before I realize I look like a teenage boy and not like the man who needs to make the next move. "It was more than once." I'm grinning like a lovesick fool. But then I think of leaving or, worse, Sparrow choosing Jacques when I leave after all . . . because he'll be here. "Graham?"

He uncrosses his arms.

"I've never loved like this before," I admit.

Graham rubs his chin with his hand and then pauses, a sad smirk on his face.

"What do I do? How do I make this right?"

He stands and walks toward the door. It's only when he's halfway through that he turns to look over his shoulder. I motion for him to tell me whatever is on his mind and immediately regret it when I hear his next words. "Are you still leaving?"

I nod briefly. I have to go, even if it's just to Nashville for a bit.

"Then tell her. Oh, and you remember she has a best friend, right?"

I think of Lily and her fierceness for Sparrow and sink deeper, hoping the sound of the door shutting behind Graham isn't a sign for what's to come.

I love you, but there's no way I'm letting you leave the house like this."

She gestures to my outfit and slinks onto my couch, her legs draped over the side and her head propped on a pillow. Lily lifts one hand higher up in the air, her fingers holding a glass of rosé that swirls as she speaks.

"Lily, you've gotta help me."

She smirks. "Well, that's obvious."

I groan. "Lily, you don't understand. This was never supposed to happen. And you should've seen his face. Devastating."

"Well, he likes you. I've been saying that from the start, I'll have you know. You were just too stubborn to see it." She crosses her arms in a satisfied-with-herself way, and I watch as Lily checks out my current state.

My hair is in a haphazard bun. I'm wearing sweats with a coffee stain on them. I can feel a speck of icing or some sort of sugar on my cheek, and my eye makeup hasn't been removed since last night. She doesn't approve.

Rafe and I kissed. Heaven and earth moved. And when it was over, and he left my apartment, I ... panicked. It was the kind of kiss that changes your life, and you feel it while it's happening. I've been moved across countries and across worlds with that kiss. But my life is here.

Which is why, for the first time, I've called out of work to avoid a man who is going to haunt me for the rest of my life. He's been calling, and I've ignored him. He's been texting, and I've silenced them all. He broke through my walls, and I can feel myself building them up again like I'm trying to defend myself from an oncoming war. I hated the look of confusion in his eyes when I avoided him at the café yesterday. After we shared our kiss, I was walking on clouds ... until I fell into the abyss. It was all so real. Too real.

"What am I going to do?" I say quietly.

"About what? The fact that you met a beautiful man from whom even you can't find a way to hide or that you look like a deranged raccoon?"

My mouth drops open. "How. Could. You? I am fragile. I am vulnerable. I am shook."

Lily smirks and takes another sip of her rosé. "You're not on social media. So, my comments actually help build your resilience. I express my love in a multitude of ways."

I love her too much to fight, so instead, she gets a throw pillow chucked at her head. Her hand goes higher into the air to avoid impact, and a tiny drop of rosé falls from the glass onto her cheek. Lily's eyes go wide, and I let out a laugh. I might as well have sprayed her with a water gun for the dramatics of her wiping the one spilled drop from her cheek. She shakes her head as if she can't wait to retaliate, and I sink deeper into the couch.

"I don't think Paris is for me. And when I say 'Paris,' I really mean all of it." The confession slips out before I pass it through a mental filter.

It's a moment before Lily recovers, and I see her eyeing me again. This time, she wants details. "You don't normally talk like this . . ."

I look out at the rain gently forming drops on the windowpanes and watch as one seems to make a fragmented path toward the sill. While most of the drops join and create streams of water, it's the one on its own that I can't seem to shake. "I feel like I'm being punished—that's how it feels."

I turn to catch a glimpse of Lily's face as she takes in what I just said. Her blue eyes flash with empathy. "Rory . . ."

"No, let me get this out."

I wipe a rogue tear, much like the one from the wet glass, and look my best friend in the eyes. "I missed my number. I can't seem to get over this frustration that feels like, at some point in my life, my number came up, and I was on a call, or I missed my name being called . . . It's like everyone got a manual except me." I manage to get that much out before swallowing.

"I feel something with Rafe . . . so deeply," I choke. "And before I can make sense of it, before I can talk myself out of walking away . . . my heart is locking itself up, with or without my permission." I stand up and start pacing in front of the record player. "And I'm lonely. And I'm . . . scared."

I look toward a picture of my parents and me when I was a little girl. Next to it is an image of my mother standing on a bridge, looking out at the Seine. "And I'm mad." I clench my fists but can't seem to raise my voice.

"I'm so mad, Lily." The anger is making its way into fatigue. My limbs are heavy with it.

Lily stands and leans her head against my shoulder and watches the rain with me, the weight of my words sinking into my bones.

"Can't you just tell him? Tell him that you're scared. Tell him you don't want to lose him. Heck, tell him that you're bleeding out because you miss him."

I wipe my face with the edge of my sweatshirt and look around my cute little apartment with so much character it could have its own novel. "I—I don't think I trust myself to love him. And if I'm too scared to try and too scared to let go, then that leaves me exactly where I am now. And he's too beautiful to get caught in that."

It's the first time I've articulated what's really going on in my heart—the fight of fear that's been warring within me. What if I ask Rafe to stay, and he resents me and leaves anyway? What if I don't let Rafe in on how I feel about him and realize no one will ever make me as happy as he does? What if I try to find a way to do long distance with Rafe and realize I was never what he needed all along?

"Lily, I'm so glad I have you. Honestly, I can't imagine my life without you. I'm grateful every single day—even when you keep me humble with your comments."

Lily grins. "I don't have all of the answers, but whatever is happening here . . ." She motions across her mind. "And here . . ."—she points to her heart—"is not letting you really live. Trust me, I'm living in it too."

I want to ask her what she means, but she's already shaking her head as if to say, "Don't go there." I nod but make a mental note that there's something Lily hasn't been telling me—and I get the feeling she doesn't want to burden me. But one day, when she's ready to open up, like she's waited for me to open up to her, I'll be ready to listen.

"He doesn't deserve to have anyone mess with his heart," Lily continues. "I know you don't mean it, but you're hurting him. In your silence, you're hurting him."

"I know. And it's killing me."

"But the thing is, life isn't certain. I know you know this. Tragedies happen. People let us down. Even happy moments don't last. And so, it's up to us to hold on to what we can." She leads us back to the couch and takes another sip of her drink. "And out there, probably three or four streets away, is a very attractive man, who happens to play guitar and put up with me . . . which is a miracle, honestly. And he happens to have a love for 'Sugar.'"

I sniff and cast my eyes onto the blanket I've wrapped myself in. The truth of it cuts like a knife. A sharp one. "Yes, there is."

Lily stays for a little longer before I decide to work through some of my doubts by going to the place I love most: the bakery. I plan to try the French muffin recipe I've been perfecting again and methodically meld ingredients so that I can feel a sense of accomplishment in seeing them come together to bring someone else joy. If only there were such a recipe for my heart.

The air is heavy with something I can't quite name. While the faint smell of sugar and melted butter waltzes with the scent of roasted coffee, another feeling lingers. My father would've said it's the "fallen soufflés." The moment you know that the heat of life has created a hole inside that will knock you to your knees as soon as it gets the chance. Sometimes, you think you can outlast it, but there's a moment when you realize there's nothing you can do to avoid it.

Another memory floats in of Rafe and me dancing in the corner of this bakery. He had asked me to make a wish and hold onto it. And I did. But what he doesn't know is that the wish I made was for him. I wished I could let the pain out and trust myself to love him freely. But that wish hasn't come true, which is why I can't seem to do the thing I want the most: hold him for as long as he'll let me. I don't think I'm very brave after all.

I haven't answered his messages. I know I need to, but I haven't been able to bring myself to get past the words that are caught in my throat. They beat against my heart and race through my mind.

After baking a few batches of French muffins, I also make some crème brûlée macarons. The air now smells like cinnamon, butter, and caramelized sugar. I've even reorganized the pastry case and arranged all the supplies and ingredients for the morning pastry chef. I should arrange the coffee shipment and organize it for the open mic night tomorrow, but I don't. It's too close to the stage, and that would make it someplace *he* has been recently.

There's a chill in the air as I look around the empty shop, and the memories flood my brain. The place where Rafe and I first officially met. The stool where he sits and keeps me company in silence (mostly). The feeling when I heard him sing for the first time. The croissant kiss that has ruined me for all other kisses. It hits me that this town is now filled with him. My safe place has become fragmented, and I'm not sure how to move forward.

I want him deeply, but he's not what I expected. After talking with Lily and baking furiously, I'm only more convinced than ever that we're not going to work. He's had enough people close to him try to take his dreams from him, and I won't be one of them, even if letting him go ruins my chances of living mine. Because, in such a short time, he's become my dream. But after my father passed, my secret is that I promised myself I wouldn't ever let another person into my heart who could shatter it. And after feeling how much his kisses would shatter the plans I've made for my life . . . well, there's only so much a woman can take.

It's a prince or a promise, and I'm a woman of my word.

No matter how much I may want to feel what it would be like to wake up with him next to me. Or to know what his voice sounds like first thing in the morning. Or to switch out his coffee grounds at home so he accidentally drinks decaf. Or to hide his guitar picks so he's constantly on an Easter egg hunt. Or to think that if I could only give in to my heart, I could walk home to him one day. The thought takes my breath away until I notice my hands are burning. The towel between my hands is wrung dry, and my hands are flaming red. I was so lost in thought I hadn't noticed.

The overhead bell jingles, and I turn to see Rafe standing in the doorframe as if conjured from my dreams. His hair is glistening from the light rain falling outside. I take him all in, and my eyes burn with the beauty of him. I used to think he was handsome, but now that I know him, he's so much better than what is visible on the surface.

Rafe looks at me like he needs me. It's a look that's

going to haunt me. I'm sure of it. It's a look I'll remember when I'm older and someone references the one they let get away. He shrugs off his navy sweater and places it on a chair to dry.

The white t-shirt he's wearing underneath grips his biceps and the planes of his chest. The air feels dry and taut. I lick my lips to try to keep them from sticking. He slowly moves his right hand through his cinnamon hair and shakes his head slightly.

His bottom lip gets stuck to the side of his mouth in a death grip, the emotion humming between us. Finally, he looks up. "I'm leaving," he says.

My stomach drops. My eyes begin to burn, and I will my hands to stay where they are. I feel the desperation aching in my fingers. I feel the hope in me dying, its wings slowly clipped with each passing moment. If he notices the shift, he doesn't let on. He walks toward me and away from me at the same time and stands in front of the coffee station.

He reaches for a coffee cup on the drying rack and spins it in his hands. He won't crush it, but he toys with it like he could. I watch his fingers flex and grip and wish I were that hunk of ceramic right now.

I hear the sounds of the shop, the ice machine, the refrigerators, and none of it matters. The whole shop could crumble, and I wouldn't have the heart to rebuild it. He's leaving. And I pushed him away. I want to say *don't*, but the word is caught in my throat. This time, my silence is slicing us apart rather than bringing us together.

"When?" I instantly hate how gravelly the word sounds from my mouth.

He doesn't look at me, but I see his jaw shift. "Tomorrow."

"Tomorrow?" I gasp. His gaze shoots up in question. I compose my face and lift my chin. I'm too good at pretending to be unaffected, because his shoulders slump slightly, and he resumes spinning the cup.

His brows indicate he's debating internally, but I see the moment he gives up. His eyes search the ceiling, and it's maddening. The way he affects me is unfair. I keep trying to convince myself that he's not what I want. *He can't be what I want.*

He lets out a mirthless laugh, spins to the small sink, and places the ruthless ceramic into the basin. I watch him reach for the soap and rag and turn on the water. His muscles are tense and unyielding. He's now washing the cup he touched, and I can't help but feel like he's doing the same with me.

Only, I'm not a cup. And all the years of me being on a shelf and keeping men away from my heart doesn't magically wash away because Rafe demolished my walls. Because he did. I can admit that. And I don't think there will ever be enough material to rebuild when he's gone.

"Why?" I whisper.

Rafe grips the mug in one hand and presses the heel of his hand into his eyes. This is the move he makes when he's frustrated. This is the move that he makes when he can't think straight. Since he didn't dry his hands first, drops of water run down his face, making it look like he's crying. And when he wipes them and opens those forest eyes toward me, I wonder if the water left on his face actually is some of his own.

"You know why," he says, defeated. There's no blame. Just truth. He turns back toward the sink, and I hear a sniff from his direction.

And suddenly, I'm thinking about how, at this time

tomorrow, he'll be gone. I won't have to worry each time I hear the bell over the door. My heart rate will get a break from the times he brings in his guitar and sings quietly in the corner. I'll finally be alone to sort through my emotions and fear.

But he sees me.

Which is the only explanation for why I'm suddenly at his back, my hands clasped around his waist and my cheekbone digging into his back. He stills, the water still running. I feel the muscles of his shoulders stiffen against my face, but I don't dare move.

Being this close, listening to him breathe, the in and out feeling of it against my own body, I feel him still doing his best to heal me.

And I'm too late.

He relaxes slightly and shuts off the water, allowing me to hold him like this. He stretches one hand to put the cup in the drainer but doesn't move farther, as if afraid to break the spell unfolding between us.

"Sparrow?" he whispers.

I shake my head. He reaches for a towel, and I feel it brushing my hands, still lodged against his middle.

When his hands are dry enough, he folds the towel and sets it next to the sink. His semi-dry hand, both warm and cool from his heat and the water, rests on top of my own.

"Sugar," he continues. He's no longer asking. "I know you won't let me love you," he says.

I hold my breath and feel my face heat.

"I wish you would," he chokes out. I hear him swallow, and my eyes burn.

I tip my head slightly, feeling a hot tear spill onto my face. And suddenly, they're flowing freely. I won't loosen my grip, so I rotate my face so the salty water won't reach his shirt. He must know I'm crying, but I refuse to have him take my tears along with my heart.

Instead of yelling at me or calling me on my lies, Rafe pulls me toward him gently. It isn't a hug for dear life but one of sympathy. "I'm sorry you're afraid," he whispers over his shoulder.

He grips my hands tighter in an act of kindness. He's being my anchor, even as I'm cutting the rope between us. I'm holding him and letting him go at the same time. And he knows it.

"You deserve this kind of love," he says.

I swallow, careful to keep my face angled away from his back. He lets the implied question linger until I'm able to answer. "What kind?" I breathe out.

I feel him slowly move his finger in a pattern across one of my hands. Back and forth, his calloused hand brands me. I focus on what he's saying and bite my lip the moment I realize what he's drawing: a heart. The movement stops as if he realizes I've gotten the message, and he gently unclasps my hands from his waist.

Without looking, he lightly shifts me away from him and moves toward the door. His shoes shuffle against the floor, a marked difference from his typically confident stride.

He stops at the entrance, his hand—the one that just wrote on my own—loosely holding the doorknob. I swallow, trying not to let out a sob. With every shallow breath, I feel a piece of myself breaking. But I'm too scared to let this turn out differently. What do you say when it's the end? As much as I hate this, I'm dying to find out.

"Rafe?" I plead. He pauses but doesn't look back, as if I could turn him to salt with one look. I inhale shakily. "What kind of love?"

Rafe turns the doorknob and cracks open the door. He breathes in the night air and tilts his head to the sky. This is goodbye. And it's a moment that is marking me. I'm sure of it. He turns his face slightly, his profile etched against the night.

"The full kind."

The bell jingles as the door closes, and I grip the counter before sliding to the floor. I cover my face in my hands and silently scream as I smell him, that beautiful cedar-and-coffee smell, heavy where his arms touched mine.

I've lost so many pieces of myself with each person who has left my life, and the one person who wants to show me love, the man I've fallen in love with . . . I don't have the strength to confess what he means to me. Running after him will only hurt him more if I can't get the words out. And I don't think my legs would move me anyway. Everything is spinning.

Can we ever come back from missed moments? It's like the words are suffocating me, and now I'm too late. Suddenly, the lies I've been telling myself turn to dust. Because he's worth all of it, and I denied myself my dream. His dream too. So I let the sorrow haunt me for tonight after all.

Chapter Twenty-Three

Rafe

Getting on the train this morning was one of the hardest things I've ever done in my life. No, actually, leaving Sparrow last night was one of the hardest things I've ever done. I knew she wasn't ready to let me into her heart completely. But, oh, how I had hoped.

I was ready to tell her all of it. Everything. But I knew that could sway her opinion. Again. And there's no way I'm going to have her in my life because of circumstances and not commitment. I've lived enough of my life for the expectations of others. My parents are the ones who tell me things to try to sway my behavior. And as much as I knew it could work in my favor, there was no way I was giving Sparrow any more incentive to choose me. She had to decide that herself. And she didn't.

If I didn't love her as much as I do, I might be bitter. Angry. Resentful. But I'm not. I'm sad for her. Because I know I would've spent the rest of my life showing her how much she's worth. And I would've been near her through every hard moment. I would've held her as we fell asleep, and I would've sung to her . . . anytime she wanted to listen. I can't say I won't write more songs about her because that's inevitable. The woman is my muse, and she will be for as long as I live, whether she knows it or not.

When Noémie took all my music, I thought I would never get over it. I thought it was the worst thing that could possibly happen to me. Now I'm realizing that while I loved her, I was never fully in love with her—there's a difference. So much of a difference that it's like standing in a shallow pond versus trying to stay afloat in a rushing river. I never had a chance to fight the current that is Sparrow. She pulled me under the second I saw her asleep on the train.

I'm now at Boston Logan airport, waiting at my gate before I head to Nashville. I have a few meetings I've set up there with the singer I met in Boston and some other country singers who are looking for a change in their style of lyrics. I even have a studio interested in my mixing abilities. I guess my demo got me further than I thought it would.

All in all, I should be so excited, but I'm not. It's the bittersweet feeling of your favorite show in its final episode. You loved it, and its leaving, and you know you'll never get a new episode to love again. It's trying to let go of something that you never wanted to say goodbye to in the first place.

The screen near my gate lights up with a message as my phone does the same. My flight is delayed. And instead of seeing this as a sign to stay or wait until a later date to figure out if Sparrow will break through her fear, I choose to put in my earbuds and go over a track that

I've been mixing, which may or may not be about the woman I'm leaving behind.

When people think of Nashville, they often think of country music and all the things that go with it. While they're not wrong, I've found Nashville to be the place I go when life doesn't make sense. It has rescued me a few times because of the connections I have and the feeling I have of being capable of anything while I'm there. I hope it can rescue me again.

After leaving my heart in a small town near Boston, I've been holed up in a studio used by some of the biggest country artists. Am I writing country music? No. But I am creating. It's been a week since I've left Birch Borough. I keep telling myself that it will get easier, that I won't miss the way Sparrow greets me in the morning. I tell myself, as I chew on a mediocre bagel and sip a slightly burnt cup of coffee, that I don't miss Sparrow's Beret and its maple croissants. To be fair, Nashville has great food. But I grabbed whatever was left over in the break room at the studio so I didn't have to go out in public and face . . . people.

I look out the windows that give a view over the street and see tourists milling about with their cameras out and ready. A guy in a cowboy hat just got stopped by a bunch of teenagers and is now crouched down and taking pictures with them. I don't envy him. It's wild to me how Broadway Street in Nashville looks like Hollywood Boulevard got replicated. But instead of fake awards in the windows, it's cowboy boots. And instead of street performers, it's open windows flowing with cover songs.

I'm not recognized here, and that's more than okay. But I am lonely, and so, in between recording sessions, I decide to call Graham. It's only two rings before he answers.

"Hey, buddy," he says. "Already missing me?"

The truth is, I am. But he already knows that. Still, I indulge him. "Something like that."

"Hmm . . . Nashville isn't enough this time?"

I look out of the window at the skyline of the city. This place where I've often found so much comfort just feels . . . uncomfortable. I feel like I'm hiding out instead of finding refuge.

"She's fine," he says clearly.

I hold my breath and wait. I wasn't going to ask him about her, but if he's bringing her up, then I'm willing to hear about it. I want to hear about all of it.

"I didn't think you'd ask about her, but I stopped by and saw her. She looks . . ." I remind myself to keep breathing because I'm starting to see spots. ". . . distant. She looks distant," he concludes.

I know why, but I don't want to comment any further. I don't think my emotions would allow me to speak anyway. I manage a hum and then will myself to keep talking. I fill Graham in on my parents and the ways that they're disappointed in me yet again. I fill him in on all the time I've spent in the studio. And then I decide to ask him the question that's been bothering me for so long.

"Do you think I could be both?"

He doesn't need me to explain. He knows how I've split my life up and all the ways I have been hiding behind my music. "I think you need to think about what you'll regret. I know it has never ended the way you wanted in any city or town you've been lately, but that doesn't mean you shouldn't keep trying. Keep risking."

There's silence on the line for a few seconds as I twirl an unimportant to-go coffee cup in my hands. Unlike the ones from Birch Borough, there's no joy in it. "I thought it was bad when I left LA, and it was. I was burnt out. I wasn't creating. But now . . . I don't know, man . . . It's like I finally felt alive and then woke up to a nightmare." I take a deep breath because this is the thing that's been haunting me since I left. "I really don't know how to move on without her."

Graham lets out a knowing sigh. "I know. In more ways than I've ever told you."

I'm taken aback by his confession. I've suspected there's a heartbreaking story beneath his cool, businesslike facade. "You'll get the full story soon. But, in the meantime, just know that we really don't regret trying. It's when we don't try that it kills us. Slowly and painfully."

"Graham, I still think it has to be her. I don't want other options."

He sighs. A long, drawn-out sigh. But not the kind that tells me he thinks I'm not thinking clearly or that I have the wrong idea. It's one that seems to get what I'm saying and knows this feeling of there being no going back. "Ok, so what do you need me to do?"

"Do you think . . . Do you think you and Lily could help me get her back?"

"Absolutely not. Not with her."

His response is unnerving. I knew he didn't have a great impression of Sparrow's best friend, but I didn't think he would be this adverse to being near her.

"But you're *my* best friend. And she's Sparrow's best friend. See where I'm going with this?"

He sighs again, this one out of frustration. "I

understand. But you don't know what you're asking of me. There's . . . history there."

Wow. I really may have underestimated this situation. "No, it's okay. I'll figure this out on my own." Silence. I know I'm making the right decision. Whatever happened between him and Lily, he's not ready to face it. And I have to respect that too.

"If there's anything I can do myself, I will. You know that, right?"

I grin. "I do. Thank you. For inviting me. For letting me stay at your place. I know I've probably brought more emotions and feelings—and loud music—into your world than you ever would've wanted, but you've been great, man. I appreciate it."

"Anytime. And I'm rooting for you, for what it's worth. I hope you get your girl." If his voice wasn't so hollow, I would laugh or find it to be a tad dramatic, given that we're two guys talking about the women we've loved and lost. But he's right. We're hurting, which doesn't make it the least bit amusing at all.

"Graham? Thank you. For all of it."

"I'm always here." And I know he is.

We hang up, and I run my hands through my hair. It's then that what I've been holding deep inside starts to creep into my consciousness. Words that I've been scared to say. Words that I'm terrified to speak out loud. But somehow, I know these are the words that need to be said.

The lights are blinding but comforting. I'm onstage at Nashville's newest venue for indie artists, Lyric. The irony isn't lost on me. I decided before I came out to perform that I was going to leave my absolute all on the stage tonight. It's the last show I have planned for a while, and it's important to me that I finish it well.

I sing through an entire set list, my heart pounding and my throat straining with all the emotion I channel. Songs about love. Songs about heartache. Songs about chemistry and finding a home. Songs about a woman I don't want to forget. The atmosphere is thick with all the things that I've left unsaid. All the things I wanted to tell her and didn't.

What is it about life that it's only when we're through a moment and on the other side that we can see it for what it was? Some moments we know we'll never forget, but why is it the ones we never expected that stick, making homes in the corners of our heart and reconstructing it in a way it wasn't before? My heart isn't the same as it was before I met Sparrow. There are new rooms with different views. There are new words I've learned that describe what love could be. It's like she's retuned some notes, and I couldn't play the way I used to before I knew her, even if I wanted to. And even now, I wish she was here.

With one more song left before the end, I take a moment to look out at the crowd. A few cheers ring out, and there's some whistling that gets a smile out of me. I ask for the lights in the house to be brought up a bit, and I make eye contact with the people in the audience. Somehow, it feels like it will be easier if I can see the people I'm talking to and tie a human connection to it all. I don't recognize a single face. And while this is actually ideal, I close my eyes and pretend for a moment that I see hair the color of dark honey, a blue ribbon melded throughout it, and eyes like melted chocolate in the front row, with a smile that warms my heart. I choose to think it could give me courage.

"Good evening. Or *bonsoir*." I swallow. "If nothing else, I hope you've felt something here. I hope you heard honesty in the sound of what I created tonight." I clear my throat.

"I'm not famous for my music . . . yet." I give a little grin when some polite laughs make it through the crowd. "But if I can reach people in this way." I tap my guitar. "If I can unlock notes and help people move forward . . ." Sparrow's words from the festival ring in my head. "If the music can help people *heal* . . ." I smile, even though it physically hurts. "Then, to me, I've found success.

"There's a French band that most people wouldn't know here. It's called Histoire. I'm not able to say much, but it used to be my dream. And now I have a new dream." I shift my guitar in my hands and take a deep breath. A catcall rings through the crowd that breaks some of the tension and has me shaking my head with a forced smile.

"Thank you. I guess." I laugh lightly, even though it feels a bit hollow. "I'll stop talking soon, but I just need to say—feel that I need to say—that I love to play and sing, but it's writing music that means the most to me. And it was brought to my attention that maybe the creativity I thought was once lost was just finding a way to return to me." I begin to tune my guitar, for something to do with my hands, and try to imagine this room is full of people who are my friends. I try to imagine I'm back at the piano at Aesop's Tavern. I'm in a café, strumming my guitar. I'm back in Birch Borough.

"Sometimes, we run from people who've hurt us, and sometimes we run from ourselves. I don't want to run from myself anymore." I pause, my gaze catching on my guitar pick that has landed on the stage near my feet.

I missed it slipping from my hands.

"And I guess that's what falling in love will do to you. Love makes you not want to hide. *J'ai eu un coup de foudre.*" *A bolt of lightning, or it was love at first sight.*

My thoughts drift to Sparrow, and I shake them away.

"So, tonight, I thought I would officially introduce myself. As if we were friends. As if I'm not hiding. *Bonsoir!* Good evening! I'm Raphaël Durand. I'm French, it's true . . . although, I've now spent most of my life in America. I recently fell in love with a woman in a small town in New England. And I—I don't know what's next for me, except to play for you tonight." I see light hitting the smiles of those in the crowd. I'm being real. Tonight, I refuse to worry about putting all of myself out there. Because without Sparrow and without worrying about my parents, I have nothing left to lose.

"*Enchanté. J'espère que vouz apprécierez ma prochain chanson.*" I pause to swallow. Man, it feels good to be speaking in French again too. "For those who didn't catch that, I only said it's nice to meet you . . . and I hope you enjoy my next song."

Lily's eyes are wide as she runs into the back of the bakery. She's in pajama bottoms and slippers, but her hair is done, and she's wearing a sweater. I freeze in the middle of piping a tray of madeleines. She's pointing at the screen of her phone, and all I can hear is a muffled voice speaking and what sounds like a guitar. Possibly some singing. It sounds a bit familiar, but I can't make it out over the noise in the front of the café.

"Lily?"

She's panting, her mannerisms wild. "He's. He told. I can't. NO."

"What on earth is happening?" I rush to her side and look down to see that on the screen is none other than Rafe. My heart constricts. "What is happening? Is he okay?" Panic enters my voice, but I couldn't control it if I wanted to. "Lily!"

That seems to get her attention as she pulls me from the back, the bag of madeleine batter falling to the floor. She's still pulling me as we move through the café, past

Anna, who's working the front of house today, and out into the street.

I shake Lily off me and point toward her phone. "Lily, tell me! Is Rafe okay?"

She's pacing back and forth and throws her phone into my hands. "I needed air. And I didn't know—I didn't know this is how you would find out." She's waiting for a reaction from me, and I'm suddenly too scared to feel whatever she's expecting me to feel.

"Find out?" My stomach drops to my toes. It's the same feeling as when you're on a roller coaster and are plummeting toward the ground from the highest height.

I pull up the screen and see the headline of the video: "Histoire in Nashville." My brows furrow because that can't be right. Rafe did say he knew them, but this can't be right. The video says, "Histoire in Nashville." But Rafe is the only one onstage.

My brain won't compute. He's sitting on a stool, and I can't even hear the video correctly. I shake the phone like it's an old-school Etch A Sketch and realize that doesn't wipe the image or make it start over. I move to the beginning of the video and hear him tell the world that he's done hiding. And that his dream was Histoire . . . he's Histoire. He then starts speaking in French. And then *singing* in French. My heart rate accelerates, and all of the past several weeks of me with him and me without him flash through my mind. It's a kaleidoscope of emotions, from anger to hurt and embarrassment to full-on longing.

The video keeps playing as I hand Lily the phone, tears falling down my face. I pushed away the one man I needed and didn't even know he was everything I wanted. Because he's beyond what I could've imagined. And fear kept me from telling him the truth. He wanted to give me love. The full kind of love. And I let him leave.

"What are you going to do?" Lily is beside me, hugging me.

And I can't move. My limbs feel like they're not my own. I can barely even compute that this is real life. She releases me, and I mumble something about taking over the store for me for a bit. I walk toward the sounds of the river, ignoring people in my peripheral vision that I've known my whole life. I don't think I could focus on them if I wanted to. Rafe is French. And while that doesn't affect the way I love him, it does affect how I see everything that has happened between us.

I've walked all around town, and now I'm running, my ballet flats catching at the bottom of one of the grooves in the cobblestones. I pass my apartment and run toward one of the oak trees across from the gazebo and lean my back against it. My chest is heaving, and my ribcage doesn't feel like it could hold what's trying to break out of me.

He's French. All this time, he's been beside me, around me. He *kissed* me, the earth moved, and I felt light move throughout my spine. And I pretended he didn't matter to me as much as I matter to him, and the shame that creeps through my bones rattles me.

He didn't tell me. He heard my announcement to the world . . . twice. And he didn't sway me. In his mind, all it would've taken for me to fall in love with him was for him to tell me who he really is. And he didn't. He wanted me to love him for him. And isn't that what he was telling me all along? I must listen better.

I curl my knees up to my chest and turn inward,

letting my tears soak through my skirt and the apron I'm still wearing, leaving an uncomfortable feeling on my face. My father always told me that I would know when I found my person. And the truth is, I did know—I just wouldn't let myself love him.

The emotion is too much, and all of a sudden, the heat of rage crawls through my limbs. I stand to my feet and start to pace.

He didn't tell me.

Why didn't he tell me?

He *knew* what I was waiting for. What I wanted. And he pretended like he wasn't the person who would fit the bill. He acted like who he was would never matter to me. Not like it should. And suddenly, I'm sunk. Like the "fallen soufflés," my stomach falls as the truth comes through.

The conversations. The memories. And I walk it back . . .

The moments he told me his family only wants him for what he can do for them.

The times he said that he left LA so he wouldn't have to become someone he didn't want to be.

The sweet way he would smile and try to remind me that it's not the qualifications that make up the person; it's who they are when no one expects anything of them. And who is he? He's wonderful.

I'm still mad that he didn't tell me, but my anger starts to dissipate and turn into an ugly knot that is hard to unwind in my gut. Because if I were him, I wouldn't have told me either. If he had come into my bakery and declared that he would never date anyone who made croissants (not the same, but close), I would've hidden my history too. To see if I was worth the risk. To see if he could persuade me that I was. To prove to him that I was worth more than whatever stipulations he put on himself and his heart.

And he told me so many times.

I walk it back again, and the memories seem to imprint in new ways within my mind, rewriting themselves as they really were. The way he seemed to understand all the pastries we sell. The way he cringed when he tried to mimic a really bad French accent. The way he held his breath when I mentioned Histoire. The way his eyes lit up any time I said anything in French. His sense of style. The fact that he lived in Paris. Seeking out my bakery his first day in town. And when I saw him, the feeling that something I had lost had suddenly been found.

I used to catch him furrowing his brow when he heard someone speaking in French, and he had such angst toward Jacques. And every so often, I would catch a shift in his accent when he was tired from staying up late writing songs or helping me in the kitchen.

It was right there all along, all in front of me. And I missed it. Or maybe I was too scared to see it.

Because what *do* you do when the thing you've wanted is also the thing you need? How can one handle such happiness?

The sun is almost set when I manage to climb up to my apartment. Earlier, Lily sent a text to tell me that she took care of everything in the store, and Anna was going to help close. I couldn't even manage to feel bad about abandoning the store at that moment. My whole world has collapsed.

I've been sitting on my couch, still in my work clothes (including the apron). My eyes are red and swollen. I've watched the YouTube video at least a dozen times. If I didn't love him so much, I almost wouldn't believe it. His voice changes when he speaks French. It's deeper, and there's more grit in it. When he speaks English, it's seamless, and he speaks in a bit of a higher tone. It's managed so well, but French is where it's rapid and fast, and a grin breaks through his face with almost every word he speaks.

If English is the lyrics, French is his melody. It's him strumming his guitar without looking. It's him eating a croissant and closing his eyes to savor it. It's him pulling me close and dancing with me in the middle of an empty bakery.

I pick up my phone a handful of times before I finally get the courage to write something. My fingers hover. Waiting. I've been waiting my whole life.

I start to type and then quit. I agonize over what to say. And when I'm exhausted, I finally get the courage to write.

Sparrow: I know.

Then I turn my phone on focus mode and carry myself to the bedroom, where sleep will be out of my grasp. When I hit my bed, I let out a sob—one that I've been holding in since before I met him. It's the one that's been waiting at the door of my soul, knocking to let it out.

And so I do. I cry until I'm almost coughing, and my pillow is soaked through. I cry like I've lost the love of my life. Because I have.

It was the baseball cap on the train. It was his laughter as I hid guitar picks. It was him tapping his pencil on the counters my father made. It was the million little things that told me I was with the person I was meant to be with all along. When our worlds collided, it wasn't a breaking but a mending. And I confused my hesitancy with my healing.

Chapter Twenty-Five

Sparrow

I'm walking home, the river so loud it's blissfully overtaking my thoughts. We've had so much rain recently, pouring in sheets and sheets, that the river is high. Its chaotic and rushing flow seems to match the level of my disappointment. I thought this would all be different. If only I had been like the river, rushing toward Rafe instead of away from him. Then maybe I could've been swept away instead of thrown ashore from the emotion of it all.

But that's the thing. It's not just emotion I'm experiencing. It's a hunger for commitment. To be the one who knows what it's like to hang my jacket on a hook next to his. To share toothpaste. To know what it's like for his cologne to mix with the smell of my perfume. To see his shampoo bottle in the shower and his dirty t-shirt on the floor. Do people know what a gift it is to share space with someone? Do they realize how sacred it is? When you spend so much of your life alone, as I have, knowing a man would want to wake up to me every day just because he can seems like a miracle. A dream too far out of my reach.

Except, it was within my reach. For a moment, I saw it. I saw it all. Rafe wanted to show me how much he loved me, and I wouldn't let him.

I'm brushing tears from my cheeks, unaware of the people shuffling around to get out of the cold. The cold feels good to me tonight. It reminds me that I'm alive. It's sharpening the ache into something a bit more manageable.

It's only when I'm leaning on the stone bridge over the river, watching the water swirl below, the cold seeping through the sleeves of my jacket, that I feel an arm wrap around my waist. I startle and turn to find Ivy. Her hair is pulled back under a chic little hat, large mittens covering her graceful hands.

Suddenly, I'm back in the dance classes we took together, our tights bunching around our ankles and our hair pulled back in a bun with sparkly clips. While we don't meet at the barre anymore, she never stopped dancing. I think it's her anchor. And being at the bakery so much, I know how important having one can be.

"Oh, Ivy. I'm sorry. I know I'm a mess."

She shakes her head. "Never apologize for letting your emotions out, Rory. It's what keeps us alive. If I didn't dance, I would be out here crying with you."

"What happened?" I ask, my focus shifting toward her.

"Nothing worth mentioning. Another bad date is all." She shrugs, but I see the hint of sadness behind her eyes. "Grey keeps asking if I'd like to write a book about all the terrible dating experiences I've been having lately. But I keep telling her there's no way I want to relive them. I'm trying to get out of this level of hell, you know?"

She laughs, and for a moment, I grin. I do know how terrible it can be out there. Which brings a memory of Rafe's arms wrapped around me, and the tears start streaming again.

"I'm sorry, Rory. I know you love him."

"How do you know?" I ask as she leans her head on my shoulder, connecting us and keeping us a bit warmer from the wind.

"Because I've never seen you cry over a man before. Except your dad."

We stay there for a moment before we both decide we're absolutely frozen. Ivy has to return to the studio but stops with me to get a hot chocolate at Eloise's Chocolates before we part. I'm rounding the corner to my place when I spot a light on at Gladys' place. I can't help but grin as she spots me walking by and throws her dish towel in the air to run to the porch.

"Come in, come in, Rory!" She's all energy and excitement, and I'm the opposite. She looks me up and down and makes a *tsk* sound. "Oh, the things men can do to us, eh?"

I have no response to this except to grip my now cold to-go cup of hot chocolate a little tighter. She waves me toward her, and I welcome the warmth from her heated porch. She's known for spying on the town and bought herself a new porch swing last fall. It's her pride and joy. And even though I'd rather be invisible tonight, I'm grateful for her need to keep tabs on everyone at the moment.

"I'm afraid I'm not much company right now," I say, a slight shrug of embarrassment washing over me.

"Oh, that's okay, dearie. I know what it's like to be heartbroken. Don't you fret."

Tears fill my eyes as she hands me a steaming cup of tea. She dumps the rest of my hot chocolate, and I'm too tired to protest.

"Now, tell me. Did he hurt you?"

I nod.

"You hurt him?"

I nod again, shakily. She lets out a sigh.

"Isn't that the way? Don't always know what we're worth until we lose what we wanted all along."

She gets up to sit beside me on the cushioned porch swing and gathers me in her arms. It's such a motherly thing to do and such a comforting gesture that it's all it takes before I'm undone. She smells like tea and lemon, and I remember all the times this eccentric woman has stepped in when I needed a mom. The Band-Aid on my knee when I fell off my bike. The flowers she gave me at every one of my dance recitals. The way she sent food to my house when my father was ill. She's always made sure I am taken care of. And I've never been more grateful.

"Let it out, dearie. Let it out," she whispers in a gentle yet commanding way. She's giving me permission to release some pain. And I do, the sound of my regret like the nearby river, pouring out from somewhere deep within.

Eyes still swollen and heart a little less burdened, I'm back home, reheating a piece of pot pie from Gladys, who insisted I shouldn't waste away after letting out so much emotion.

One of Rafe's sweatshirts is still on the back of the couch. I may or may not have smelled it several times (I have) or used it as a sort of pillow so I could go to sleep last night (I definitely did).

I shift my gaze to a photo of my father and me when I was a little girl. I had just made my first batch of croissants. The oversized oven mitts cover half my arms, my hair haphazardly brushed across my face, and my father so steady, so proud.

My father was the best man I've ever known. Consistently kind, gentle, and unassuming. He was the type of person who filled up a space without ever announcing his presence. Never calling attention to himself, he gave freely, and the absence of his presence was devastating. He was the one who practiced French braiding my hair so I didn't look motherless at school and was overly concerned about making sure I never felt less of . . . anything, really.

I wish I could say that I remember every single moment my father and I shared, but I'm human. And sometimes words fall short. Even when I look back on old cards or journal entries, they're fragments of what we shared and not the whole story. It will never be the whole story. Because when you lose someone, through the force of life or through time, we're still in the middle of our own story. All the pieces become fragments, chapters ending or new worlds beginning, and all of it brings me back to the moment, two years ago, when I saw my father awake for the last time.

He was sitting up in a hospital bed. I brought him a special treat—cookies my mother used to make. It was her own recipe. We never sold them in the shop because my mother said that while she loved everyone, she loved my father the most, and he deserved to have a cookie from her that was only made for him.

I now move through my own kitchen, gathering the

ingredients and getting the mixing bowls. I turn on the oven and set my phone to Ella Fitzgerald while I work, getting lost in the movement of it all. The music of it all.

Even though my father was too sick to eat the cookies during our last moments shared here on earth, I still remember the smile across his face. He looked at those cookies like they were an old friend. And I guess, considering the memories he had shared with my mother, they were.

In honor of him and my mother, for two years, I've made the cookies on the anniversary of the last time I saw him. Although he passed away the next day, this is the day that I do the most remembering and hiding and processing away from the world.

As I spoon the dough onto the cookie pans, pop them in the oven, and set the timer, I take deep breaths. Reaching into my pocket, I find one of Rafe's guitar picks I took the last time he played music in the café. It was early morning, and he had decided to play a new song for the customers while they ordered their coffees and pastries. I rotate it around through my fingers, careful not to let it fall. And it's then I make a decision: I will never let love slip through my hands again. Hope beats hard and fierce within my chest. Maybe love is never really lost after all.

I'm waiting at the edge of town, at a café I rarely frequent. It's a chain one, and we don't do chain stores in the heart of town. But I needed a place where I wouldn't be too scarred from the memories of what's about to go down. I shift in the uncomfortable seat, listening to the sounds of baristas yelling and calling out orders like we're at an auction. It's then that I notice him.

Jacques gives a sheepish smile and walks over to where I'm sitting. "Did you want anything?" He motions to the counter.

"No, I'm good," I say politely. He nods and walks over to the pickup area for a tiny espresso cup, which he obviously ordered ahead.

I grin at this. Rafe would never have ordered without me. It sends a bit of a sting, but I'm learning that perspective is everything. And having him in my life for the time that he was is more than I could've ever hoped for. He opened my eyes to what's possible. And what being loved by someone who doesn't have to—who isn't family and doesn't require anything of me—feels like. He never responded to my last text. I didn't expect him to after I reached out once I found out the truth. Rafe may have said he had fallen in love with me at his show, but that doesn't mean he'll be returning. I have to accept that my hesitation may have turned his feelings to the past tense.

When Jacques is seated before me, I take a moment to really look at him. He's still the polished French man who makes women swoon everywhere. His style is still impeccable, and he's meticulous in how he carries himself. And somewhere within him is a puzzle piece hinting that he might be as uncomfortable with himself as I have been with my own life.

"Jacques, I'm sorry."

He arches a brow. "Why are you sorry? I should be the one apologizing."

I nod politely, but we're both to blame. "I shouldn't have gone out with you." His eyes widen. "Not that there's anything wrong with you," I add. He relaxes slightly. "But I shouldn't have gone out with you when I knew I was in love with someone else."

At this, he smirks and looks toward the window. "Ahh, love." He plays with his now empty paper espresso cup and then looks up at me with an earnest expression. "You really love him?"

I nod quickly.

"And he loves you?"

I hesitate. "He did."

"He still does." He's so sure, but I don't contradict him. "Then, to me, you're lucky." He won't meet my eyes. "Not all of us know what that feels like."

We don't stay long. We wave our goodbyes, and Jacques promises to stop by the bakery again, but we both know he won't. He'll be off to another French bakery in the area, looking to fill a void he hasn't yet named.

When I step back into my bakery, I wrap an apron around myself and take a deep breath. For as much as it can be, this is home. I take in the sight of a mother and daughter sharing a croissant at the corner table and Johnny texting at the bar while drinking an Americano. I wave at Gladys, who's eating macarons and having tea on the other side of the space and reading the latest town newsletter. Lily steps out from the back and raises a brow to ask if I'm okay. I nod and give her a grin.

"Good girl," she says while pulling me into a side hug. I take another moment to look at the cream trim throughout the store. Everything feels so warm and cozy. The whole place smells like butter, coffee, and a hint of caramelized sugar. And there's a look of peace on the faces of those who are here. This is home. And I'm ready to share a piece of it with the world. My mother had it right: Share a space with others to make them feel loved and watch the love that fills your life.

"Hey, Lils? What do you think about finally helping me open that online store?"

"Finally!" she yells. "So, what are you thinking? Like, we launch a website, and then what? Should we sell maple croissants first? Nobody's selling those except us." The look of pride and determination on her face has me grinning. Can't have a home without a little fire, can we?

"Or what about the macarons? I mean ... if someone doesn't like a macaron, I truly question their character."

"Oh! Or our marshmallows! Those are perfect for shipping!"

I shake my head and move to the back of the store to get started on some dishes and to brainstorm the best ways to keep things fresh during shipment. I haven't told Lily yet, but I'm thinking the first items we put online should be French muffins.

I'm sitting in a booth at the diner, my head slightly throbbing. I got home, and after all the excitement of the day, I assured Lily I was fine, but as soon as I got in the door, I was hit with sadness again. Not wanting to heat up any more frozen food, I recognized my need for a real dinner and the bravery required to leave the apartment or the shop yet again.

Lucy already brought me a water, but as soon as she sees my face, she brings over the biggest pumpkin pie milkshake I've ever seen in my life and tells me it's free refills tonight. I haven't even told her I'm not sure I can eat much when the door swings open, and my best friends walk in. Just the sight of them makes me want to cry.

Lily leads the way with Grey and Ivy close behind. Spotting me, they head my way, looks of concern etched across their faces.

"I told you it was bad," Lily says to them as if I'm not here, waiting for them to tell me why they've decided on what looks like an intervention.

"Rory, Lily filled us in," Ivy says quietly.

"And you're here to tell me what a mistake I've made?" I sniffle and wipe my eyes with the edge of my sleeve.

"No," Grey says. "We're here to tell you how much we love you."

Lily scoffs, and I see the way her jaw tightens. "And to tell you what an idiot you've been, but you already knew that." She winks at me, and I let a laugh escape.

They don't mention Rafe directly. I think they're waiting for me to bring him up. And it's a relief to know they're not pushing for answers. We order food and sit and eat as they fill me in on what's been happening in their lives. Grey's waiting for Boston, her childhood best friend, to return from a business trip so they can take their own adventure up north to see the leaves changing. It's a bit late for it, but there should be some good moments, just the same.

Ivy doesn't say much about her own relationships except to tell me how much she loves her ballet students and how she'll never get over seeing them in their baggy tights and slippers that never seem to keep the bows tied. They're already practicing for their Christmas show, and I promise I'll attend. She and I met in ballet class and took classes together all throughout high school. After I had some problems with my hips and things picked up at the bakery, Ivy kept dancing and spreading that joy with our town. I could never imagine a different life for her.

Lucy makes good on her promise to keep refilling our milkshakes, and with my friends, I'm able to eat a proper meal for the first time since Rafe left. My heart sinks thinking about him.

It's only when we're laughing about the latest shenanigans from Lily's adventures on a dating app that I admit to what's been brewing all along. I can't seem to find the words to describe what this man has done to my brain and to my heart.

The thing is, Rafe is like the difference between the famous *The Great British Bake Off* (it's the UK title) and the French version, *Le Meilleur Pâtissier.*

I love the British one. I'm obsessed with it. But then you see the French one, and you honestly can't believe they're amateur bakers. They make American baking competitions look like school art projects. And I don't even mean that to be condescending, because I don't know if I could last in the French one . . . and I own a bakery. But, yeah, Rafe is like that. Like every other version of a man I've seen is just a hint, scratching the surface of what's possible.

He must've thought the way I communicate is through a lack of words and croissants. My grace and elegance seemed to erode whenever he was near, because I was apparently undone by a man who called me "Sugar" and used to send me GIFS of French bulldogs wearing striped shirts and berets. He also used to send me GIFS of Joey from *Friends*, usually from when he tried to speak French.

So, let's talk.

Let's talk about the fact that I want to run into his arms, wrap my legs around him, and hug him so tight I know what it's like to be cling wrap. My body is itching to do it. He's like a magnet. And the more I'm pulled away from him, the more powerful the feeling becomes.

It's like there's a remote control somewhere that's exponentially increasing my attraction to him. So much so that when he would leave and come back before, I'd be incrementally more excited and simultaneously more gutted when he left again. What is this enchantment?

I remember every detail of those days with him. His hands that were too big for the tiny coffee cups we use, so his thumb always stuck out a bit when he tried to pick it up. The eyebrow with the scar through it, lifted when he was trying to determine what kind of mood Lily was in. His eyes would flash whenever he saw me for the first time . . . and he did it every time. Even when I came back and forth from the kitchen to the front of the store, it happened (I checked). I remember the way he ran his hand through his hair when he was writing new music and the lyrics were frustrating him. The way he laughed nervously when something was awkward. The way his stubble crossed his face like a master artist had drawn perfect shadow lines across his features. The way he swallowed whenever I got close to him.

Blast. This man has single-handedly redefined my definition of love.

"I really messed up," I whisper quietly. So softly I don't think anyone heard. But there's an immediate clanging of forks and spoons as they drop on the plates and table. Lily has a forkful of pie hovering near her mouth, which is currently half open. She lowers the fork slowly and then reaches for my hand. I avoid her eyes, not wanting to see pity, but when she clears her throat, I look up. There's only warmth there and a bit of a fierce look that lets me know she means business.

"You did. But the question is, do you know why?"

This is . . . not what I was expecting her to say. I look

up to Ivy and Grey, who look surprised by this question as well. But the more I ponder it, I do know why.

"Because I thought hiding was safer." I shrug my shoulders. "You were right."

"I'm always right," she says as she lets me go to wave her hand like that's the most obvious conclusion anyone could come up with at this moment.

We all laugh a little, except Lily, who just has a grin on her face. She motions for me to continue.

"And I was scared."

"There it is!" she yells in the diner. Some customers look at us but then go right back to digging into their breakfasts-for-dinner and burgers.

"Why were you scared?" Grey asks kindly, a hint of something in her eyes like she'd like to know the answer to some questions she's been asking herself.

"Well . . ." I begin. "Because he was more than I ever expected." I move the straw around in my milkshake, chocolate swirls blending with the whipped cream. "And when love was right in front of me, I didn't think I was worthy of it." I swallow, but it's challenging to not let emotion get in the way.

"What do you love about him?" I look up at Ivy, who's sweetly waiting for my response. I grin and think of all the ways Rafe has changed my life.

"Apart from the fact that he's gorgeous," Lily adds.

"Yes, he is." I smile, thinking of the secret behind his scarred eyebrow and the laugh lines that only deepen when he's really happy. From his nervous tics to his forest stare, I'm his. "Everything," I whisper. "I love everything about him."

Just then, my phone pings with a text, and as I reach for it, I nearly drop it.

Rafe: I'm sorry.

My heart rate keeps time with the three little dots. After days of silence, he's responding.

Rafe: *Tu me manques.*

He misses me. I cover my mouth with a surprised laugh as I bolt upright. Part French, part English. So us. My fingers shake as I type, my friends squealing their approval.

Sparrow: Are you here?

I bite my nails and wait for the response past the dreaded three little dots.

Rafe: Nashville. Recording for the next week.

The three little dots appear and disappear.

Rafe: Save a dance for me, Sugar.

I lean back, my head falling to the back of the booth, and feel the smile overtaking my face. I pull my phone up to my face and type out my response without overthinking.

Sparrow: Always.

Rafe: *Fais-toi confiance.*

Trust yourself. Hope beats hard and fierce within my chest. Maybe what was lost won't really be gone after all.

"Lily." I look right at her, courage growing in my heart. "Can you watch the store for a few days?"

She lifts a hesitant brow while Ivy and Grey lean back in their seats. "Yesss," she drags out.

"Great." I grab my purse and start to put on my coat, catching the faintest hint of Rafe's cologne on one of the sleeves. I swallow. "I think it's time I visit Nashville."

I'm running out of the diner when I hear Lily yell behind me, "But you've never been on a plane!"

Chapter Twenty-Six

Rafe

The next day, I'm in a recording booth in the studio, headphones plastered to my head and a weight still in my lungs. I'm doing my best to move through it, but there's not much more I can do other than to throw myself into my music. It always seemed to work before, but now, it's a temporary bandage to my heart as it bleeds out.

Sparrow texted me, and I responded. But the uncertainty of when I'll ever see her again has me reeling.

We've gone over this song at least a dozen times, and each time, my studio sound engineer, Evan, has something to change or add. Some inspiration hits, and he's ready to capitalize on it. Normally, I'd be down for the creative flow, but today, I just want to finish this song and keep moving.

In between recording sessions, I've been hurriedly planning a way to show Sparrow that I'm still here if she wants me. While I've sorted out the details, I've been doing everything I can not to hop on a plane. Her last message had me looking up flights.

And somehow, during the last song, the air has shifted. It's almost like I can feel her near me, which I know is impossible. The click speeds up a bit, and I feel the energy pulse through my body. With Graham's and Lily's help (separately, of course), there's a possibility that Sparrow and I may have another chance at this—a real chance from the start.

"Can we try it again?" Evan says, the sound of the click still keeping time in my ears.

I run my hand through my hair. "Are you sure? Because the last take felt like the best one so far, and I know that I've struggled a bit today, but I just want—"

"The full kind of love."

I shake my head, the visceral reaction of hearing the angelic voice—her angelic voice—in my ears. I look toward the booth, but the glare isn't showing me a clear picture.

"What—what did you say?" I ask into the void, a hint of desperation lacing my voice.

"Rafe." I hear her again. "I want the full kind."

I rip the earphones off my head and race out the door to the sound booth, where, standing near the digital mixer, is the most gorgeous woman I've ever seen in my life. Her eyes are full, her chocolate depths swimming with hope.

I brace myself on the door frame and wait. Everyone else has left, sneaking away to give us a moment, no doubt. "Sparrow?"

She nods and takes a step closer, then one more. I do the same, and we're now inches apart. My heart is hitting my rib cage, and for a moment, my voice is gone as I hungrily take her in.

"Rafe?" She reaches for me, and I feel the cracking

in my heart.

I'd built a wall around it when I left her town, piece by piece, but now it's falling, brick by brick. I can almost hear the demolition between my ribs. Since we seem to do the silent thing so well, I reach toward her and let out a deep breath when our skin makes contact. She inhales sharply, and then her shoulders drop. We're home. I allow my palm to mix with hers and slowly slide it up her arm until my hand is curved around the back of her neck. She's shaking, and I can't help but notice I am too.

Her breathing is shallow, like she's waiting to see what I'll do next. Now that she's with me, I wonder the same thing myself. I reach my other hand forward and almost moan when my palm moves over the curve of her hip bone and up and around to catch her waist. Holding her and feeling her near me has my spine humming. Her hand reaches out and brushes against my chest, settling over my heart. I grin at this. This would be where she would go first since she owns it anyway.

Not wanting to let her go but needing to see her fully, I slide the hand near her neck up, pushing the pad of my thumb across her blushing cheek to catch a falling tear.

When I lightly lift it from her face, I'm met with the eyes I've been dreaming about. Her eyes. The ones that are melted chocolate mixed with spun gold. Another tear falls down her face, and her eyelashes flutter. She opens her mouth to say something, but nothing comes out. Instead, she lets out a little cry, and suddenly, she's clinging to me like I'm her favorite thing in the world.

Sparrow's arms are tight around my neck, her body pressed against mine. She buries her face in my neck, her eyelashes brushing against my collar bone as she nestles in. She's as close as she could possibly get to me, and I'm holding on to her for dear life. I nuzzle my nose into her shoulder and clutch onto her like she's my everything. Because she is.

With one arm pinning her waist against me, the other caressing her, and my whole hand covering the base of her neck, I hold her.

She smells like butter and sugar and every future I could ever imagine for myself that's worth writing about. I whisper over and over again all the things I've been wanting and waiting to tell her. How much I love her. How much she means to me. How she deserves everything that I could ever give her. How I'll spend the rest of my life trying to make her believe how valuable she is to me. How she's everything I could've dreamed of. I switch back and forth between French and English, knowing she'll understand me. It feels good to be fully myself and have her still hold on.

We're both a blend of two worlds that happened to collide. And now we get to create a new world together. One where she knows she's my favorite forever.

When we finally release our hold enough to look into each other's eyes, Sparrow reaches up and gently wipes the tears that have fallen down my own face. "Rafe, I'm so sorry," she whispers, her eyes searching mine.

"I'm sorry too," I whisper back, my voice rough to my own ears. I brush a section of her hair away from her face and slowly tuck it behind her ear. "I should've told you sooner."

She nods but then says, "Yes, I was upset. But I do understand." She reaches up to play with the back of my hair, her kindness pulsing through her fingers. "But I also should've told you how I felt. That night—when you left."

I tip my chin quickly to show her I know what she

means. My brow furrows. "Why didn't you?"

She traces the line I've created in my forehead, and I don't miss the way her fingertips trace the scar over my eyebrow. She focuses on it before her eyes drop to mine, the warmth in them removing any remains of fear I have as to whether or not she'll let me close this time.

"Because I loved you too much." A grin hovers on one side of her face, her dimple starting to shine through. "Oh, my darling Rafe. Do you still doubt how valuable you are?"

I don't waste another second before I lean down and catch her perfect mouth with mine. It tastes even better now that love has been spoken between us. It's sweet and soft until I feel her make a hum that vibrates across my bottom lip. I take the kiss deeper, lifting her up until she's wrapped her legs around my waist. I set her on the nearby stool, her hand sliding on the console. A weird music mix is now playing throughout the studio, but I can't bring myself to care as I allow my hands to rediscover the curve of her waist while her hand wanders across my chest and back before sliding up to play with the ends of my hair.

"Keep it PG, you two!" I hear from outside the door.

And we do (mostly). But we're desperate for each other, the distance and space and honesty creating a new sense of excitement between us. After being starved of this kind of love for so long, we're so darn hungry. It's familiar and altogether new. It's heartbreaking and healing. It's her and I choosing to move forward. Together.

We spend the next three days enjoying Nashville. Since

Sparrow has never been and Evan has an extra spare room, I want to show her pieces of my world that she's never seen before. We've been visiting every coffee shop possible for "research" and stopping by every ice cream shop and pastry shop possible. Sparrow even tried to convince one of the owners that they needed to add French muffins to the menu. They gave her their card.

Mostly, since I told Evan I'm leaving to head back to Birch Borough as soon as possible, we've been holed up in the studio. And it's the best feeling in the world. I have my girl and my music, and it's so much different than before.

Not wanting her out of my sight, Sparrow has happily agreed to sit in the recording booth with me, so I get to sing while looking at her. After all, the songs are really about her anyway.

When we finally land in Boston again, with her hand in mine, we take a ride to the North End before catching our train home. We wheel our luggage through narrow streets to get some fish and chips and look out over Boston Harbor as the sun sets over the ocean. With my arm wrapped around her, I realize this is what it feels like when you start to feel whole.

When we step off the plane in Boston, the surprise of my life is finding my parents waiting with a car. I don't know what methods they used to get the information on my travel plans, but it's not beneath them to do such a thing. My mother dressed in an elegant dress, her hair long and flowing, her face familiar and yet hollow, despite the work she's had done to imply that she's much younger than her age. My father stands in a suit, his aftershave carried on the wind. I smelled them before I saw them.

Their driver opens the car door, and my father motions for me to get in. I move a step closer to them before placing my guitar case near my feet, shaking my head. They don't even notice Sparrow, who has wrapped one of my hands between her own.

"What are you doing here?"

My father looks bored. I would think he didn't care except for the bit of red coloring that's now creeping up his neck. He's irritated, but he can't lose his cool in public. There could be a video taken, evidence obtained by anyone carrying a cell phone, which is . . . everyone. We don't normally have our standoffs in public, so I decide to use this to my advantage. There's no way I'm getting into the car.

"I have a train to catch."

"Yes, you do," my mother says, her accent creeping through her words. They don't like to speak French in public, and I'm tempted to speak French just to spite them. But they're the reason I was in America and learned how to get rid of every trace of my French accent. It's possibly more annoying to them than anything else. "You're coming home with us. To Paris."

I shake my head again. "Quit doing that," says my father, his jaw clenched.

"I won't be going back to Paris. Not without the woman I love."

Their eyes briefly scan over Sparrow, and I feel a growl in the back of my throat.

"The woman you . . . ?" My mother takes in a breath. "Noémie is getting married! You can't possibly be thinking of breaking up a wedding. Especially all these years later!"

I shake my head and roll my shoulders back. "She's

not the woman I love."

Suddenly, it dawns on my mother that I'm speaking about the woman beside me. Her posture stiffens. They are controlling if nothing else.

"Another one to steal your songs, hmm?" My father raises a brow, smug with himself for trying to get a jab in while I'm already vulnerable. Too bad for him that he doesn't realize how much my past doesn't affect me the way it used to.

I wrap my arm around Sparrow's waist. "She would never. Are we done here? If you stay much longer, you're going to get soot on your clothes." At my cue, a bus pulls up nearby, releasing some passengers, the smell of exhaust filling the air. My mother waves it away like she does all her problems.

"When are you going to come to your senses?" she asks.

"When are you going to stop following your thirty-three-year-old son around, trying to get him to do what you want?"

My mother leans back. I'd feel bad for her, except her narrowed eyes tell me she's already plotting another way to strike. And this is how it goes. Back and forth, back and forth. They've built me to fight with them, and I'm suddenly . . . tired. I'm not doing this anymore. I'm a grown man, and whether they like it or not, I can make my own way.

Sparrow hasn't said anything, her presence enough to clear my mind. I lean down to pick up my guitar without letting go of her, finally ready to say goodbye to the people who can't get out of their own way.

"If you would just do what you're told, we wouldn't be having this problem." My father steps closer to me, his anger radiating through his own designer suit.

I nod. "You're right. We wouldn't be having this problem. We'd be having another problem." I pull my shoulders back and grip my guitar case's handle and Sparrow's hand tighter.

"What problem is that?" my mother whispers.

I look at her with a bit of empathy. I don't know what happened in their lives to make them this way. They don't seem to realize they've created my desire to run. "Me. You don't see me. You never have."

She scoffs, her heels clicking on the concrete as they hurry toward me. I notice the hollowness around her eyes, the crease lines that should be more prominent but have been smoothed by years of surgeries and treatments. For a moment, I wish for her to hug me, to tell me that I'm worth their attention, just as I am.

Instead, she rolls back her shoulders and looks at me, a chill settling behind her eyes. "You didn't want to be seen. Isn't that the real problem?"

I lower my gaze. "No, Mom." I never call her Mom. "The real problem is that you still think an image is the solution. And loving me means outsmarting me. Outperforming me. That my love is a game that you have to win." I look at her, compassion filling my frame. "Except, I never wanted to play. The only thing I've ever want to play is music."

We turn away from them and have only walked a few steps when I hear my dad's voice pierce through the chilly air. "Do you know what you've lost?"

Without looking back, I project my voice to be loud enough for them to hear even though I'm facing the other way.

"No." I shake my head, looking into Sparrow's eyes. "I know what I've found."

Chapter Twenty-Seven

Sparrow

It's early morning on a day that will forever be known to me from here on out as Celebrate Rafe Day. It's his birthday. And since we'll be celebrating tonight, I had to get some more work in to keep up with orders, so I'm doubling what we normally would create.

"Ah!" I yell as something furry lands on the counter next to me. It's Philippe, the raccoon. I turn around, and there's Rafe, wearing a light-blue sweatshirt that reads *Charmant Français* or "French Charming." Boy, is he ever. "You scared me!"

"I've already had two Americanos and a maple croissant." He grins, the guitar pick that used to be in Philippe's grubby hands on display. "I got it back. And I still don't think it's sanitary."

I shake my head and try to hide my smile, the batter in front of me unaffected by the intrusion.

His arms wrap around my waist, and I feel his mind working. "Wait. What are you making? I haven't seen you make this before."

Drat. I wince slightly.

"Sparrow," he says in a low register that causes my heart to pick up speed.

"It's nothing." I shrug. He moves around me so that his back is against the counter, and he can get a good look at my face.

"Why won't you tell me?" His dimple is on display, and my willpower is crumbling.

"Don't you cave back there!" Lily yells through the swinging door.

Rafe's eyes narrow as I see him calculating how willing I am to play (I'm willing). He leans closer and starts to lightly rub his hand up and down my back. Okay, so he's in for a slow melt. And I'm here for it. Moving around to my back, his steady arms wrap around my waist once again.

"It's just . . . I . . ." I whisper, losing my train of thought when I feel his stubble start to scratch the edge of my cheek and feel his breath brush the side of my neck. "It's your birthday cake!" I yell.

Lily groans in frustration from the front of the café, and I turn around in his arms to let out a laugh before it dies when I see Rafe's face. He's staring at me as if he can't believe what I just said.

"You . . . you're making me . . ." He trails off, taking in the ingredients all around us.

I nod and give a small smile. "I mean, it is tomorrow, isn't it?" He nods his head, and I watch as his forest eyes start to swim with unshed tears. He clears his throat, and I move to hug him, forgetting that my hand is covered in flour. And now flour is all over his sweatshirt. His mouth hangs open, and I stifle a laugh.

"I'm sorry! I didn't mean to—" I'm stopped in my tracks when he places his calloused hand in a nearby container of flour and holds it up between us.

"You wouldn't," I dare. He would. His hand cups my jaw and slowly trails down my neck and shoulder to my waist. I'm covered. It's my turn to give him an *I-dare-you* look, and I swear, even covered in flour, he's the most attractive man I've ever seen. Like: *Here are all your dreams in one moment . . . try to stay conscious.*

Determined not to let him win this round, I bring my other hand around and cup both hands around his jaw, smirking as I see the flour getting stuck in his stubble in the most satisfying way. He raises his scarred eyebrow. *Happy?*

I nod, but just to prove me wrong, he lifts me up and onto the counter. My pants are now covered in flour as he keeps grabbing little piles and tossing them my way. I'm laughing uncontrollably, tears running down my face, before he gently touches the edge of my jaw. I'm instantly quieted, my eyes taking in the flour hovering in his long lashes, the dusting on his nose with the tiny beauty mark on one side, and the eyebrow with the scar from his childhood. I use my fingers to lightly brush the flour away from his full mouth, his bottom lip pliable beneath my thumb.

He studies my face before leaning in, the warmth of his kiss and the taste of maple, coffee, and a hint of flour filling my senses.

We're standing in front of the farm at Wicked Good Orchards, Rafe's hand in mine. I convinced him we'd finally get to go on a hayride and see a pumpkin patch before Thanksgiving. Little does he know I've invited (and recruited) the entire town.

"Close your eyes," I whisper, hugging him from behind and reaching up to cover his eyes so he can't see anything. He stills and reaches up to touch my hands. I expect him to move them away, but his thumb makes small circles before he puts them back down with a smile. This man.

We manage to make it up to the entrance—sometimes tripping, always laughing—when I stop to stand in front of him.

"Rafe, darling," I whisper, hardly able to contain my excitement. I grab his hand and reach up to kiss his cheek, his hum causing the motion to vibrate through my lips. I take a step back and to the side, never letting go. "*Joyeux Anniversaire.*" Happy Birthday.

He opens his eyes, and his mouth falls open.

Here, across every space in the barn, are people from Birch Borough. There are tables with cider, hot chocolate, and apple-cider donuts. There are stations to paint pumpkins next to more pies from Angie's than we could ever eat. When I headed to Nashville to find Rafe, I used the time while traveling (and avoiding my nerves from my first time being on a plane) to send out the signal to everyone I know that we have someone who needs to feel like they belong. A man who needs to be reminded that he is worth the celebration.

"You did this?" he whispers, his eyes taking in all the details. I see them catch on the flowers in the corner, the bales of hay for seating, the lanterns on every surface, and the makeshift stage in the corner where Liam plays softly. I hug Rafe's arm and lean my head against his shoulder.

"I'd do anything for you. Honest."

Gladys is one of the first to step up to us, her excitement unrestrained. "I'll tell you what, when I found out . . . Oh, when I found out!" She turns to face the others in attendance before lifting a fist in the air. "She got herself a Frenchman! Woo-hoo!"

I'm both horrified and cracking up with most of the others as Lily whistles with her fingers between her teeth.

"It's time to wish D'Artagnan a happy birthday!" The whole town starts singing, and I look at Rafe, whose eyes are calm and peaceful. He swallows, and I know how much this must mean to him. I've been with him all day, and never once did he bring up his parents. And here we are, a tiny town in a spot he never planned to stay, showing him just how much he has a place here.

After having our fill of coffee, birthday cake, and maple croissants (of course I made more for him), we end up on the makeshift dance floor. Couples dance about. Grey with her friend Boston, and Lily with a concerned-looking Ted, while Graham watches her from the corner with a clenched jaw.

My thoughts are interrupted from wandering toward what that could be about when Rafe leans to whisper in my ear, "I love you. Thank you."

I wrap my arms more tightly around his neck, my fingers playing with the bottom of his hair and the pieces that flip out when he wears a baseball cap. The love of my life is back in this beautiful misfit of a town, and my heart is full. "Are you happy?"

He studies my face with what can only be described as awe. "Never been happier."

"Good. That's good," I confess, tipping my head to give him a smile.

He pulls me closer to him, his strong hands wrapping around my waist. "From the first moment we met, I knew." I study his face, no trace of playfulness about it now. He leans in closer and hugs me tight. It's the kind of hug that heals. "Thank you for letting me hold you," he whispers against my ear. "It's all I've ever wanted when it comes to you."

Chapter Twenty-Eight

Rafe

I'm waiting for a call for a potential opportunity, which is why I'm pacing across Sparrow's living room floor. The rogue remaining leaves on the trees outside are swirling and lightly hitting the windows in all their fall glory.

My demands were fairly simple and straightforward, but I'm still nervous. I've been burned before. So burned. But a woman has changed how I see the scars, and I'm ready to hope again. I've also learned not to be so trusting when it comes to protecting my creative work, so I asked for fair royalties and credits on each of the songs. I know artists sometimes get caught up in asking for less because they want to break into the scene, but I need this win. After losing everything, you realize how much you can still lose in the future.

Sparrow went to work at the bakery, and I've just been waiting. So much waiting. Apparently, a man named Ben was in the audience at my show in Nashville, and he is a fan of Histoire. Knowing I'm in the States, his company wants to meet with me to see what may be possible for a future collaboration and is interested in seeing what can be created with some of the American artists who are also fluent in French. All I know is that I'm so close to seeing my dream realized. To have one or more of my songs out in the world. I never wanted to be in the front or on the stage, and this gives me the chance to live out the dream and still earn my own way.

The ring of the phone cuts through the air, and I nearly jump. "Yes, hello?"

"This is Ben Carmine. Is this Rafe Durand?"

I take in a breath. "Yes, sir, it is."

"Great. We've reviewed your requests for a collaboration, and everything looks good. We would like you to meet with some of our premier artists, get a feel for them in person, and collaborate with their teams on some of the directions they'd like to go in. We'll start with one of our artists who is fluent in French. She's looking to expand into the French market and has an affinity for some of the songs you've written. Do you have a manager?"

I freeze. This isn't great. Of course I'd need one for this type of deal. But then I remember I have a friend who said he'd do anything for me. And I realize in an instant that he'd be great at it. Time to take another chance. "Yes, sir. I do."

"Excellent. Send us over their information, and we'll send over a contract within the next twenty-four hours."

"Great. Thank you, sir. I'm grateful." And I am. I feel the emotion filling my lungs and hold my eyes to avoid any tears leaking out. It's been such a long road, and if I hadn't met Sparrow, this would definitely seem too good to be true. But she makes me believe that good things can happen. So I'm going to accept this for what it is—a gift.

"We're glad to have you. I know I'm a businessman, but I have a good feeling about this."

"So do I, sir. Thanks again."

"We'll be in touch soon. Oh, and I understand another congratulations is in order for you getting your girl."

A full smile breaks out on my face. "Yes, she's my dream."

"Well, good. That's how it should be—or so I hear. Feel free to bring her with you when you come back to LA."

"She'll love that. Thank you, sir."

"Of course. I look forward to meeting you both in person. Bye now."

He's gone, and I'm staring at the phone in disbelief and elation. I did it. I got the contract. All the nights. All the long hours. All the pain of knowing my ex is living off my old creativity. I have another chance to build something of my own—to build a family of my own. And this time, I'm not going to let it go.

"So, you may need to head to LA?" Sparrow asks as we walk through town, her hand in mine. I'm never not touching this woman again. If we're in the same space (which is always the plan), then it's a new rule of ours— one that she doesn't fight me on in the least.

"I need to get my stuff at some point," I say, leaning over to wrap my arm around her shoulder. Even though it's early evening, it's pitch black outside. The windows in the shops are all lit, casting a romantic light on the sidewalks. Now that Halloween is over, it's strictly decorations that are autumn related with a hint of Thanksgiving. For the first time, I'm actually looking forward to this American holiday.

Sparrow stops outside of Marlee's Books. "Oh! Can we go in?" She turns to face me, a hint of excitement on her face.

"Of course, Sugar. Lead the way."

She places a far-too-quick kiss on my lips and bounces up the steps before turning back to me and reaching for my hand. I told you . . . we must be touching at all times. It's a truth I will never complain about.

We walk into the quaint shop, the smell of paper and old bindings in the air. For a moment, it's almost as if I'm back in a Parisian book shop. It's amazing how the love of books translates into every language. Although I've been here before, I've never been here with Sparrow.

Grey looks up from her book, a warm smile on her face as she reaches from behind the counter to hug Sparrow. I'm pulled along, and it isn't two seconds later before Grey has wrapped me up in her arms too.

"Oh! I'm sorry," she says. "Were we supposed to do the kiss thing?"

I hold back a laugh. Sparrow shakes her head in amusement, fully knowing Grey is the most innocent of all of us. Plus, I'm pretty sure if she did mean anything by it, her best friend, Boston, would end me. "No need—unless you're wanting to be very French." I give her a wink as she laughs and sits back down.

"That's okay. I'll leave that to you two."

"Good idea," Sparrow says with a grin and a look that tells me she wishes we were alone right this moment. I pop up an eyebrow and give her a look that I hope implies she's got fair warning that her wish is my command. The blush running up her neck is enough of an indication that my message got across just fine.

The sound of a throat clearing has us both looking back to Grey, who has both a horrified and amused look crossing her face. I would say sorry, but I couldn't in good conscience. I'm undone by the woman beside me.

"Rory, what are you looking for? I know it isn't love."

Sparrow laughs, and I watch as her face lights up. "Oh! Paris!" She looks at me with a smile that's brighter than any light I've ever seen.

"Paris, huh?" I whisper while I rub my thumb across the back of her hand.

Sparrow looks from me to Grey before confidently saying, "Paris."

"Yes!" Grey jumps up and heads to a travel section a few rows away from us. The store is small, so we can see her even from across the room. She's busy sorting through books and mumbling to herself when Sparrow turns toward me, wrapping her arms around my waist.

She rests her chin on the front of my coat as she lifts her face. I brush a piece of hair from her forehead, letting my fingers trail the side of her face. When she's situated, she studies me, my hands now on her waist, her eyes flaring with desire. We stare at each other and do a dance with our eyes, moving between our lips and our eyes, back and forth. Grey clears her throat, and Sparrow laughs, the tension broken for now.

"What did you love about Paris?" Sparrow asks me, her gorgeous, melty-chocolate eyes lighting up with possibilities.

"Uh—well, I didn't."

Her eyes grow almost comically wide, and her mouth opens slightly. "What do you mean? You *didn't* like

Paris? That can't be true. It just can't." Her spine stiffens.

This may take a turn for the worse, but I have to be honest. "It's true."

She shakes her head. "How? Why? I don't understand."

"Well, it's busy . . ." I begin.

"You love cities."

"And the music—"

"You're a singer."

"And the art—"

"You're an artist."

"And the food—"

"You're a foodie."

I take a breath because she is not going to let me give anything other than a from-the-heart answer. "Not many good memories there, I'm afraid."

"I'm sorry for that," she whispers. "It feels like Paris should be magical for everyone. I recognize that doesn't make it true. Of course you feel that way." Her hand is wrapped around my arm, smoothing small circles over my coat.

"Sparrow, were you hoping my answer was different because you want to love Paris so much or because you want me to love Paris as much as you think you do?"

Her eyes dance back and forth between mine again as we hold each other's gaze. "I don't know," she finally sighs. I want to kiss away the worry hovering near her eyes. "Rafe, I understand if you say no. I won't ask you to do something that would be hurtful for you. But someday, if you ever feel like you could, will you go to Paris with me?"

For a second, I stop breathing. Not because it hurts to think about returning to Paris, but because, for the first time in years, returning actually sounds like something I would want to do—as long as Sparrow is with me. She misinterprets the silence.

"I mean, of course, you don't have to," she says as she takes a tiny step back, holding her head up to try to hide any disappointment. "It's clear that it wasn't a place that felt good for you." She doesn't want to pressure me, and it makes me love her more.

Lifting her face up by cradling her jaw in my hand, I meet her gaze. I nod briefly. "True. But I have a feeling it would be different now. And I need you to know I'll go anywhere with you." And I mean it.

"I hear Paris is lovely in the spring?" she asks, her eyes lighting up with excitement.

I grin. "Yes, it is. Grey, looks like we'll need that book on Paris for my girl. We've got a trip to plan."

Sparrow kisses my cheek before giving a little squeal. Looks like the image I had of picturing her in Paris will come true after all.

Chapter Twenty-Nine

Sparrow

I've been waiting to find out if our shop is going to be featured in *The Seacoast Gazette* magazine. I sure hope so. We've been working so hard to get everything in order, and I just know my parents would be proud. We're finally doing what my father and I planned, and we're honoring my mother in the process.

I'm wrapping up some online orders we launched just last week when I hear a bang on the window. I look up to find Gladys, her nose pressed almost fully to the window, waving with one hand and frantically tapping the glass with the other. Seeing that I've noticed her, she holds up her phone and yells, "He's wearing those jeans again!" She smiles and then rushes past the store. I shake my head at her antics. I'm going to have to take that phone from her soon.

Not two minutes later, another knock is at the door. I lift my eyes to see Rafe. My cheeks instantly warm, my body continuously reminding me that I'll never get enough of him. I slowly walk to the door, creating a moment where I almost feel like Rachel in the coffee shop, walking toward Ross to let him in. Rafe patiently waits as I walk toward him, the emotion on his face so open and genuine I can hardly breathe. I unlock the top lock, the sound of it opening so satisfying. And as I reach for the bottom lock, we make eye contact.

My heart hammers. I lick my lips and see how he traces the movement, a grin causing his dimple to make an appearance. He puts his hand on the doorknob, and we go to turn it at the same time. As soon I open it for him, he steps in and takes me in his arms.

"You okay?" he asks me. Darn his kind and considerate ways. "I could sing to you," he says matter-of-factly.

"Ha!" I say a little too loudly, knowing full well that singing would lead to other things.

"Sugar, did you see the news?"

I'm too distracted by thoughts of his mouth to make out what he's saying. I lean back enough to meet his gaze, his forest eyes full of sunlight. I shake my head as he pulls a newspaper from his back pocket. He grabs my hand with his free one, and we walk over to the bar. The same place he sat the first day we met.

Opening the paper to page ten, I see a spread that I didn't realize until now I've been waiting to see for a very long time. The newspaper features Lily and me outside of the shop. There's a picture of me rolling croissants, and one of Lily melting chocolate, and lastly, an image of me in my apron holding a picture of my parents.

My hand covers my mouth as I don't know whether to laugh or cry. And there, right at the top, is the headline: BIRCH BOROUGH'S FINEST LOOKS LIKE SPARROW'S BERET

I can't even read the article because my eyes are

swimming. "We did it," I whisper. Looking at Rafe, I see his smile is as wide as my own. I throw my arms around him and jump into his arms. "We did it!" Now I'm squealing and yelling and laughing. "Lily! I have to call Lily!"

"I already did. She's on her way."

I grin at how adorable and thoughtful he is. I'm back to covering my face with my hands in disbelief. This changes everything. The website is featured. There are directives on how to order online. This goes out to the whole Seacoast area and beyond. There's no way this isn't the step that we needed to get this business to the next level. Soon, even more people will be traveling here or ordering maple croissants and a piece of my mother's legacy.

"Incoming," Rafe whispers.

"Oof!" I yell. No sooner has the door swung open than I am attacked by my best friend before I even get a chance to face her. Good thing Rafe warned me.

"Rory, we did it!"

And now we're jumping and yelling and laughing. Lily pulls Rafe in so now we're in some sort of group hug, and I wish I had a picture of this moment to frame as a new memory for this next phase.

As if reading my mind, Rafe takes a step back and takes a picture of Lily and me holding up the article. And then, in true Lily fashion, she turns the camera around for a selfie, Rafe photobombing behind us, only the corner of the article visible in the picture. That's my favorite one, for sure.

I'm elated. I'm motivated. We did it.

"So, it's official. Sparrow's Beret is going to be seen around the world." He grins. "Or at least New England."

I lean back on my couch and watch Rafe's shoulders, which fit his t-shirt like a glove. He's sitting on the edge, playing some new songs he's been working on for the past half hour. I'll never get tired of hearing his voice, especially now that I know he can switch back and forth between English and French. It's a dream. But more of a dream is the way that we've eased into being around each other. How we've relaxed into falling in love.

"It's official." I grin as he peeks over his left shoulder, a guitar pick hanging slightly out of his mouth. I reach up and wrap my arms around him. Gently pulling the guitar pick from his lips, I lift it over my head and lean in to kiss him. It's soft and sweet. Like we have all the time in the world. He gives a little hum, and it's enough for me to lean back and guide him back with me this time. Rafe lets it happen, his head now cradled between my neck and shoulder.

He's still holding his guitar as the top of his perfectly tousled hair tickles the side of my face. I rest my cheek on his head and let his smell of cedar and coffee fill me. I hope my shirt smells like him after he leaves tonight.

"Are you smelling me again?" he asks as I let out a laugh. Rafe starts strumming and making up a love song to his cologne for all its benefits. I'm cracking up with laughter, and he's seriously trying to keep going when I run my fingers across his forehead and start to play with his hair. He slows his hands and starts to softly play a song I recognize from some of his earlier work. A sweet love song about how he'll know he's home when he feels safe in the arms of his love.

I nestle closer to his face, my nose brushing his stubbled jaw as I place a kiss on the line between his cheek and his facial hair. I can't get enough of him. The feeling of him close to me, his weight resting against my side. I can't believe I once let him go.

"I love you," I whisper in his ear. I hear his smile more than I see it, his chest vibrating through my own as he keeps singing. I get it. It's calming. And also very attractive (not that he needs any more help in that area).

I play with his hair again, loving the feel of it between my fingers. His singing slows, and I notice that he's not trying to move from my arms. Soon he's only humming, his eyes slightly closed. And it's not long before he's completely asleep, his breathing even and sweet. I gently reach over to remove the guitar from his loosened grasp and pull him back with me so my legs are stretched out, his head in my lap. My eyes travel over the lines of his face, and I'm spellbound.

He's the most beautiful man I've ever seen in my life. There's a bit of grey coming in at the sides of his temple and a bit throughout his stubble. His mouth is relaxed, and the laugh lines around his face are waiting to be activated again when he awakens. I let my fingers trace his profile before moving them through his hair again. He turns his face toward my stomach, and I inhale as I watch his chest rise and fall. With my free hand, I place it on top of his as I kiss his forehead, the feeling of his hairline softly greeting my nose and his skin beneath my lips, warm and sweet.

My eyes fill a bit as a tear slips out. It's amazing how we pass by thousands of people, and then one can change our whole world. A world in which holding him feels like a gift. Where being able to see him up close— the humanity, the mistakes, the beauty—is worth every day I didn't have him. I never thought that my time alone would ever make sense. I thought I would grieve it when

I finally opened my heart up to someone. I thought I would beat myself up for the missteps. But all I can feel is grateful. Because I remember what my life was like before I met him, and I feel so deeply the miracle it is to choose someone and have them choose you in return.

Of all the things we've done so far and all the times he's proven how much he loves me, holding him is my favorite. I've never told him, and maybe I should when he wakes up. But for now, I'll hold him close and keep these quiet moments like the miracles that they are— sacred and valued.

"Lily! The baguettes, hurry up!" I sing the words in my best *Beauty and the Beast* villager imitation, laughing as Lily gives me a glare that's so satisfying it was worth the effort.

Our table is still full of food. Of course we have bread from the café, but there's also homemade cranberry sauce. I found a beloved recipe for my grandmother's pumpkin bread that was tucked inside a recipe book at the bakery, so I made a few loaves of that as well. (Rafe has already had three slices.) And Lily made a vegetarian concoction that Rafe is poking at while muttering under his breath in French.

We—and by we, I mean Lily, Rafe, and I—are sitting in Lily's makeshift dining room, which really means that one of us is technically sitting in the kitchen, one of us is in the living room, and one of us is straddling the space in-between (me, it's me). I'm surrounded by my two favorite people. Lily's studio apartment is so "her," and it's delightful. There are pictures of flowers all over the walls, most of her items are from vintage and thrift stores, and there are candles throughout.

I love being here. It's more eclectic and free than my own space and somehow feels organized at the same time. Rafe wore an easy smile on his face while Lily moved about in the "kitchen" (which is really only a tiny stove with four mini burners), quietly muttering at anything boiling on the stove. Now, we're settled with some herbal tea, an espresso, and an Americano with cream, full from our traditional dinner.

This is the most grounded I've felt in a long time. I still feel the tinge of sadness that quietly knocks on my heart and the ghost of grief left by the void of my parents. But I also feel hopeful and as if all the things I dreamed of have somehow found their way to me—most of which I owe to the man sitting to my left. The gorgeous human who has transformed not only how I see myself but what's still possible. I don't fear being abandoned, and it's a beautiful space to be in.

We've had to work through our words, sure. We sat down and talked through all our reasons for keeping each other at a distance. We are pulling our fears away one by one, like flakes from a piece of puff pastry.

He's turning into my partner and my best friend. And that, I believe, is really what my father was talking about when he said to wait for the French kind of love. He had a partner with my mother, and she just happened to be French. Same is true for my Rafe—my music-loving, South-of-France-meeting-Paris, multi-layered man who's all of the best things I've known in human form.

I feel him looking at me, and as we make eye contact, the grin hovering on the right side of his mouth tells me that tonight will end very well for us both. My cheeks blush at the thought, and I hold back a laugh as I meet

Lily's gaze, who's now staring at me all-knowingly.

"Look, lovebirds—no pun intended, Rory," she says to me. "Actually, yes, it's intended. For that dreadful baguette comment." She rolls her eyes.

"Ha. Ha," I say but still can't hold back a smile.

She hovers her finger between us and puts on a hint of an annoyed glare (except, I know she's not mad because she's sitting cross-legged. And she only sits that way when she's comfortable). We've been having holidays together forever, especially since Lily's parents have been doing humanitarian work overseas since they retired a few years ago.

"You've got a beautiful thing happening here, but I don't need to be reminded of it every second of every day, okay? And no, you're not being subtle with your pining glances whenever you're in the same room."

Rafe smirks while he draws on the table with his finger, the swirling motions somehow making me warm too. Ah, love.

"Lily—or Lils," he laughs as she winces. She doesn't shut him down for the nickname, though, which means he's officially in. "What kind of person is your type?"

She shakes her head furiously. "I don't have a type. I just pray over myself and keep moving forward."

"Huh," is all that Rafe says.

Suddenly, I remember the man from the train station. My eyes light up as I turn to look her way, an idea striking me like it came from the heavens. "Lils," I say, looking pointedly at Rafe to get one of his signature grins. "What about the guy I mentioned at the train station? I still have his card somewhere . . . probably."

"Is he handsome?" Lily asks far too intensely.

"Wouldn't suggest otherwise."

"And what's his name? You know I have a thing

with names. They need to work together." She points her finger between me and Rafe again. "You two lucked out."

She's not wrong. But I see the way she's tensing, covering up for something I know has been locked away in her emotional vault since a few years ago. I would say it was around the same time as the loss of my father, but I don't know if that's my perspective because of where I was in my grief or an actual observation.

"Greg? No . . ." I tap my fingers on the table. Suddenly, I picture him clearly. "Oh! Graham. His name is Graham."

Lily's eyes widen, and I watch her face turn a shade paler.

"Lily, are you okay?" I ask, placing my hand on her forearm.

Rafe sharply turns his head toward me and lifts a brow. "Wait. Did you say *Graham*? As in my best-friend-turned-manager and soon-to-be-ex-roommate Graham Winnings?"

I grin innocently and watch as he puts two and two together.

"I can't deny he has good taste. But you two wouldn't have worked. He seems more suited for . . ." He looks up at Lily before focusing intently on the table. "You know, there's a story there. I think he really loved someone, and . . ."

"Mashed potatoes!" Lily nearly screeches as she rises to her feet, a finger pointing in the air like she just made an earth-shattering declaration and not the bizarre response she actually gave.

There's silence. Crickets, really, as Rafe and I look at Lily. I catch a glance and see his mouth slightly open, and I force mine to close. Before either of us can say anything more, Lily is at the stove, frantically stirring a pot that's been off the heat for an hour.

"Thanks, but no thanks, Rory. I just remembered I've sworn off men, and now it's time for our pie," she says casually while I'm still trying to catch up.

"But you just said . . ." I don't get a chance to finish before a pie plate is dropped in front of us, the whipped cream shifting a bit at the velocity with which it was placed on the table. Rafe carefully grabs the slicer from Lily's fist and starts dishing out the pumpkin goodness to our plates. I don't like pumpkin pie as-is, so Lily always makes a pumpkin cheesecake for me with pumpkin macarons on top and calls it "pie." She says that anything in a pie tin can be called a pie, even if it isn't one. I know she just doesn't want me to feel bad, so add it as another reason why she's a gem of a friend, even if she has seemingly lost it in the past two minutes.

"Are we going to talk about—"

"No. So, Rafe, how's the apartment search going?"

And that's how we transition from one of the most awkward moments for Lily I've ever seen in my life. Rafe, bless him, never mentions the outburst, and I place a hand on his leg and squeeze gently as a sign of gratitude. He softly smiles at me and shifts his attention back to Lily. And this is how we continue for the next few hours. Light and fun conversation, lots of laughter, extra slices of our "pie," more espresso for Rafe, and even a Christmas movie on in the background while we play a board game. It's a magical evening, and I don't miss the way my heart seems to lift at the beauty that is me and the two people I hold most dear spending a quiet holiday together. And after the mention of Graham, I also don't miss the way Lily's hand shakes each time she lifts her spoon to her mouth.

Chapter Thirty

Rafe

Sparrow and I stop at the market in town to get some things for dinner. We both had a photo shoot today—her for pictures for her upcoming cookbook and me for new headshots for my music. I used to think those things were miserable. But they got my best side today, for sure, since I was looking at her the whole time.

She's been adorably talking about Paris, and for the first time in a long while, I really do feel ready to go back again. My father has not reached out since our run-in in Boston, but my mother did ask about my address. In her note, she mentioned that it was no bother to send me some sweaters from their last collection that didn't sell as well, but I recognized one on the top of the pile that was featured on their most famous model. I took that as a sign that she was trying.

Speaking of trying, Sparrow and I have been scouring the aisles for the last ten minutes. It's taking us ages to walk through this tiny store as we keep stopping every few ingredients or aisles to look into each other's eyes and talk about nothing. It's not productive at all. I love it.

"How about a picnic?" I ask, my eyes focused on her chocolatey eyes.

"In the freezing cold?" She grins, a knowing look that tells me she knows I haven't been paying attention to our mission in the least.

"We could have one on your living room floor. Play music. Grab some wine. It will be great."

"Honestly, sometimes you're just so . . ." she trails off.

"French?" I add with a smirk. She's laughing as I grab her hand and push us through the aisles until we're standing in front of a giant section of assorted cheeses, *les fromages*. "Charcuterie?"

She nods as I start to find the best options for us tonight. "You know, I have a few recipes of my own I can make."

Her eyes light up as she grabs a block of cheese without looking at it. I know she won't like that one, but it looks like she's not paying much attention either.

"Oh! Like *coq a vin*, or *tarte tatin*, or *crêpes*? Can you make *crêpes*?" Her expression is positively elated at this possibility.

Because I can't help teasing her, I furrow my brow. "What? No. I was thinking about *escargot* and *foie gras*."

"Hmm." Her color lightens a shade, and I try to hold back a laugh.

"I mean, you are French too, right?"

"I suppose." She's now studying the block of cheese like it's a magic portal to take her away from this conversation.

"Don't let him tease you too much, darling," I hear over our shoulder. It's Angelina, an older woman who often visits Sparrow's bakery when she's in town to visit her grandson. She moves with the elegance of royalty and the fashion sense of a runway. Her accent is strong but poised—the beautiful French I'm used to hearing and probably would've sounded more like before I made it a point to get rid of all traces of it when I speak English.

As if she seems to know what I'm thinking, she reaches out to Sparrow for the kiss on each cheek, or *la bise*, and does the same to me.

We easily begin speaking French, and Sparrow's eyes fill with a look of pride. She's happy that I am owning this part of myself once again, and I'm grateful to her for making me realize that not all of me was tainted from another life. Even the best cities of the world can be challenging if you're not whole when you're there.

As much as I was trying to sound very American while in the States, I realized I have a deep love and pride for being French, even if it's been hard for me to process all that took place in my homeland. It was a place of great pain, and I needed to leave for a while. Some memories needed time to heal, but Sparrow is helping me to reframe my past with her love. Now, I can see the noteworthy moments previously overshadowed by grief. The taste of croissants when you're breathing in the air of Paris. The look of the Seine in different facets of light. The glow that hovers across the boulevards and bridges every evening. The distinct sound of ambulances and mopeds meeting the tune of conversation and clinking of coffee cups. The faint scent of tobacco and fresh bread lingering in the air. When I see Sparrow, I suddenly miss it all.

Angelina picks out a different cheese for Sparrow and gives me a warning look. I laugh as Sparrow just shrugs in her adorable way. She looks us both in the eyes, one at a time, and says, "*Je suis fière de toi.*" *I'm proud of you.*

She starts to walk away but not before turning over her shoulder and saying, "Save me one of your cookbooks when they're ready, yes?" Sparrow nods and reaches for my hand.

We're not much closer to having dinner put together when Sparrow grins at someone behind me.

"What's for dinner, you two?" It's Graham. He's dressed in his impeccable business attire, a grin hovering on his mouth.

"Oh, this and that," I say, reaching for a nearby jar of apricot jam.

"What's up, lovebirds?" Lily yells from the other end of the aisle. She's rushing toward us when she stops in her tracks and gives a look that would put the fear of God in anyone. All her energy is focused on Graham. I take a step toward Sparrow, who looks at me with wide eyes. This should be interesting.

Trying to lighten the mood, I decide to finally discuss what it has taken us ages to talk about. Turning to Graham, I ask, "Did you really hit on Sparrow at the train station?"

His mouth gapes open as Lily gives what can only be described as a wicked grin. Sparrow is holding back a laugh so intensely that tears are starting to fill her eyes.

"He did," she barely gets out as Graham says, "I did."

Lily gives a slight roll of her eyes, her jaw flexing as she looks between them, a hint of mustered bravery in her voice. "Can you imagine these two together? Please. Winnings is far too much of a corporate man for the likes of our sweet, French American girl." Her confident smile says she's teasing, but her eyes seem to really be asking if it's a legitimate option.

"We never would've worked," Graham says quietly while nodding at Lily. He turns to give Sparrow and me a full smile.

"You're a lovely man, Graham. And I'm honestly surprised we never met sooner," Sparrow says, her arm lightly touching his. She's too much of a giver to have him feeling bad for too long. And she's right. As much as I'm grateful she didn't say yes—more because it would've been torture to see them together—he's a good man. I'll give him that.

"Did you just growl?" Sparrow looks at me, incredulous. I didn't realize I had, but I guess just the thought of them together still has me on edge.

"Don't worry, D'Artagnan. You're the only one who's ever gotten through to her." I give Lily a grin as she picks up a round of Brie cheese.

"The only one who ever could." Sparrow's chocolate eyes melt into mine. I kiss her forehead and breathe her in.

"Enough already! We get it. You love each other, blah, blah, blah," Lily says. That brings another laugh as Lily also picks up a bottle of champagne. "We've got a picnic to have. Winnings can come too, I guess, since he's suddenly everywhere I go these days anyway." She pauses, an eyebrow raised in challenge.

They're in a stare-off. Sparrow and I could leave now, and I don't think they'd notice.

"You go ahead. I've got work to finish elsewhere."

Lily nods and forces a smile. "We've got a trip to Paris to plan for you both. Let's get to it." She turns away and starts to walk to the front of the store.

"See you around, Lily," Graham says quietly.

Lily freezes but doesn't turn around. Pushing her

shoulders back, she gives a brief shake of her head. "Don't count on it!" she yells, resuming her steps toward the checkout counter while clutching the Brie and champagne like a lifeline.

"All right," Sparrow says cheerily without commenting on Lily's odd departure. "Graham, it's been lovely to see you again. I would like to have you over for dinner sometime. Especially since we've now made the connection that you're the best friend and now the manager of this guy." She grabs my arm and looks up at me so sweetly I can't help but smile back.

"Definitely," Graham says while he stares off at Lily, who's now outside the store, pacing. I see the look of disappointment etched across his face. Maybe it's because Lily never uses his actual name. Graham doesn't seem to notice, or if he does, he doesn't let on. But I do.

Chapter Thirty-One

Sparrow

SPRING - *Un voyage à Paris*

I recline on a bed in Paris, the sounds of traffic and fresh air streaming in above my head. The windows are open, and I'm cozied up, fidgeting with the wedding band on my finger while reviewing edits to the recipes for the book I'm creating for my mother. For the opening epigraph, I am including one of my favorite quotes from *Sabrina* with Audrey Hepburn, where she writes to her father from Paris. I've decided to write it for both of my parents.

"I have learned how to live, how to be in the world and of the world, and not just to stand aside and watch. And I will never, never again run away from life. Or from love, either."

I grin as I think of my life now, set apart from the rest of my days as pre-Rafe life and life now with him. Gently putting the papers all around me aside, I stretch to stand and walk toward the window, Parisian rooftops etched against the bright-blue sky. The sounds of people making their breakfasts and living their lives brings a smile to my face. A light breeze blows across my face, billowing the sheer drapes with it.

"I made it," I whisper into the air of Paris.

Since our engagement last Christmas, Rafe started going through pictures I had of my mother when she was a young girl and making a list of places in Paris to visit. He recognized many of the locations and has made it his mission to move us across the city so that I can take similar pictures in the places she's been. He says I'll want them someday, and I think he may be right. Even though my limited memories of her keep fading, like a dream you remember the feeling of without remembering much of what it was about, I feel closer to her here.

I'm obsessed with how I feel in this city. It's the only time in my life that I've ever been someplace and felt like I was returning instead of seeing it for the first time. I love the way I feel alive and awake while trying to find my way in a new place. And I also love how our breakfast trays include mini jars of Nutella to go with our croissants and coffees.

It's spring, and Rafe and I are here on our honeymoon before he collaborates with a new singer on songs for their album and before I finalize the cookbook and add another item to our online store. So far, we've been selling chouquettes, macarons, and an apron with our logo. Lily lobbied for stickers that say *Pain of chocolate*, and the next item we're going to be able to ship is French muffins (Rafe was right; they're a hit), followed by maple croissants.

I'm so proud of Rafe. After officially moving to Birch Borough, he's been hunkered down between the studio in town and the ones in Nashville and LA, writing with so many artists. My heart couldn't be prouder of him. He continuously calls me his muse, but I think, really, that we unlocked something within each other that only we each had the key for. And I know, without a doubt, that he has my heart.

Our wedding was more than I could've ever dreamed it would be. The town showed up in both small and big ways that I will never forget. Everyone pitched in, and even Graham and Lily, as best man and maid of honor, respectively, somehow didn't kill each other. It was a day the deepest parts of my soul will remember as a core memory for the rest of my life.

Speaking of Rafe, I smile as I hear him humming through the bathroom door, the smell of his shower gel swirling with the fresh air. We're staying in a boutique hotel that used to be a newspaper office. It's darling, and I never want to leave.

I hear the door open and turn to find Rafe standing there in glasses, hair disheveled and slightly darkened from his shower, stubble already catching the morning light in delicious ways. He's been threatening to shave it, but I know it's all talk, especially given how much he knows I enjoy the way it feels against my skin when he nuzzles into my neck. I take in his bare chest and my eyes catch on the top of the towel around his waist. Words leave me.

A wicked grin settles over his face as if he knows what I'm thinking. He slowly walks toward me, leaning over and dropping a kiss on the side of my neck. His slightly wet hair has me giving a little squeal. It's cold, but he's so warm—a contradiction in temperatures. A chill runs up my spine as the wind from the spring air hits the drops of water now on my shoulders.

Rafe laughs and looks through my open window. I

see the way he looks at it. Like the view is so familiar and yet new.

"What is it like being home?" I ask as I wrap my hand around his forearm. I lightly rub my hand up and down his arm as his gaze trips back to me. He leans down until his lips are brushing mine as he says, "It's like being with you."

Paris has been everything I've ever dreamed of and more. We've taken river cruises on the Seine, the river murmuring below us as we floated past groups of people dancing on the banks or sharing picnics. We passed the floating bars and night parties, the French flag waving high above the banks.

We've never walked so much. I had the best ice cream of my life, *Berthillon* from *Le Flore En L'Ile* (yes, the café featured on *Emily in Paris*). It was otherworldly. I'm going to be dreaming of that ice cream for some time. Rafe fed me spoonfuls of it—I think because of how much he realized I was enjoying it. He really does love to see me smile.

We also strolled across *Pont Neuf,* the oldest existing bridge across the Seine. Turns out, the Seine really is a character with its own personality and style. I adored walking around its edges, having our own picnic as the sun set and dancing our way around its ledges with the bands and the other couples who decided to rest in Paris for a while.

In Montmartre, we got our portrait sketched (I'm framing it immediately when I get home), walked through the *Sacré Cœur,* and kissed in front of *Le mur des je t'aime,* or the Wall of Love. It's in a tiny garden in

Montmartre and has *I love you* written 311 times in 250 languages. We've had more coffees than we can keep track of, and Rafe has been an angel through it all. He says that it's because even though he grew up here, all of it is new when he's with me.

Rafe has been passing out business cards to people and asking them to come to America, aka Birch Borough, to taste the best croissants they will ever have outside of Paris. I typically laugh and push him along, apologizing for my husband, who has taken it upon himself to be my very own marketing agency. He's also slightly changed his style while we've been here by wearing pieces like a button-down shirt paired with suit pants, Chelsea boots, and a fitted suit jacket to complete his Parisian look.

We've been stopped quite a few times for people to take selfies with him or get an autograph, mainly because of his parents, but for the most part, people have been respectful. And if any woman has tried to get a little too friendly (I get it, he's gorgeous), he's quick to put his arm around me or pull me into a bone-melting kiss.

The patisseries are enough to keep me inspired for the next several decades, and we've even traveled across the city. Turns out, Rafe is quite adept at riding a moped. It's both one of the scariest and hottest things I've ever seen in my life (as if he needed any other reason to have me melt). We drive all throughout Paris, weaving in and out of back roads and streets that are hidden from tourists and full of life. He even talks of getting one when we get back to the States. I wouldn't hate it.

He speaks only in French unless we're on our own. He says he wants me to feel like I have the full French experience when we're on the streets of Paris. It's adorable how much he wants this trip to be everything of my dreams. But what he doesn't fully realize is that it's only this way because I'm with him.

So, when we're riding on the metro all over Paris, and I see the Eiffel Tower, *la tour Eiffel*, in the distance (some of their metros are above ground), I'm taken back to the moment I first saw Rafe and how much our lives have changed for the better. How funny to think I was once afraid to let myself love him, when now the only fear I have is of one day not being able to remember every moment we share together.

Now, I'm leaning on the ancient stone wall of the *Pont Alexandre III* bridge, the wind playing with my hair that's caught in a low bun, the light dress I'm wearing billowing around me. The air smells different here. Like croissants and cigarettes that carry a different smell of tobacco. And coffee. So much coffee. The sounds of the Seine move around us, along with the sounds of Paris traffic. I thought it might be strange for me to hear French all around me or that I'd feel out of place, but really, I feel at peace.

"You look happy," Rafe says as he rubs small circles on my lower back and brushes his beautifully calloused fingers across the diamond ring on my left hand.

"I am happy," I say as I turn to look at him, the setting sun causing part of his face to glow. "I'm with you." I smile. "Husband."

He grins before stepping behind me and wrapping his arms around me. I cover his arms with my hands and lean back onto his shoulder, allowing one of my fingers to trace his strong wrists. He marks a trail of small kisses beneath my ear and down my neck before lifting his head so that his cheek is resting beside mine. I reach one hand back to rest against one side of his face, enjoying the feel of his stubble beneath my palm.

And this is how we stay until the sun sets and the lights turn on. We hold each other while the Eiffel Tower glimmers and the city becomes the City of Light it's known to be.

Time begins to lose meaning, except that it gives us these moments, and I think of all the ways I would try to describe how I feel. I don't think I'd ever be able to explain it fully. Lily once asked me when it was that I knew. And it had to have been somewhere between a train and guitar picks, a dance and a very memorable croissant. But years from now, when I look back on our story, I know I'll have no regrets for opening my heart. I'll think about the ways I moved through fear and how he moved through fear for me. I'll recall moments like this when I held him as my own. And oh, the way that I loved him. With a full heart, I loved him (in French).

Epilogue

Rafe

NEXT FALL

I stand in our kitchen, the stove light creating a soft glow within the space. It's cozy and comforting and reflective of my days and nights since Sparrow and I started our life together. I listen as the espresso drips into the cups we bought in Paris last spring. Seeing her light up in the City of Light felt like the first time I really saw Paris, and it's all thanks to Sparrow. I smell a sunflower I pulled from our petite garden this morning and set it on the wooden breakfast tray. It's a little late for breakfast, but I know she'll appreciate the gesture.

My girl is waiting for me upstairs. And if what I smell is correct, she's got a bath running and some candles burning. I smile to myself and run my hand through my hair, the fire that she sparks in me kindling at the thought of us being able to spend the rest of the day together— preferably under blankets.

Sparrow is my everything, my home. I waited for

someone to really see me, and she didn't just see me, she saved me—from loneliness and especially from myself. I hum one of the songs I've written for her recently (because they're all about her now) and brush my hand over the scruff on my face.

The oven timer dings. I timed it perfectly. I pull out the warmed French muffins that have made our store and my latest album famous and nearly burn myself. I put my thumb to my mouth and wait—can't have myself burnt. Worse than this pain would be not being able to feel Sparrow underneath my fingers.

Satisfied that I'll make it, I pop some muffins from the tin and allow the steam to melt pats of butter through the cut pieces. As it melts and flows onto the dish, I dip my finger in the melted butter and cinnamon-sugar mixture and savor it with contentment.

To imagine that my life at this point last year was me hightailing it out of LA to find the most beautiful woman I'd ever seen passed out on a train and then to spend the next several weeks trying to win over her heart . . . well, I never saw it coming.

My eyes catch on the pictures of us on our refrigerator because, yes, I am the man who is sentimental enough to get them printed at our local pharmacy just so I can stare at us every time I get cream from the fridge.

There's a photo of Sparrow when we first went to the diner, and she looked at me over her shoulder. One of the two of us on Halloween when I played the piano, and she sat beside me (Lily took that one). One of us at Thanksgiving, passed out on the couch (Lily took that one too).

Then, there are more recent photos. One of us in Paris, in Montmartre, holding the illustration an artist drew of us. One of us in Nashville, attempting to line dance. One of me laughing with my eyes closed as Sparrow kisses my cheek so hard that my face is squished. One of us in Boston Common, sitting under a willow tree and drinking coffee. One of us in LA, at the Hermosa Beach Pier near the Pacific Ocean. One of me as I play the guitar while Sparrow hugs me from behind. She does that a lot these days and snuggles her face into my shoulder each time. One of me on one knee in front of Sparrow, on the local train platform, with a ring box in my hand. One of us as we make vows to each other under hanging lantern lights in an old stone church.

I hear a quiet humming and gather the tray so I can make my way upstairs. I love looking at pictures of us, but seeing her face in real time is even better.

Sparrow continues to hum softly, the sound echoing throughout the bathroom. It greets the door where I stand on the other side, adding to the richness of her voice. I crack open the door and hear the gentle splash of her surprise. Holding up the tray as an offering, I gently put it on the counter near the towels.

Her eyes warm toward me, and I feel the swirl of love within my stomach. The gritty kind of love. The one that's going to love this woman even when we no longer look like ourselves from the weathering of age.

A candle flickers on the corner top of the tub, casting warmth throughout the room. The diamond on her left finger sparkles in the firelight, briefly catching my attention before my mouth goes dry. The scent of rose combined with her sweet skin arrests me, and I'm not leaving her side. No chance.

"Hello, darling," she says softly.

"*Mon cœur*," I respond. My sweetheart. I often speak to her in French because she may have lost the sound of it in her life for some time, but she'll always have it now with me. I'll make sure of it.

Her eyes catch mine, and we linger there, a dance of who will make the next move. Without hope of a standoff, I move toward the tub and crouch down, my jean-clad knees touching the porcelain. Her breath catches, and her hands quickly try to coax the bubbles over herself. Even though I can't see anything, it's no use. My hands have already memorized every part she's trying to cover. Even my semi-burnt thumb pulses now. Her body is a magnet, so I slowly dip my finger into the water as if osmosis might work this time and get me even closer to her.

I slowly turn my face toward her mouth and focus on the bright pink of her lips, deep rose in the candlelight, then the curve of her neck arching against the arc of the tub. Her pulse gently greets me under her neck, and I grin. She inhales slowly.

"What are you thinking?" she whispers.

I hesitate. Allowing myself to fully feel what I do for this woman is still somewhat new, even if I welcome the discomfort. The candlelight flickers on her features.

"I'm thinking that I need you." My voice scratches through the air. "How I always need you," I add. Her eyes widen, and I swallow. "But I think you already know that."

"Oh."

Her eyes trace the outline of my face, landing on the parts she says are her favorite. My scruff. The dimple on my right cheek. The scar on my left eyebrow. She looks in my eyes for a fraction of a second before sliding closer to me. The sound of the water gently flowing around her curves has me frozen. I feel the heat of the water turn cool as her hand wraps around my neck, casually dripping bath water down my back.

"So sorry." She hesitantly moves her hand, but I catch it before it returns to the water.

I lightly grip her hand and slowly kiss the center of her palm. Her eyes flutter closed as she leans closer to me, and I pause to hungrily take in her face. No matter how much I stare at her, I'm still willing to find out more, to see another angle I've missed.

"And I'm thinking that we never did finish that book," I say with a grin. She smiles back at me, resting her arms around the edge of the tub. We've started a tradition where I read to her while she takes a bath. Sometimes, it's a fantasy book. Other times, it's a classic. And lately, it's been poetry. Love poems.

I stand and move the wooden stool from the corner to place it beside her. I pull the paperback from my back pocket, already prepared for this moment, and settle in, reading to her in French as the candlelight flickers off the porcelain tub and the millions of tiny bubbles surrounding Sparrow.

Later, when we're sitting on the couch, another day tucking away into the quiet of evening, I strum my guitar and listen as Sparrow hums beside me. I don't even know if she realizes how much she sings lately. I carefully place my guitar on its stand near where we sit, Sparrow twirling one of my guitar picks between her hands. With her hair pulled casually into a low bun, dressed in my shirt and some oversized grey sweats, she looks like comfort and hope.

I lean toward her, lightly catching her bottom lip with my own. Wrapping my arms around her, I slide my hands around her ribcage and down the length of her spine, now curved toward me. I bury my face in the side of her neck, the feel of her warm, soft skin unlocking my reason. I can't be this far apart from her for another moment.

"Sparrow?" Slowly sliding my mouth up her throat, I lightly place a kiss on the pulse point that was calling to me earlier.

"Mmm?" She happily sighs.

"Let's go on an adventure."

She lets out a laugh that's laced with desire. "Ready when you are," she whispers.

I sense how shy she still is in this way when it comes to me, but when she kisses my scarred eyebrow, I know that's my cue. Without hesitation, I scoop her up, and she squeals, some coffee in a cup spilling onto the little table. I don't care. I'll clean it up later.

I set her down in our bedroom, the vulnerability in her eyes a lightning bolt. She still doesn't know how desirable she can be. Still. But it's okay. I have the rest of my life to show her.

A candle flickers on the bedside table and on her features, one side of her face now more lit than the other. She stares at me openly, almost reverently, and I don't want to waste this sacred moment. My eyes burn from the emotion threatening to come through, so I pull her even closer, until our breath is one.

"Je t'aime, Sparrow."

She closes her eyes and softly kisses a trail along my neck and collarbone. I tuck my chin down to meet her gaze. Hovering her mouth near mine, she kisses me slowly, smiling against my mouth before deepening the kiss. I can't get enough of her. She tastes like croissants, Nutella, and dreams. Lots of dreams.

Sparrow breaks the kiss only to catch my eyes again, the light between us branding my heart. Pulling at a piece of my hair falling over my forehead, she slowly twirls it between her fingers before letting them outline my jaw. Grinning, she rises on her toes to get closer to me and softly inhales.

"Rafe?"

I nod slightly.

"I love you too."

"In French?" I mumble, barely able to wait before I plan to capture her sweet mouth once more.

"*Oui*." A slow, soft kiss. "*En français.*"

Acknowledgments

To you, dear reader, thank you. I'm so grateful that you've read my first book, and I hope that somewhere within it, you've found words to hold on to. This book was the one that I needed during the time of my life in which it was written, and it's truly been a joy to write. I hope you've felt the love throughout the pages.

Britt, I'm so grateful to you and for you. I truly couldn't imagine this book being in the world without you. Thank you for your endless kindness, patience, and for answering the questions that kept me up at night. I know God is kind, but the fact that I got you for my editor is beyond what I could've ever hoped for. I'll never forget it.

Jenn, thank you for your kindness, for catching what I couldn't, and for being the second person in the world to ever read my book. I appreciate you.

Elijah and Ashlee, thank you for creating the space for me to confidently create. You are my people, and I'll never get over how you've taken me in. You're more than my friends, you're my family. Let's keep creating and dreaming together for another twenty years (and more).

Alyssa, I don't think I'll ever get over the fact that I

get to have your art on (and in) my book. Your friendship has meant more than I can say over the years. Thank you for your thoughtfulness and for noticing all of the details. Thank you for dreaming with me and for laughing with me as I clumsily tried to articulate what was on my mind. You created a cover (and more) that was beyond what I could imagine. How lucky am I?!

Tay! My friend. My support. You have loved me so steadily and have always made me feel like I'm so important to you. Your kindness has not gone unnoticed. I can't believe I get to be friends with you (and thanks for loving me even if I ever decide to change genres…).

Kylie, you are the little sister I always needed. I can't believe we've gone from Christmas productions to dreaming through this book. Thank you for being my sounding board in so many ways and for your endless support.

Jen Grisanti, words aren't enough. Thank you for believing in me before I truly believed in myself. You've seen me and believed in me as a writer when I couldn't. To know you is a gift. I hope I never stop learning from you. I have felt your support. Thank you for getting excited about my stories and for telling me how proud you are of me. It has meant more to me than I could ever convey.

Liz and Shana, thank you for being dear friends and for celebrating this book before it was a book (and, Liz, thanks for asking for extra chapters! I'm glad you had the first ones with you for the plane).

Derek and Leah, years later, here we are. You saw a book in me when my confidence was fractured. Your kindness wasn't wasted. I will think of you with each book I write.

Amber, thank you for telling me that you're proud of me.

Virginia, thank you for the celebratory macarons and for being my friend who happens to be family.

To my family and my friends (who are also my family), I honor you. To anyone who has ever supported or encouraged me in my writing, it mattered more than you know.

Mama, thank you for introducing me to books, for letting me read extra chapters before bed, and for always believing that I'm a writer. I'm forever grateful for your support and for loving me so selflessly. Your endless faith in me over the years has helped me move through some of the darkest moments of my life. There's always a spot for you at my book table.

And I couldn't close this book without giving thanks to and for Jesus—the One who has been my constant. Thank you for never letting me go and for the gift that is creating. I am so grateful.

ABOUT SARA NORTH

Sara North is a New England native who often dreams of Paris. While books held her heart first, Sara's training included writing and story development for both film and television scripts and fueled her desire to create with heart.

With a passion to cheer on creatives and writers across art forms and industries, Sara recognizes the power of stories to bring healing, hope, and happiness. When she's not writing, her loves include 90s rom-coms, Old Hollywood films, Hallmark Christmas movies, beloved sitcoms, music to match her mood, café hopping, baking, and celebrating all things fall.

AuthorSaraNorth.com | @AuthorSaraNorth